Grace's New Frien[d]

"Why do the guards bow ...   ... asked.

"Because I'm *Samael*," Samael said smugly.

"I'm going to need a bit more than that."

Samael sighed. "I'm one of the original Rebels. Part of the nobility of Hell."

"Nobles still exist down here?" she said innocently. "I thought people here worked, what with the money and all?"

He glared at her, and Grace grinned.

"Some do," he said.

"Do you?"

"No. I'm *noble*."

Grace smiled. "So you mentioned."

"You're an annoyance, you know that?"

Grace tilted her head slightly, looking at him. He couldn't quite conceal the glimmer of amusement in his eyes. "But you like me anyway," she said before she almost ran into him as he suddenly stopped in front of a pair of golden doors.

"We're here," he told her. "And I most certainly do not. I find you entertaining. That's all."

SAVING HELL

MARIA SJÖSTRAND

GUARDBRIDGE BOOKS
ST ANDREWS, SCOTLAND

Published by Guardbridge Books,
St Andrews, Fife, United Kingdom.

http://guardbridgebooks.co.uk

SAVING HELL.

This is a work of fiction. All characters and events portrayed in this book are fictitious, and any resemblance to real people or events is purely coincidental.

Cover art © Jacqueline Abromeit.

ISBN: 978-1-911486-85-5

Printed in the United Kingdom
on 100% Recycled paper.

To my publisher who took a chance on an unknown author,
My teachers who taught me to write,
And my parents who at least attempted to teach me the rest.

With a special thank you to author Sascha Christensen
My mentor and personal cure for procrastination.

CHAPTER ONE:

A Joyful Tragedy

Who'd have thought dying would be so much work?

The doctor certainly kept talking about experimental treatments to try, medicines to take, discussions to have with her insurance company. It all sounded rather fancy to Grace, who'd assumed that death was a relatively simple affair.

Perhaps she would have been paying more attention if the doctor hadn't had one of those kinetic toys on his desk. Grace watched the balls move back and forth with a little smile, finding them a delightfully playful touch to an otherwise serious-looking office.

The doctor apparently took her silence for shock as he explained to her that while they would do everything they could, the chances of survival were slim.

"How slim?" Grace's niece asked him, voice cracking. She was sitting on the edge of her chair, looking at the doctor with desperation.

The doctor's answer seemed unnecessary long and technical, but Grace got the gist of it. She was going to die.

"Well, I guess it can't be helped," she said.

The doctor's eyebrows rose a notch. "Miss O'Neill, I'm not sure if perhaps you've misunderstood me," he said.

"Oh, no, I think I understood you well enough. I used to be a nurse, you know. You give me what? About a month?"

"I... yes. Approximately. Of course, it's impossible to say for sure, but when the tumour is this aggressive..."

"A month should be time enough to get my affairs in order," Grace noted and turned to her niece. "Oh, dear, I have so much to do. I should probably put the house up for sale? Unless you want it, Anna, dear?"

Her niece looked at her with a shocked expression.

"No," she said. "No, I mean... I don't know. It's so much to take in."

"Now, don't be silly. People die every day. At 93 years old, you can hardly suggest that I'm too young?"

"It's still too soon."

Smiling, Grace patted her hand. "That's sweet, dear," she said, mentally composing a list of things to do. There were letters to write and documents to sign. And the funeral arrangements. It would be a nice excuse to bring the whole family together.

She should buy some nice stationary to write the list on. Or maybe Matthew could show her how to download one of those app-things. There seemed to be one for just about anything these days. Marvellous, really.

"Miss O'Neill," the doctor said. "If it's acceptable to you, I would like a word with your niece?"

"Of course, doctor. It's no problem at all."

Leaving them alone, Grace walked into the hallway outside the office. She wondered if Anna had noticed how handsome the doctor was. Kind too. And it had been five years since Anna's divorce. A nice little doctor might be just what she needed.

Humming under her breath, Grace looked at the bare walls around her. Some paintings would really liven the place up.

Maybe she should paint them a little something? She wasn't an artist, but a few splashes of colour could hardly be much trouble? She would buy a bit of paint and a canvas on the way home. And maybe she'd swing by the funeral store as well. Browse around for a coffin and a tombstone.

She wondered what to write on it. Maybe some joke about the zombie apocalypse? Or she could have it engraved with the recipe for that strawberry pie everyone complimented her on?

She could work out the details once she was home and could jot down her ideas. Maybe she could convince her neighbours to have a poll and pick the funniest one?

Grace heard the door open and turned around to send Anna a pleased smile.

"All done, Anna dear?"

"Yes, auntie."

"Wonderful. I have such lovely ideas for the tombstone."

Anna burst into tears.

Grace blinked in surprise before she hurried over and embraced her niece.

"There, there," she said. She noticed that the doctor still hadn't left but was merely looking on awkwardly. He probably needed a bit of a push if Grace wanted them together before the funeral.

"Would you like me to slip him your number before we leave?" she asked in a whisper.

Anna pulled away to stare at her. "You have a tumour," she said.

"I know that, dear," Grace said. She'd thought the doctor had made himself clear enough.

"It's in your brain."

"So I've heard."

"You're not yourself."

"Of course I am, dear. Who else would I be?"

"But you're not! You don't even care that you're going to die! It's not *normal*."

"But, dearest, isn't going happy far preferable? Even if it isn't the normal way?"

"I… yes, I… I suppose it is."

"That's my girl. Now, tell me, if I was to paint something for this place, do you think I should go with a mixture of red or green colours?"

Her niece didn't answer.

* * *

Cheerfully swinging her legs in tune to the song blasting from the stereo, Grace was currently perched on the dining room table, looking over the assembly with satisfaction.

Ever since the news of her cancer had come out, everybody had treated her differently. Her family visited her more, friends stumbled awkwardly in conversations in the most amusing way, and even the mail man had taken to giving her encouraging smiles.

That part was probably due to Rosalie, who lived three doors down. The biggest gossip Grace had ever met. Though of course still invited to her going-away party. Everyone was. Grace O'Neill would go out with a bang. Loud music, good company, and a piñata the shape of a goat.

The others had at first refused to oblige as they, apparently, thought it in poor taste. Grace had argued. What could be poor taste about a going-away party, when she was the one going away? She was hardly going to offend herself.

Then, even after they'd all showed up, they'd been positively glum.

No one had said anything above a whisper, and not a single person had made a move towards the piñata.

Thankfully, all it'd taken to turn it around had been a little alcohol. Well, a lot of alcohol. And suddenly people were singing, dancing, and furtively swinging a baseball bat. Her vase collection had suffered, but it wasn't like Grace could take it with her.

Raising a glass over her head, she gave a cheerful shout.

"Is everybody having fun?!"

A scream of affirmation met her. Jerome had started his own makeshift bar, loudly telling everybody in his nearest vicinity to just call him Jim. Harold was currently taking his turn at the piñata, using his tie as a blindfold, while Sarah was attempting the moonwalk.

Grace laughed. Lately, she'd tired more easily, but she refused to spend this night sleeping.

Grabbing an energy drink from beside her, Grace decided

that Red Bull was an even better invention than coffee. Ignoring the warning on the label, Grace poured the golden drink into her glass before she added a bit of vodka. The combination was absolutely delicious. She couldn't believe she'd never had one before.

Grace smiled at the scene in front of her. Her family and all her friends. She'd never seen anything so beautiful, even including Sebastian, whose dance moves appeared more as if he were riding a horse than actually dancing.

Grace congratulated herself on the successful party before she yawned in spite of her earlier determination. She got off the table and made her way to her favourite armchair; a hideous but comfortable thing. Sitting down, she yawned again. Maybe she could sleep for just a moment? Her eyes closed. Just a couple of minutes, and she'd be ready to go once again.

* * *

It was quiet.

That was the first thing she noticed. She must have fallen asleep, and everybody had gone home.

Then she realised that it wasn't completely silent. There was an odd buzzing sound, almost too low to hear. Grace opened her eyes and saw only whiteness.

Clouds, she thought. Then she blinked and realised her mistake.

She was looking at a clear, white sky, without a cloud in sight. Nor, for that matter, a sun, a moon, or any other celestial object.

Slowly sitting up, she tried to make sense of her surroundings. The ground consisted of dark soil, and near her was the foot of the longest staircase she'd ever seen, so long that she couldn't even see where it ended. The steps and railing were made of ordinary wood, not even that well-crafted. Someone could easily get a splinter climbing up that thing.

Looking away from the staircase, she located the source of

the buzzing. She was sitting near a moving walkway, like the ones they had at the airports. It led in the opposite direction of the staircase, was made of sleek steel, and moved faster than any other she'd ever seen. It also had no safety railings of any kind. It might, in fact, be even less sensible than the crude staircase.

Grace stretched her back and cracked her neck. She felt better than she remembered feeling... well, ever really. She looked down at her hands. Gone were the wrinkles and brown spots, leaving nothing behind but smooth, unblemished skin.

Her movement had caused her hair to spill forward, despite it having been shaved off just a month prior. Not only had it grown back, but it was once again the dark brown she remembered from her youth.

Touching her face, she felt tight skin, and when she pinched it, she could feel it snap back like a rubber band.

She was young again.

How neat.

Looking back and forth between the staircase and the moving walkway, Grace quickly came to a conclusion. She'd been wrong.

She had never been a religious person. She'd tried to be, once upon a time (mostly for her mother's sake), but it had never made sense to her. One quick perusal of the bible had shown her dozens of inconsistencies, and Grace had declared defeat. She couldn't have faith when it went against the facts, and most religions rather depended on the faith.

But now she was standing in front of what could only be the staircase to Heaven, and what, by the process of elimination, had to be the walkway to Hell. Both there for the taking.

Perhaps good people got to choose, though Grace couldn't imagine what sane person would ever pick Hell. Looking up the staircase, Grace was thankful to have her old body back. It *was* rather long.

Taking her first step up towards Heaven, Grace couldn't help but think that it was all rather anti-climactic. Where were the angelic choirs? The ethereal light? There was nothing here but ground, a white sky, and a crude staircase.

No matter. Heaven was still a nice surprise. Humming slightly under her breath, Grace began to make her way upwards.

And upwards.

And upwards.

And upwards.

Twelve thousand, eight hundred and forty-six steps later, Grace finally found herself in front of the Pearly Gates.

Well, the Wooden Gates, really.

They couldn't be more than six feet tall and had no ornaments or engravings of any kind. Just two closed, plain doors, unconnected to any wall.

Trying one doorknob, she quickly established that the Wooden Gates were, indeed, locked. With a shrug, she lifted her hand and knocked four times.

Nothing happened, but Heaven was undoubtedly big. It'd probably take them a while to make it to their front door. Mentally, she began to count backwards from a hundred.

She'd just made it to fifty, when the door opened, and an angel came out.

Taking a step back, Grace stumbled over her own feet and landed on her behind with an undignified bump.

If the door to Heaven had been disappointing, the angel guarding it certainly wasn't.

Beautiful beyond words, and so bright that her eyes hurt just looking at it, she found herself unable to discern whether it was male or female.

"Um... hello," she said. "I'm Grace."

"I know." Its voice was beautiful, unnerving, and emotionless. The latter two might've been connected.

"Right. Of course, you do. It's… eh… it's a real long staircase you have here. Ever thought about installing one of those moving ones?"

"No."

"Right. Guess that's not really… heavenly or anything."

The angel neither agreed nor disagreed.

"The body's really neat," Grace told it, mostly to break the silence. "Being, you know, young and all."

"Your current form reflects your mind. Your body has been left behind. Your soul and mind remain as they were."

"Right," Grace said, picking herself up from the ground. She forced herself to look directly at the angel. "So… can I get in?"

"No."

"No? What do you mean, no?"

"You may not enter the sacred grounds of Heaven."

"You're kicking me out?"

"I deny you entrance." The angel began to turn around, and Grace realised that it was about to leave.

"No, wait! *Why* are you denying me entrance?"

"You are not a good believer of God."

"Sure I am! I'm a good person! I haven't murdered anyone or anything."

The angel seemed to be looking at her contemplatively, though it was hard to be sure.

"Do you think that not committing murder is enough to get you into Heaven?"

"Well, no… but…"

"You have stolen."

"Once! I stole one bra *once* because my mother thought that I was too young to have one. You're going to deny my entrance because of one bra?"

"You have lied. You have cheated. You have gambled. You have taken the Lord's name in vain. And, above all, you have not believed."

"I... I have... you're going to *deny my entrance* because of that?"

"Yes."

"Then what do you expect me to do?!"

"Go to Hell. They may want you."

The angel turned around and walked back into Heaven, the doors falling closed behind it.

Staring in shock at the now empty space, Grace considered her options.

She looked down on the seemingly endless steps. Couldn't they put up a sign or something? *Must be religious to get into Heaven. Bra-stealers not welcome.* Would have saved her an awful lot of trouble.

With a sigh, Grace began to make her way downwards.

At least it's easier to walk downwards than upwards, she thought. *And when I get to the bottom, there's that neat walkway.*

Still. The thought of Hell seemed quite unpleasant. And there was no angel to tell her she couldn't just... hang around. Forever.

But no sooner had she decided to stay up here than the steps suddenly evened out and weren't steps at all any more, but rather one long slope. Scrambling for footing, Grace shrieked as she slid downwards, faster and faster.

I wonder if you can die again if you're already dead, she thought madly, nearing the ground in an impossible speed.

She hit it with a resounding smack that would have broken several bones if she'd been as old as she was that morning. As it was, it merely hurt like hell.

How ironic.

Slowly, Grace got to her feet before she made her way to the moving walkway. It seemed she didn't have much choice in the matter. But she supposed what would be, would be and all that. C'est la vie.

And at least it'll be a lot less effort than that staircase.

Grace took a step out onto the walkway and gave a shriek as she was once again moving faster than what should be possible.

Highway to Hell indeed.

Desperately wishing that there was something to hold on to, Grace fell on her knees, squeezed her eyes shut, and hoped for the best.

And then, just like that, it ended. Knocked forward by her own momentum, Grace ended up on her face this time. She'd certainly established that it was, indeed, possible to feel pain after death.

Picking herself up from the ground, she looked at the door in front of her. This one was made of wood, too, but in a darker colour. Other than that, it quite resembled the door that could have led her into Heaven. Grace doubted, however, that this would lead anywhere particularly pleasant.

Maybe she would just stay out here, after all. She really wished she'd brought a book. Or perhaps a deck of cards.

And then the door opened, and a demon came out. It was seven feet tall, dark red, and horned.

It looked at Grace. Grace looked at the demon.

"Good evening," the demon said.

"Good evening," Grace answered, decades of polite conditioning kicking in.

"I do hope you had a pleasant trip?" the demon asked her.

"Well, you might consider putting a safety rail on that walkway," Grace said.

The demon smiled, showcasing a mouthful of unsettling sharp teeth. "A marvellous idea," it said. Every word coming out of its mouth was perfectly enunciated, and Grace was reminded of how they spoke in certain old movies. She was charmed.

"I do hope you are not hurt," the demon said. "I would feel just terrible if we bruised yet another newcomer."

"Nothing to speak of," Grace assured him. Then she hesitated. "Perhaps, if you don't terribly mind, I could stay out here?" she suggested.

"Of course, Miss...?"

"O'Neill."

"Miss O'Neill. Are you waiting for a friend? People die together more often than you might think, but to be frank, I must say that it would be more comfortable waiting inside. If you give me your friend's name, I will be happy to keep an eye out for them and let you know."

"Eh... that's mighty kind of you, but I'm not waiting for anyone. I just thought that I could wait out here for a century or two?"

The demon smiled. "I understand," he said. "Hell does not have the best reputation, and I deeply regret the worry this may have caused."

"That's... that's no trouble."

The demon bowed slightly. "You are too kind. I can assure you that while we undoubtedly have our faults here, we do have standards that we are very proud of."

"Standards? What standards?"

"Well, we do not accept murderers except for under certain circumstances, and we never accept rapists or child abusers."

"Those are... pretty loose demands," Grace noted.

"It is a bit more complex than that, but we are admittedly not as exclusive as they are upstairs."

"So... what? No eternal torture?"

"Oh, no, none at all. Well, we do have some masochists here, but it is all perfectly consensual, I assure you. And I would not go as far as to call it torture, though I know that others may disagree."

"Screaming demons?"

"We do occasionally scream, but no more than you humans do, if you'll forgive my saying so."

"A burning pit?"

"We do have a barbecue."

"Oh."

Grace thought it over.

"Well, that sounds rather nice," she decided.

The demon positively glowed.

"I agree," he said. "Would you like a tour? It can get confusing here at first and having someone introduce you can take much of the pressure off."

"That's awfully kind of you... I'm sorry, but I don't believe, I caught your name?"

"It is Reigh, Miss O'Neill. Reigh the Horned. But do feel free to just call me Reigh." He bowed once again before he offered her an arm.

With a smile, Grace took it. Arm in arm with a painfully polite demon, she entered Hell.

CHAPTER TWO:

Hell

The first thing that met her was the smell. Burning wood and something sugary she didn't recognise. After that came the heat. It wasn't a scolding, burning-your-skin-off kind of heat, but it was definitely warmer than fall in Boston. Glad that she'd worn a relatively thin shirt, she wished that she'd opted for a skirt rather than pants.

"Why is it so warm?" she asked Reigh, who'd been waiting patiently beside her.

"I regret to say that I do not know, Miss O'Neill," he answered. "Some people believe that it is because we are so close to the Earth's core, but that is not true. We are not even in the same dimensional layer."

Pretending she understood, Grace just nodded along, too busy looking around to really pay attention.

Hell was dark, and Grace thought with regret back on the sun, which she'd never feel again. The dark, however, was broken by little lights, and Grace realised that they were standing on top of a hill, looking downwards. In the distance, she could see a great building, and Grace strained her eyes to make out the details.

"What's that?" she asked Reigh, pointing at the building.

"Lucifer's palace," he told her, and Grace gaped at him.

"Lucifer?" she said. "As in the Devil? Right. I guess that makes sense. Find the Devil in Hell and whatnot."

"Yes. Most newcomers are nervous around him, though they have no reason to be. Why, he has not as much as pillared anyone in over a decade!"

"Pillared?" Grace repeated.

"Yes, to hold them while they await judgment."

"And what could cause such a judgment?" she asked, thinking it'd be nice to know what to avoid.

Reigh smiled. "Do not worry, Miss O'Neill," he said. "The Devil is only involved in severe cases. I doubt that you will ever meet him. It has been centuries since he has personally greeted a new citizen."

Grace was most definitely not disappointed by this. The one angel she'd met had been unsettling enough, and Lucifer had stood up against God.

"I met his wife once," Reigh added, unmistakable pride in his voice.

Grace frowned. "Lucifer is married?" she asked. She sure couldn't remember hearing about that in Sunday school.

"Yes. Lilith is one of the most wonderful woman who ever lived, created by God's own hands."

"She's human?" Grace asked, surprised.

"Yes. The only marriage to have ever taken place between an angel and a human."

"I thought Lucifer hated people."

"He would hardly open up his Hell for them if that were the case. And he certainly loves his wife."

Grace thought it over. It was surprisingly sweet.

"What's she like?" she asked.

Reigh seemed to think it over. "I believe that she is the strongest woman whom I have ever met," he told her. "Of course, she would have to be, being married to Lucifer. I'll admit that he can occasionally be a bit... intimidating, if you'll forgive my saying so."

"I bet," Grace murmured, her head swimming from everything that had happened. Perhaps none of this was real. Perhaps the cancer had caused her to lose her mind, and she was just imagining it all.

If that were true, Grace saw no reason why she couldn't enjoy it to its full extent.

She looked up at the demon standing at her side.

"So, Reigh," she said. "Does Hell have alcohol?"

* * *

Reigh took her to an outdoor bar, complete with little huts with straw-roofs and tiki-lamps. He proceeded to pay for two colourful drinks with small coins that appeared to have been made of copper.

"You use money down here?" Grace asked.

"Of course, Miss O'Neill. Money was originally created in Hell."

Grace frowned. "I don't have any way to repay you," she said.

"Please don't concern yourself with it. Few people bring money with them nowadays."

She would still have to get some eventually, and Grace wondered absent-mindedly if there was any need for nurses down in Hell. She decided to worry about it later.

Instead, she took a sip of her turquoise drink and blinked in astonishment.

"This is delicious!"

The bartender sauntered over with a grin. "For that, you'll get your second one for free," he told her with a wink.

Grace stared at him. Was he flirting with her? She hadn't been flirted with in decades, and she felt butterflies flutter in her stomach. She'd missed flirting, though she felt terribly rusty at it.

"Thank you," she said, looking him over. He was human with tan skin, brown hair, and green eyes. Handsome, and aware of it.

"I'm Grace," she added.

He offered her his hand. "Raoul," he said.

Grace shook his hand. "This is Reigh," she introduced her guide, not wanting to leave him out.

Raoul grinned. "I know. I'm his favourite bartender. He loves those little umbrellas I put in the drinks."

Grace might have been wrong in the low lighting, but she was pretty sure she saw the 7-foot demon blush. Taking another sip from her drink, she decided that she could get used to Hell.

"Samael!" Reigh suddenly exclaimed.

Grace looked up to see a black cat make its way across the bar.

"Reigh," it answered before it sat down and licked itself.

Grace stared. Talking animals. Okay then.

"Aren't you supposed to greet a newcomer today?" Reigh asked.

The cat stopped licking itself and looked at him in annoyance. "It's boring. All that screaming and crying and insisting that they don't belong here. And since I saw that one of the newcomers was registered to be at this bar, I figured this meeting could at least include alcohol." The cat smirked.

That would probably be her. She should introduce herself.

"Hello," she said.

The cat looked at her.

"Hello," it answered.

Yep. Definitely talking.

"This is Miss Grace O'Neill," Reigh introduced. "She's new here, so I thought I would take the liberty of showing her around."

The cat's round eyes got even rounder as it stared at Grace.

"You're the newcomer?" it asked with clear astonishment. "But you're not crying. When did you come to Hell?"

"I just arrived," Grace said.

"Just arrived?"

"Yes," she said. "I tried the big staircase first, but they didn't want me, and to be completely frank, this place seems better anyway. I mean, admittedly I never really *saw* the other place, but it seems nice here. The drinks are delicious, if nothing else."

Raoul grinned at her.

The cat jumped up on the bar in front of her and sniffed at her drink before it turned accusatory eyes on Raoul.

"Did you put something in her drink?"

Raoul held up his hands in a surrendering gesture. "I would never!" he said.

The cat looked at Grace with mistrust.

"They made you say that, didn't they?" it asked.

"Not at all," she assured it. "You don't like it here?"

"Of course I do. I helped create this place, you know. But it usually takes months for newcomers to realise that we're not going to start poking them with pitchforks." The cat rolled its eyes, an utterly bizarre sight.

"Oh. Well, I have been a tad more optimistic lately," Grace said.

"Such a normal feeling for the dying," the cat answered, sarcasm clear in its voice. "Unless it was a nice, sudden death? Let me guess. Automobile accident?"

"Brain cancer."

The cat seemed to consider it. "Well, I suppose that does explain it. You've gone bonkers."

"Well, at least I'm not someone's pet," Grace said.

Raoul almost fell over laughing.

"Pet?!" the cat shrieked. "Pet?!"

It seemed to flicker, and before Grace had time to process what was happening, a man sat on the bar in place of the cat. He was dressed old-fashioned in a pair of black trousers and shirt. He had olive skin, black hair, and equally black eyes, which seemed to shine with fury as he looked down at her. He was devilishly handsome and clearly extremely insulted.

"I am nobody's pet!" he said.

"Oh. Sorry. My bad."

The man looked at her with the same mistrust that the cat had shown. "Are you making fun of me?"

"No. Are you always this suspicious?"

"Yes."

"Well, you were a cat right before. How was I supposed to know?"

The man glowered at her. "I am Samael!"

Grace tilted her head inquiringly. "I'm afraid I don't recognise the name," she said. "I don't think they covered you in Sunday School."

"They did," the man said. "Extensively. I'll have you know that I am *very* important."

"Oh. Who are you then?" Grace asked. "In the bible, I mean."

The man snorted. "That written pile of propagandic garbage? Hardly a credible source of information." Despite his words, he wasn't quite meeting her eyes. "Besides, it doesn't matter much anyway."

Raoul grinned at him. "Since when have you been this modest?" he teased. "I thought you would *love* a new audience to tell the same old stories?"

The man gave him the same offended look that Grace had been subjected to.

"Do shut up," he told the bartender before he turned his attention back towards Grace. He held out a hand.

"I'm Samael," he formally introduced himself, far more calmly than before.

Grace looked him over. Clearly easily offended, he seemed to get over it just as quickly. She decided that she liked him. She reached out and shook his hand.

"I'm Grace," she said. "Though I guess Reigh already told you that."

Samael snorted. "Reigh is hellbent on being the official welcome committee of Hell," he said.

Grace smiled up at the horned demon next to her. "And I'm very happy he is," she said. "If he hadn't, I would still be out there, determined to wait out eternity."

Next to her, Reigh blushed once again.

"Most people do have to be carried in," Samael said. "Though I don't see why we bother."

Grace was starting to realise that perhaps Samael wasn't the most compassionate of beings.

"Well, I think it's awfully nice of him," she said, still smiling at Reigh. Samael did not look amused.

"Have you met your lost ones yet?" he asked.

Grace frowned, not sure what he meant.

"Who?" she asked.

Samael sighed. "Your lost ones," he repeated. "Friends and family members who died before you."

"Oh. No, I haven't."

"We can find them in the Book of Souls," Samael said and jumped off the bar. "Follow me."

Grace hesitated. "I don't want to leave Reigh behind," she said. "And I haven't finished my drink."

Still, she couldn't keep the longing out of her voice. It would be nice to see her parents again.

"Please don't worry about me, Miss O'Neill," Reigh said. "I shall be fine on my own. I would not want to be a bother. And I'm sure that Raoul would not object to you taking your drink with you." He looked imploringly at Raoul, who shrugged.

"Sure," he said. "Why not?"

Grace smiled at them. "Thank you," she said. "And thank you for talking me into Hell."

"It was my pleasure, Miss O'Neill. Please come visit me at any time. My name is in the Book of Souls."

"I'll do so," Grace said, and apparently Samael thought that he'd been waiting for long enough because he began to drag her with him.

Following him through Hell, Grace quickly came to the conclusion that Samael liked the sound of his own voice.

"Don't you ever stop talking about yourself?" she asked, interrupting a story about winning some poker game against a guy called Asmodeus.

Samael stared at her. "Are you always this frank?" he demanded to know.

"More so recently, yes. So do you?"

Samael scowled. "Why don't you tell me about yourself?" he said, sounding like the words were awfully hard to get out.

Grace grinned. "Why, I'd love to! Thank you for asking; it was very considerate of you."

Samael huffed, and Grace smiled at him. He was entertaining enough. You just had to interrupt him if he went off on a tangent. Which he seemed to do quite often.

Looking around with curious eyes, Grace watched with delight the mixture of demons and humans who seemed to inhabit Hell, along with the centuries upon centuries of different fashions and architectural styles. Rapidly nearing the palace, Grace craned her neck up in an attempt to take the whole thing in.

It was black, she realised, thinking that a bit of paint would really warm it up. Preferably a warm colour, like a dusty rose.

Maybe she should at least try not to mention that.

Finally, they entered the palace, and Grace found herself in a treasure chest masquerading as a building. Every inch of the place seemed to have been carefully crafted, there were jewels embedded in the walls, and every piece of furniture was a masterpiece.

There were also guards, she noticed. Each of whom bowed whenever she and Samael walked past, and she felt relatively sure that they weren't bowing to her.

"Why do the guards bow to you?" she asked.

"Because I'm Samael," Samael said smugly.

"I'm going to need a bit more than that."

Samael sighed. "I'm one of the original Rebels. Part of the nobility of Hell."

"Nobles still exist down here?" she said innocently. "I thought people here worked, what with the money and all?"

He glared at her, and Grace grinned.

"Some do," he said.

"Do you?"

"No. I'm *noble*."

Grace smiled. "So you mentioned."

"You're an annoyance, you know that?"

Grace tilted her head slightly, looking at him. He couldn't quite conceal the glimmer of amusement in his eyes. "But you like me anyway," she said before she almost ran into him as he suddenly stopped in front of a pair of golden doors.

"We're here," he told her. "And I most certainly do not. I find you entertaining. That's all."

With these words, he threw the doors open, and they entered the library.

It was just as ostentatiously done as the rest of the palace, but it was also filled with books. Hundreds of books, thousands, millions. It stretched on farther than Grace could even see, and she looked at the sight in amazement. Black wooden shelves continued seemingly for eternity, and when she looked up, the shelves disappeared into a fog, a hundred feet or so above them. The white, marble floor was inlaid with gold, and the room seemed to echo with every step.

"How many books are in here?" she asked.

"Every book ever written in every language ever spoken," he answered.

"We could spend days trying to find our book."

"Space here doesn't work the same way as on Earth," he told her. "Besides, we want that book." He nodded towards a book lying on a lectern approximately twenty feet in front of them.

"Oh. Well, that's neat."

"It's the book most often used for reference," he said, walking towards it. "What was your full name again?"

"Grace Rose O'Neill."

"Grace Rose O'Neill," he murmured, opening the book at a seemingly random page. It was full of symbols she couldn't decipher, but Samael appeared to have no such problem.

"Your father is here," he said. "At the Offices to be exact. Your mother is in Heaven."

That did make sense. Her mother had been a good person as well as a religious one.

"Why isn't dad in Heaven?" she asked. Hadn't he believed in God too?

Samael flipped through the book. "Greed, workaholic tendencies, and problems with gambling," he told her. "Heaven is too goody two-shoes to take someone like him."

"Reigh called it exclusive."

"Reigh is too polite for his own good."

He *was* impressively polite. Grace rather liked it.

"So we're going to see my dad?" she asked, trying not to realise that she would probably never see her mom again.

"I think not. It sounds unbelievably dull."

Grace shrugged. "Fine. I'll go on my own then."

Samael looked annoyed. "You don't know the way," he said.

"I'll ask for directions."

"Only people incapable of finding their way need other people's help."

Grace shrugged and turned around to leave. After a few steps, Samael followed her.

"A bloody annoyance," he mumbled. She ignored him.

"How do you become a noble in Hell?" she asked instead.

He looked at her in utter disgust.

"*You* couldn't," he told her. "It's not for humans."

"You're human."

"I most certainly am *not*." He made a disgusted face. "*I* am a shapeshifter."

Well, that explained how he'd been a cat before. Still...

"You *look* pretty human to me."

"It's just the shape I've chosen," he said, but he did turn back into a cat, so maybe she'd hit a nerve.

"Besides, isn't the queen human?" Grace asked.

"She is," he admitted. "And a human could *theoretically* become a noble. Either as a reward for something they've done, or if they marry someone who is. Marriages between humans and demons are rare though. I only know of four."

"I thought the only one was between Lucifer and Lilith."

"That's the only marriage between a human and an angel. Not demon." He began licking his paw.

Grace thought back on the angel she'd seen earlier. Frightfully beautiful — and utterly genderless.

"Is Lucifer male?" she asked.

"Yes. He's an angel. They decide their own gender. If they decide on one at all."

"I see," Grace said, considering it.

Making their way through Hell once again, Grace tried to soak in as much as possible. They were walking on a red brick road, and both sides of it were lined with small houses. The road was both too uneven and too narrow to allow for cars (at least if they came from opposite directions), and dandelions were found in the cracks between the bricks. The flowers didn't appear to notice the utter lack of sunshine.

Grace saw humans and demons playing cards, arguing, going for walks, and laughing together. She could hear live music playing in the distance. She thought it sounded like Michael Jackson, but she wasn't sure.

Samael clearly knew where he was going, and so Grace followed him, too busy staring to really see where they were going.

The trip could have taken hours, but Grace hardly noticed. She hadn't had this much energy in years, and there was just so much to see.

Eventually, Samael stopped in front of small building that couldn't have been more than ten square feet.

"It's here?" Grace asked doubtfully.

Samael smirked. "You forget. Space works differently here."

With these words, the doors opened before them and showcased a room that was much, much too big to fit inside.

Grace entered, staring. It was packed with people. People yelling at each other, shoving at each other, walking around like they knew exactly where they were going. She'd been to the stock market in New York once, and she thought it was much the same, except this place was bigger, busier, and occasionally included a horned demon.

"My dad's in here?" she asked, but it did make sense. Her dad had been a stockbroker, and he'd lived for his job. This piece of Hell would be Heaven for him.

"Yes. Now let's go find him."

Grace rather thought that might be an impossible feat, but she wouldn't actually know unless she tried, and so she squeezed herself into the crowd.

She couldn't move.

For all the youth of this body, she might as well have tried to part the red sea, and all the shoving in the world didn't seem to even phase the people around her. They were probably used to it.

Beside her, Samael turned into a bull.

"That's better," he said and sighed in satisfaction. "They should be grateful none of them stepped on my tail."

Grace looked at him. She had to admit that it was pretty impressive.

"Can I ride you?"

"No." He began to walk through the crowd.

Even this crowd had to make room for a bull, though several people complained loudly as they went by. Grace followed him closely, careful not to let the crowd separate them.

They made their way through the grand room without too much difficulty. Above them was a huge chandelier, consisting of thousands upon thousands of crystals. It was beautiful but Grace was seemingly the only one to look up and see it.

Looking like he knew where he was going, Samael led her

out of the grand room and through narrow, grey hallways, occasionally stopping to talk with people. Grace rarely understood the words, except in one instance where he spoke French.

Biting her lip to keep herself from laughing, she tried to convince herself that however much fun it'd be, she still shouldn't tell Samael that she knew he was asking for directions.

And finally, the shapeshifter stopped.

"Your father's in there," he said, craning his head towards a door. In his current form, it looked bizarre. He was also much too big to fit through the modestly sized door.

Apparently, Samael realised the same as he changed back into a cat. He walked to the door and looked expectantly up at Grace. Never had he looked so much like a normal cat.

Smiling at the thought, Grace opened the door and found her father on the other side.

For half a second, she was nine again, so familiar was the sight in front of her. The back of her father's head as he sat pouring over some papers on his desk.

She cleared her throat.

"Is it important?" he said, like countless times before. He still hadn't turned around.

"Dad?" she said. "Dad, it's Grace."

She watched in anticipation as the figure slowly straightened out before it turned around to look at her.

"Grace." He gaped at her. "Aren't you much too young to be here?"

"I'm 93."

"Already?"

She thought she remembered them having a conversation just like this, back when she'd been eight.

"Yes, dad." She smiled at him. "Missed me?"

"Of course I did, sugar pie," he said, smiling at her, before he glanced backwards. At the paperwork. "Won't you come over to dinner sometime?" he said. "Here's my card. It has my address on it."

Grace accepted it, not quite understanding.

"Sure," she said. "But how about now? I haven't seen you in decades."

Her father hesitated. "I have an awful lot of work to do." He came over and kissed her on the cheek. "Tomorrow, sugar pie. I promise." He walked back to his paperwork.

It seemed a heart attack hadn't changed him one bit, but decades worth of living, however, had changed Grace.

"Why don't you come over when I've found a place?" she said and waited for his absent-minded affirmation before she turned around and walked away.

Samael turned into a bull again, and they made their way out of the building in uncharacteristic silence.

Once outside, he turned back into a human.

"Are you going to cry?" he asked her.

She looked at him in surprise. "No. Why would I?"

"I've seen warmer greetings between strangers."

Grace shrugged. "It's not like I didn't know how he is," she said. "It is what it is."

"It is what it is," he repeated. "Grace, you're really odd, you know that?"

"Thank you."

"Wasn't a compliment."

She smiled, pushing the meeting with her father out of her mind. "I didn't think it was."

She was sure that she would know other people down here. People who'd make time for her.

"What now?" she asked.

Samael glanced at her. "What do you mean?"

"What are we going to do next?" she said.

"You don't think dying, going to Heaven, going to Hell, going to a bar, going to the palace and finally going to see your father for the first time in decades counts as enough for one day?"

Well, when he put it like that.

Still though.

"I'm not tired," she said.

"Of course you're not," Samael said. "You're *dead*. But unless there's any reason to postpone sleep, I wouldn't recommend it. After a few weeks, you start hallucinating. Besides, if you go to sleep, *I* don't have to stick around, so why don't you just go to bed, little girl?"

"I'm 93 years old," she argued. "Hardly a little girl."

"You are compared to me."

"Really? How old are you?"

"Old. Do you have a place to sleep?"

"Of course not." She shrugged. "I'm sure I'll figure something out."

Sleeping on the street didn't sound so bad. It was warm, and there were plenty of people out. Why not sleep outside? It could be fun.

"There's plenty of housing available for newcomers. You should get one of those huts down at the beach. They're nice for someone like you."

"Oh."

"Are you actually disappointed?"

Grace grinned. "Just a little bit. But the hut thing sounds nice."

Crashing waves, open windows, and the sounds of the ocean. Perfect.

"And I could always sleep on the street some other time," she added.

Samael didn't answer.

"So where do you live?" Grace asked.

Samael looked at her with clear suspicion.

"Why?"

"Well, I was thinking that I could just sleep at your place for tonight."

"No."

"Why not?" she asked, surprised.

"I don't share."

"You never have people sleeping over?"

"No."

"Then I guess this is a good time to start," she said and walked in the direction she felt relatively sure the palace was in.

Samael had no choice but to follow.

* * *

Samael spent their trip telling her why she absolutely, under no circumstances and under no dire situations could ever crash at his place. He seemed to get so much enjoyment out of complaining that Grace couldn't bring herself to tell him that she could sleep somewhere else.

He was good at it though. Complaining. She had no idea how someone could complain for that long a period of time without ever repeating themselves. Though the reasons he gave her became more and more absurd.

"You're afraid that I'm a hit-man?" Grace asked.

"You could very well be an assassin," he said, though for all his suspicions he didn't look overly worried.

"Well, I'm not."

"Ah, but that's exactly what an—" He cut himself off midsentence as he caught sight of something behind her. Or someone.

"My Lord," he said, bowing respectfully. A completely different person, and even before Grace turned around, she knew who'd be standing there.

Dark.

Ominous.

Lucifer.

CHAPTER THREE:

Lucifer

Grace stared. She'd assumed that Lucifer would be as dark as the other angel had been light, but his wings were just as bright, as white, and as horrifyingly beautiful.

"Samael," Lucifer said, and Grace rather thought that he could whisper and still be heard among shooting cannonballs.

Samael seemed to shrink ever so slightly.

Then those grey eyes turned towards her, and Grace found herself unable to meet them.

"I see you have made a new friend."

"She's not my friend, my Lord."

It was somehow reassuring to know that even when Samael tried to be respectful, he was still kind of annoying.

"I'm Grace," she said, forcing herself to meet the Devil's eyes for the briefest of seconds. "My Lord," she added quickly.

"Grace Rose O'Neill," Lucifer said, causing her to gape at him. "Recently deceased. Tried to enter Heaven, but was denied entrance."

"Um, right. So I guess you already kind of know me."

"Yes."

Lucifer turned his attention back to Samael and said something in an unfamiliar language. Samael answered, and Grace took advantage of their inattentiveness to examine the Devil. Surprisingly tan skin, black hair and grey eyes, though it was none of these details that made him so very intimidating.

There was something undeniably frightening about him, though she couldn't quite put her finger on what it was. Maybe it was just knowing that he was the Devil.

But he looked tired too, she noted, once she was able to look past the brightness of his wings. There was something about the way he held himself, something in his eyes that made her think that he could probably use a couple of days in bed. Ruling over Hell was evidently a stressful job.

She'd seen how quickly Obama's hair had turned grey after he'd been elected. There must be an awful lot of stress involved in a job like that. Still, the nurse in her felt uncomfortable at the sight.

"Are you resting properly?" The words were out before she'd had a chance to stop them.

Samael stared at her in horror, while Lucifer frowned.

"Grace!" Samael hissed. "Now is not the right time to be yourself!"

"But he looks tired!" she argued and forced herself to meet the Devil's eyes once again. "You should remember to rest," she said. "I know a world isn't ruled by itself, but it won't help any if you allow yourself to fall ill."

"*Grace!*" Samael tried again. "I've realised that you're not always in control of what you're saying but *try!*"

"Well, I've seen men hold themselves like that during the war, and it never ends well. I'm a nurse. If I can't tell someone that they're hurting themselves, how would they know?"

Samael turned towards Lucifer with a mortified expression.

"I apologise, my Lord," he said. "Do forgive her. She's not right in the head." He sent Grace a withering look.

"It's no matter," the Devil answered, looking at Grace with contemplative eyes. "Samael, you keep odd company." With these words he left them, Samael sagging with relief, and Grace frowning ever so slightly.

"I really haven't done anything you should apologise for," she said, and Samael groaned.

"Not done anything! You don't tell the Devil that *he needs to rest.*"

"Well, he does! Has he always looked this tired?"

"Lucifer is not tired. He's never tired. And come on. Are you going to sleep at my place or not?"

Grace looked at him, trying to figure out what had happened in the last few minutes to make him change his mind. Samael wasn't looking at her, but rather in the direction the Devil had disappeared. He didn't look happy.

"Sure," she said. "Thanks."

She tried to push the encounter out of her mind.

But the Devil *had* looked tired.

* * *

She woke up on a couch many hours later, for a moment confused about where she was. Then everything came back to her. Death, Heaven, Hell, Samael, the Devil.

She'd ended up crashing at Samael's place, which turned out to be an apartment located inside the palace. She'd commented on how pleasant it was, and he'd told her that an apartment like that wouldn't be given to commoners like her.

Slowly, she sat up. Samael was already awake, sitting at a desk at the other end of the room. He was writing, though he soon looked up with an annoyed expression.

"Finally!" he said. "You've been sleeping for *hours*. I was just about to have you thrown out."

"Sure you were." Grace yawned. "Is there any breakfast?"

Samael glared at her. "At the table," he said, gesturing towards the middle of the room.

Grace looked over and saw a variety of bread, fruit, and an impressive amount of cake.

"Bit of a sweet tooth, huh?"

"No."

With a shrug, Grace went over and started to butter a piece of toast. Then she frowned.

"I'm not hungry," she noted.

"So?"

"Well, shouldn't I be? I haven't had anything to eat in, what? At least a day?"

"Hunger is a problem for physical bodies."

Looking down, Grace thought that she appeared quite physical. Still, she should've been hungry by now.

"If you don't need food, why is it here?" she asked.

"I happen to like eating. Now stop badgering me. I have work to do, you know."

Taking a bite of toast, Grace didn't bother with a response. She had an entire Hell to discover. An exciting new world.

"Do you have a spare toothbrush?" she asked.

"No."

"Then I guess I'll go without." She grinned at him. "I'm going exploring. Do you want to join me?"

"No."

"Not a morning person, huh?" Grace said. "Well, come find me if you change your mind."

Samael frowned. "You're actually going to explore Hell alone?"

"Sure. If truly evil people aren't allowed in, then what's the harm?"

Samael looked at her in exasperation. "I'll tell you what the harm is," he said. "You'll probably walk directly off a bridge somewhere and end up at the bottom of a river, and *I'll* get the blame. Just because I was supposed to show you around." He snorted. "Which I did."

"That you did," Grace agreed.

"And it's not like a whole week is even necessary." He rolled his eyes. "Like half an hour isn't enough to tell someone what they need to know. This is Hell. Don't get in my way. Don't get in Lucifer's way. See? Easy. Certainly didn't need a week for that."

"You're supposed to stay with me for a week?"

Samael shrugged. "Whomever I had the misfortune to show around, anyway." He sent her a doubtful look. "Are you going to be okay if I let you wander around alone?"

Grace smiled, pleased to hear that he did worry.

"Because I don't want to be blamed just because you had the idiocy to get yourself in trouble," he continued.

"Well, then come with me," Grace said.

Samael snorted. "I think not." He gestured towards the papers in front of him. "I have important things to do."

"But you're supposed to show me around."

"I'm *supposed* to get you 'acclimatised'. Which you can do just as well here. So sit still and don't bother me."

"Yesterday, you were going to let me sleep alone."

"Even Lucifer can't expect me to spend all twenty-four hours in your company." He frowned. "If I just spend my days with you, he certainly can't fault me. In fact, he really should be impressed. I'm *Samael*, and yet I'm spending my time on a puny human. So don't bother me. In fact, try to make me forget you exist. Let that be your new ambition in death."

"No, thank you," Grace said. "I'm going exploring." She walked towards the door.

Samael got up and followed her. "No, you're not," he said. "I don't feel like going anywhere."

"Then stay," Grace said. "I won't tell on you."

"I can't do that!"

"I'm sure you can if you just give it a try."

Samael scowled at her. "No," he said. "I can't. I'll get in trouble." He grimaced. "I'll go with you. We'll walk around for ten minutes, *only ten minutes*, and then we'll go back, and you will sit quietly and pretend you don't exist. Understood?"

"Sure," Grace said, bouncing slightly, barely able to contain her excitement.

"Only ten minutes," Samael repeated as they left his apartment.

"Sure," Grace said again. "Now let's go. I suppose it's too late to go to that concert I heard yesterday?"

"I said ten minutes!"

* * *

Thirty minutes later, they were standing in front of Reigh's front door, Grace having insisted that it was only polite to stop by.

She'd been delighted to discover that Hell wasn't dark. Now that it was (apparently) daytime, she could see the roof of Hell, which consisted of a yellowish white ceiling so far away that it was impossible to gauge the distance. Grace guessed a few miles at the least. It appeared to glow above them, as if the sun had been stretched out to fill the whole sky.

Reigh's house certainly fitted with the sunny ceiling. It was three stories high and buttercup yellow. It was surrounded by a white veranda, and both the door and the window trimmings were painted a dark blue. Grace found it absolutely adorable.

More so because it was squeezed in between two skyscrapers, which each appeared to have been cut directly from a mountain.

Grace knocked on the blue door and noted with delight to Samael that the door knocker was shaped like a sunflower.

He grumbled in reply.

A few seconds ticked by before the door was opened by Reigh, who lit up at the sight of them. "Miss O'Neill!" he said.

She smiled at the horned demon. "Hello," she said. "Samael and I thought we'd stop by."

She ignored Samael's derisive snort.

"I hope it's okay that I didn't call first," she said. "I don't have a phone."

"Well, of course, Miss O'Neill. I always welcome visitors." Reigh was practically radiating with happiness as he led them inside. "Would you care for a cup of tea?"

"That would be lovely," Grace said, looking around with interest as Reigh led them from the entrance and into the living room.

A fire was burning cheerfully in the fireplace that took up an entire wall. Three couches were all facing it, each covered with so many pillows that you could hardly see the cushions underneath them. A soft, white rug covered the floor, and a young woman was sitting on one of the couches, smiling shyly as they came in.

"I already had company," Reigh said in an apologetic tone.

"The more the merrier," Grace assured him and held out her hand for the woman to shake. "I'm Grace," she said.

"Mei Lien." The woman's handshake was firmer than Grace had anticipated. She was pretty, Asian, and delicately built. Her smile was shy but friendly.

Grace sat down across from her and looked on in amusement as Samael glared at the many pillows before he simply brushed an armful of them on the floor.

"I'll just make that cup of tea," Reigh said, fidgeting nervously. "I won't be long."

"A cup of tea would be lovely," Grace said, and (with a blush and a quick glance at Mei Lien) Reigh left the three of them alone.

"Don't forget the biscuits!" Samael yelled after him.

"So, how do you know Reigh?" Grace asked Mei Lien in the silence that followed.

Mei Lien blushed. "He convinced me to enter Hell," she said. She spoke with a slight accent, but Grace wasn't knowledgeable enough to place it. "I'd gone up the staircase, but when I got there, I was told that I couldn't get in."

"Not religious?" Grace asked her, remembering her own rejection.

Mei Lien's blush deepened. "No, that wasn't it," she said. She stared intently down at her hands.

"Well, what then?" Samael demanded to know. "What were those halo polishers upset about this time? Did you wear lipstick to church?"

The woman took a deep breath before she looked up at them.

"I killed my dad," she said.

"You did the right thing," Reigh said firmly as he walked back into the room, holding a tray of tea and biscuits, which he placed on the coffee table.

Mei Lien smiled at him.

"Reigh said that murderers are sometimes allowed entrance into Hell," Grace remembered. "Depending on the circumstances."

"So why did you off your old man?" Samael asked.

Reigh frowned. "That's not a polite question," he reprimanded him softly and sat down next to Mei Lien.

Samael stared at him. "Not a polite—?! Do you think I bloody care?!"

"He hurt my older sister," Mei Lien said. "And she just put up with it. She could've run away, but she stayed because of me." She took a deep breath. "Because he'd do it to me, if he couldn't do it to her. So I killed him. To make sure she never had to bear it again."

"That was very brave of you," Grace said.

The woman frowned. "Perhaps. I was just a child. No one on Earth ever found out, but when I got to Heaven, they knew. Refused to let me in. I spent the next five days outside the Gates of Hell." She sent Reigh a fond smile. "Reigh kept me company the entire time," she said. "Until he finally convinced me to come in."

Grace looked back and forth between her and Reigh. "That's nice," she said. "I just died yesterday. At least I think it was yesterday."

The woman gaped at her. "You only needed *a day* to be convinced to go to Hell?" She looked at Reigh for confirmation.

He nodded. "Yes, Miss O'Neill came yesterday." He looked at Grace. "And if you'll forgive my saying so, I did find it slightly peculiar how quickly you agreed to enter Hell."

"You must be very brave," Mei Lien said.

"Or very stupid," Samael muttered.

Grace looked at him in confusion. "But Hell is wonderful. Seems like it was a good decision to me."

"Well, it *could* have ended badly," Samael said. "As things tend to do when you don't think them through. It was a stupid, misinformed decision." He nodded decisively.

Grace looked at him for a few seconds before she decided that her focus was better spent elsewhere. She turned back towards Mei Lien. "So what do people do here in Hell?" she asked. "Besides going to bars and listening to Michael Jackson, that is."

Mei Lien considered it. "I suppose it depends on the person," she said. "A lot of people still work, though. Even with free housing and no need for food, you still need money if you want other stuff. Clothing. Furniture." She shrugged. "Concert tickets."

Grace mused it over. "I suppose I could go back to nursing," she said. "If that's still an occupation down here?"

"It is indeed," Reigh assured her. "Though people no longer get sick, accidents still happen. There will be plenty of broken bones and bruises to take care of."

"Lovely!" Grace exclaimed. "And I have all this energy as well! I'm sure I could work twelve hours a day without tiring."

"Twelve hours probably isn't necessary," Mei Lien said.

Grace smiled. "Or maybe I could get another job," she said. "Try something new. I've always wanted to be a musician. Are you still tone deaf after you die?"

"That depends," Samael said.

"On what?"

"On whether you were tone deaf back when you were alive."

"Oh. Well, being a nurse is nice too." She looked at Reigh. "How do I apply for a job here?" she asked. "And where do I get a house? Not that I mind crashing at Samael's place."

Reigh looked at Samael in surprise. "You allowed her to stay at your place?"

Samael scowled at him "Well, I couldn't… it wasn't like… she wouldn't leave!"

Reigh didn't look any less baffled.

"Your assigned guide will help you with that sort of thing," Mei Lien assured Grace. She looked at Samael, who was currently glaring at Reigh. "I assume that would be Samael?"

"I think so," Grace said. "He'll help me with all that?"

Mei Lien hesitated. "He's supposed to. I'm sure Reigh would be happy to help though."

"It would be my pleasure," Reigh assured them.

"Good," Samael said. "Then perhaps you can take her off my hands now?"

Reigh frowned. "You're supposed to look after her for the first month."

"Month?" Grace repeated. "I thought it was a week."

Samael shrugged. "Well, a week should be more than adequate time," he said. "No use wasting anyone's time. Especially mine."

Reigh frowned. "Lucifer did ask you to volunteer as a guide," he said.

"Ask isn't the word I'd use," Samael said. "And since you've offered to relieve me of my current assignment, surely this means that I'm off the hook for the month."

Mei Lien frowned. "That's not fair," she said. "He only offered to help."

Reigh reached out and gave her a gentle pat on the hand. "It's no trouble," he assured her. "I'm sure that showing Miss O'Neill around will be a pleasure."

"Great," Samael said and stood up. "Good luck with it then." He reached out and grabbed three biscuits from the tray in front of him before he made his way through the living room. At the door to the entrance, he hesitated before he turned around. "I'm going back to the bar tonight," he said. "I suppose it wouldn't be completely intolerable if you guys were there as well. As long as you don't disturb me, that is." With those words, he left.

Grace looked over at Reigh and Mei Lien. "Samael mentioned something about some huts down at the beach," she said, deciding to ignore the shapeshifter's sudden exit.

"Yes, I think I know the ones," Reigh said. "They are lovely, but there is, unfortunately, a waiting list for them. They're only given to new inhabitants if someone of high social standards speaks on their behalf. I'm surprised that Samael wasn't aware of this."

Grace considered it. She wondered if the shapeshifter perhaps *had* been.

"I suppose it can't be helped," she said. "And I'm sure there's plenty of other wonderful places." She grinned. "Besides, if I'm not growing any older, a waiting list is really only a matter of patience." She leaned forward to take a cup of tea from the tray. "So tell me," she said, looking back and forth between Mei Lien and Reigh. "How long have you two been dating?"

Reigh gaped at her while a crimson blush spread across Mei Lien's pale cheeks. Grace smiled with satisfaction. It was always nice to be right.

* * *

Grace looked around with approval. Her possibly future apartment was cosy, light, and absolutely perfect.

"It *is* rather small," Mei Lien said.

"Well, I'm only one person," Grace said. "And it's a lot bigger than the apartment I had back in nursing school."

Mei Lien peeled a sliver of paint off the living room wall and shot Grace a dubious look.

"And as it needs repainting anyway, I can pick any colour I want!" Grace said, already picturing it. Maybe a light green or a periwinkle blue. She needed money for paint, though, which meant a job.

"It's perfect," she said, smiling at Reigh.

He smiled back, clearly pleased to be helpful. "I'll make sure they put you on the list," he promised.

Grace's smile grew. "Thank you," she said. She stretched, still not used to having so much energy. "What about going to the jobcentre then? If you're up for another excursion, that is?"

Reigh hesitated.

"I can go by myself," Grace hastened to assure him. "You might be tired."

"No, not at all, Miss O'Neill. I would be pleased to. It's just that... well, your guide is supposed to be your reference when applying for a job. I was hoping to speak with him about it tonight."

"I can't get a job without Samael there?"

Reigh hesitated. "You can. It's just more difficult. Unless he agrees to hand over his duties as your guide."

"We'll just get him to do that then."

"He might not be willing to," Mei Lien said. "Officially turning his guardianship over would require paperwork. And he would then have to help someone else adjust." She frowned. "I still think he's a poor choice for a guide. Reigh was mine when I first came to Hell, and I still had trouble adjusting. I can't imagine Samael helping you find a job or getting you enrolled in the language school."

"Language school?"

"For Demoniac," Reigh explained. "The official language of Hell. Though it's not unusual for people to learn other languages with the time we have on our hands. Eternity can be long if you don't keep busy."

Grace considered it. If Samael was supposed to help her with these sorts of things, she was going to hold him to it.

"Perhaps we can meet up again later?" she asked Reigh and Mei Lien. "Tonight? At the bar?"

They looked surprised.

"Of course, Miss O'Neill," Reigh said. "Where are you going?"

"To the palace," Grace said. "To speak with a certain shapeshifter."

"He might not be too pleased," Mei Lien cautioned her.

Grace shrugged, not caring in the least. "He'll live," she said. "Now which way was the palace again?"

* * *

Walking down the hallways of Lucifer's palace, Grace was caught up in her own thoughts. She would get a job, which would be an experience in and of itself. Getting back to work. And learning Demoniac sounded like an exciting third language.

Not to mention all the other things she hadn't been able to do for decades. Snowboarding. Kayaking. Being part of a dancing flash mob.

The possibilities were endless, and she'd do them all. And she'd find new adventures, new rushes she'd never gotten to experience alive.

And then someone grabbed her by her collar and slammed her into the wall.

If she'd needed a reminder that dead people could indeed feel pain, this would've been it. Blinking repeatedly until the black spots in front of her disappeared, Grace looked into the face of a stranger. He had his lower arm up against her throat, and as Grace tried to wiggle herself free, he added to the pressure. Grace stilled, trying to get a good look at him.

The man's appearance was unkempt. He clearly hadn't showered in days, and he had just enough of a stubble for it to almost be called a beard. He was dressed in clothes that reminded Grace of her youth, and his teeth were straight but yellow.

"Hello," Grace said.

The man looked at her with wild eyes.

"Um, you're kind of hurting me," Grace told him.

"Why you and not me?!"

"What?"

"We're both sinners. Why did you fucking get to go to Hell, and I found myself *there*? Do you have any idea how long I was there for?!"

"Well, I understand it's not pleasant if your greeting committee was late, but there's really no reason to take it out on me."

The man didn't appear to have heard her.

"We're both sinners! Why were you welcome, and I wasn't?!"

More pressure was added to her throat, and Grace gasped for air.

"I'm sure you're more than welcome," she said. Or at least she tried to. "And perhaps you'd be so kind as to let me go?"

"I wasn't, though. In the end, I *begged* them to let me in, begged Hell to take me, but they just bloody *wouldn't*."

Grace got a hand under his arm and pushed it back an inch or so. Taking several deep breaths, she looked at the man in realisation.

"You're one of the sinners even Hell won't have," she said.

"But I got in!" he gloated. "They wouldn't have me, but I got in all on my own, yes I did!"

"Good for you. Now please let me go."

"I think not." He grinned at her, and she saw that there was a knife in his other hand.

"I wonder," he said, eye twitching. "I wonder what happens when you kill a dead person. Care to find out?"

"If it's the same to you, I'd rather not."

He pressed the knife against her cheek. Blood trickled down.

"I care to find out," the man whispered before he leaned over and licked the blood off. "I bet it's real interesting."

"Let her go," a voice commanded. A low voice that would have been heard over shooting cannonballs. Lucifer.

The man turned around, pulling her with him so that she was between him and the Devil.

"You wouldn't let me in," the man said. "I screamed, and I begged, and I cried, and you wouldn't let me in."

"Your presence was not desired."

The knife was touching Grace's throat now.

"What about now?" the man said, and Grace realised that he was crying. "When I have one of the sinners you *wanted?*"

"No."

The man disappeared. He simply turned into dust behind her, and Grace fell to her knees as he no longer held her up, knife falling harmlessly to the ground.

Grace spent several seconds gasping for air. Then. Then she looked up at the Devil.

"What was that?"

"An Undesirable Sinner."

"Yeah, I kind of got that. But how did he come in? And are there more like him? Why did he attack me?"

Lucifer looked at her, and Grace fell silent.

"Sorry," she mumbled.

"He came in through a hole in the wall. There are more like him, though they are still few in numbers and easily dealt with once found. I assume that he attacked you out of jealousy for your place in Hell."

"Oh," Grace said. "Okay. And, um, thank you. For not letting him kill me, I mean. *Could* he have killed me?"

The Devil didn't answer, but merely turned around and started to walk away.

"Follow me," he said, and Grace hurried to stumble after him. She guessed snowboarding had to wait.

"You are not to tell anyone what has happened," Lucifer told her.

"Sure."

"Both Heaven and Hell have held out Undesirables for millennia."

"Not very well, it seems."

Lucifer stopped and turned to look at her.

"Miss O'Neill," he said. "Hell has successfully kept out people like him for millennia. Until three weeks ago when the first one entered."

"What has changed?"

"Much," he said and started to walk once again. "Now be silent."

Grace was silent.

CHAPTER FOUR:

Lilith

In the end, the Devil took her to what appeared to be a bedchamber. A bedchamber that made the Royal Suite at the Four Seasons look like the place behind a dumpster at McDonalds. Priceless paintings hung upon the walls, and luxurious rugs covered the floor. It was a museum as much as it was a bedroom, and the only thing ruining the image was the unmistakable stench of sickness in the room.

In the middle, lying on a large canopy bed, was a woman. She must have been beautiful before the sickness had gotten to her. Now, however, her hair lay limp around her face, her black skin stretched over frail bones, like leather over a drum, and her every breath sounded like a struggle for air.

She was surrounded by doctors, who all looked up as they entered, only to immediately return to their work.

"My wife," Lucifer said. "Lilith."

Grace stared at her. "She's sick."

"She became ill a bit over a month ago. Nothing has helped. Then, about a week later, the first Undesirable entered Hell. You, however, are the first resident they've dared to attack."

Grace looked at the woman in the bed.

"Why have you brought me here?" she asked.

"You are a nurse."

"Yes. Once upon a time. But... you must have the best doctors imaginable down here, and I wasn't... I was good, but I wasn't the best in my field."

"I am aware of your situation."

"My situation?"

"Your unyielding sense of optimism. I require someone who is unable to see how bad things are."

Grace frowned. "It's not like that," she said before she realised that she probably shouldn't argue with the Devil. Still though. In for a penny, in for a pound.

"I'm aware of when things are bad," she said. "*This* is clearly bad. I just... I just look at the bright side, that's all."

Lucifer looked at her, and if he'd seemed tired before, he now looked as if he hadn't slept for centuries. "My wife has an uncanny ability to tell when someone is lying," he said. "When the doctors tell her that she will be fine, she knows that it is a lie. You, however, honestly believe that it might work out for the best. She could use a little of that belief."

"So you brought me here to be her companion?"

"Your skills as a nurse are an asset as well," he said. "And you have already been made knowledgeable about the current state of Hell. I would prefer not to inform more people than necessary."

"But don't people deserve to know?"

"Panic makes people do stupid things, and I do not desire distractions."

"And you... you trust that I won't tell anyone?"

"I do not. You would not willingly betray a secret, but you are currently showing an inability to hold your thoughts to yourself. I shall have someone keep an eye on you."

"I'm getting a warden?" Grace asked.

"Think of him as your companion."

"Who?"

"Samael will have to do."

Grace stared at him. Samael had hardly allowed her to sleep over, and Lucifer wanted him to spend his every moment with her? Then she remembered Samael's changed attitude when they'd run into the Devil. If Lucifer told him to do something, Grace was willing to bet just about anything that Samael would do it.

"Okay," she said. Because after all... what else could she say?

* * *

Samael stared at Lilith with a horrified expression.

"How could this happen?" he whispered and looked at the Devil with desperation. "Why haven't you healed her?"

The Devil narrowed his eyes, and Samael shrank back ever so slightly.

"Do you think," the Devil said, voice cold, "that I would let her suffer like this if I knew how to change it?"

"No, I just— I mean— No, of course not, my Lord," Samael stammered. "It's just... it's you. I just assumed that..." he trailed off.

"Keep an eye on her," Lucifer said. "She is your responsibility. Try to live up to it."

Samael cringed. "Yes, my Lord," he muttered, looking at the floor.

The Devil turned around to leave.

"Wait!" It was Samael, though the shapeshifter looked horrified by his own audacity.

Lucifer turned. "Was that an order you gave me?"

Samael flinched. "I didn't mean it as an order, my Lord," he said. "I just... it's me. I could help. Perhaps. If I just knew what has happened."

Grace moved over to stand next to Samael, wanting to show her support. She couldn't quite bring herself to stare defiantly at the Devil, but she did put her hand on Samael's arm. The shapeshifter stiffened ever so slightly, but he didn't pull away.

For a long time, the Devil merely examined them in silence.

"Come," he then said.

He brought them into an office, which consisted almost entirely of bookshelves. In the middle of it stood a single desk, and there was a bowl of apples on a nearby table.

"I know that Samael is familiar with my history, but what about you? What do you know of the Devil?"

"You were kicked out of Heaven," Grace said. "You had a

disagreement with your dad."

The Devil's eyebrows lifted ever so slightly. "True," he said. "Though I have never heard it described like that before. So tell me. What happened next?"

"God threw you into Hell and condemned you to torment the souls of sinners for all of eternity," Grace said. "Except... except that part is obviously less correct."

"Indeed. I was not condemned to this place. I travelled here myself, to lick my wounds as you humans are fond of saying. I found that I liked the place. I determined to make it the kingdom I thought Father's should have been."

"It's nice," Grace said. "Certainly better than advertised."

"And herein lies the problem. Not everyone agrees with the truth of Hell. They prefer Dante's version." His lips curled ever so slightly at the name. "And if I will not give them the version they desire, they plan to create it themselves."

Grace frowned. "But... I mean, people can't just change Hell."

"They can if they have the Voice of God."

Grace frowned. "What's the Voice of God?" she asked, but her question was completely drowned out by Samael's yell of alarm.

"A human got their hand on the Voice of God?!" He sounded horrified at the mere thought.

"No," the Devil answered calmly. "But a human has gotten their hands on a part of it."

"Um, excuse me," Grace tried again. "But what exactly is this Voice-thing?"

"The Voice of God," Samael said, voice grave, "is an ancient tool with the power of the Trinity."

"The power of the what?"

"The Trinity," Samael repeated, sending her a reproachful look. "It means that it has the power of the mind, the body, and the soul."

"Oh." She paused. "I still don't get it."

Samael sighed. "The power of the mind can bend the will of angels and demons, the power of the body can create or destroy the walls between the worlds, and the power of the soul can create or destroy souls."

Grace considered it. "That sounds bad."

"Bad doesn't begin to cover it. It's a catastrophe."

"Not yet," Lucifer said. "Only one part of the Voice has been found. The part of the body. Without the others to increase its strength, it can open holes in the walls between the worlds, but it cannot tear them down nor build new ones."

"So kind of like a broken elevator," Grace mused.

The Devil looked at her, eyebrows slightly raised.

Grace felt herself blushing. "Well, you know, how a broken elevator can't go from floor to floor, but you can still force the doors apart and slip through. Though doing so is probably a bad idea."

The Devil continued to look at her, and she fell silent.

"We have to find the other parts before they do," Samael said.

"I have already sent out a search party," the Devil said.

"Send me as well!" Samael demanded before he flinched. "I mean, please consider sending me as well, my Lord. Let me help."

"You have proven yourself reckless. I have better people to send." Lucifer seemed to hesitate before he walked over and placed a hand on Samael's shoulder. "It is better that you remain here in Hell."

Grace looked at the pair in surprise. Considering Samael's obvious respect for Lucifer, it seemed odd that the Devil would now call him reckless. Samael was clenching his fists, a pained expression on his face. He didn't, however, argue.

Lucifer let go of his shoulder.

"Now go," he commanded. "Return to my wife. Comfort her."

Grace opened her mouth to protest, only to gasp in pain as

Samael stepped on her foot. Hard.

"Yes, my Lord," he said. "As you command."

He bowed to Lucifer before he dragged Grace with him out of the office, leaving the Devil looking more tired than ever.

* * *

"I should go," Samael said for the tenth time.

Grace watched him pace back and forth in silence. They were the only two people left in the chamber with Lilith after she had briefly woken up and ordered everyone out. They had been the only ones to defy the order, though Grace wasn't sure if Lilith had even been aware of what she was saying. She'd immediately fallen back into unconsciousness.

"Except, Lucifer told me I shouldn't," Samael added, once again.

Grace remained silent, watching his internal struggle with fascination.

"He told me not to go the last time, and I did, and it was an utter disaster."

"What happened?"

Samael looked up, seemingly surprised to still see her there.

"What? Oh, I gave an apple from the Tree of Knowledge to Eve. Still don't see why *I* was to blame, though. I mean, she could have just not eaten it."

"You were the snake?"

"Yes." Samael made an annoyed gesture as if he couldn't believe she was focusing on such a trivial matter at a time like this.

"But how could I just stay here?" he continued. "I fought beside Lucifer during the rebellion. Well, I mean, technically I was a scout, but still. I helped build this place. I've been by his side for millennia. I can't just do nothing while a human threatens everything we've built."

He seemed to hesitate, and as he turned towards Grace, she could see the fear in his eyes.

"But he would be so angry," he said.

"You should go," a voice croaked, and they both turned towards the bed in surprise.

Lilith was struggling to sit up, and Grace hurried over and stuffed a large pillow behind her back.

"Thank you," Lilith whispered before she turned her attention back to Samael. "You should go. My husband—" She was cut off by a coughing fit. "My husband can be stubborn," she said, once she'd regained her breath. "He doesn't forget. Even when he should."

She looked at Samael with a grave expression, and Grace could see the queen that she must have been. That she still was. She could see herself following this woman through catastrophes and triumphs alike.

She wanted to help her.

"Have you been diagnosed yet?" she asked, flipping through the options in her head. Probably not cancer, considering the retainment of her hair. Ischemic cardiomyopathy would explain the fatigue but would likely have resulted in a weight *gain* rather than loss. And Samael had assumed that Lucifer could just magically heal her, so they were probably dealing with something rare and not easily diagnosed. Something like—

"It's the curse of God," Lilith croaked.

"I'm sorry, what?"

"The curse of God," Samael repeated, impatience clear in his voice.

"I went against God's plan," Lilith said. "He gets angry when you do that, and he still hadn't learned to—" She was cut off by another coughing fit. On her nightstand was a pitcher of water and an empty glass, and Grace hurried to fill it. Before she could offer it to Lilith, however, the coughing had stopped.

"Hadn't learned… how to appropriate his reactions," the sick woman said. "And so he cursed me." She closed her eyes and took several deep long breaths. Her breathing was louder than it should've been, and there was a raspy quality to it that concerned Grace.

"I sought asylum in Lucifer's new kingdom. It was the only place where the curse couldn't—" Another coughing fit. Grace held the glass up to Lilith's lips, and the woman forced down the water between coughs. Finally, the fit subsided.

"Thank you," she said. She looked at Grace with exhaustion clear in her gaze. "Lucifer denied me entrance at first, but I always was a stubborn one." She smiled weakly.

"That's why you're sick," Samael said, his horror evident. "Because there are holes in the walls protecting you."

"Yes. But my sickness—" She cut herself off, and for a second, Grace thought that she was about to cough again. Instead, Lilith held a hand up to her mouth, and Grace realised that the risk of vomiting was far more likely.

Nothing came up, however, and Lilith let her hand fall back down on the blanket covering her. She was taking long, deep breaths, her eyes falling shut. Grace wondered if she'd fallen asleep. Then the woman opened her eyes again.

"If someone gains control of the Voice, my sickness is the least of our concerns," she said. "So go. Find the pieces and bring them here."

Samael nodded once, shakily. "I will," he said before he looked at Grace. "Will you...?"

"I won't tell," she promised. "Or at least I'll try not to, but sometimes things just seem to slip out."

A raspy laugh came from the woman in the bed.

Samael only gave her a strained smile. "I've noticed," he said. "But that wasn't what I was going to ask."

"What then?"

"Would you go with me?"

Grace stared at him. "With you?" she repeated. "Why are you asking me? You hardly know me."

"That's true." Samael took a deep breath. "But you're the only one down here who might be moronic enough to go against Lucifer's wishes. Besides..." he trailed off, but Grace saw in his eyes what he couldn't bring himself to say out loud.

He didn't want to go alone.

"Yes." The word slipped out of her mouth as easily as breathing. "Yes," she repeated. "I'll go with you."

"It's going to be dangerous," Samael warned her.

Grace grinned at him, eyes sparkling.

"Sounds like fun," she said.

CHAPTER FIVE:

The Brother

"I can't believe that people can just leave," Grace noted.

"Why not?" Samael asked as he pushed open the doors leading out of Hell.

The outside was almost as Grace had left it. A ground that consisted of dark soil, a white sky, and a sleek, fast-paced walkway. Except said walkway now sported a safety railing, and Grace wondered if Reigh was the one to thank for that.

A shove to her back caused Grace to stumble forward, more due to the surprise of it than any real force. She regained her balance and glanced back at the shapeshifter, who was looking far too innocent as he followed her out.

"Bit clumsy, are we?"

Grace ignored the taunt. "Hell doesn't exactly have the best reputation," she said instead. "I thought demons would stop people from leaving. At least at first."

"Not if they're with me," Samael said smugly as he closed the door behind them.

Grace returned her gaze to the walkway that would lead them to the Gates of Heaven. It couldn't be more than twenty feet away from the entrance to Hell, and it was such a bizarre link between the two worlds that she couldn't help but smile.

"What's that stupid grin about?"

"I was just thinking that the afterlife has more in common with the average airport than I had anticipated. It's kinda funny." Grace looked out into the horizon. She couldn't see the end of the walkway, but if she squinted, she could just barely make out the stairway as a thin line out there in the distance. She wondered exactly how far they'd have to walk.

She looked back at the moving walkway. "Can't we use it?"

she asked. "Isn't there some button or something that'll make it go the other way?"

"No."

"Could you turn into a horse then? I could ride you there."

He gave her a look of disgust. "Absolutely not. And I'd die before I'll carry a human, so don't bother asking again."

Grace grinned and made her way over to the moving walkway. At least they had the world's easiest directions to follow, which was to walk beside it until they were there. Easy-peasy, lemon squeezy.

They began walking, Grace eternally thankful for the return of her youth. Her entire body seemed to be brimming with energy, and their brisk walk was quite pleasant.

Samael, however, kept glancing nervously around as they walked, and Grace wondered what he had to be so nervous about. There was nothing around them but dark soil and white sky.

"What's eating you?" she asked.

"What do you mean?"

"Well, why so nervous?"

Samael stared at her. "Do you have any idea how angry Lucifer is going to be when he finds out about this? It's a bloody miracle he hasn't already."

Grace shrugged. "I'm sure he'll forgive you," she tried to comfort him. "You're doing what you think is best."

"Yeah, well, the road to Hell and all that. He still hasn't ended my punishment for the apple-incident."

"You're being punished?"

"There certainly aren't any other nobles forced to be part of the welcome committee of Hell."

"Doesn't seem like much of a punishment."

"Not much of a—! It's *demeaning*."

Grace considered it. "Well, I'm glad it caused us to meet," she said.

"Of course, you are. Besides, it's not leaving Hell that's a problem. It's entering Heaven that's going to be the real challenge. In case you haven't realised, I'm not exactly popular up there."

"Heaven?"

"We're going to see Adam. If anyone would know where the Voice of God might be, it'd be him. Annoying little snoop."

"Oh." Grace considered it. Going to Heaven did sound pleasant, even if it was only as a visitor. And maybe she could see her mom while she was there. If they stayed long enough, there might even be enough time to share a sherry between them as in the old days.

"I'm sure they'll let us in once we explain things," she said.

"Your optimism is sickening."

Grace smiled. "I thought that you liked that about me."

"I'm starting to wonder if it's just masquerading stupidity. Heaven is not going to just let us in."

"Well, why not? It's not like we're asking to move there. And if they won't let us in, we can just ask them to send Adam out."

"We could," Samael admitted. "But Adam hates me even more than most people up there. I doubt he'll be willing to meet."

"We'll just have to make sure he knows it's an emergency. That we need his help."

"I don't think he's interested in helping out anyone from Hell," Samael noted. "Besides, he's been so awfully paranoid since that little misunderstanding with the apple."

"That seems pretty understandable."

Samael shrugged. "He could've just said no," he muttered. "No one forced it down his throat."

"Maybe don't say that when we talk with him?"

"Of course, I won't. I'll have you know that I can be *very* charismatic. I did convince them to go against God back then."

"Before you made Adam all paranoid."

"And good thing I did too. If he hadn't been so overly

suspicious, he wouldn't have that annoying need to know just about *everything*, and we wouldn't even know where to start."

"You really think he knows where it is?"

"Probably not," Samael admitted. "But if someone has heard anything, it'll be Adam. And it's the only lead we have."

They walked in silence from then on, every attempt of Grace's to start a conversation being immediately shut down. The staircase in the distance was slowly moving closer.

And then, finally, they were there.

The crude staircase was as long as Grace remembered, thousands upon thousands of steps before them. With a shrug she took the first one, knowing that the trip wouldn't become shorter by her staring at it.

"Wait," Samael said.

She looked back at him. "What?"

He turned into a cat and jumped into her arms. "Okay, you may go."

Grace looked down at the cat. "You want me to carry you?"

"Yes."

"What happened to not carrying each other even if our lives depended on it?"

"I said that I wouldn't carry you. There's no reason for you not to carry me. You should consider it an honour."

"I don't," Grace informed him but continued upwards just the same. He wasn't heavy.

Step by step they made their way upwards. Around eight thousand steps later Grace refused to carry Samael any further, and he reacted to this refusal by loudly complaining about that fact for the next thousand steps or so.

Grace let him; it seemed to soothe him.

Far later, Grace was thoroughly exhausted. It was fortunate that she was dead, and it therefore took more to tire her out. She was still grateful, however, when she once again stood in front of the Wooden Gates.

Except, this time someone was already there.

The man was human by the looks of it. He was Caucasian, with brown hair, kind eyes, and a nose that seemed to have been broken once and not healed properly.

"Hello," Grace said politely.

Samael, however, glared at the man. "You're not dead," he told him, sounding mortally offended at the thought.

The man stared at the talking cat before he seemed to pull himself together.

"No," he said. "I'm not."

Grace frowned, confused. "How can you be here if you're not dead?" she asked.

"Drugs," Samael answered for him. "And an impressive quantity of them as well."

The man flinched. "I'm currently in a coma," he told them.

"Brought on by drugs," Samael added.

The man sighed. "Brought on by drugs," he admitted. "But I had to."

Samael snorted, a bizarre sound coming from a cat. "I'm sure you did," he said. "You *had* to. I hope you're not stupid enough to believe that Heaven accepts that excuse? You humans have been using it for millennia."

The man lifted his head proudly. "I'm aware that my choice might have barred me entrance into Heaven," he said. "But I don't regret making it. My brother is my responsibility, and I have to make sure that he won't hurt anyone."

"Yeah, well get lost. Whatever reason you're here for, ours is far more important, so why don't you just leave and stop wasting our time?"

"Samael!" Grace scolded and turned towards the man. "I'm sorry," she said. "But we are in a bit of a hurry. Do you think perhaps this issue with your brother can wait a couple of minutes?"

The man shook his head. "No," he said. "I can't waste time. I have to stop him."

Samael rolled his eyes. "I've seen millennia full of the worst acts a human can commit. They're rarely important in the big picture, so what, pray tell, is your brother planning to do that's so crucial that it can't wait?"

The man fidgeted nervously for a few seconds, looking everywhere but at them.

"He's trying to rule Hell," he said.

* * *

For several seconds Grace and Samael could only stare at the man.

"Your brother is the one who's found a piece of the Voice," she realised. "And you're trying to stop him."

The man nodded, miserable. "Dad was a priest," he told them. "He loved God, and he taught us to love God as well."

"It's hardly love that makes someone want to rule," Grace noted, while Samael seemed to be too infuriated to speak.

The man winced. "Our religion meant everything for dad," he said. "Every day, hours would be dedicated to the study of the bible. He even taught us Hebrew. We needed to be able to read the Testament as it was meant to be read." He smiled slightly. "Apparently it lost something in the Latin version. My brother learned every word by heart. We both did. But Jacob — that's my brother's name — he became fanatic in his studies. Suddenly it wasn't enough to believe. He had to know. So he came here."

"What a bloody buffoon!" Samael hissed.

Grace knelt down to soothe down his ruffled fur. "He died?" she asked. "Seems like a steep price to pay for a bit of impatience."

The man smiled bitterly. "Perhaps I'm explaining myself poorly. He came here the same way I did." He looked down. "I'm still shocked that my brother would go to such lengths when we already knew the truth. These drugs... they're dangerous. You can never be sure that you're going to wake up again."

"But he did," Grace noted. "Though I still don't see how

knowing the truth would make him want to rule Hell."

The man avoided her eyes. "I was there when my brother awoke," he said. "He was... frantic. Kept talking about how the worlds needed to be corrected. How he was going to right the wrongs. He said that the rules had been twisted, and he told me that... that..."

"That *what?!*" Samael demanded.

"That he hadn't been allowed entrance into Heaven."

"The angel told him to go to Hell," Grace guessed, remembering her own meeting with the guardian.

"Yes. He never forgave that."

"But why go against Hell?" Grace wondered. "When Heaven was the place that rejected him?"

"Because Hell rejected him as well."

"He's one of the Undesirable Sinners," Grace realised, wondering what exactly the religious man had done to have Hell refuse him as well.

"Yes. Being rejected by Heaven was one thing, but by the place that was supposed to be the condemnation of all sins... He couldn't take it. He concluded that something was wrong with both Heaven and Hell. He plans to make them as they ought to be. He asked me to join them. He got... angry, when I refused."

"Them?" Samael repeated. "Who exactly are 'them'?"

"Him and his... he calls them his apostles. His followers."

"A cult then," Grace mused. She'd heard of enough men pretending to be the next messiah.

The man frowned but didn't object.

"How does he get them?" Samael demanded to know. "These so-called apostles of his? He doesn't sound horribly charismatic. Or clever."

Grace wondered if Samael *liked* to annoy people. It would certainly explain a lot.

"He met them in Limbo."

"Limbo!" Samael stared at him. Then he scowled. "And he

just happened to tell you that?" he asked, clearly suspicious.

"My brother was convinced that I would see reason. He was telling me about the successes he'd already had."

"So he was bragging?" Grace translated.

"How many of these followers does he have?" Samael asked. "Are we looking at dozens? Hundreds?"

"Eleven."

"Eleven," Samael repeated. "There are thousands of desperate souls in Limbo, and he gets help from *eleven?!*"

"Well, I met eleven," Daniel said. "But he's able to call forth more than that. He brought one to our world when I was there. The man was... thankful. At least until my brother sent him back."

"How long did it take him?" Samael asked.

They looked at him in confusion.

"To call forth someone from Limbo," Samael clarified. "How long did it take him?"

The man frowned. "Why?"

"If we ever meet your brother, I'd like to know how long we have before his backup arrives."

The man appeared to think back. "I'm not sure," he said. "Around twenty minutes?"

Samael nodded, thoughtfully. "Should be long enough," he murmured. Suddenly, he looked up at the man with sharp eyes. "Why are you telling us all this?" he demanded to know. "You don't know us."

"I'm not stupid," the man said. "I'm aware that Hell must be fighting against my brother. I assume that you're here for the same reason that I am. We're on the same side."

"We most certainly are not! I'm on the side of Lucifer."

"And I'm on the side of God. But we want the same thing. To allow things to stay as they are. Who am I to question God? If he did not allow my brother into Heaven, he must have had his reasons."

"You don't sound like a very good brother," Samael noted callously.

"I hope to save my brother as well. It's not too late to repent. But I need to find him first. I haven't been able to locate him since our last meeting."

"And how exactly are you planning to do so?"

"I'm going to ask God for help."

Samael laughed, but it wasn't a cheerful laughter. It was loud, and it was mocking.

"Ask God," he ridiculed. "God doesn't answer to neither angels nor demons, and he certainly won't answer to you."

"God always listens."

"Listens, yes. But answers?"

"Samael," Grace scolded. "Be nice."

"He's being ridiculous!"

"And so are you. This man knows who's doing all of this. Do you really think alienating him is in your best interest? Lucifer's best interest?"

Samael glowered at her, but he fell silent. "I guess he could join us," he finally said. "Temporarily. Until I say otherwise."

Grace smiled at him. "Thank you," she said before she turned towards the man and held out her hand. "I'm Grace."

The man took it with a baffled expression. "Daniel," he said. "You're... human, I presume?"

"I am, yes." Grace smiled.

"And yet you are travelling with this demon?"

"He's really not as bad as he seems."

The man, Daniel, looked at the hissing cat with a dubious expression, but he didn't contradict her. "The Devil sent you as well?" he asked.

"No, actually he didn't send—" Grace cut herself off. Maybe the truth wasn't in their best interest. "No, only Samael was sent," she said. "I just decided to tag along."

"Why?"

Grace frowned, confused by the question. "Well, he asked," she said.

"He… asked?"

"Yes. And since we've all agreed that we want the same thing, perhaps we should concentrate on getting into Heaven? My last attempt was quite a failure."

The man nodded in agreement. "I've been waiting for hours," he said. "But if they mean to test our patience, I do not intend to fail."

"Well, patience has never been one of my virtues," Grace noted before she walked over and knocked on the door. Nothing happened, and so she hammered on it instead.

Neither Daniel nor Samael made a move to help her. Apparently, sinners and saints alike were equally incapable of being gentlemen. Grace's hands started to hurt, so she used her feet instead, kicking insistently on the doors to Heaven. She was starting to get downright peeved. The least they could do was answer. Anything else was just plain rude.

Suddenly the angel was there, appearing as abruptly as the monster in a bad horror movie. Except terrifying.

Shielding her eyes against the light, Grace glanced back at her companions. Daniel was concealing his eyes altogether, while Samael stared at the angel in defiance.

"What do you want?" the angel asked, and it was impossible to say if it sounded annoyed or not. Grace shook off her surprise at the sight of it.

"I'm terribly sorry for being rude and whatnot, banging on your door like that," she said. "But we need to be let into Heaven." She forced herself to look the angel in the eyes even as tears streamed down her face from the pain. "Please and thank you," she added.

"No," the angel answered, and Grace was starting to kind of dislike that word.

"Not permanently," she assured it. "You've made that

impossibility perfectly clear, thank you very much. But we do need to make a visit. A little one."

"No."

"It's important."

The angel didn't answer, and Grace looked towards the door. She pulled at the handle. Locked.

"Please?" she asked.

"No."

Samael stepped forward. "I've been sent by Lucifer himself," he lied, sounding awfully regal for a cat. "A danger has come forth, threatening Hell and Heaven alike. It is time to join forces and together fight this threat. To do so, we need to speak to Adam, and I must, therefore, ask you to make an exception and allow us entrance. For angels and demons alike, for all of mankind, and for the greater good."

"No."

Samael's regal look was replaced with a scornful glare. "You angelic piece of detritus, who do you think you are to—"

The rest of what he wanted to say was cut off when Daniel hurriedly sat down next to him and held a hand over the cat's mouth.

"I apologise for the inconvenience," he said. "But it *is* for the greater good. We need to stop my brother, and I beg you to help us do so."

"No."

"May I at least ask why not?"

"Your companions are not worthy of Heaven, and you are not dead."

Daniel stood up and stepped towards the angel with a pleading expression. "I'm seeking a meeting with God," he said. "If you won't let us in, please ask Him if He would give us a few moments of His time."

"God's time is valuable," the angel noted.

"And I can't even imagine how much," Daniel agreed. "But I

think this is worth it."

"We could talk with Adam instead," Grace added helpfully. "If God is unavailable."

The angel looked at them, the pleading man, the scornful cat, and Grace.

"Very well," it said. "You may enter Heaven under supervision and during a period of time which I determine. Follow me."

With these words, the doors to Heaven opened by their own accord, blinding Grace as light poured out. Squinting her eyes, Grace walked towards the light and into the Kingdom of God.

* * *

Pastel.

That was the first thought that popped into her mind. There was something bright, and light, and undeniably pastel about Heaven, and though it all seemed perfectly pleasant, Grace missed the barbecue and Michael Jackson music of Hell.

Or considering that she hadn't actually experienced either, perhaps she really just missed the idea of them.

Bird chirping filled the air with cheerful song, and as far as Grace could see there were green plains, blue sky, and countless small buildings spread about, too small to be called houses, but too big to be called huts.

It was a bit anticlimactic, if she had to be honest. This seemed more like a Disney movie than anything else. Looking at her companions, she smiled as she saw their vastly different reactions to Heaven.

While Daniel was looking at the scenery with awe, Samael looked almost nauseous, and he kept glancing at the birds with predatory eyes.

The angel was already walking, and as they followed it, Grace scooped Samael up in her arms.

"Behave," she told him, keeping her voice down. "They're not going to help us if you eat one of the residents. Even if it is a bird."

Samael looked insulted. "I wouldn't eat a bird!" he declared. "Unless it was cooked first, that is. All those feathers." He shuddered theatrically to show his repulsion before he shot another hungry look at one of the birds.

Grace ignored him.

"Does God live far away?" she asked the angel, whose light seemed to have dimmed considerably since they entered Heaven. At least he wasn't blinding them any more.

"I am not taking you to see God," the angel said.

"Oh. Okay. Adam then?"

"Yes."

"You're a person of few words, aren't you?"

"I am."

Grace stopped for half a second before she resumed walking. Was the angel joking? She glanced at its serious expression. Probably not. What a shame.

"Is it far to Adam?" she asked instead.

"Yes."

Samael made a dissatisfied sound. "What do you mean, it's far? Can't you bend space here?"

"Yes."

"Then why aren't you?"

"Shortcuts lead to Hell."

"You have got to be bloody kidding me!"

"Samael!" Grace scolded and looked up at the angel with an apologetic expression. "I'm sorry," she said. "But we are in a bit of a hurry. Could you perhaps bend the rules just this once?"

"I let you in."

"And we'll be out a lot quicker if we used a shortcut," Samael noted.

The angel didn't answer, and Grace wondered if it simply didn't want to bother, or if it actually considered his words.

"Of course, I'm sure it's preferable to break one rule over two," Samael added, and Grace looked down at him in surprise.

"After all," Samael added. "All rules are equal, aren't they?"

A sound came from the angel that reminded Grace of a gust of air through wind chimes. She realised that it was a sigh.

"They are not," the angel said. Admitted. "Do not think, shapeshifter, that I am unaware that you are manipulating me. You are, however, correct in your estimation. Letting you stay here longer than necessary would indeed be worse than bending space to arrive faster."

It was the longest coherent speech Grace had heard from the angel so far, and she squashed down a sudden urge to praise it for its growing social skills.

The angel lifted its hand, and Grace looked on in awe as the air in front of them *cracked*, fracturing like a porcelain cup.

"That is awesome," she whispered, thoroughly impressed.

Daniel smiled at her enthusiasm, while Samael merely snorted. The angel reached out and seemed to take hold of one side of the crack, which it pulled open until a hole was revealed, big enough to easily fit a grown man. Through it, Grace could see a flowery meadow and a sunny sky.

"Go," the angel ordered them. "I will not keep it open longer than necessary."

Samael rolled his eyes but jumped through it all the same, quickly followed by Grace and Daniel. Finally, the angel entered through, and the hole closed, leaving behind no trace of its existence.

They were surrounded by more flowers than Grace had ever seen. Colourful flowers of every shape and size, and in a quantity far beyond anything she'd seen on Earth. Not too far from them sat a beautiful woman with dark brown skin and long, black hair. She looked up in fright at their arrival.

"Hello," Grace said.

The woman let out a shriek and ran away.

Grace frowned, relatively sure that it hadn't been anything she'd said.

"What was up with her?" she said.

Samael cleared his throat, sounding almost embarrassed.

"That was Eve," he said. "There's a slight possibility that she doesn't remember me fondly."

"I thought you had appeared as a snake."

"I did. You know, that last time."

Grace looked at the cat at her feet, who was currently licking his paw. She wondered if he appeared that indifferent on purpose.

"You went to see her more than once?"

"Of course. You think I could've made her take a bite after only one meeting? It took weeks."

"What happened to her just being able to say no?"

"She could. And she never did. Not even once. She just... took a while to say yes."

Grace sighed. "They're not going to want to help us, are they?" she said.

Samael switched paws, not bothering to answer.

"I'm sure they'll help," Daniel said. "They're good people. They'll know it's the right thing to do."

Samael rolled his eyes. "Bit idealistic, are we?"

"Daniel is probably right," Grace said. "Besides, there's no harm in asking. Though we should probably start following her soon. She was in quite a hurry."

She turned around to ask the angel if it had any advice, only to discover that it was gone. She looked at the empty space in surprise. Then she shrugged and went off in the direction Eve had run. After a few steps, she looked back at the man and the cat.

"Well, are you coming?" she asked. "We have a woman to calm down, and her husband to convince to help out the demon, who led them both into temptation. We should probably get to it."

CHAPTER SIX:

Adam

To say that Adam disliked Samael would be like saying that the French Revolution gave a couple of nobles a slight headache. No, as Adam looked at Samael, Grace understood why people had once believed that The Evil Eye could actually kill people. And why you'd feel safer burning whoever looked at you like that.

As Adam glared at the cat in front of him, his handsome features were drawn into something that wasn't pretty at all. He was Black, Grace was unsurprised to notice, having come to expect it after seeing both Lilith and Eve. It still felt a little odd, however, as she was used to the Caucasian depiction of him. His dark hair fell in tight curls around a high forehead, and his brown eyes shone with rage. Eve stood behind him, shivering in fear.

"You," Adam said. "*Snake.*"

"Hello, Adam," Samael answered. "What has it been? Couple of millennia?"

"Nowhere near long enough."

"Missed me?" Samael smirked as only cats can. "Or perhaps the missus has?"

"Samael!" Grace exclaimed, while Daniel gasped in horror behind her.

"What?"

"Manners!"

Samael sighed. "Fine." He looked back at Adam. "I apologise," he said. "Both for that admittedly dreadful joke, and for that unfortunate incident with the apple."

"Unfortunate incident?!" Adam stared at him in disbelief. "You had us exiled from *Paradise!*"

With a flicker, Samael turned back into a man. He held up

his palms in the universal sign of peace.

"And I apologise," he said, his voice kinder than Grace had ever heard it. "I realise now that while you both made a choice, I shouldn't have tempted you to begin with. I'm sorry."

"Who do you think you're fooling?" Adam snarled. "That fake compassion might've worked last time, but I've gotten wiser. Everything you say is a lie. It doesn't matter what shape you take. You'll always be the snake."

"We're not here to ask for forgiveness," Grace said. "We're here to ask for help."

Adam looked at her in disbelief. "I don't know what you're doing with the snake, girl. But trust me when I say this: Get away from him, or you'll come to regret it."

"With all due respect," Grace said. "I find myself regretting very little. Samael needed my help, and I'm not about to go back on my word."

"The words of demons are worth nothing," Adam said. "So why should promises made to them be worth any more?"

"Someone is changing Hell," Daniel cut in. Probably a good idea. Grace rather got the impression that they could use a change of topic.

"I've heard," Adam said. "And they need to be stopped."

Grace faltered, surprised. She'd spent a good part of their trip trying to come up with arguments as to why exactly they *had* to stop the transformation of Hell. And now it seemed Adam had gotten there all by himself.

"So you'll help?" Daniel asked.

Adam looked at him. "I'll do what I believe is right," he said. "God decides over Heaven and Hell. We shouldn't question his decisions. I will not, however, go into a partnership with any demon, least of all *that one*."

"That's fine," Grace assured him. "You don't have to talk to him at all. Just pretend he doesn't exist."

"If only that were true."

Grace smiled, relieved that Adam at least didn't need convincing. "I've been told that you might know where the Voice is. Or where we could possibly find Jacob."

"I don't."

Grace frowned. "You must know something?"

Adam sighed. "A sinner was denied entrance to both Heaven and Hell. He now refuses to accept his fate, as all sinners do. This one, however, has a piece of the Voice of God."

"So basically," Samael said. "You know squat."

Grace sent him a look. "We were hoping for some new information," she translated.

"I do know something," Adam said.

They waited, but he made no move to continue.

"Might we inquire what it is?" Daniel asked.

Adam sent a suspicious glance towards Samael, and Grace realised the issue. So, apparently, did Samael.

"Oh, for the Sake of Hell," he muttered. "Whether you like it or not, Adam boy, I'm part of this expedition, and you'll just have to make your peace with it."

Privately, Grace thought that it was somewhat of a miracle Samael had been able to tempt anyone into anything. Personally, she didn't find him much of a people-person.

"Samael," she said. "I think you should leave."

Samael stared at her. "It's my mission!"

"Not leave permanently, of course," she assured him. "But if Adam feels his information would be harmful to tell you then that's his choice."

Samael made a rude noise. "Perhaps you should've gotten into Heaven after all," he muttered as he walked away.

Grace ignored him and turned her attention back to Adam. Eve, who'd been standing behind him, seemed to relax as Samael moved out of hearing range. She crept forward so that she was now standing beside Adam rather than cowering behind him.

"I know where God is," Adam said quietly.

"I... okay. Neat," Grace said, not sure why that was vital information.

Daniel, however, looked impressed.

"We could ask God," he whispered reverently. "We wouldn't have to get an angel to lead us to him. We could simply go ourselves."

Adam nodded, pleased. "I'll go," he said and sent a look towards Samael. "The snake stays behind. And you two will stay to watch him."

Grace was relatively sure she'd just been demoted to babysitter, but as Adam was essentially telling them that he could ask *God* for advice, she figured it a fair trade.

"Thank you," she said, because manners never hurt anyone. "And good luck."

"Good luck to you as well," he said, voice low and serious, as if Daniel and she were to guard a ferocious demon and not, well, Samael. "And..." He hesitated.

"Yeah?"

"Don't trust him."

With these words he walked away, Eve following in his steps.

Samael, seeing them leave, returned with a scowl.

"Where are they going?" he demanded to know.

Grace brushed a lock of hair away from her face as she tried to find a way to tell him that Daniel and she had essentially agreed to just sit around and keep an eye on him.

"Well," she said. "It seems that you're considered in need of guards."

There. Guards sounded better than babysitters, didn't it?

Considering Samael's smug expression, she'd made the right choice.

* * *

Grace wasn't the least surprised when Samael proved himself utterly incapable of sitting down and waiting for Adam's and Eve's return.

Pacing back and forth, he ignored the amused glances from her, continuously muttering that really, how long could it take to ask God one stupid question?

Grace wondered if perhaps now would be a good time to sneak off and share a quick sherry with her mom. She had kind of promised that she'd keep an eye on Samael, but perhaps she could take him with her?

"Samael, does Heaven have a Book of Souls?"

He frowned at her. "Of course."

"Could you read it?"

He looked at her like a teacher might look at an exceptionally dull student. "*Of course.*"

"Lovely. Would you be open to the idea of making a quick visit to my mom?"

"You're going to leave?!" Daniel exclaimed.

Grace looked at him in surprise. "Well, just briefly."

He looked at her in a horrified manner, and Grace frowned as she tried to figure out what was wrong.

"Oh!" she said. "I'm sorry. I didn't mean to make you feel excluded. You're welcome to come along."

"We can't just leave! We're waiting for *Adam*. Who's speaking with *God!*"

"Yeah?"

Daniel stared at her, and Grace realised that he'd already made his point. "We'll come back," she assured him. Then she frowned. "Though if you're coming too, there'll be no one to tell Adam where we've gone. And it is rather rude to just leave." She considered it. "Do you think it'd be okay to leave him a little note?"

Samael smirked. "Sure thing. Dear Adam, we're hanging out with Grace's mom, having a bit of tea. Fancy a cup?"

"Sherry."

"What?"

"We'd be having sherry."

Samael grinned. "Even better. Unfortunately, however, we can't."

"Why not?"

"While I'm perfectly capable of reading every Book of Souls, I'm certain that they're not going to let me near a ten-mile-radius of it. Your visit will have to wait."

"Oh." Grace considered it. Maybe later she could ask the angel for directions to her mom? She decided that it couldn't hurt to ask. For now, however, she turned her attention towards Daniel. "So when did you realise your brother was cray-cray?" she asked.

He stared at her. "Excuse me?"

"Well, you know. Cray-cray. Isn't that how you young people say it?"

"My brother isn't crazy."

"Do you prefer eccentric?"

"That's not what I... Jacob isn't crazy. He's just... sensitive."

"No kidding," Samael muttered.

"He was kind to me," Daniel said. "Three years older, but he always made time for me. We were best friends. We used to pretend we were holy soldiers, travelling the world together and slaying demons." He suddenly blushed, looking at Samael. "Eh... Not that I'm going to... I mean..."

Samael snorted. "Save it, choir boy," he said. "The idea of you slaying me is as laughable as a mosquito slaying a lion."

"Maybe it could," Grace argued, "if it had malaria." She frowned. "Wait, can lions get malaria?"

Samael's face twitched. "Fine," he said. "A fly then. Like a fly slaying a lion. Happy?"

Grace considered it. She did have trouble seeing how a fly could possibly slay a lion. "Yes," she said. She looked back at Daniel. "Oh, I'm sorry," she said. "You were saying?"

He had a puzzled expression on his face. "Have you two... known each other long?" he asked.

"No," Samael said. "It just feels long because she's so annoying."

"I... see," Daniel said. "You just seemed..."

"Well, spit it out, choir boy."

"You seem like good friends," Daniel said.

"Good friends!" Samael sputtered. "We're most definitely not *good friends*. I am Samael! I'm not friends with a puny, brainless human!"

"Sure, we're friends," Grace said.

Samael turned towards her with a stormy expression, and she quickly decided to change the subject.

"So your brother," she said, focusing intensively on Daniel. "You said he was sensitive?"

"Yeah, he wasn't like... he just didn't... some things were just harder for him, you know?"

"Like what?" Grace asked, now honestly curious.

Daniel ran a hand through his hair. "I don't know how to explain it," he said. "It was... I suppose I first noticed it when I was four or so. Mom usually packed our lunch, but one day she'd been sick and asked our dad to. He forgot." Daniel frowned. "Jacob cried," he said. "And refused to leave for school without one. It didn't matter that our parents gave us money for lunch instead. In the end, my parents gave in and let us stay home. We played boardgames. It was a lot more fun than going to school. But I just never..." He trailed off.

"Never...?" Grace prompted.

"I just never forgot. He wasn't faking the tears, and I'd always considered my brother fearless." He smiled wistfully. "When we chased after demons, he'd even dare to go down in the basement. And when someone broke into our house, he told me to hide under the bed while he'd stand guard."

"That was brave," Grace noted.

"Yes, hallelujah," Samael said. "Let's hold a bloody parade for the nutjob."

"You can be brave and crazy at the same time," Grace admonished him.

Samael rolled his eyes but didn't otherwise comment.

Grace turned back towards Daniel. "It's nice," she said, "when older siblings look after their younger ones."

He smiled bitterly. "It is," he agreed. "And I tried to protect him as well. Since he could face the big dangers for me, I could face the small ones for him."

"What's a small danger?" Grace asked.

"Mostly himself," Daniel admitted.

"He'd hurt himself?"

"Not on purpose," Daniel said. "But when things got hard for him, he'd… express himself."

"How so?"

"He'd have a fit," Daniel said. "Yell. Throw things. Sometimes he'd hurt himself, and sometimes…he'd hurt other people." He brushed his temple with his fingertips, and Grace wondered if he remembered an old injury. "Never on purpose," Daniel quickly added. "And he'd feel terrible afterwards. But during the fit, he wouldn't really think about it. He'd just… have it, you know?"

"It must've been hard to grow up with him," Grace noted.

"Hard?" Daniel sounded surprised. "No. Well, yes. But God helped."

Samael snorted. "Sure," he said. "We all know what kind of a hands-on kind-of-guy God is."

Daniel squared his jaw. "Just because you don't see Him, doesn't mean He's not there. And He did help. Gave Jacob the strength and patience to calm down. Before he hurt anyone seriously. His faith brought him peace."

Samael opened his mouth, and Grace hurried to cut in.

"Isn't that why a lot of people become religious?" she said. "Because their faith brings them peace?"

"Yes," Daniel said. "Knowing that God loves you gives you a peace of mind that you can't possibly find elsewhere. And it truly did give my brother peace. Dad taught us both about God, and Jacob *devoured* his teachings."

"But you didn't?" Grace asked.

"I believed, of course," Daniel said. "It's the only thing that makes sense. But for Jacob, it wasn't enough. He had to know. He consumed every book he could find on the subject, every article, every sermon. He soon knew the bible better than dad did." Daniel frowned, thinking back. "But it still wasn't enough."

"So your brother didn't actually *believe* in God?" Grace translated. That would certainly explain why he didn't get into Heaven, though the Hell-part still confounded her.

"Of course he believed in God," Daniel said. "How can anyone not, once they truly study it? It just makes sense. For both of us. At least until our mom..." He trailed off.

"For Hell's sake, choir boy," Samael said. "Would you finish a bloody sentence?"

Daniel shot him an annoyed look. "When our mother died," he said. "Religion helped. I was seven at the time, and mom was pregnant." Daniel smiled bitterly. "We were going to have a little sister, but mom developed difficulties in her last trimester. Bled out in an elevator in a friend's apartment complex across town."

"I'm sorry," Grace said.

"What does that have to do with religion?" Samael demanded to know, offering no condolences of his own.

"He..." Daniel hesitated. "The funeral was over," he said. "I'd hated it. We sat there in stiff, black clothes, and strangers kept patting our heads. I was so relieved when we got to go home. Jacob wasn't. He begged dad to let him sleep in the church." Daniel sighed. "Perhaps things would've been different if he'd said yes. It was, after all, his church."

"What happened?" Grace asked.

"We came home; dad locked himself in the office, and Jacob..."

"Yeah?"

"He had a fit. I tried to calm him down, but he kept throwing stuff and screaming. He hit me with this old statuette that'd belonged to mother. I started bleeding, and I couldn't see anything, and he just kept screaming. He'd never had a fit that bad before. He hadn't even had one in over a year." Daniel sighed. "So I told him she was in a better place now."

"Yeah, people do say that," Grace mused. She'd certainly heard it whenever someone she'd loved had died. When she'd been diagnosed, however, nobody had said it to her. In fact, it had rather seemed like people had gone out of their way to avoid talking about it at all. The conversational version of the floor is lava.

"Jacob didn't accept that though," Daniel said. "He wanted to know how I could *know* that. How I could know that she'd really gone to Heaven and not Hell." Daniel shook his head. "Though how he could have even contemplated that she might've gone to Hell is beyond me." He looked at Grace with a sheepish expression. "I mean... sorry."

"None taken," she said. "What did you tell him?"

"That she went to Heaven because she followed the rules. And he just... calmed down. From one moment to the next. It was wonderful. He just calmed down. Just like that. So I told him that if you follow the rules, you're a good person and you go to Heaven, and if you don't, you're bad, and you go to Hell. He liked that." Daniel grimaced. "So I started to remind him of the rules whenever he was difficult. They always calmed him down. And it worked so well; I just kept at it. Whenever he was difficult, I'd tell him about the rules... It was just so *easy*."

Grace was about to note that Jacob hadn't sounded all that easy to her when Samael cut in.

"How ridiculous," he said. "If he threw stuff at you, you should've just thrown something heavier back. Let him deal with his own problems. You don't see me trying to solve everyone else's problems, do you?"

"Isn't that kind of what we're doing right now?" Grace asked.

Samael sent her a look. "No," he said. "We live in Hell, which makes it our problem. If his brother was only interested in changing Heaven, I wouldn't have bothered."

Grace smiled at him. "Maybe you shouldn't mention that to Adam," she said.

"I'm not an idiot. And how long can it take to ask one bloody question anyway?" He went back to pacing.

Grace sat down next to a nearby tree and leaned back against the tree trunk. "It'll take however long it takes," she said philosophically. "Be patient."

When they finally returned, however, Grace was feeling anything but. It felt like they'd been waiting for *days*.

Adam and Eve looked demoralizingly glum.

"He said no." There was not a hint of surprise in Samael's voice.

Adam flinched. "He reminded me that ever since Eve and I ate the apple, humans have had free will. Including Jacob. We are free to stop them, but He is not."

"So basically," Samael said drily. "His plan is to do nothing."

"He can't interfere with free will."

"Of course not. Bloody old geezer."

Both Adam and Daniel grimaced at the words, looking around as if they were scared God might overhear. He probably did.

"So what now?" Grace asked.

"We could go to Earth," Daniel suggested. "Ask around. Maybe someone in my brother's acquaintance can tell me where he is."

"Why didn't you try that first?" she asked. "Seems easier than almost dying."

Daniel looked embarrassed. "I did," he admitted. "But I think some of them lied. Hopefully, we can make them see reason."

Samael smirked. "Bring me with you," he said. "And I can definitely make them see reason."

"We are *not* going to torture anyone," Grace said firmly.

Samael blinked innocently. "Who, me? Why, I would *never*. But what's torture anyway? I mean, is sleep deprivation really torture? Or isolation? It's really a grey area when you think about it."

"It's really not," Grace said. "We are *not* going to torture anyone."

"Well, then I hope either of you have a better suggestion," Samael said.

"I'll find one," Daniel said.

Samael rolled his eyes. "Don't hurt yourself trying," he said. "And be grateful that you don't have to. I've already come up with a backup plan in the *unlikely* event that God wouldn't just magically fix our problems."

"Really?" Grace said. "Samael, that's brilliant."

Samael seemed taken aback. "Yes, of course it is," he said.

"Well?" Adam demanded. "What is it?"

"We'll go pluck an apple from the Tree."

For several long seconds, Adam only stared at him, shock written across his handsome features. Then his expression darkened.

"You almost tricked me," he said. "But it's been your plan all along, hasn't it, snake?"

Samael sighed. "I'm not asking you to eat it, you idiot. I just need you to point us in the right direction. You must know where it is?"

"You must think me a great fool, if you believe that you can trick me a second time. If I let you near the Tree of Knowledge, disaster will strike us all."

"Isn't that a bit melodramatic?" Grace asked.

"The last time cost us *Paradise*."

"And obviously that was very bad. But I still have to side with

Samael on this one."

Samael looked at her, surprised. "Really?" he asked.

"Well, it was a really shitty thing you did," Grace told him. "But it's not fair of him to only blame you. Especially since you weren't even the one who convinced him as far as I recall. Wasn't that part Eve?"

Eve made a squeak when all eyes suddenly turned to her.

"Besides," Grace added with a shrug. "I think Adam's being mean."

All three men turned to stare at her, and Grace frowned slightly. She'd hardly said anything shocking.

"How do you figure?" Daniel finally asked.

"Well, this doesn't only affect him, does it? Every inhabitant in Hell is basically going to be tortured for all of eternity, and now he refuses to do what he can to help, just because he's scared? That's pretty selfish."

"I'm not... that's not... I'm *not* being selfish," Adam said. "I just refuse to go against God. For the second time."

"How are you going against God? What, he's told you to never give directions?"

Adam hesitated. "No," he admitted. "But... that *cat*. I don't trust him."

Grace looked at Samael, who was still very much in his humanoid form. "He's not a cat," she said. "Besides, I'm not asking you to trust him."

Adam grimaced. "You remind me of the cat," he said.

Grace smiled. "Thank you," she said.

"I'll walk you to the Tree," Adam said. "I will not touch any of its fruit, and if you try to convince me to, you may burn in Hell for all I care."

Grace grinned. "Deal," she said. "Though people don't really burn in Hell." She reconsidered her words. "At least not yet," she added thoughtfully.

* * *

"I thought the apple would only give knowledge of good and evil, or something like that," Grace said to Samael as they were making their way through Heaven. Adam was leading them, which unfortunately meant that sherry with her mom had once again been postponed.

They passed by rolling hills, creeks of bubbling water, and little patches of small forests. Grace wondered if space here worked like it did in Hell. Maybe every patch of forest was the size of the Amazon, and every hut they passed by was a palace within.

Daniel looked around with a besotted expression that made it clear he would find it marvellous either way. Samael did not. He was once again a cat, and Grace suspected that it was so that she could carry him.

"Not quite," Samael said. "The Tree of Knowledge contains knowledge on everything, every apple containing something different. The apple that Eve and Adam ate contained the knowledge of good and evil."

"So we would want the apple containing the knowledge of what? Where to find lost stuff?"

"Basically."

Grace thought it over.

"What happened?" she asked. "Adam and Eve just happened to pick that particular apple rather than one teaching them... I don't know. Algebra? Or French?"

"There wasn't more than one language back then," Samael said. "And perhaps there's a slight possibility that they didn't just happen to pick that one. I might have pointed out that if one was to take an apple, one might as well take the best."

Grace sighed. "Samael," she scolded gently. "You really should apologise."

"I did!"

"Sincerely."

"Oh. I can't do that."

"Why did you even do it?"

Samael yawned rather than answering.

"Don't give me that," Grace told him, making sure to keep her voice low. "There's no way that you risked going against Lucifer just because you felt like it."

"I didn't know he'd be so angry."

"I still think there's more to it than that," Grace insisted.

"Well, there might be. Happy?"

"Generally so, yes. With you? Less so."

Samael sighed. "You're an annoyance," he told her, flicking his tail in irritation.

"Why did you tempt them?" she asked again, not allowing him to distract her.

"Because I wanted to punish Adam. Eve was just collateral damage. And I hadn't expected things to go that far. Honestly. I just wanted them to get in trouble. How was I to know that He would actually kick them out?"

"Why did you want to punish Adam?"

"He hurt Lilith."

Grace tried to make sense of his words. "What?"

"He hurt Lilith," Samael repeated. "Lilith was originally created to be the mate of Adam. But she wasn't interested. And when the crybaby complained to God, she was kicked out of Paradise."

"For turning a guy down? That's harsh."

"Indeed. And Adam got his way. Lilith was kicked out, and he got Eve. Though he must be insane to believe it an improvement."

Grace looked over at Adam and Eve. Eve had both her arms around one of his. She was looking downwards, ever so often glancing up at Adam next to her. She was as beautiful as Lilith, but far... less.

"I guess he didn't deal with rejection that well."

Samael snorted. "He was a spoiled brat. Getting kicked out

of Paradise was the best thing that ever happened to him. Forced him to grow up, it did. At least some."

"Well, he seems... okay."

"He's prepared to let us burn in Hell if we try to make him take a bite of a fruit."

"Okay, so maybe he's a bit... rough around the edges. But everyone matures with age. I'm sure he'll improve."

"You sicken me," Samael told her, but he smiled, nonetheless. An odd sight on a cat.

Grace smiled back. "You like me anyway," she said.

Samael sighed dramatically.

"You're... acceptable," he said. "But don't let it go to your head."

"We'll keep each other humble," Grace promised him. "Though I think it might be more of a challenge for me."

Samael eyes gleamed as he looked at her.

"It might be," he agreed with a Cheshire grin.

* * *

The Tree of Knowledge wasn't as much a tree as it was a mountain that just happened to be shaped like a tree. Grace stared at it in awe, craning her neck back to see it all. It *was* a mountain, she realised. The tree was made entirely out of rock, and a botanist would probably tell her that it wasn't a tree at all, for all that it had apples growing on it.

It was certainly big. The tree had to be measured in miles rather than feet, and upon its branches hung thousands upon thousands of apples, all gleaming red in the sunshine. Perhaps, however, it looked bigger because there was nothing around it. They'd left behind the forests and creeks and were now surrounded by nothing but grass. Still, even among the skyscrapers from back home, it would have seemed enormous.

"That is a very big tree," she said.

"Well, it has grown for over two hundred thousand years," Samael noted. "What did you expect?"

"Not this. This is *spectacular.*"

"How are we supposed to pick the right apple?" Daniel asked, looking at the tree with dismay. "They all look exactly the same."

"Maybe to your untrained eye," Samael said.

"So you can find the right one?"

Samael looked up at the tree. "It *has* gotten bigger since the last time I saw it," he said. "Back then it hardly took up more space than a small village."

"How minuscule," Grace said. "Can you find the right apple now?"

"Of course. I'm *Samael.*" He hesitated. "It might take a while though. Even back then I had to spend over half an hour finding the right apple."

"How long do you think it'll take you this time?" Grace asked. "An hour?"

Samael looked up at the thousands of apples. "Maybe more," he admitted before he jumped down from her arms and turned into a hawk.

"It'll go quicker like this," he said. Then he took off and soared towards the very top of the tree.

"We shouldn't let him out of our sight," Adam said, following the bird with his eyes.

"Worried he's going to fly off?"

"I worry he'll try to take some of the apples with him."

"You're accusing him of stealing?" Grace asked, surprised.

"It wouldn't exactly be his first time."

Grace was about to deny it when she realised that she'd really only known Samael for a couple of days.

"I think he's nice," she said instead, looking at the hawk above them. "And I'll keep an eye on him while we're here," she added.

"Good. I don't want to spend another moment looking at him."

Grace tore her eyes away from Samael. "What?" she said.

"We're leaving. We've led you to the Tree of Knowledge. Our involvement ends here. We won't spend a second more with that *thing* than absolutely necessary. Our part in this endeavour is done."

He turned around and made his way over the grassy planes, Eve following him with only a shy, parting smile for Grace and Daniel.

"But you're a part of this!" Daniel shouted after him.

"I'm not an inhabitant of Hell," Adam said over his shoulder.

"You can't let it happen just because it won't affect you!"

"I've done my part," Adam said.

Grace ran up to them and blocked their way. "What about you?" she asked Eve, ignoring Adam. "Will you come with us?"

Eve stared at her with wide eyes.

"We can't," she said.

"Well, I only asked you."

"Oh." Eve blushed. "I'm sorry," she said. "But I can't."

"Why not?"

Eve smiled shyly. "These sorts of heroic deeds are best left to the men," she said. "You're going back to Hell yourself once you've gotten your apple, aren't you?"

"What? No. Of course not."

Eve frowned. "But the next part might be dangerous," she said.

"You were kicked out of Paradise," Grace said. "You must have faced dangers before."

"Yes, of course. But I would never seek them out myself." She looked up at Adam with a smile. "And if only I'd listened to Adam to begin with, we never would have left Paradise at all."

"Didn't he take a bite as well?"

"Oh, but that was only because I tempted him. I shouldn't have done that."

"I see," Grace said, thinking back on the strikes she'd been part of, back when she and the other nurses had fought for better working rights. She'd gotten fired, and only going to her parents for a loan had saved her from starvation. A lot of the other nurses hadn't had that option, and many of them had folded.

Grace suspected that Eve wouldn't have been part of the strike to begin with.

"I wish you the best of luck," she finally said. Watching them walk away, she wondered if they were happy. Thinking back on Lilith, she tried to envision her with Adam.

Perhaps it had been better for all parts that Lilith had left Paradise behind, not least of all for Lilith herself.

With a last glance at the pair, Grace returned to Daniel and answered his questioning glance with a shrug.

"Looks like we're on our own," she said.

"And Samael?" he asked. "Will he follow this to the end?"

Grace thought back on Samael's frustration that Lucifer wouldn't allow him to try and save the place he called home.

"Yes," she answered. "I believe he will."

* * *

When Samael returned a bit more than an hour later, he had a shining apple held victoriously in one of his claws. Flying over them, he released it from his grip. As she reached out to grab it, Grace watched him turn back into a human just before he hit the ground. He looked quite pleased with his landing, surreptitiously glancing over to see if Grace and Daniel were watching.

"Where's Adam and Eve?" he asked.

"They left," Daniel explained, voice stiff. "Apparently they felt like they'd done their part."

"Well, good riddance," Samael said. "Now let's find out where they keep the Voice of God. Grace, be a dear and take a bite."

Grace looked at the apple in her hand. It did look rather appetising. Willingly, she lifted it to her mouth before she blinked in surprise when Daniel reached out and pushed down her arm.

"What's wrong?" she asked.

"Perhaps it's not such a wise idea," Daniel said. "After all, Samael is…" he trailed off.

"Samael is what?" the shapeshifter asked. "Samael is a demon? Samael will lead you into temptation?" He rolled his eyes. "Scared of the demon, choir boy?"

"Samael," Grace scolded. "I'm sure that's not what he meant."

She looked at Daniel, who didn't meet her eyes.

"Oh," she said. "That *is* what you meant."

Daniel looked at Samael. "Why don't you take a bite yourself?" he asked.

"The apples only work on *humans*. For me, you idiotic boy, this is nothing but a particularly tasty-looking apple. It won't grant me any extra knowledge about, well, anything."

"Then I'll take a bite," Daniel said. "I can't let her commit that sin for us."

"It's a sin to eat an apple?" Grace asked.

"It's an apple from the *Tree of Knowledge*. It's the Original Sin. The sin before all others."

"Oh." Grace looked down at it with fascination. It looked like a pretty normal apple to her. Perhaps a bit shinier. A little more red.

"But wouldn't it also be a sin if you ate it?" she asked.

Daniel nodded. "It would," he said. "But we're trying to stop my brother. He's my responsibility, and it's only right that I'll pay the price."

Samael snorted. "Quite the little saint, are we? What does it matter anyway?"

"I can't let her sin because of my brother," Daniel said.

"She's already a sinner," Samael reminded him. "Comes from Hell and all that. Or perhaps you've forgotten?"

"Samael is right," Grace said. "I'm already denied entrance into Heaven. You're not. You have so much more to lose than I do. It only makes sense that I'll take the bite."

"Absolutely not," Daniel persisted. "I'm responsible for my brother. I should be the one to take on the sin."

Grace frowned, trying to come up with some argument that would make Daniel realise that it was just sensible to let her take the bite. Seeing the look in his eyes, she realised that no argument would make him reconsider. She also realised that she didn't, in fact, need to convince him.

So she put the apple to her mouth and took a bite.

CHAPTER SEVEN:

Knowledge

It was the single most delicious thing she'd ever tasted.

Moaning when the taste hit her, Grace closed her eyes. If Samael had convinced Eve to take a single bite, Grace understood why she hadn't been able to stop. The only question was how she'd been able to share with Adam. Or stop after one apple.

Taking another bite, she hummed softly. It wasn't sweet. It was... fresh. With just a tint of bitterness. Grace took another bite, wondering when the magical powers would kick in. She'd expected to see images or hear voices, but no such thing occurred.

Perhaps it would be okay to finish the apple before she told the others.

Taking her third bite, Grace wondered whether it'd be possible to sneak some more apples with them. Sure, they didn't *need* food, but it couldn't hurt, could it?

The apple was plucked from her hand, and Grace's eyes popped open.

Daniel was standing in front of her with a worried expression, holding that unbelievably delicious apple in his hand.

"I was eating that!"

"A bite should be enough."

"But why take the chance? And if I've already sinned, what's the point of stopping now?"

Daniel looked far from impressed with her argument.

"Besides," she added. "I know nothing more than what I knew before. So maybe it won't work until I've eaten the whole thing."

She reached furtively for the apple.

"Of course it has worked," Samael said.

"No. It didn't. No images, no words from God. Nothing."

Samael gave an exasperated sigh.

"Grace, where's the Voice of God?" he asked.

"In New York City," she answered. Then she frowned. The words had simply slipped out. But as she'd said them, she'd known they were true. The Voice of God was to be found in New York City. Marble Cemetery, 41½ Second Avenue.

Maybe she didn't need any more of the apple.

How disappointing.

"Are you sure?" Daniel asked.

"Of course, she's sure," Samael answered. "It's the Tree of Knowledge. Not the Tree of Pretty Good Guesses."

"We should leave then," Daniel said, sending a suspicious glance at the tree behind them. Holding the apple at arm's length, he walked over to the foot of the tree and carefully placed it on the ground before he wiped his hands on his jeans.

He walked back to them, still looking somewhat anxious.

"Do any of you guys have some water?" he asked.

"Why?" Grace asked absent-mindedly, looking towards the apple.

"I'd like to wash my hands."

"Whatever for?"

"He's scared," Samael said.

Grace tore her eyes away from the apple to look at Daniel. "Of what?" she asked.

Daniel hesitated. "It's a sin," he said. "To eat the apple. And I got some of its juice on my fingers. I don't want to eat anything later, and accidentally…" He trailed off.

"I don't think that'll count," Grace said. "I think you need to do it on purpose. Otherwise, it would've been a lot easier for Samael to simply wipe a bit of juice on Adam's or Eve's fingers as they slept."

Samael grinned at Daniel. "It was more satisfying to

convince them to do it themselves." He glanced at Grace, who was once again looking towards the apple. "I take it you enjoyed it?"

"Yeah. I understand why it'd be hard to resist after you've taken that first bite. Seems unfair to make it so delicious and then forbid people to eat it."

"Not everyone likes it," Samael said.

Grace gaped at him. "You can't be serious. It's without a doubt the most delicious thing I've ever tasted."

Samael shrugged. "Not everyone is fond of the taste of knowledge. Some people prefer their temptations a little sweeter."

Grace shrugged. She'd rather enjoyed that slightly bitter after-taste. She shook her head. They were on a mission, and she'd allowed herself to be distracted by a piece of fruit.

"Okay," she said. "So New York City. How do we get there? Angel express?"

"Yes," Samael said. "I imagine that they'll be quite pleased to get rid of us."

Grace nodded, knowing he was probably right. "How do we get in touch with them?" she asked.

Samael shrugged. "We call. Angels hear everything that takes place in Heaven."

Grace considered it. "Okay," she said. She took a deep breath. "ANGEL-PERSON! WE'RE READY TO LEAVE NOW!"

"There is no reason to yell," an angelic voice said, and Grace turned around to face it. It was the same angel who'd allowed them entrance into Heaven.

Daniel bowed. "If it pleases you, we would very much appreciate a lift to New York City," he said.

The angel looked at him. "I hope that we will see you here again," it said, and Daniel nodded quickly.

"I'll do my best," he promised.

The angel nodded gravely before it lifted a hand. The air

before them cracked open, and smoke came out. Grace breathed in. She was met with the unmistakable smell of cigarettes and forgotten trash.

With a provoking grin to the angel, Samael pulled the crack open and stepped through, quickly followed by Daniel.

Grace hesitated. "I realise that it's a bit last minute," she said. "But is there any way I could come back some time and visit my mom?"

"No."

"Oh." Grace decided not to dwell too long on that thought. She would just have to convince it otherwise, once Heaven and Hell weren't in immediate danger. Or maybe her mom could visit her?

"Would you tell her I said hi? She'll be downright peeved when she hears that I was here and didn't visit."

The angel looked at her, and Grace met its eyes square on.

"I will," it said. "And be careful on Earth."

"Careful?"

"You have died once. You may die a second time, but it will be a Demon's Death. A cursed death."

"I… see. Thanks for the heads-up, I guess. You're actually rather nice."

The angel didn't look particularly pleased, but Grace sent it a parting smile nonetheless. Then she stepped through the hole and left behind Heaven.

* * *

The contrast was striking.

Grace hadn't realised how quickly she'd gotten used to the sunshine and soft colours of Heaven. At least not until she was suddenly surrounded by the smell of garbage and car exhaust.

In front of them stood a group of young men. Boys, really. They each had a cigarette in their hand, though none of them were actually smoking. Instead, they all stared at the two men and Grace in confusion.

"Where the hell did you come from?" one of the guys said.

"Actually, you've successfully guessed as wrong as possible," Samael quipped.

"What?"

Samael sighed. "Never mind. Now scram. We're here on important business, and you're in the way."

Impolite as he was, he was quite right. They'd been transported into a narrow alley that was surrounded by red brick walls on three sides. One of the walls had a door, but it was blocked by several black garbage bags. And even if they moved them all, the door would most likely be locked.

Meaning that the only way out was currently blocked by the group of boys.

One of them stepped forward, throwing his cigarette to the side as he did so. He looked displeased, Grace noted. And judging from his slightly stumbling walk, he was probably drunk as well. How bothersome. She stepped forward.

"What my friend was trying to say," she said. "Is that we're in quite a hurry, and we would greatly appreciate it if you would let us through."

"Don't bother," Samael told her. "I'll take care of them."

"You'll do no such thing," Grace told him.

The guy laughed. *"Take care of us?* Protecting your little girlfriend, are you? What an idiot!"

Grace frowned. "There's no reason to be impolite," she said.

"Shut it, doll face."

Grace pursed her lips, considering.

"Samael," she said.

"Yeah?"

"I've changed my mind. Go ahead. Please."

He grinned, eyes shining with delight. "I thought you'd never ask."

He began to change. While his other transformations had been done in the blink of an eye, this one was slower. His body grew larger, fur seemed to grow out of his skin, and his face transformed into something that became less and less human by the second.

Finally, a grizzly bear stood in Samael's place. What had to be the biggest, meanest-looking grizzly bear that had ever existed. He roared.

A whimper brought Grace's attention back to the boys. Three out of five of them were staring at the bear in shock. Trembling with fear, they looked nothing like the self-assured group from before. A fourth guy had run away, while a fifth one was lying in the alley, passed out.

Grace smiled sweetly at them. "Would you be so kind as to let us pass?" she asked. Behind her, the bear roared again as if backing her up.

The three remaining — and conscious — boys turned around and fled.

Grace laughed, spinning around to face Samael. Burying her hands in his fur, she hugged him as best as she could. The bear put his heavy paws on her shoulders and gave her the slightest push away.

"That was awesome!" she said, grinning so broadly that it hurt.

"Was it really necessary to scare them like that?" Daniel asked. "Seems like an unnecessary risk."

"Well, it was certainly effective," Grace said as she looked at the grizzly bear shrinking down until a man stood beside them once again.

"Daniel might have a point," Samael said, once he was fully human. "We shouldn't attract too much attention."

"But a little attention is okay, isn't it?" Grace asked. She'd rather enjoyed the experience of having a bear have her back. "Like when Samael showed off before, transforming so slowly. You have to admit that it looked pretty cool."

"I didn't slow down my transformation in order to show

off," Samael told her. "It's harder to transform here on Earth. My body is heavier. Less adaptable." Then he smirked. "Of course, it would have been utterly impossible for a shapeshifter without my talent."

"And great belief in himself," Grace added, walking over to the unconscious guy. With a quick glance towards the end of the alley, she squatted down next to him and began to search through his pockets.

"What are you doing?" Daniel asked.

"If we're back on Earth, we'll need money," Grace noted. "Besides, they were awfully impolite. And I'll leave enough for the subway."

Daniel hesitated. "Money would make our mission easier," he said. "But do we really need to steal it?"

Samael walked over to help Grace in her search. "We're kind of on a deadline here," he noted. "And stealing is a lot easier. Besides, you don't need to help us."

"I should help though."

Grace smiled at him. "Don't worry about it," she said. "Unlike you, Samael and I are going back to Hell anyway."

It didn't seem to reassure him.

Feeling confident that they'd gotten what money the boy had on him — and after a short discussion with Samael about whether or not they should leave him a little — they left the alley behind, effortlessly becoming a part of the crowd of New York City.

"Where are we?" Grace asked the others.

"Shouldn't you know that?" Samael said. "You said the Voice was in some cemetery, so just bloody point us in the right direction."

Grace hesitated. Then she lifted her hand and pointed. "That way," she said.

"Great. If only that stupid angel had dropped us off in the actual cemetery, we could've saved ourselves all this walking."

"It did save us the trip from Heaven to New York," Grace reminded him.

Samael shrugged, entirely unimpressed.

"It's kind of an odd place to find it, isn't it?" Grace mused. "A cemetery."

"Not really," Samael said. "Humans tend to feel when something is beyond this world. Someone was probably buried with it."

"*Buried?!*" Daniel exclaimed. "Are you telling me we're going grave-robbing?"

"Probably."

Grace considered it. There was something undeniably gross and yet fascinating about the thought. Though it seemed awfully rude to disturb someone's final resting place. Still, if the person had known how important it was, they probably would've agreed anyway.

"Shouldn't we buy a shovel?" she asked.

The others stopped and looked at her.

"That's a good idea," Daniel said. He looked pale. Grave-robbing was apparently harder for him to accept than thievery.

Samael nodded thoughtfully. "Grace," he said. "Where's the closest place we can buy a shovel?"

"This way," she said, beginning to walk in the right direction, followed by the two others. "Is this thing permanent?" she asked Samael. "Me working as a human compass?"

"Yes."

"Oh. That's pretty neat. Though I still kind of wish we had taken more than one."

* * *

In the end, it took them forty minutes to get to a store that sold good, old-fashioned shovels.

A clerk immediately came up to them.

"Is there anything I can help you with?" he asked.

Grace smiled at him. What a pleasant, young man. "We need

three shovels, please," she said. "And a rake," she added, figuring that it would make their purchases look slightly less creepy.

"And a large bag," Daniel said.

"And a flash light," Samael added. "And a crowbar if you have it."

Well, so much for not seeming creepy.

The man's smile never wavered. "Of course," he said. "Are there any specific brands you prefer?"

"We trust your judgement," Grace assured him.

"Of course. Anything else?"

"No, I think that's it. Oh! A rope would be nice."

"Of course. If you'll just wait here, I'll be right back." He left.

"A rope?" Samael asked. "What do we need a rope for?"

Grace shrugged. "I'm not exactly sure," she admitted. "Seems like the kind of thing you may need for anything that *has* to take place after dark. We may need it just to get into the cemetery. They might lock it off to avoid vandalism. Or, you know, grave-robbing."

"I pick locks."

"Of course you do." Grace stepped to the side and looked through a pile of gardening gloves. Then she looked at the prices.

"We may have to change our order," she said. "I don't think we can afford everything we just asked for."

"We have a wide variety of prices," the clerk assured them.

Grace jumped, and turned around. She hadn't heard him come back and she wondered how much he'd heard. Hopefully not much, considering that he still had his professional smile plastered on.

"What's your price range?" he asked them.

Grace gave a number.

"Ah. I'm afraid that won't cover everything you want. What are the most important items on the list?"

"The shovels," Grace said, deciding to ignore how alarming it sounded. It wasn't like he was going to call the police just because they bought some shovels. "And the crowbar. And a bag to have it in."

"Still a bit out of your price range," the clerk told them. "Could you make do with a single shovel?"

"Sure," she said, figuring that someone would have to stand guard anyway. "One will do just fine."

"If you'll come to the register, please?"

Following him to the register, Grace ignored how Samael was eyeing the items in the store. She was sure Daniel would keep an eye on him.

Having paid for their purchases, Grace wished the clerk a pleasant shift before she dragged Samael with her out of the store, Daniel following behind them.

"Why do you feel the need to *drag* me?" Samael complained. "I'm perfectly capable of walking by myself."

"Because I can," Grace answered absent-mindedly before she glanced up towards the sky. "How long would you guys say we have before sunset?"

Samael shrugged. "A couple of hours perhaps," he said. "Why?"

"They probably don't lock the gates to the cemetery before then."

"So?"

"If we can get in before they lock it off, we can simply hide until after dark."

Samael stared at her. "I am *not* hiding in some bushes."

Grace sent him an exasperated look. "I'm not asking you to. You can turn into a sparrow and hide in a tree or something. Daniel and I are going to hide in some bushes."

"In that case, it might be a good idea to smear some mud on you, when we get that far. For camouflage, of course."

"Of course," Daniel said. "I'm sure that you're only thinking of what's best for the mission. Not for you own amusement."

Samael smiled. "I'm deeply offended. Really."

"I'm sure you'll get over it," Grace said. "Now come on. I may be able to tell you which direction we have to take, but I still have no idea how far it actually is."

* * *

Five hours later, Daniel and Grace crawled out from under the bushes they'd lain in for the last four hours.

Stretching, Grace was once again reminded that physical discomfort wasn't just for the living.

"I'm so glad I didn't have to do that in my old body," she said. "I'm not sure I would have ever gotten up."

Daniel grimaced as he stretched, while Samael was smirking at them from where he was standing. He'd spent the last four hours sitting in a tree, occasionally flying around to scout the area.

"*I* feel wonderful," he said.

They both ignored him.

"Where are we going?" Daniel asked Grace, who gestured towards a nearby grave.

"There it is," she said. "The Voice of God."

They looked at the tombstone in front of them. Annabelle Hale, born 1840, died 1918. Daughter. Sister. Mother.

"Okay, so let's dig her up," Samael said, thrusting the shovel towards Daniel.

Daniel took it but made no move to start digging. Instead, he knelt down beside the grave. "I'm very sorry for having to do this," he said. "But I'm afraid it's for the greater good. Wherever you are, I'm sure you understand, and I want to thank you for your sacrifice."

Samael rolled his eyes but stayed uncharacteristically quiet. Then he shrunk down, and Grace looked on in fascination as his face flattened and fur grew out.

"Is a *badger* really the best choice?" Daniel asked. "Not something... bigger?"

The badger ignored him, already digging, and after a

moment of hesitation, Daniel joined in.

Having already tried and failed to convince Daniel to allow her to do the digging, Grace walked away in order to keep an eye out, in case anyone heard them. It would be an unfortunate situation to explain to the cops.

The graveyard was quiet, and she could hear Samael and Daniel behind her all too well. Straining her ears, she took a moment to appreciate her vastly improved hearing before she decided to test her new knowledge.

She supposed it would be nice to know if anyone was close by. She could serve as a distraction if there was.

Closing her eyes, she tried to formulate an internal question. *Where is the closest living human being?*

She frowned as she instinctively knew that it was right behind her. Where Samael and Daniel were.

So much for specifications. She tried to re-frame the internal question.

Where's the closest person who might discover what we're up to?

Same answer.

She frowned thoughtfully. *Where's the closest person to us, who doesn't know anything about the Voice of God?* she asked instead, reassured when she finally got a different answer.

Repeatedly asking herself the same question, she continuously got a different answer than Marble Cemetery. Meaning that she could safely ignore it.

Finally, Daniel called her over.

They'd made quite an impressive hole in the amount of time they'd spent, and somehow they'd even gotten the coffin out of it. The fact that Samael looked half-human and half-bear probably had something to do with that.

Grace looked at the grave in fascination as Samael completed his transformation back to his human shape. She realised that she was probably lying in a coffin somewhere too.

It was... odd.

As was the coffin in front of her, as it had apparently been nailed shut. By about a hundred nails.

"Are coffins usually that... protected?" Grace asked.

"It used to be more common," Samael told her as he put the crowbar to the lid and tried to force it open. When it didn't budge, he frowned and changed his arm into something that was half human and half... something else. "When grave-robbing was an actual problem, the upper-class would use all kind of methods to keep their belongings safe." He forced the lid open.

Both Grace and Daniel stepped closer, looking into the coffin with fascination.

Somehow Grace had expected a classic skeleton, but her first impression was rather that of a mummy. Leathered skin stretched over sharp bones, loose rags covered a thin frame, and strands of hair still hung limply around a hollow face.

Ignoring the corpse as best as she could, Grace tried to locate the Voice of God. There were plenty of items to choose from. A rather ugly brooch was the most obvious choice, and the woman also wore several rings, bracelets and necklaces. Grace suspected that they were inlaid with genuine jewels. The woman had been buried with a fortune. No wonder they'd nailed the coffin shut.

Trying to feel if any of the items gave off a feeling of the otherworldly, Grace realised that she was being foolish. Closing her eyes, she asked where she could find the Voice of God, and instantly she just knew.

With a deep breath, she reached out and grabbed the corpse's leathered hand. It was holding what appeared to be two rather common-looking sticks, entwined together. The corpse held the Voice tightly in its grasp. It was as if the woman had used her last strength to keep it close, even in death. Maybe her relatives had buried her with it out of necessity rather than choice.

Finally, the hand was opened, and Grace softly ran her

fingers over the Voice of God. The wood was smooth beneath her fingers, but the two separate parts still felt infinitesimally different in their textures.

"I think we might have found two of the pieces," Grace noted to the others, pleased by the discovery. "It feels like two pieces of twigs entwined into one."

Two for the price of one, she thought to herself and resisted a sudden urge to giggle. She had a feeling neither of her companions would appreciate it.

"Definitely two pieces then," Samael said. "All the better reason to keep it out of that lunatic's hands. I don't even want to think about what he could do if he got to combine all three."

Grace nodded and closed her hand around the intertwined pieces. She'd expected to feel something. Power. Magic. A light sizzle, if nothing else. But the Voice of God felt exactly like a common, wooden stick.

How sub-standard.

And then an iron grip closed around her wrist, and Grace gave a shout of alarm.

The supposedly dead lady had reached out, face twisted in rage at the sight of the would-be-thief. She opened her decaying mouth, screamed in fury, and pulled Grace towards the grave.

CHAPTER EIGHT:

Annabelle

A shout came from behind her, but Grace paid it no heed. Instead, she tried to stumble backwards, only to be yanked forward by the grip on her wrist. Losing her balance, Grace fell into the grave, her face landing in the crook of the corpse's neck.

The stench of rotten flesh surrounded her, and insects were crawling on her skin. The grasp on her wrist disappeared, and Grace was struggling to escape the embrace of the corpse when she felt two thin hands circle her throat and squeeze.

The old lady's bony hands tightened their grip, pushing Grace away until she was held at arm's length, staring down at the corpse beneath her.

The lady's decaying mouth was stretched into a triumphant grin as she attempted to choke Grace to death. World turning hazy, Grace desperately scratched at the old woman's face. The grip around her throat didn't loosen, and Grace forcefully dug both of her thumbs into the eyes of the corpse. A scream of fury met her before the old woman simply laughed. Grace could feel her strength slipping away.

A set of abnormally large and hairy hands suddenly circled her throat, but rather than attempting to choke her as well, they fought to remove the old lady's hands. The grip around her throat loosened, and Grace gasped for air.

Tearing herself free, Grace tripped over her own feet in her haste to get away. Landing on the ground, she looked in silenced shock at the scene in front of her.

It consisted of an old lady, partly decomposed, having a wrestling match with a fully-grown orangutan. The cemetery, otherwise so eerily quiet, was filled with the old lady's furious screams.

Clambering backwards, Grace grimaced as she put her hand directly into a pool of muddy water. Never taking her eyes off the fight, she scrambled to her feet and wiped her hand against the fabric of her pants.

Warm hands grabbed her shoulders, and Grace looked up to meet Daniel's worried eyes.

"Are you okay?" he asked. Even in the darkness, his face looked pale.

"Yeah," she croaked before she looked back at the fight. "Samael?" she asked.

"Yes. He started to transform the second she grabbed you. I just—" He cut himself off. "I'm sorry."

"For what?"

"I didn't... I didn't do anything. I just *froze*."

"It's no matter," she said, looking at the fight. She and Daniel should be helping, but neither of them had any weapon, and they were more likely to be a distraction than any help.

"She was dead," Grace said, trying to clear her head. "The coffin was nailed shut. Did she return? Like us?"

"No," Daniel said. "We're not here in our real bodies. The old lady... that's the body she died in. Or should've died in."

"Then how... I mean, zombies don't exist. Do they?"

"I don't think so. But I have a guess as to why she isn't really dead."

"The Voice of God," Grace breathed. "We need to get it then. Force her to cross over." She looked at the fighting pair. "Help Samael distract her," she told Daniel.

"Distract her? Distract her from what?"

"From me getting the Voice of God."

With these words, Grace made her way to the coffin, attempting to ignore the sound of the fight happening nearby.

She jumped back into the grave only to find the coffin empty. Rather than giving up, she tore at the fabric, hoping that the Voice of God had somehow gotten lost in its folds. It was no use. The Voice was gone, and Grace climbed out of the grave once again — quite thankful that her young body was able to do so.

Looking around her, Grace inwardly cursed the darkness that made every random stick look like the Voice of God. Behind her, she heard a snap and an exclamation of horror from Daniel.

Ignoring it as best as she could, Grace fell to her knees and allowed her fingers to guide her rather than her sight. The Voice of God couldn't have fallen far from the grave. If it wasn't in there, it must have been thrown away during the fight.

Unless the old lady was still holding onto it.

With this realisation, Grace whipped her head around so quickly that it hurt and gasped at the sight that met her. The snap she'd heard earlier had been the old lady's neck being snapped, but it hardly seemed to slow her down. Instead, she was trying to scratch out Samael's eyes, while her own head dangled to the side. It was an utterly bizarre sight, and Grace wasted seconds staring at it, mouth agape.

Then she pulled herself together and strained her eyes. Was that the Voice of God held in the corpse's hand?.

"Fudge!" she whispered. The old lady still had it.

"Daniel!" she yelled, running over to the fight. "She still has it! It's in her hand!"

The old lady turned towards Grace, who quickly realised that she would serve better as a distraction than a direct opponent.

"Annabelle!" she shouted. "Annabelle Hale!" She bent down and picked up a rock.

The corpse looked over at her.

"We're going to take your stick!" Grace yelled at her. "And there's nothing you can do to stop us." She threw the rock, and it hit the corpse's right shoulder with an impressive smack.

"I thought us old ladies were supposed to stick together," Grace yelled, picking up another rock. "So why don't you show a bit of female camaraderie and hand it over?!" She threw the rock, and the corpse made a pained sound when it struck her chest.

Samael took advantage of the distraction to grab hold of Annabelle's hand and pry it open, causing the Voice of God to fall to the ground.

Both Grace and Daniel hurried over and fell to their knees beside each other. The Voice couldn't have fallen far, but it was dark, and they were essentially looking for a stick. Again and again, Grace mistakenly mistook a twig for the Voice of God.

Above them the orangutan roared, and Grace looked up just in time to see Annabelle throw herself at them.

It was Daniel she attacked, however, and Grace gave a shout of alarm when the corpse reached out in an attempt to strangle him.

Samael's hand closed around the corpse's upper arm, pulled Annabelle away from Daniel, and flung her backwards. She landed on the ground with an impressive thump but didn't stay down for long. Within seconds she was running towards them, head dangling to the side.

Grace pulled herself together and went back to her search for the Voice, using her hands as well as her sight.

Rather than the Voice, however, she suddenly touched bone.

With a gasp she pulled her hand away and looked in disgust at the severed hand in front of her. Annabelle's.

With a grimace, she gave it a hard smack, sending it rolling across the ground.

Above her, she could hear Daniel and Samael fighting against the corpse, but she ignored it to the best of her ability. One of them needed to get hold of the Voice, and she trusted them to have her back.

Finally, her hand closed around two intertwined pieces of wood, and Grace practically jumped up, holding the Voice up in victory.

In front of her, Samael was holding a severed arm while Daniel's face was covered in blood. The corpse, however, was focused solely on Grace.

"Annabelle Hale!" she yelled. "I... uhm..." She hesitated, only now wondering what words would kill the undead. "I command you to cross over!" she finally yelled, finding the words suitably dramatic.

The old lady hissed at her.

Grace frowned at this lack of reaction. "I command you to cross over," she said again, shaking the Voice of God for good measure.

A scream was all the answer she got before the old lady flew at her throat.

Throwing herself to the side, Grace wasn't quite fast enough. A thin hand got hold of a lock of her hair, and Grace yelled in pain as the old lady pulled with all her might.

And then Grace fell to the ground, free from her grasp.

Scrambling away, Grace didn't waste any time looking back before she was once again on her feet.

The old lady was staring down at her hand, which was holding what appeared to be a thin rope. Grace realised that it was a lock of her hair.

Backing away, she had a growing suspicion that she shouldn't have shown the old lady that she'd found the Voice.

"Samael!" she yelled. "Why isn't it working?"

The orangutan slowly got closer while answering with some animalistic and completely incomprehensible sounds.

"You're not speaking one of the languages," Daniel shouted at her.

"What languages?!"

The old woman now looked at Grace, face contorted in rage.

"One of God's blessed languages. Like Hebrew. Or Arabic."

"You need a specific language to use this thing, and you're telling me *now?*"

The old lady threw herself towards Grace, only for Samael to grab hold of her.

"Maybe there's a university or something nearby," Grace said, preparing herself to make a run for it. Samael would have to keep the old lady distracted for quite a while if they needed to find a translator in the middle of the battle.

"I speak Hebrew," Daniel said.

Grace gaped at him.

"Who speaks *Hebrew?* Actually, never mind that, just catch."

She threw the Voice of God towards him.

The fight in front of her stopped as both corpse and orangutan looked at the Voice, flying through the sky above them.

Then the old lady reached up, hand grasping desperately for her most beloved treasure. Abnormally large, hairy hands grabbed her pulled her down, and she wailed in despair as the Voice of God was once again out of her reach.

Only to end up in Daniel's waiting hand.

He spoke, unfamiliar words ringing through the air, and the old lady gave off one last, despairing wail before she collapsed in front of them.

Silence.

Grace slowly inched closer.

Half expecting the old woman to suddenly jump up, she knelt down next to her and turned her around.

The old lady's empty eyes were staring into the sky without seeing. There was no mistaking that vacant stare. She was dead. Truly, really dead.

"So..." Grace said. "Was that it?"

"What do you mean?" Daniel asked, coming over with a careful expression. He was holding the Voice of God tightly in his hand while staring fixedly at the corpse.

"I mean, we've found the Voice of God. That was the whole point, wasn't it? So, we're just... done now?"

To Grace, it felt rather anticlimactic. Perhaps it always felt like that after someone got their adrenaline pumping, and the danger was simply over.

"We still need to bring the Voice to Heaven," Daniel noted.

"To Hell, you mean," Samael said, having returned to human form during their conversation.

Daniel stared at him. "It belongs in Heaven," he said.

"Yeah, well, finders keepers, losers weepers. It was Grace who found it, and Grace is an inhabitant of Hell. All *you* did was play catch."

"What about the last part of it?" Grace interrupted, figuring they could continue the argument somewhere where they didn't have a dead body and an open grave next to them. And after making quite a bit of noise as well.

They both turned to look at her.

"Daniel's brother still has the last part," Grace reminded them.

"That's true," Samael agreed. "Even if we've removed the possibility of him gaining the other parts, we should get the last one as well. After we've gotten the rest of it somewhere safe."

"And you want to take it to Hell?" Daniel asked, horror in his voice. "The Voice of God doesn't belong in Hell!"

Okay, so apparently, they *were* doing it here with the corpse and the open grave.

"I think we should give it to Lucifer," Grace said. "The only place that would be safer is with God, but since he's staying out of this…"

Daniel looked appalled. "We can't give it to the Devil," he said. "The Voice of God belongs in Heaven, and the angels have already proven themselves willing to help. One of them would be the best choice."

"Lucifer is an angel," Grace informed him, proud of her new knowledge.

Daniel sent her a look. "An angel that *hasn't* turned its back on God," he clarified.

"Oh."

"We're not giving it to one of those *goody two-shoes*," Samael said, in the same tone someone else might use to describe a cockroach. "Good for nothing unless you're in need of a flashlight."

"They got us to Earth," Daniel said. "I'd say that was good for something."

Samael snorted. "Fine," he said. "Flashlights and chauffeurs then."

"They do guard the Gates of Heaven," Grace noted helpfully. "Though I can't see why Lucifer would be such a bad choice either."

Daniel stared at her. "But he'll—" He cut himself off.

"He'll *what?*" Samael asked.

Daniel was quiet. His grip on the Voice tightened, and Grace watched with fascination as his knuckles turned white.

"He'll what?" Grace repeated with genuine curiosity.

"He could use the Voice of God in a second rebellion," Daniel finally said. "That kind of power in the hands of the Devil…"

"Don't be daft," Samael said. "Lucifer fought against God because he refused to bend down to humans. He convinced plenty to join him. His cause was the ultimate freedom. Enslaving others would be more than a bit hypocritical."

"Some people believe that the ends justify the means," Daniel said.

"Well, of course they do," Samael said. "But you see, choir boy, I'm taking the Voice of God to Lucifer, whether you like it or not."

"Easier said than done," Daniel said, lifting the Voice slightly as if to remind Samael who was holding it.

"Enough!" Grace said, raising her voice. "You're being stupid, both of you." She stared them down, daring them to contradict her. "We need to get the Voice of God away from

Earth," she said. "I hope we can agree on that?"

Daniel nodded while Samael gave a lazy shrug.

"Good," Grace said, wondering if she should make them shake hands. Better not. Best to quit while ahead.

Samael scowled at Daniel. "Lucifer can't use the Voice of God anyway," he said. "No angel could. Or demon for that matter. It's a weapon meant for humans."

Daniel stared at him. "Why didn't you just say that?!"

"I didn't feel like it, choir boy!"

"Well, it's still not a reason not to take it to Heaven!"

"It would spare my life," Samael said.

Daniel looked at him in incomprehension. "What? How?"

"If I have to go back to Lucifer and tell him I gave the Voice of God to a bunch of angels, I might actually die of shame," Samael declared. "I'm Samael. I can't rely on the help of a bunch of glorified watchdogs."

"I think we should take it to Hell," Grace noted, causing Samael to smirk at Daniel. "Lucifer is probably the second most powerful entity there is, and since the most powerful is staying out of it, it makes sense to give it to him."

"But..." Daniel hesitated.

"But what?!" Samael demanded.

Daniel opened his mouth, seemed to think better of it, and closed it again. He shook his head. "Nothing," he said.

"Okay, so I guess we're going back to Hell," Grace said. She looked at Annabelle's corpse. "Poor woman," she said. "We should rebury her, shouldn't we? As a sign of respect?"

"She tried to kill you!" Samael exclaimed.

"I'm already dead. Besides, it didn't seem like she was in control of herself. She wasn't exactly... coherent."

"I agree with Grace," Daniel said. "We opened her grave to steal something she obviously treasured. The least we can do is to put her back."

Samael snorted. "Idiots, the both of you. Wasting time on

some ridiculous, insignificant human."

"No human is insignificant," Daniel said.

"Besides," Grace added. "The more time we spend arguing about it, the longer before we're out of here. So how about just helping us bury her and save us the time?"

Samael glared at her. Then he grimaced. "*Fine*," he said. "Let's bury the old crow." Slowly, his body started to transform, growing both bigger and heavier, until a full-size bull was standing before them.

"Why a bull?" Grace asked, tilting her head slightly in befuddlement.

The bull sent her a look, which Grace guessed was meant to be exasperated. Then he walked over to the old woman's corpse, put his head to the ground, and unceremoniously started pushing Annabelle towards her dug-up grave.

"Samael!" Daniel exclaimed, horror written across his every feature. "That is *not* respectful!"

The bull ignored him, completely indifferent to the dirt he was pushing the woman through.

"We should carry her," Grace said, rushing over to him. "Between Daniel and myself, she shouldn't be too heavy."

The argument might've been sound, but it was also given too late. The bull had made his way to the grave, and with a last push, the woman was dumped back into it.

Grace winced at the hollow sound it made when the corpse hit the coffin. It might've been more respectful just to leave her lying underneath the night sky, after all. Though she'd feel rather sorry for whoever happened to stumble upon her in the morning.

With a sigh, she went to get the shovel. She had trouble imagining they'd be able to entirely cover up what they'd done, but they might as well give it a try.

"I'll do it," Daniel said and came over.

"You dug her up!" Grace protested.

"Which is why I owe this to her," Daniel said and took the shovel out of her hands. Next to them, Samael had already started using his large head and horns to shovel dirt back into the hole.

Realising that Daniel needed to do this, Grace focused on the rest of the graveyard. It was quite obvious that *something* had taken place, and she started putting everything back as best as she could — stamping down dirt, brushing off gravestones, even replanting some flowers to the best of her ability.

Finally, they were done, and if it rained heavily enough before anyone got there, they might not notice that anything had taken place.

She looked over at Daniel and the bull. The latter was shrinking down, and Grace watched in fascination as he straightened up on his hind legs before he was entirely transformed back into the familiar shape of Samael.

"There!" he said. "Are we done?"

"I'd like to say a prayer," Daniel said.

"Oh, for the love of—!" He looked at him in exasperation. "Well, be quick about it, will you?!"

Daniel ignored him. Instead, he folded his hands in front of him and closed his eyes. Whatever he said, he didn't say out loud, and Grace remained silent as a sign of respect. Which made the sound of Samael's impatient pacing all the more prominent.

"Finally!" he said when Daniel lifted his head. "Let's get going! Hell's awaiting!"

Grace frowned as she realised something. "How do we get back to Hell anyway?" she asked. "I don't suppose you have a phone number to Heaven?"

Samael grinned. "Earth is full of entrances to Hell," he told her. "Haven't you read any of the stories from Ancient Greece?"

"So you know where to find an entrance?"

"No."

"No?"

"Well, I've used one in Crete before, but I can't remember exactly where it is, and I know of two which have collapsed since then. But it's going to be easy to find the one closest by." His eyes were glinting at them in the darkness, much like a cat's might.

"After all," he said. "We do have our very own human compass, and I know just the question to ask her."

* * *

"Why do you speak Hebrew?" Grace asked Daniel later, twisting in the seat of the cab to look at him.

Samael and she had won the discussion about how to commute to their next destination. While Daniel had voted that they walked, both Samael and Grace had been too impatient. In the end, Samael had turned into a small bird and stolen money straight out of people's hands. Money they had then used to pay for the cab they were currently in.

Samael had since then transformed back into a cat, and he was now lying contently on Grace's lap, purring ever so slightly as she petted him. Out the window, they could see skyscrapers slowly give way to houses.

"Dad insisted," Daniel answered. "He believed that anyone who truly wanted to understand the words of God should read the bible in the language it was originally written in. At least, the language it was mostly written in."

"So I'm guessing your brother speaks Hebrew as well?"

"Yes. Otherwise, he wouldn't have been able to get as much power out of the missing piece as he has."

Grace thought it over. "What about the old lady? Annabelle? She spoke, what? Arabic?"

"Probably not. Even without a language, the Voice of God still contains some power. It must've been the reason she hadn't been forced to cross over."

"But how do you think she got a hold of it to begin with?" After all, if Grace had been asked to place a bet on who'd have the Voice of God, she would've put it on someone from the church. A bishop, perhaps, or even the pope. Or possibly a treasure hunter, like Indiana Jones.

But she sure as Lucifer wouldn't have placed it on Annabelle Hale.

"I don't know," Daniel said. "She could've bought it, I suppose."

"Why would anyone buy a stick?"

"Throughout history, people have paid vast fortunes for religious artifacts. Fragments of the cross, or the bones of saints."

"I once heard of a guy who tried to sell Jesus' toenails on eBay."

The cat in her lap made an odd sound, almost like he attempted to laugh.

"*Important* religious artifacts," Daniel said. "People want to feel closer to God."

"I didn't feel any closer to God when I held it," Grace said. "Did you?"

"I wasn't really… contemplating my feelings at the time," Daniel said. "I was distracted by…" He glanced at the cab driver. "Well, you know."

Grace took that as a no. "It felt like a stick," she said.

"But there must've been stories. Even if the Voice is only half as powerful as I suspect, there must've been incidents. And people are willing to pay for things with a story behind it."

"You really think she just went into a store and bought it?"

"I was thinking an auction or something," Daniel said. "But it's just a theory. It might've been an heirloom, or… I don't know. I mean, there could've been hundreds of ways for her to get it. I doubt we'll ever know."

"Well, we could ask her."

"What?"

"We could ask her. She did try to kill me, so she's probably heading to Hell. Once we get there, we could ask her. I *am* kinda curious. I mean, who gets buried with a stick in their hands?"

Another almost-laugh from Samael.

"What's up with the animal sounds, anyway?" Grace asked the cat, ignoring the look she got from the cab driver. "Can't you speak while you're a cat here on Earth?"

The cat shook his head.

"Are we getting close to where we're supposed to go?" the cab driver asked. He looked nervous.

"Not at all," Grace said. "But the place we need to go lies in that direction." She pointed.

"Right," the cab driver said. "But you can't tell me how far?"

"Well, I don't know. Would you like me to try?"

"No, that's... that's not necessary."

"Are you okay?" Grace asked. "You look a tad... warm." Sweaty, really, but that would be impolite to say.

"I'm fine," he said.

Grace shrugged. She assumed that if he were feeling ill, he'd let them know. She refocused her attention on Samael.

Finally, the cab turned one last corner, and Grace let the driver know that he could stop wherever. She was thankful that they hadn't opted to walk. That would have taken hours.

She got out of the cab as Daniel paid the driver, who quickly drove away. Grace looked around.

They were standing in what appeared to be a normal, if somewhat poor, neighbourhood. The house in front of them was not only the smallest of the block but also the one being taken the least care of. Paint was peeling off its walls, and broken toys lay scattered around the yard. Next to her, Samael turned back into a human.

"Should you really be doing that here?" Daniel asked, looking around with a worried expression.

Samael shrugged. "It's too early for people to be out and about, and we'll be in Hell soon enough anyway. Besides, if anyone actually saw me, they'll think it was a figment of their imagination. They usually do."

"Still, there's no reason to take the risk."

Samael ignored him. "So what about it, Grace?" he asked. "Where's the nearest Gate to Hell?"

"There," she answered, pointing towards the garage of the house. She walked over, bent down to grab the handle, and pulled up the garage door in one, sliding motion.

There was nothing inside.

Well, technically there was. An old car that didn't seem to be able to drive, a child's bike leaning against one wall, and several empty beer cans lying scattered on the floor. Against one wall, there was a grey cabinet.

Thinking it was the only gate-like or even door-like thing in the garage, Grace walked over and opened it.

Inside it were four shelves, all filled with tools of different kinds.

Disappointed, she closed it again.

"Are you sure it's here?" Daniel asked.

"Of course she's sure," Samael said, rolling his eyes. "The Gates of Hell aren't designed to allow anyone to just stumble upon them. Here. I'll show you how it's done."

He pulled Grace away from the cabinet.

"Careful," he told her. "Sometimes the Gates are full of traps." He closed his eyes and said something in an unfamiliar language before he opened the cabinet once again.

Grace blinked.

Inside the cabinet was a short hallway. A red carpet covered the floor, and beautiful paintings lined the walls. A door at the end of the hallway was engulfed in flames, and someone was resting next to it. A bald, silver-skinned person with no nose, wide-stretched lips, and a thick tail. He rather reminded Grace of a lizard. Demon, probably.

He was sitting on the floor, his head resting against the wall a few inches away from the flaming door.

"One of the Gatekeepers," Samael told her. "Asleep on the

job, I see."

"Well, it's probably a really boring job," Grace defended him. "How much excitement can you get guarding a hidden door? No wonder he's asleep."

Samael frowned. "I'll still reprimand him. It's unbecoming for a Keeper." He walked over and grabbed the demon by his shoulders before he gave him a firm shake. The sleeping demon didn't react at all. Samael, however, paled.

"What's wrong?" Grace asked.

"Stay back," Samael told her. "You too, Daniel."

They both walked over. Samael was staring down at the Gatekeeper with a grim expression.

"He's dead," Grace realised.

"Killed," Samael said.

Grace stared at the demon. "What can kill a demon?" she asked.

"A stronger demon. An angel. None of whom would have any reason to do so."

"Can a human?"

Samael considered it. "Maybe with the right weapon," he said.

Grace looked at the dead demon. She wondered if he'd had a family. "What happens to demons if they die?" she asked.

"They get stuck in Limbo. A place of nothingness and insanity."

"That sounds... bad," Grace said. "Hopefully he'll find his way out. Like the man who attacked me back in Hell."

"Doubtful. But we can't afford to worry about him now. Jacob might have killed other Gatekeepers. We need to find one that's still alive before he's killed as well."

"You don't know if it's my brother!" Daniel said. "And how do you even know he's been killed? He could have died of any number of things — a heart attack or something!"

"A heart attack is a privilege left for you humans."

"And even if he was killed, someone else could have done it!"

"Like *who?*"

"I don't know. You said yourself that another demon could've killed him!"

"No demon would kill a Gatekeeper on duty! And it's a bit too much of a coincidence that someone else just *happens* to kill a Gatekeeper after your brother has declared war on Hell!"

"My brother... he wouldn't kill anyone," Daniel said.

Samael stared at him. Then he looked back at the dead demon. "Clearly, he would."

"He wouldn't! Maybe one of his followers did it. Without being told. Maybe they thought they ought to. He *was* a demon."

"Meaning what exactly?"

"He might have... I don't know! Demons are generally known to be evil!"

"You think we should be killed off? Rooting for a bit of a genocide with brother dearest, are we?"

"Of course not! Just... my brother wouldn't kill someone. Anyone. Why would he even want to kill him?"

"Are you a complete idiot?!" Samael snapped. "The Gatekeepers are not only here to keep people away from Hell, but also to let them in. They're the only ones who can open the Gates. If they're dead, we're stuck here on Earth!"

CHAPTER NINE:

Pray

For several long seconds, none of them spoke. Finally, Daniel seemed to pull himself together.

"We could still go to Heaven," he said. "Give it to an angel."

"The way to Hell *was* the way to Heaven," Samael said. "The Gateway of Hell might be known under that name, but it's just the Gateway to the In-Between. The place that leads to both Heaven and Hell."

"So what do we do now?" Grace asked, bending down to examine the corpse. She wondered how he'd been killed.

Samael shrugged. "We could find another Gateway to Hell," he said. "But I doubt it's going to make a difference. The only real reason to kill a Gatekeeper is to make sure that no one can enter or leave Hell."

"Someone killed him so that we won't be able to go to Hell?" Grace asked.

"Probably," Samael said. "Well, partly. Lucifer did send out several demons to search for the Voice. I assume that it was so that none of them could return."

"What if someone killed him in rage?" Daniel suggested. "If he refused to grant them entrance?"

"It's possible," Samael said, not sounding terribly convinced. "And I guess there's really only one way to find out, isn't there?"

"We have to find another Gateway," Daniel said. "And see if its Gatekeeper is still alive."

"Not quite what I had in mind."

"What then?"

"We simply need to ask the right question," Samael said. "Like this. Grace?"

"Yeah?" she said, looking up from the dead Gatekeeper. She

could find no outward signs of a struggle.

"Where's the nearest Gateway to Hell with a Gatekeeper who's alive and well, capable of letting us back?"

Grace frowned, getting no sudden insight. "I don't know," she said.

"And if our human compass can't point us in the right direction," Samael said, "it means that there is no right direction. You can't find what doesn't exist."

"There has to be another way to Hell," Grace said. "Another question you can ask me?"

"You can't find what doesn't exist," Samael repeated, running a frustrated hand through his hair.

"What if I die?" Daniel asked.

Samael and Grace both looked over at him.

"What are you talking about?" Samael asked.

"I'm not dead," Daniel said slowly. "Unlike Grace, I still have a body here. What if we went to the hospital where I was lying in a coma and killed me? Would that send me to Heaven?"

"It might," Grace said, considering it. There was no reason for Daniel not to ignore the Staircase and go straight to Hell. As far as she knew, there was no rule keeping the virtuous and innocent out of Hell. And even if Daniel could only get into Heaven, it would still be a safe place to keep the Voice.

"It won't work," Samael said.

"Why not?" Grace asked.

"While Daniel would pass on, he couldn't take the Voice with him. Only the soul is transported to the other side."

"Reigh said some people brought coins."

"They aren't transported though. A copy is created. Like with your clothes. It wouldn't work with something that has the sort of power as the Voice of God. All you'd have is a stick."

"What if I passed on a message?" Daniel suggested. "Asked an angel to come bring you guys back?"

"An angel?" Grace asked. She'd been under the impression

that he'd take a small detour to Hell on his way to eternal bliss. "I thought you were stopping by Hell," she said.

Daniel paled. "I am *not* going to Hell," he said. "What if you can't change your choice later? I'll ask an angel for help."

Samael stared at him. "Absolutely not!" he said. "I won't lower myself to the help of *them*."

"Fine," Daniel said calmly. "Then *you* die and pass on a message."

Samael glared at him.

"I'm not going to Hell," Daniel said again. "There's no way I'm handing the Voice of God to Lucifer. If I'm going to get help, I'm going to Heaven. And since it's the only option we have, you'll just have to accept that. Unless you think it's better to wait around here for my brother?"

Samael was silent.

"Samael?" Grace asked.

"I'm thinking."

Grace rolled her eyes. "This isn't the time for personal dislikes," she said. "No matter how little you care for angels. But what about Daniel?"

"What about him?"

"Well, he'd probably prefer a method of travel that wouldn't literally kill him," she said.

Daniel shook his head. "No," he said. "I mean, I do, but this... this is too important for me to worry about myself."

Samael sighed. "Of all the companions we could've had," he said. "We had to get one that Jesus himself would call a goody two-shoes."

"I'm sorry if my willingness to die irritates you," Daniel said.

Samael smirked, ready to retort when Grace put a hand on his arm.

"Samael," she said.

Samael sighed and turned his attention towards her. "Grace, where is Daniel's body?" he asked.

"In Phoenix," Daniel said.

"In Baton Rouge," Grace corrected him.

Daniel looked at her, confusion written across his face. "Baton Rouge?" he repeated. "I live in Phoenix. Why would they move me to a town I've never even been to? Where was my body originally sent?"

Grace shrugged. "I don't know."

"She knows where things *are*," Samael said. "Not where they *were*. And as to why you've been moved, I can think of one option."

"My brother."

"And if he's moved your body, I doubt he has left it unguarded. He must have moved it for a reason."

"He might just want to keep my body safe."

"Even then, it's too much of a risk. We can't bring the rest of the Voice to him. And I can't leave you and Grace to guard it alone." He ran his hand through his hair again. Grace thought that he looked quite stressed.

She turned her mind back to the problem at hand, only partly listening to Samael's and Daniel's discussion. It seemed that they'd agreed to kill Daniel, and Samael was currently suggesting they make his brother so angry with him, he'd do the job himself. Daniel, however, was insisting that while Jacob had lost his way, he would never kill his own brother.

"He's no Cain," he said.

"He might be," Samael said. "I've seen worse betrayals than the one between brothers."

"He won't kill me," Daniel insisted. "I *know* him. I don't know what your time in Hell has taught you, but my brother isn't an evil man. He's simply lost his footing."

"He's trying to control Hell!"

"Well, maybe that isn't such a bad thing!"

Samael stared at him. Then he smirked. "Ah. The truth comes out. In cahoots with your brother, are you? Should've known."

"Of course not! He's trying to decide who gets to go to Heaven! But maybe... maybe gaining control over the demons wouldn't be such a terrible thing. You can't deny that it might be safer. Just to make sure that they don't do anything... bad."

Samael lifted an eyebrow. "Such as?"

"Well... you know! Torture. Killing. Stuff like that. Imagine a world where demons aren't allowed to spread devastation!"

"The world wouldn't be all that different!" Samael said, voice rising. "Humans have been perfectly capable of doing those things on their bloody own!"

"But fewer bad things would happen if we controlled the demons!"

Grace, who'd been looking back and forth between the two of them, considered the argument. "Fewer bad things would happen if humans were controlled as well," she noted.

Daniel looked at her. "But that would be going against their free will!"

Samael took a step closer to him, looking for all as if he were about to knock him out. "We have free will as well!" he hissed. "And we fought for ours!"

Daniel took a step back. "It's not like I want demons to be enslaved," he said. "Just... controlled."

"Oh, yes," Samael said. "There's a world of difference there." He curled his lip in disgust. "I think it would be better if Grace held on to the Voice of God," he said. "Hell, I wouldn't even trust you to be killed if we had any other options!"

"What about a prayer?" Grace suggested.

They both turned to look at her.

"What?" Samael said.

"As another option. I've heard people pray to Jesus before, or the Virgin Mary. Couldn't we... send a prayer to an angel?"

"I... we could," Samael said, not sounding all that pleased. "Even an angel might hear a prayer from a... devout believer."

"So probably Daniel."

Samael grimaced. "Which means we're stuck with the damn choir boy."

"I'm sure Daniel just wants to do what he thinks is best."

Samael snorted. "So does his brother."

Daniel flinched. "I'm sorry," he said. "I expect it sounded worse than I meant it. I only meant to order demons not to hurt people."

Samael stared at him. "Can you honestly not see how that might go wrong?"

"What do you mean?"

Samael sighed. "You can't." For some reason it seemed to calm him slightly. "If you would hand over the Voice of God?" he said.

Daniel hesitated.

"It wasn't a request," Samael said sharply.

Daniel handed the Voice of God to Grace.

"Thank you," Samael said, not sounding grateful in the least. "And I'll let your immense stupidity excuse you. For now."

Daniel opened his mouth to reply, and Grace cleared her throat. "That's Samael's way of saying 'you're forgiven'," she said. "I think."

Samael snorted. "We would need to go somewhere holy," he said. "God might hear everything, but his angels don't. If we want an angel to hear our prayer, we need a place of worship."

"A church then?" Grace asked.

"Or a mosque or a synagogue or somewhere similar. It just has to be a building that has been blessed as a place to reach Heaven."

Grace smiled, happy that the verbal minefield seemed to be behind them. "So rather than going off and getting our friend killed," she said. "Why not start by asking me the right question?"

* * *

The church they ended up in was surprisingly cosy.

Grace had never spent much time in churches, but she still remembered the one her mother had used to drag her to, back when she'd been a little girl. It had been beautiful, but it had felt too large and imposing for the young Grace. She'd hated to go there. It had made her feel small.

This place, however, could make her understand why people might go to church. She could see a small community gathering here, exchanging news and enjoying the feeling of belonging somewhere. It was a place that made you feel welcomed.

"Out! Out, I tell you!"

They turned around. Behind them stood a priest, wielding a cross in front of him. He was an elderly man around seventy, whose wrinkly face shone with determination. His white hair was receding, and he was clean-shaven. He looked like a kind man if you ignored the look of righteous fury on his face.

"Are you talking to us?" Grace asked. They were the only ones in church, so she couldn't see who else he would be talking to, but she couldn't imagine what they'd done to make him so angry.

The priest stared at them with fury in his eyes. "You think I won't recognise a demon in my church!" he said, looking at Samael.

"I'm a shapeshifter, if you want to be precise," Samael said.

The old man didn't seem to consider it much of a distinction.

"You hail from Hell," he told him. "You hail from Hell, and you bring evil with you!"

Samael looked at Grace. "She's actually decent enough once you get to know her," he said.

Daniel stepped forward. "We're here to pray, Father," he said. "Please allow us to do so."

The old man stared at him. "You don't have the stench of Hell hanging around you," he said. "And yet you keep company with these sinners. Repent, son. Repent before it's too late."

"Now, listen here," Samael said. "We're not here to lead you into temptation, or whatever it is you're worried about. We're just here to send a quick prayer upwards, so if you would let us do so in peace, that would be just bloody outstanding."

The priest ignored him. "I will protect my flock against all evil and temptation," he said. And that was apparently all the warning they got before he grabbed the nearest bible and hurled it at them.

Samael swore as he just barely had time to duck. "Damn it, old man, we're on your side!"

"I will not listen to your poisonous words, demon!" the priest said before he grabbed another bible. "Now begone! Begone and never come back!" He hurled it in Samael's direction.

The shapeshifter ducked again, swearing at the old man, who seemed intent on chasing them out with the holy book, one way or another.

"Distract him!" Samael told Grace. "I need time to change."

"You can't attack him," she answered before she barely avoided being hit with a flying book. "He's only trying to protect his flock. It's sweet, really."

"Yeah, it's downright adorable," Samael hissed before he threw himself to the side to avoid getting a book thrown in his face. "What do you suggest we do then?!"

"Run," she said before she grabbed his hand and pulled him with her out of the church, Daniel following behind them. Finally, they were outside, away from the priest's bible-throwing vicinity.

"What now?" Samael said.

"Perhaps I should go in alone," Daniel suggested. "He seemed less intent on chasing me out. He might allow a single prayer."

"And if not, we can always find another church," Grace said. "We can't be chased out with bibles in all of them, can we?"

"I'd rather not waste any time," Samael said. "I guess we'll just have to send Daniel back in. I just hope he's good at ducking."

"I don't understand how he knew you were a demon though," Grace said. "Do priests have some sort of mental sensor to feel that sort of thing?"

"Some people can feel the presence of Hell," Samael said. "Making your vocation that of your God, whoever that might be, would only enhance that talent. He certainly didn't like me very much."

"And that's without knowing about the whole apple-incident," Grace said, impressed by the old man's intuition.

"I'll go back in," Daniel said. "If he doesn't allow me to say a prayer, we'll simply have to take the time to find another church. We can't harm a priest for doing what he believes is right."

"A quick smack to the head will hardly leave any permanent damage," Samael argued. "And we only need him out cold for a couple of minutes."

"Absolutely not," Daniel said. "I'll go in, and I'll pray, and we're not going to hit some old man in the head. For all we know, we might accidentally kill him."

"Would that be so horrible?"

"Yes!"

"Well, he's probably going to Heaven anyway!"

"He probably has a *family*," Daniel said. "We're not going to harm an old man just because you're impatient."

Samael sighed but refrained from arguing, and Daniel turned around and stalked back into the church.

Grace and Samael waited in silence for a few minutes.

"Do you think the priest will allow him to say a prayer?" Grace finally asked.

Samael shrugged. "Who knows? I still think we should just give him a good knock on the head."

"I doubt Daniel would allow that."

"Okay, so you punch the old man out, and I'll keep back Daniel. Problem solved."

"I think not," Grace said. She looked at the church. "He has a nice church," she added. "I understand why he wants to keep it safe."

Samael stared at her. "You're really odd," he told her.

Grace was about to retort when Daniel came running out of the church once again.

"What, he chased you out?" Samael asked.

"I hit him."

"What?"

"I hit him!" Daniel said, close to hyperventilating. "He came in, and he attacked me, and I *hit* him. I didn't mean to! He just surprised me, and now he's bleeding, and I don't know how to make it stop!"

"You hit him hard enough to make him bleed?" Samael asked, sounding impressed.

"No! I hit him, and he fell, and he hit his head against the floor, and now he's bleeding, and what if he ends up dying, and I've killed someone!"

"Daniel," Grace said firmly. "I used to be a nurse. We'll go inside, I'll take care of the old man, and you'll send a prayer to Heaven."

Daniel nodded, relieved, before he turned back around and hurried inside, followed by Samael and Grace.

The priest was lying in front of the altar, a small pool of blood at his head.

Samael let out a low whistle. "So much for not harming him, huh?"

Daniel sent him an angry look before he fell down on his knees in front of the alter and started to pray.

Meanwhile, Grace examined the old priest. The damage wasn't as bad as she'd feared it'd be. His pupils reacted when she lifted his eyelids, and he was already beginning to show signs of consciousness. She felt his pulse, which was beating steadily. Slowly, he opened his eyes.

Grace held up four fingers.

"How many fingers am I holding up?" she asked.

"Four," he mumbled.

"Well done," Grace complimented him before she lowered two of her fingers. "What about now?"

"Two," he said, beginning to sit up.

Grace held him down. "What's your name?" she asked.

"Frederic Samuelson," the man said.

Grace nodded and asked him a couple more questions to ensure no permanent brain damage had taken place. The priest willingly enough answered her questions, confusion clear in his voice. Then, suddenly, his eyes filled with realisation.

"Demon!" he gasped. "You were with the demon!"

"And we're leaving now, so there's no reason for you to chase us out," Grace said, looking up to make sure that Daniel was done with his prayer. "I do, however, want you to call someone to take you to the doctor. You might need stitches or at least glue. If necessary, I want you to call a cab. Don't try to drive yourself."

The priest looked disoriented once again, and Grace gave him a quick pat-down to make sure he had a phone on him. Satisfied, she met the priest's eyes.

"Call someone," she said, speaking slowly and clearly to make sure he could hear her. "Okay?"

"I... but... okay," the priest mumbled.

"Grace, we need to leave," Samael said.

"I know," she said, still looking at the priest. He'd made no move to take out his phone.

Suddenly, she heard voices coming from outside.

"Someone is coming," Samael told her. "They'll take care of him, so unless you want to explain how he got hurt to begin with, I suggest we leave *now*."

Grace nodded and followed him and Daniel out of the church with a last glance back at the priest. Outside, they passed two men heading into the church, both of them smiling and nodding as they walked past.

Soon after, Grace heard their exclamations of horror.

"Run," Samael said. They ran.

Finally, they stopped, feeling confident that they were far enough away that the men wouldn't find them.

"When are they coming?" Grace asked. "The angels, I mean."

Daniel grimaced. "I couldn't get any contact," he said. "They were supposed to answer, weren't they?"

"Yes," Samael said. "With something like this, they were. Meaning that we need to go back to our plan of killing you."

Grace gnawed on her bottom lip. She hadn't considered that her plan might fail. They might actually have to kill Daniel. She wondered if people in Heaven could visit people in Hell. She hoped so. She rather liked Daniel.

"So how do we do it?" she asked. "Will Daniel stay behind with the Voice, while we try to get to his body? Or will Daniel try to kill himself? I mean, if they kill him while he's trying, that will only work to our advantage, won't it?"

"No," Samael said. "If Daniel's spirit is destroyed, he won't go to Heaven. That's for when your body dies. It's better if we…" He trailed off. "Did you hear that?" he asked.

"Hear what?" Daniel asked.

Samael frowned. "It was like a… pop."

"A pop?" Grace repeated before she heard it as well. A pop very much like the ones you heard when you were making popcorn.

"I did hear that," she said. "What is it?"

"I don't know," Samael said. "But whatever it is, I'd feel a lot better if we— *aargh!*" His words turned into a scream.

A knife was sticking out of his shoulder, having seemingly come out of nowhere.

Daniel and Grace stared, speechless. Then Grace's experience kicked in, and she ran forward to help.

Black blood was oozing out of Samael's shoulder, and Grace hesitated as she realised that his physiology might be quite different from a human's.

"Just pull it out," Samael hissed at her.

"But—"

"Just do it! I know what I'm doing!"

Gritting her teeth, Grace followed the order, ignoring Samael's sounds of pain as she yanked the knife out.

"We need to stop the bleeding," she said, making a move to tear off a piece of her shirt.

"There's no time," Samael said. "It was only the first attack."

"What?" Grace asked.

She heard something flying through the air and felt a searing pain in her left arm.

The second knife hit the ground. It had only grazed her, and Grace looked in the direction it had come from, getting the first look at their attackers.

Two men were standing on the opposite side of the street, each wearing a... sheet?

No, a cloak, Grace corrected herself. Both men were dressed in a white cloak, but they couldn't otherwise have been any more different.

The one closest to them was young, barely out of his teens, with a slight build and a delicate bone structure.

The other man was older with clear, blue eyes and an impressive mane of white hair. Both of them were armed with long, silvery daggers.

"Undesirables!" Samael hissed.

Grace didn't look away from the two men. Undesirables. Lucifer had used that same expression, meaning that these people belonged in Limbo. Jacob's apostles.

Suddenly, the two men set in motion, running towards them. Their eyes were focused on Samael, ignoring Grace and Daniel completely.

Grace didn't stop to think. Instead, she bolted towards the young man and slammed her entire body weight into him, which caused both her and him to fall to the ground in a confusing heap of limbs and weapon, Grace underneath the young man.

In the background, she could hear another struggle taking place, but she didn't know if the older man was fighting Samael or Daniel. She risked a quick glance over and saw that Daniel had tackled the older man to the ground.

A hand grabbed her chin and forced the back of Grace's head down on the concrete. Her eyes flickered back to the man on top of her. He was pressing her down on the concrete with his left hand, while the other raised the knife into the air. Hatred was burning in his eyes as he looked down at her.

The knife sliced through the air.

Gasping, Grace thrust her hands out and got a hold of the man's wrist before the knife reached her.

The man wasn't particularly strong, and yet Grace found herself struggling. Her left arm was still burning in pain, and he had the upper hand. Still, inch by inch, Grace got the knife further away from her, staring into the man's eyes as she did so. She'd never seen such utter disgust.

This man meant to kill her. *Wanted* to kill her.

She brought her knee upwards as hard as she could, and the man gasped in pain as she successfully kneed him in his private parts. The knife fell from his hand, leaving a slit down Grace's cheek as it fell uselessly to the ground. She let go of the man's wrist to blindly grab for it, and her hand met cold metal. Clutching the knife tightly, she didn't give the man time to think. Instead, she slammed the hilt of the blade into his temple.

The man fell down on her, unconscious.

Breathing heavily, Grace pushed him off of her and got to her feet. She looked towards Daniel, who was currently holding the other man down. One of Daniel's hands was holding both the man's wrists while he struggled to get hold of the knife the man still held in a tight grip. It was obvious that Daniel had the upper hand, but he seemed reluctant to hurt his opponent.

Grace had no such qualms. She hurried over and fell to her knees next to them. The man seemed to double his efforts when he saw her, but Daniel was undoubtedly stronger than him. He was helpless.

Grace knocked him out with the hilt of the stolen knife.

Not giving herself a moment's pause, she immediately got to her feet and ran over to Samael, who was in the middle of a transformation. Four legs, fur and hooves. A horse, she realised. It seemed to take him longer than ever, and his face was contorted in pain. His wound was still bleeding, creating a small puddle of blood on the concrete beneath him. Grace stared. The wound seemed to alternatively stretch and contract as he was slowly transforming. It looked horribly painful.

"Stop changing," Grace ordered him. "We've taken care of it."

Samael didn't answer but continued to transform.

"There might be more," Daniel said, looking at Samael with a pale face. "I doubt they were sent here alone."

Pulling herself together, Grace tore off a piece of her shirt to use as a bandage for herself.

She wished she had something to clean the wound with, but settled for licking it instead before she covered it with the bandage. At least it had stopped bleeding, though she wished she could say the same for Samael's. How did one treat a wound if the wounded person was slowly transforming into an animal?

They had to get him to a hospital after this.

It seemed to take an eternity for Samael to change, and he seemed to backslide towards a human shape every so often. Grace tore her eyes away from this slow transformation.

Instead, she and Daniel kept an eye out for more enemies.

Then Grace heard it. Another pop.

It came from behind her, and she spun around to face her new opponent. She felt her mouth fall open. She was looking at a giant.

No, not a giant. At least not in the strictly technical term.

It wasn't the kind you found at the end of a long beanstalk. However, the man was without a shred of doubt the largest man Grace had ever seen. He was Asian, and must've been at least seven feet tall and as wide as a small shed. Grace gaped at him. The man consisted apparently of nothing but muscles, and Grace had no doubt that he would be able to pick her up and snap her in two like a dry twig.

Another pop sounded, and this time Grace saw it happen. A man simply appeared next to the giant, as suddenly as if he'd always been there.

Another pop came from behind her, and Grace spun around once again. Another two pops sounded, followed by a pause, followed by another four pops. She waited with bated breath, but finally, it was quiet.

Eight men in total then, not counting the two unconscious ones. Eight men who were carrying weapons and standing in a circle around them, slowly closing in.

Behind her, Samael was struggling to stand up, finally fully transformed, and Grace wondered why he hadn't turned into anything more ferocious. Perhaps he merely wanted to run away.

She took a step backwards and put a hand on his mane, all the while keeping a careful eye on the men.

"Do you want us to ride you?" Grace whispered into Samael's ear.

The horse moved his head up and down.

She signalled with her eyes for Daniel to come closer, trying to tell him the plan without alerting the men around them.

Daniel nodded, a tiny little jerk of the head that was barely discernible. Then he jumped.

Samael wobbled as Daniel landed on top of him, but he stayed upright. The men swore, but Grace didn't wait around to give them time to realise what they were doing. Instead, she grabbed Daniel's outstretched hand and was hauled onto the horse.

Samael set off, and the men moved forward. Several knives flew through the air but largely without the precision of that first throw. Only one knife hit its target, but the horse didn't even slow down as it dug into his side.

The horse jumped, and for a second they were flying through the air, above the head of one of the men.

Then the hooves of the horse hit the ground hard, sending an mighty jolt through Grace that almost caused her to fall off.

Samael didn't pause but continued running with both of them still on his back and a knife sticking into his side. Behind them, the men were running. Grace was thankful that no men, at least, popped up in front of them. Hopefully, the teleportation had been a one-time kind of trick.

The men fell behind, but Samael kept running, and houses seemed to fly by as they made their way down the streets. Finally, Samael came to a halt. They were eight blocks from where they'd started, nowhere near safety, but Samael was shaking beneath them. Suddenly, he fell over, and Grace and Daniel barely kept themselves from being squeezed beneath his huge body.

Thankfully, he'd fallen on the side without a knife in it, and Grace looked around for inspiration. They needed to get away, but it was clear that Samael couldn't take them any further.

Not far from them, a man was standing in the street, staring at them in shock. Behind him was his van, door half open. There was no other people around. Running over, Grace kept her stolen knife hidden as well as she could until she was right beside him. She then took a deep breath and pointed her knife at the man.

"We need to go to a hospital," she said before she changed her mind. "No. A vet. We need to go to a vet, and we're going there in your van. You're going to help us get that horse into your van. If you do, no one needs to get hurt. Do you understand?"

The man nodded, eyes wide with terror. Grace ignored his fear as she signalled Daniel closer. To her relief, he didn't scold her for threatening the man but merely got to work.

The horse was heavy, but Samael was conscious enough to help them as well as he could. With their help, he successfully stumbled into the van, which sagged with the added weight.

With a last glance around them, Grace lifted the knife and used the hilt to hit the man in the head. He fell over, unconscious, and Daniel yelped in protest.

"We have to take him with us," she said. "If we leave him, they might learn to keep an eye out for a white van."

Daniel nodded, eyes worried as he looked at Samael. He helped her get the unconscious man into the van.

"I'll drive," he said. "Keep him alive until we get to a hospital."

"A vet," Grace corrected him.

Daniel gave her a dubious look.

"He clearly isn't changing back," Grace said, gesturing towards the horse. "We would probably be better off with someone familiar with a horse's physiology."

Daniel nodded. "You stay with him," he said.

"You don't need me to point you in the right direction?"

Daniel opened the front door and shook his head. "It's got GPS."

Grace nodded. There was no doubt that in this instance it'd be better than the apple, which took no heed of such details as buildings blocking their way. She got into the back and closed the door behind her.

The van set into motion, and Grace focused her attention on Samael. Gnawing on her bottom lip, she knew that she couldn't do much. Even just removing the knife would probably do more damage than good. She'd been a nurse, not a vet.

After having done what little she could, she gently stroked Samael's mane. The only thing she could do now was to hope that he would stay alive until they could get him help.

Hope and pray to herself, as it was becoming clear that no one else was listening.

CHAPTER TEN:

The Next Step

Grace and Daniel both looked up when Samael came out of the veterinarian's operating room. Though paler than usual, he looked far better than when they'd brought him in. As well as far more human.

"I guess we should've brought you to a regular doctor," Grace said.

"This one turned out to be quite adequate," Samael said with his trademark smirk. "Even if she does usually operate on animals. Which I was — for the most part."

"Where is she now?"

"Inside, getting drunk."

"Drunk?"

"Quite impressively so. And I suggest we take advantage of this situation and leave."

Grace nodded. "And then what?" she asked.

"And then we go kill off Daniel," Samael said with glittering eyes.

Daniel sent him an annoyed look. "It seems to be our best option," he admitted. "As we've already tried asking Grace where we can find a Gatekeeper."

"In Montreal," Grace said. She blinked in surprise. "That counted as a question?" she asked.

Samael, however, was focused on other things.

"There's a Gatekeeper who's still alive?" he asked.

Grace frowned at him. "I wouldn't know," she reminded him. "I only know where stuff is."

"He might be dead," Daniel said. "The Gatekeeper in Montreal."

Samael frowned, looking thoughtful. "Grace, where can we

find a Gatekeeper who's alive?" he asked.

"In Montreal," she said.

"So, not dead then," Daniel surmised. "Whoever he is."

"We could still go kill off Daniel," Samael said. They turned to look at him, and he shrugged. "Still a perfectly viable option," he said. "To avoid going on what is possibly nothing but a wild goose chase."

Daniel didn't look entirely convinced. "I would prefer not to die," he said. "If there's another solution. And weren't you against asking the angels for help unless it was our very last option?"

"I might've said something like that."

"Isn't it just a matter of asking the right question?" Grace wondered. "To figure out if this is a wild goose chase?"

"It should be," Samael said. "If we knew what the right question was. But we can certainly try. Grace, where is the nearest Gatekeeper, who's capable of letting us back into Hell?"

"In Montreal," she said.

Samael frowned. "I still don't understand why we didn't get that answer the last time," he complained.

Grace shrugged. Who cared why it hadn't worked the last time, if only it worked this time?

"Shouldn't we get going?" she said. "What with the drunk vet and all?"

"We should," Samael said. Then he hesitated. "I think it's best if I don't transform for a while," he admitted. "Unless absolutely necessary. I heal faster than you fragile humans, but another transformation too soon might kill me. Especially if it's too biologically different from this body."

"Then why didn't you stay a horse?" Grace asked. "If transforming is dangerous for you?"

"Have you tried being a horse? Utterly humiliating. And I'm *Samael*. I can't be stuck as a *horse*." He looked disgusted at the mere thought.

Grace wasn't quite sure what to say to that.

"How do we get to Montreal?" Daniel asked, changing the subject. "We can't fly without passports."

"We'll drive," Samael said. "And walk across the border. Find somewhere unsupervised."

"How do we get a car?" Grace asked. "The van?"

She turned towards Daniel, who'd driven the van away, while Samael had been in the operating room. It would've been slightly unfortunate if the van's unconscious owner had woken up and called the police, so Daniel had left both him and his van at the nearest other vet before he'd used the last of their money to grab a cab back.

"It's probably gone by now," Daniel said. "I doubt the man has remained unconscious for this long."

Grace considered it. She turned to Samael. "Do you know how to hot-wire a car?" she asked. It seemed like the sort of thing he could probably do.

"No."

"I do," Daniel said.

Grace and Samael looked at him.

"Why in the world of all that is sin," Samael said, "does a priest know how to hot-wire a car?"

"A priest?" Daniel repeated. "I'm not a priest. I'm a mechanic."

They looked at him in silence.

"You thought I was a priest?"

"Didn't you say you were?" Grace asked. "Your dad was a priest."

"Yeah, my dad. Not me. I went to the seminary for a while, but ultimately I realised that it wasn't the path for me, so I left."

"To become a mechanic," Samael clarified.

"Yes."

"A mechanic who knows how to steal cars?"

"Well, I've never stolen a car before," Daniel said. "But I can find my way around an engine with a blindfold on. I'm sure I'll be able to start a car without too much trouble."

"How about that," Samael mused. "Our little choir boy is no choir boy at all." He grinned at Daniel. "Well, dodger boy," he said. "Whatever are we waiting for? Let's go steal a car."

* * *

"I've always wanted to do this," Grace said, watching Daniel fiddle with the car door.

They were standing in an underground parking lot, trying to steal an old Volkswagen. After having done their best to avoid the cameras, Grace and Samael were now standing guard while Daniel worked on the car.

"Really?" Samael asked.

"Well, not always. But since the first time I saw it in a movie. It went a lot faster though. It was really cool."

"Why didn't you do it then?"

"Well, stealing is wrong," Grace said.

"You could've returned it. Eventually."

"You can't just steal a car."

"Clearly," Samael said drily. "It's not like it's anything we're doing *as we speak.*"

"We're only doing it because we have to," Daniel said. "And once I'm back in my real body, I'll find some way to make it up to the owner."

"Why the bloody Hell would you do that?" Samael asked.

"It's the right thing to do."

Samael made a disgusted face. "How dull," he said. "How's it going anyway? Aren't you done soon?"

"Well, it would go faster if you'd stop asking every other minute."

"I still don't get why we're stealing *that* car," Samael said. "Why not something that won't break down before we're half-way there? Preferably one of those shiny ones?" He sent a nearby Ferrari a longing look.

"I don't wanna try anything with too complicated an alarm.

Now, would you let me work in peace?"

Samael ignored him, turning towards Grace.

"Do you think you can keep watch alone?" he asked, lowering himself to the ground.

"Sure," she said. "Why?"

"Well, while this pain medication does work miracles, I have to admit that I'm not feeling a hundred and ten." He leaned back against the car, closing his eyes. "So if you don't mind, I think I'll just close my eyes for a couple of minutes."

"Sure. Should I wake you once the door is open or wait until the engine's running?"

Samael didn't answer, already fast asleep.

Remembering her task, Grace looked around to make sure that no one was seeing their less than subtle attempt at stealing a car. They'd chosen this one partly because of the relative lack of cameras and the small chance of anyone just walking by, but it was still a pretty big risk.

"There," Daniel said, having gotten the door open. "Thankfully, starting it without the key will be easier than opening it."

"Great," Grace said. She knelt down next to Samael and put her hand on his shoulder.

"Samael?"

He grumbled in reply.

"We should get inside the car. You can go back to sleep then."

Samael groaned but stumbled to his feet, nonetheless. He crawled into the backseat of the car and immediately went back to sleep.

Grace reminded herself to keep an eye on him. She'd seen his occasional grimaces of pain, and experience had taught what could happen if someone pushed themselves too far.

Knowing that there was nothing she could do right now, she got into the front seat and looked on in fascination as Daniel started the car. That part did go a lot faster.

Finally, they were driving, and Grace rolled down her window to enjoy the wind against her face. They were once again on their way, and when they got to Montreal, the Gatekeeper would let them back into Hell. Once there, Lucifer would take over. She wondered if she could ever return to Earth again. She hoped so. Despite it all, she enjoyed having an adventure.

She looked over at Daniel and realised that she might be alone with that sentiment. He looked positively glum.

"Why so blue?"

Daniel glanced over at her. "What?"

"What's bothering you?"

"Nothing," Daniel said.

Grace hoped that she wasn't that bad a liar. She waited patiently.

It took about eleven seconds for Daniel to give up pretending. "When I fought that man..." he said. "He said something."

"He did?"

"He mentioned my brother." Daniel said.

"Well, he was one of his henchmen."

"Apostles."

Grace tilted her head to the side "What's the difference?"

"That's... never mind."

They sat in silence for a few seconds.

"So what did he say?" Grace asked.

"He said my brother was disappointed I was fighting against him."

"...Okay?" Grace wondered what was so upsetting about that. It wasn't like they'd expected Jacob to be pleased.

"Which means that he knew," Daniel said.

"Knew what?"

"Knew that they were going after us." Daniel drummed his fingers against the steering wheel. "Maybe he didn't realise they were going to attack us," he said. "He could've just planned for them to steal the Voice."

"Or maybe he just tried to kill Sammy and me," Grace added, trying to cheer him up. It couldn't be pleasant, wondering if his own brother had tried to off him.

Daniel didn't look at all cheered up. "He still wouldn't... though Samael *is* a demon... and you're from Hell..." He trailed off.

"Daniel," Grace said, gently. "I think you at least need to entertain the *possibility* that your brother tried to kill Samael and me."

"Jacob isn't... He wouldn't... I'll *fix* this. I'll calm him down. Make him see reason."

"He might not want to," Grace said. "And you can't just go around and patch things up whenever your brother messes up."

Daniel's knuckles turned white as he tightened his grip on the steering wheel. "I have to," he said.

Grace frowned. "Is that why you went to Heaven?" she asked. "To clean up his mess?"

"I was trying to do the right thing."

Grace considered his words. "For the world or your brother?"

"Both."

To Grace it sounded like it had mostly been for his brother. It was impressive how responsible some people felt for the actions of others. Daniel seemed to blame himself, which was ridiculous, and Grace was about to tell him just that.

"Can we please talk about something else?" Daniel asked.

Grace gave him a contemplative look. He looked even worse than when they'd started the conversation. "Sure," she said.

Silence.

Grace reached over and turned on the radio, letting Britney's voice blast through the car. Behind them, Samael grumbled in his sleep, and with a sigh, Grace turned off the music.

"So why did you leave the seminary?" she asked Daniel.

He sent her a grateful look. "There was a girl," he said.

Grace sat up straighter. That sounded wonderfully sinful. "And you fell in love?" she guessed.

"We did. I was sure that we would be together forever. I was wrong."

"She died?"

"What?" Daniel shot her a glance. "No. We broke up."

"Oh. Why?"

"She had to move away for work, and I didn't offer to go with her. Perhaps I should have."

"You could still go," Grace said. "Once you're back in your old body."

Daniel shrugged. "Perhaps. I just need to survive this first."

"Of course you're going to survive it," Grace said. "Why wouldn't you?"

"Thirty minutes ago, we were planning to kill me ourselves."

"Yeah. Thirty minutes ago. But I still don't get why you left the seminary?"

Daniel looked confused. "I told you. There was—"

"A girl, yeah. I got that. But since your father had children, I assume you're not Catholic?"

"No, I'm a Protestant."

"So you could've become a priest and still been with her."

Daniel smiled. "I suppose I was rather vague. April — that's her name — has a brother, who's a mechanic. They were roommates and sometimes he'd show me a couple of tricks. I was a lot happier working on an old classic than I ever was in the seminary, so ultimately I left. April convinced me. Said I should do something with my life that makes me happy."

Grace thought it over. "She sounds like a sweet young girl," she said. "I hope you two youngsters work it out."

"Grace?"

"Hmm?"

"How old are you?"

"93," Grace said and glanced down at the smooth skin of her hand. "I just remember to moisturise."

"That must be it," Daniel said, smiling.

Grace grinned at him before she decided to change the subject. "How far is it to the border?" she asked.

Daniel shrugged. "About five hours or so."

"Let's play some car games then. Ever heard of Zitch Dog?"

* * *

Around four hours later Samael woke up.

"How are you feeling?" Grace asked.

"Better," he yawned, stretching. He grimaced as he lifted his shirt and checked his bandages. "Though the pain medication is starting to wear off. Is it too much to hope that any of you guys have any on you?"

"I found a bottle of rum in the glove compartment," Grace said.

"That should work."

"Do you really think you should be drunk when we meet the Gatekeeper?" Daniel asked.

"Sure. Why not?"

"Do you feel well enough to transform?" Grace asked him as she handed him the bottle.

"I feel *better*, I don't feel *well*. And are we sure the Gatekeeper is still alive?"

"I've been asking Grace for the location of a live Gatekeeper every half an hour or so," Daniel said. "So far, so good."

"Spectacular," Samael said and opened the bottle Grace had handed him. "Here's to them still being alive when we get there," he said and took a long swig. He grimaced. "Heaven's Wooden Gates, that's disgusting. I haven't had alcohol that cheap in centuries."

Daniel glanced at him in the rear-view mirror. "Between you and Grace, I feel very young," he said.

"That's because you are," Samael informed him. "Nothing but a well-grown baby." He took another long swig.

"Well, I'm pretty young compared to you as well," Grace said.

Samael shrugged. "And yet I don't find your company completely unbearable." A third swig. "Even if you are awfully impulsive."

"So are you."

"I am not! I'm *Samael*. I'm part of the nobility of Hell." He took a fourth swig. "I'm not impulsive. Or immature."

"Immature?" Grace repeated.

"Yes. I'm not. No matter what Lucifer might've said. And I'll show him." A fifth swig. His eyes seemed to have trouble focusing. "He'll realise that I'm just like him. Noble. Mature. Perfectly capable of handling responsibilities." A sixth swig.

Daniel sent Grace a questioning look, which she answered with a shrug.

"I wasn't stupid," Samael said. "I was clever. It wasn't like I did anything wrong, anyway. I merely made a slight suggestion. They were the ones who did it. He got so angry though." He took another swig. Grace was starting to lose count.

"Who did?" Daniel asked.

"*Lucifer.*" Samael glared at seemingly nothing. "And it's so unfair as well! He starts a war, and it's all noble and shit, and then I make a teeny tiny suggestion, and suddenly it's the end of the world. Well, the end of Paradise, anyway." Another swig. "One would think he'd be pleased. It wasn't like he was fond of the idiot either. But no, *I'm* acting irresponsibly." He smiled dreamily. "He'll have to change his opinion now. None of his precious warriors could get the Voice, but I did." For several seconds, he merely smiled into the air. "That'll prove it." He yawned.

Grace smiled at him. "If you're still tired, why don't you go back to sleep?"

"I will," Samael mumbled. "The pain woke me up. I just need another shot of medication." He took a last swig of the rum before he closed his eyes and fell back asleep.

"Wow," Daniel said. "I wonder if he's okay."

"He's probably a bit stressed," Grace said. "Feeling that the future of Hell is resting on his shoulders. And then he's still in pain, which makes him grumpy. He's happy that he's not here alone, but far too proud to admit it. He's hopeful that this will make Lucifer consider him an equal. And he's also a little drunk."

Daniel stared at her.

"What?" Grace said. "He's quite easy to read, once you get to know him." She looked at the clock. "Do you need me to drive again for a while? Hasn't it been around an hour since we last switched?"

"You don't mind?"

Grace shrugged. "I like driving," she said. "And it's no use if you're exhausted once we're there. We're going to need our energy crossing the border."

"I'm sure it's going to be okay," Daniel assured her.

Grace grinned. "I'm sure it's going to be *fun*."

* * *

In the end, it was almost disappointingly easy to cross the border. At least on foot.

The place they'd decided to use consisted entirely of dense forest. If there were any patrols walking around, they never saw anything of them. In fact, it was rather like taking a hike.

They used Grace as a compass, and if Samael hadn't looked quite so pale, it would've been an altogether enjoyable trip.

He did complain, though, which Grace was grateful for. He couldn't feel too awful then. He also refused to let them support him or aid him in any other way. Instead, he insisted that he wasn't some puny human, and that he was perfectly capable of walking on his own, wounds be damned.

He couldn't walk quite as fast as usual, though, and it took them around three hours to get to the other side, and another twenty minutes standing on a dusty country road, trying to get a car to pull over.

Finally, an old, powder blue Ford did just that. Grace hurried over to it, Daniel and Samael following close behind.

"Thanks for stopping," Grace said before she repeated her words in French, unsure which language the driver might prefer. He was an elderly man with a frail build and a kind face.

"Pas de problème!" the man answered. "Ce serait bien d'avoir un peu de compagnie." *It's no problem! I would enjoy the company.* He glanced at the others, standing a bit behind Grace.

"T'es-tu malade?" he asked Samael, a concerned expression on his face. *Are you unwell?*

"Je me sens bien," Samael answered in flawless French. "Merci de vous être arrêté." *I feel fine. Thank you for stopping.*

Daniel looked at him in surprise. "You speak French?"

Samael smirked. "Of course. Don't *you?*"

Daniel rolled his eyes. "I don't," he said. "So could someone please translate?"

"Ah! Américaine?" the elderly man asked.

"Oui," Grace answered.

"Would you prefer English?"

"That won't be necessary," Samael said.

"That would be kind of you," Grace corrected, far more considerate of Daniel. "If it wouldn't be too much trouble?"

"Oh, it's no trouble at all. Climb in, climb in."

They did as instructed, thanking him again. Grace took the front seat, expecting a complaint from Samael that never came. Perhaps he was feeling worse than all his grumbling had led her to believe.

"So, where exactly are you kids off to?" their new driver asked them.

"Montreal," Grace told him.

"Ah. Lovely place, but a bit crowded for me. I lived there once when I was a young man. It was smaller back then, of course."

"Of course," Grace said. She'd seen towns and cities grow bigger as well.

"Are you sure you're okay?" the man asked Samael, frowning ever so slightly as he looked him over. "You look mighty pale."

"He's just hungover," Grace lied. The old man lit up.

"Ah, the stories I could tell you that ended with a bad hangover. Of course, that's really a young man's game, but I did have my share of fun, back in the days."

He immediately threw himself into a retelling of these 'fun days', and Grace repeatedly had to check herself before she said something that might reveal her true age.

"I'm going to Blainville myself," he told them after a while. "So I can take you all the way, no problem. What are you doing in Montreal?"

"We're meeting an old friend," Grace said.

"Lovely. I have a friend in Montreal as well. Nice fellow. Though he did once stab me in the ribs. Not on purpose, mind you. Meant to cut my birthday cake." He smiled fondly at the memory.

He and Grace kept talking, with the occasional comment from Daniel, all the way to Montreal, while Samael once again slept in the back seat. Once they got nearer to the city, the old man insisted on driving them to their exact destination; an offer they gratefully accepted.

Their exact destination was in one of the outer parts of Montreal. In fact, the neighbourhood was so far removed from the buzz of the city that it could hardly count as being part of it. Her eldest sister lived in a neighbourhood like this, where the gardeners used measuring tape to make sure the hedges were exactly four foot, seven inches.

They thanked the old man for the ride one last time, got out and watched him drive off.

"Which house is the Gatekeeper in?" Samael asked Grace.

"That one," she said, pointing. It was just as pleasant and

correct as all the others.

Grace walked up the perfectly symmetrical stone pathway leading to the front door, closely followed by Samael and Daniel. Looking around with interest, Grace noted that the garden was a lush green that probably hadn't been achieved without plenty of pesticides and artificial watering.

The door was made of dark wood and was covered in beautiful carvings, and the door knocker had the shape of a lion's head. Grace used it to knock four times.

Nothing happened.

Frowning, she knocked again. And again. She *knew* the Gatekeeper was in there, and she sure hadn't come all the way from literal Hell to walk away simply because they couldn't be bothered to open their dang door.

Finally, they did.

At least she thought it was them. It was hard to see whether it was a human or a demon standing before them in a fuzzy, pink robe, a green mud mask, and a floral shower cap. Whoever it was, he or she was currently eating a cucumber slice that seemed to have been recently removed from his — or hers — face.

"What?!" It was a male voice.

"Grace, where's the nearest Gatekeeper?" Samael asked her.

"Right in front of us," she said.

"Right. So you might as well give up on the disguise. We know who you are, and you need to let us back into Hell."

The Gatekeeper stared at them.

"I don't know what you're talking about," he said.

"Don't bother lying. She ate an apple from the Tree of Knowledge."

The Gatekeeper scowled at them. "Fine, so I'm the Gatekeeper," he sneered. "At least I was. But I'm not going anywhere near one of those dead-cursed Gates, so you find someone else to ask because *I* am not helping."

And with these words, he slammed the door in their faces.

CHAPTER ELEVEN:

The Dilemma

Grace stared at the door, appalled that anyone could be so fundamentally rude.

Squaring her jaw, she lifted her hand and started hammering on the door.

"Open up!" she demanded.

"Go away!"

"No! We came a long, fudging way, and we're not going to just leave. We need you to take us back to Hell so that Lucifer can keep the Voice safe."

The door opened slightly, and suspicious eyes peered out.

"You have the Voice of God?"

"Yes. Now let us in, or I'll do something you'll regret."

The demon cursed and opened the door entirely.

"Well, come in then," he grumbled. "I can't have you on my doorstep, yapping about something so dangerous. You'll get yourselves killed, you know that? You'll get *me* killed."

Refraining from answering, Grace stepped inside, followed closely by Samael and Daniel. Looking around with interest, she wasn't sure what she'd been expecting. It undoubtedly wasn't floral patterned fabrics and hundreds of small dog figurines placed on every flat surface within her eyesight. A collection of porcelain dolls on a side table made her shiver. Not exactly her taste in interior design.

Focusing her attention back on the Gatekeeper, Grace watched in fascination as he took off the pink bathrobe and floral bathing cap before he wiped off the green facial mask. His skin was rough and dark red, and his horns curled around themselves no less than three times.

"Well, sit down or whatever," he said before he followed his own advice and practically fell into one of his two over-sized armchairs. The other one seemed far less comfortable; for some reason it was covered in scorch marks.

Grace chose the couch.

"Thank you for your hospitality," she said.

The demon sent her a withering look.

"Perhaps you'll offer a cup of tea?" Grace suggested.

"No," he said.

"We're not here for refreshments," Samael said. "We're here because we need you to get us back to Hell."

"And I've already told you no," the demon answered. "I've retired."

"Gatekeepers retire?" Grace asked.

"Yes," Samael said. "Every job gets boring after a millennium. He, however, hasn't retired."

"I've retired," the demon insisted.

"You've filed a submission? It's been approved, and a new Gatekeeper has been appointed? You've trained him and left the Gate in capable hands?"

The Gatekeeper said nothing.

"I thought not," Samael said.

"It's not as if anything bad will happen," the demon muttered. "They had them locked up centuries ago."

"Well, that's kind of the problem," Grace said. "The Gate is useless without its Gatekeeper."

"Well, what did you expect me to do?" the demon said. "If I hadn't left, I'd be dead by now! All the others are! We stay in touch, you know, but suddenly Petrav stopped answering, and Alysi found him *dead!* And then it was Alysi herself! And when Gazol died, I knew it was only a matter of time. Gazol was the strongest of us! He could defeat an army with the flick of a hand. Not that it helped him much in the end!"

"You should have contacted Lucifer when the first Gatekeeper died," Samael said, uncaring. "Applied for help.

Protection."

"You don't think we tried? We sent messages, but they all remained unanswered. Tobas and Kristas travelled through their Gates to beg for help. We haven't heard from them since, and I know that it can only mean one thing. Death!"

"How do you know they've died?" Daniel asked. "They could've just run away."

The Gatekeeper glared at him. "Not Tobas," he said. "Not Kristas. And I sure wasn't going to follow their example and try my own Gate! I'd be killed before I got to Hell! And even if I did get there, my safety would only be temporary anyway. In these times, a demon is better off in Heaven, if you ask me. I had to hide. It was my only option."

"It's probably a good thing that you did," Daniel said.

Samael stared at Daniel in disbelief. "You got to be kidding me," he said. "Because of this... this mealy-mouthed coward, one of the Gates of Hell has been left unattended, unprotected, and utterly useless."

"Well, if he hadn't, he would've been dead by now," Daniel argued. "And we'd be even worse off."

"That's true," Grace said. "Now he can help us get to Hell."

"Absolutely not," the demon said. "What if it's an ambush? I'm not going to die just because you kids didn't think things through. And let's say there's no one waiting there to kill me? Then what? I'll send you through the Gate, and you'll be killed in the In-Between? Can you imagine what Lucifer would do to me?"

"Kids?" Samael sputtered. "Listen here, you glorified doorman, I am—"

"It's very considerate of you to think of our safety," Grace interrupted him. "But we have to take the chance."

"And what then?" the demon asked. "When you've been killed? Do you think they'll just leave the Voice of God behind with your corpses? You'll only make things worse."

Silence fell over the room. He did have a rather unfortunate point.

"What then?" Grace said. "We'll do nothing?"

"We can't do that," Samael said. "Daniel's brother might find us. If he's been able to find every Gate to Hell, he must be in possession of some sort of tracking device."

"An apple?" Grace asked.

"No. He wouldn't be able to enter Heaven, and even if he were, there's only one apple of its kind. There are other ways."

"Like how?" Grace asked.

"Magic."

"Magic?" Grace repeated. "Magic's real?"

"Well, that's your humans' word for it. What else would you call everything you've seen so far?"

"I haven't really thought about it. But what would that even mean? That Jacob is some sort of wizard?"

Samael snorted. "Don't be ridiculous," he said. "But the Voice of God isn't the only magical item out there. Most, however, were made by angels or demons and are far less powerful. During the war, countless were lost here on Earth. I'm sure you've heard stories about some of them. Excalibur. The Golden Fleece." He grimaced. "You've even had the misfortune to see one of them up close."

"I have?" Grace asked.

"The dagger that stabbed me."

"It was cursed?" Daniel asked.

"Yes. Otherwise, it wouldn't have hurt me the way it did. No ordinary knife would've been able to do that."

"But I was hit as well," Grace said. "Was that knife normal?"

"No," Samael said. "But it wasn't cursed against humans."

Grace considered it. "Well, I'm glad you didn't die," she said.

Samael smiled wryly. "So am I."

"But what now?" Daniel asked. "Are we taking our chances with the Gate of Hell?"

Samael sighed. "I don't know," he said. "We could just wait. Lucifer is bound to work against your brother from inside of Hell. He might find us."

"And if Daniel's brother does first?" Grace asked. "I think we should take the chance."

"Well, of course, you do," Samael said. "You always believe things will turn out fine. Sometimes they don't."

"So we're just going to sit around and wait?"

"No. We... I don't know what we're going to do. Just let me think for a second."

The Gatekeeper looked displeased. "I won't take you through one of the Gates," he said.

"Oh, do shut up," Samael said. "I'm thinking."

"If you won't take us voluntarily," Daniel added. "We'll use the Voice to force you."

The Gatekeeper gaped at him. "You wouldn't?!"

"I would. If it proved necessary."

"It could cost me my life!"

"I know." Daniel squared his jaw. "And it might cost me Heaven, but I'll do what has to be done."

The Gatekeeper snorted derisively, and Grace decided to cut in.

"Please do help us," she said. "I can't say that we won't force you if we have to, but I'm still asking you to do this."

"Why should I?"

"It's the right thing to do."

The Gatekeeper looked entirely unimpressed.

"Besides," Grace added gently. "How do you think Lucifer is going to react when he finds out that you not only abandoned your post but also refused to help us get the Voice of God to safety?"

The Gatekeeper gulped. "You'd tell him?"

"You don't think he'll find out on his own?" Grace asked. "Eventually?"

"I... I..."

"We're staying here," Samael said, interrupting them.

They looked over at him.

"So we're just going to hope Lucifer will come and get us?" Grace asked, dissatisfied. It wasn't the decision she would have made.

"No, we'll take our chances with the Gate," Samael said. "But not right now. I can't protect us if someone does attack. Hopefully, I'll feel closer to my old self tomorrow."

"You can't stay here!" the Gatekeeper said. "You're bringing danger with you, and I've managed to keep myself safe until now."

"Well, tough luck," Samael said. "We're staying. But please; do feel free to call the police." He gestured towards the phone.

The Gatekeeper made no move to pick it up.

"I thought not," Samael said. "Now go and make up some beds for us. And afterwards you're going to cook us something to eat, as food will speed up my healing process. Something with plenty of red meat. Because I like that."

"You think you can order me around like some common servant? I'm a Gatekeeper of Hell."

"Correction. You *were* a Gatekeeper of Hell. Wasn't that what you said yourself? That you've retired? Meaning that you've lowered yourself to the status of a common demon. So if I tell you to do something, you better blasted well do it."

Their eyes locked, and Grace got the sense that something profound was happening between them. A tense moment later, the Gatekeeper looked down, and Samael smirked.

"Fine," the Gatekeeper said and stood up. "You can stay here tonight. I'll prepare you some beds."

"One last thing," Samael said.

"What?"

"Don't try to sneak off. You'll regret it if you do."

The Gatekeeper glowered at him. "I won't," he said. "I have

enough people out to get me as it is."

"Lovely," Samael said and leaned back against the couch. "Then I think I'll take a nap." He yawned and let his eyes drift shut.

"Then Daniel and I will start on dinner," Grace said.

Samael opened his eyes to look at her. "You don't have to," he said. "He... I actually don't believe I caught your name?" he said, glancing at the Gatekeeper.

"Gregorian," he said.

"Gregorian here is more than capable of making dinner," Samael said.

"Maybe," Grace said. "But we're guests here. We should help."

"You want me to help cook *dinner?*"

"No. You're still wounded. You should rest. Daniel and I will help, though."

Samael shrugged. "Suit yourselves," he murmured, closing his eyes once again. "Wake me when it's ready."

"Will do," Grace promised. "Sweet dreams."

Samael's only answer was a slight snore.

* * *

Dinner was awkward.

Whatever had happened in the staring contest between Samael and Gregorian, it was clear that the latter was holding a grudge. He spent the entire meal glaring at the shapeshifter, who ignored him in return. Daniel ate quietly, seemingly deep in thought.

And Grace was bored.

It was a relief when dinner was finally over, and they could go to their respective bedrooms. Sleep wasn't really a necessity, but Samael had told her to get some anyway.

Grace decided to take his word for it, but when she was about to go into her bedroom, Samael grabbed hold of her sleeve. He looked tense.

"I'd prefer if you stayed in my room tonight."

Grace turned back in surprise. "You want to have sex?" she asked, hardly able to remember the last time someone had propositioned her. "Sure, I guess. I might be a bit rusty, though."

Samael laughed, his tenseness evaporating. "Not quite what I meant," he said. "I meant that you should sleep on the couch in my room."

"Oh. Okay. Sure." She walked past him and into his room. Then she turned around and looked at him. "Why?" she asked.

"In case something happens," he said. "If you're sleeping in a different room, you might be killed before I even realise it."

"What about Daniel?"

"What about him?"

"Well, won't he be in danger too?"

"Sure. I just care less about him."

"Well, I don't. I'll ask him to sleep in our room as well. And Greg too."

Samael looked at her in horror. "*Why?*"

"He's risking his life to harbour us."

"Not exactly willingly," Samael said. "And where do you propose you guys will all sleep?"

"We'll put one of the other mattresses on the floor for Greg," Grace said. "I can sleep on the couch, and Daniel can sleep with you."

"I am not, under any circumstances, going to sleep in the same bed as Daniel."

"Fine. We'll share a bed then," Grace said. "And Daniel can take the couch."

Samael considered it. "You don't snore, do you?"

Grace laughed. "Not that I know of," she assured him. "And if I do…"

"Yeah?"

"Live with it."

* * *

Lying in the darkness, Grace listened to the sounds around her. Samael's soft breathing next to her, Daniel's light snore, and Gregorian's anything-but-light snore.

"Are you awake?" Samael whispered.

"Yeah."

"Of course you are. How can anyone fall asleep with *that* noise?"

A particularly loud snore tore through the air like a pack of running bulls.

"He might have some earplugs somewhere," Grace said.

Samael didn't answer, and she was just beginning to wonder if he'd fallen asleep when he spoke again.

"Gregorian might be right," he said. "There might be an ambush waiting for us."

"There might not be," Grace said. "And if there is, we'll just have to beat them."

"You should stay away."

"What?"

"You should stay away. Find somewhere safe. Just ask yourself where that would be."

Grace frowned. "You don't want me with you?" she said. "I know I can't transform into a gorilla or anything, but I really do think I can help."

"We should keep the Voice safe. Daniel and I will get Lucifer, and he'll come bring you and the Voice back. It's risk-free."

"No, it's not. What if you guys die too?"

"Better than you... better than the Voice falling into the wrong hands. Besides, I won't die. Weeds never perish."

Grace smiled in the darkness. She knew that she would never be able to sit back and watch them go into danger without her. Even if Samael did have some excellent points.

"Daniel can keep the Voice safe," she said.

"I'd rather it was you."

"Why?"

He didn't answer. For several long minutes, Grace lay awake, listening. Finally, she decided that he must have fallen asleep. With an internal shrug, she closed her eyes and allowed herself to follow his example. She knew one thing for sure, though.

She wasn't going to sit back, waiting.

CHAPTER TWELVE:

Suburbia

Yawning, Grace opened her eyes. The room was bathed in the soft light of the morning sun, and a warm body next to hers assured her that Samael was still asleep. A continuing snoring further proved that both Daniel and Gregorian were as well.

Grace slipped out of bed and made her way to the kitchen. She should make them breakfast, she reasoned. If food helped Samael heal, they should stuff as much into him as shapeshiftingly possible.

She could make pancakes. With a smiley face made of syrup.

Humming ever so slightly, she turned on the radio and grinned as cheerful music filled the kitchen. Though music would never be as it had once been, she was thankful they'd at least gotten over that dark phase with all the screaming. She'd never understood what that had been about.

But this Ed Sheeran fellow was actually quite decent, and so she attempted to sing along as she cracked three eggs against the side of the bowl. She didn't actually know the words, but that hardly mattered.

She found a bag of flour with some difficulty, and almost dropped it when she attempted to pour some of it into the bowl. Laughing at herself, Grace realised that she should probably have worn an apron. She looked around and saw one hanging on the side of the last cabinet. It was bright blue and had little yellow ducks on it. Grace instantly fell in love.

She put it on over her borrowed pyjamas and used a bag clip to keep her hair away from her face before she struggled for a couple of minutes to locate the sugar. She found it stuffed into a jar labelled cinnamon. The rest of the ingredients were easy enough to find.

A single lock of hair stubbornly refused to stay back, and as she pushed it behind her ear, she felt herself smearing pancake batter on her cheek. She ignored it, knowing that any attempt to stay clean would be a waste of time. She had always been a messy cook.

A doorbell rang.

Having been busy stirring, Grace ground to a halt as she listened. Perhaps it'd been one of the neighbours' doorbells.

It rang again.

Definitely theirs.

She considered for a second to ignore it when she realised how stupid she was being. She'd turned the volume up so that the music was blasting out of the old radio, and her unexpected guest could undoubtedly hear it. She had been rather silly to turn it on at all.

With an internal shrug, she went and opened the door.

The man outside had his hand in the air as if preparing to knock. He slowly lowered it as he stared at her.

He looked nice, she decided. A bit dull perhaps in his pressed trousers and forest green sweater, but nice. He also seemed a bit unsure of himself.

"Bonjour!" she greeted him cheerfully.

"I... um, bonjour," the man stammered. "I mean hello. We, eh... we prefer English here."

There was something slightly reproachful in that last sentence. An English enclave, perhaps, insisting on the language of their choice. No matter. "Hello," she smiled. "Can I help you with anything?"

"No. I mean, yes. I mean, I don't know."

"That does sound confusing. Would you like a cup of coffee while you figure it out?"

"I..." The man hesitated, seemingly unsure of what to say.

"I'm Grace," she introduced herself, trying to set the man at ease.

"I'm Dick," he said. "I'm a friend of Hannah and Tom."

Grace wondered who Hannah and Tom were.

"That's nice," she said.

"Yes…" He squirmed a bit. "They told me to keep an eye on the house," he said. "While they were away."

"That's very kind of you," Grace said. "We did the same kind of thing where I used to live. It eases your mind, doesn't it? Knowing that someone is keeping an eye out while you're away?"

"Yes. Yes, it does." He cleared his throat. "Hannah and Tom never mentioned that someone was going to be staying in their house."

"Oh, they hadn't really planned to have us stay here."

"Us? There's more than just you?"

"Well, me and a couple of friends."

"I see. If you don't mind me asking, how do you know Hannah and Tom?"

"Oh, I don't. I'm Greg's guest. He's the one who's house-sitting."

"Ah! Greg!" The man visibly relaxed. "I know Greg. Good man. Hell of a lawyer."

Grace deduced that they probably weren't talking about the same Greg. She decided not to inform the man of this.

"I was just making pancakes," she said.

The man lit up. "Pancakes?" he said. "You don't say? I'm really on a diet, you see, but I must admit that I miss my Sunday pancakes." He looked at her hopefully.

Grace opened her mouth to invite him in when Samael popped up next to her.

"Who's this?" he asked.

"This is Dick," Grace said. "He lives next door. He's house-watching, and he got a bit worried when he heard us."

"That was, of course, before I knew you were friends of Greg's," Dick said.

Samael offered his hand, something undeniably sharp in his smile.

"Samael," he said.

Dick took a deep breath before he shook his hand. "Dick," he said. "As introduced by your lovely... wife?"

"We're not married."

"Ah. Well, don't worry about that," Dick assured him. "We are very liberal on this street. Alan across the street there votes for the Liberal Party. Nice fellow despite it all. He and his girlfriend aren't married either. Even though they have three kids." Dick frowned. "It's fine though."

"Well, if they don't marry before it's too late, they might just go to Hell," Samael said.

Dick gave a nervous chuckle.

"Dick was just mentioning how he misses his Sunday pancakes," Grace said.

"Ah. He's welcome in, of course," Samael said.

Grace looked at him in pleasant surprise.

Dick smiled.

"If he doesn't mind that they're gluten-free, of course" Samael said.

"Even better," Dick said. "Shouldn't have too much of that dangerous gluten."

"And vegan," Samael added.

"No worries. My wife's a vegan. I'm sure they'll be delicious just the same."

"And sugar-free."

Dick's smile froze. "Sugar-free," he repeated. "Without any sugar?"

"Not as much as a grain," Samael assured him.

"Ah. Actually, I've just remembered that my wife and I are on this new diet together. I wouldn't want to cheat."

"Of course not," Samael said. "That's very recommendable."

Dick smiled, relieved. "Tell Greg I said hi. We met at last

year's barbecue. I'm sure he'll remember me."

"I don't think that he will," Samael said and closed the door.

"That was rude," Grace said.

"Yeah, well, I'm rude. And you're stupid."

"I'm not stupid."

"So you weren't about to invite him in?"

"So?"

"You don't think Gregorian will be just a bit of a shock for him?"

Grace considered it. "Perhaps," she admitted.

Samael sighed. "Perhaps impulsive is a better word for you. Though in this instance, it did bring something good with it."

"It did?"

"Now we don't have to hide our presence as much. They're all going to think that we're house-sitting. It'd be hard to consider you a burglar, apron and all. Lucifer, they might even bring welcome baskets!"

"Oh, I love those!"

"Of course you do."

"But they won't all think we're house-sitting. I've only been talking with Dick."

"And I saw three others watching while pretending to garden. In this kind of neighbourhood, they'll all know within the hour."

"It's nice that people talk. Especially neighbours."

"I wouldn't really call it talking as much as gossiping," Samael said. "Now, how about those pancakes? I have to agree with Dick on that one. They do sound delicious."

* * *

"Another one," Samael demanded.

"Say the magic word."

Samael glared at her. "You're going to insist on that every single time?"

"Yes."

Samael sighed. "May I have another pancake, *please?*"

"You most certainly may." She accepted his offered plate and gave him his eleventh pancake.

"What about you, Greg?" Grace asked. "You've hardly eaten any."

Gregorian shook his head. His skin was almost rose coloured this morning, a pale imitation from the darkened red of yesterday.

"Does your skin change colour according to the time of day?" Grace asked.

Samael snorted. "Hardly. He's just a coward."

Gregorian inhaled sharply. "I am no coward."

"You abandoned your post!"

"I would have died if I hadn't! That's not cowardice, that's... self-preservation."

"What does your skin colour have to do with that?" Grace asked, interrupting them before they really got going.

Samael poured a generous amount of syrup on his pancake. "He's pale with fear," he said. "As he should be. I can only imagine how angry Lucifer is going to be."

"If I live long enough for it to matter," Gregorian said. "You guys are going to be the death of me. I was perfectly fine, hiding out here on Earth. Not quite as safe as Heaven would be, no doubt, but adequate before you people showed up."

"Are you sure you won't have another pancake?" Grace asked.

He stared at her. "Yes."

"What about you, Daniel?"

"I'm fine," he assured her. "Thank you." He turned his attention towards Samael. "How are you feeling?" he asked.

"Hmm?"

"Do you think you can transform yet?"

"I do feel better. I'd prefer waiting until evening, though."

Grace sent him a scrutinizing look. It was hard to notice

compared to Gregorian's shivering paleness, but she thought she detected a hint of worry in Samael's eyes.

"So you'll be good by then?" she asked. She wondered if he'd let her take his vitals. Probably not.

"No, but I'll be able to transform. I won't be able to change too many times, though. Nor will I be comfortable with anything too different from my regular body. Mammals would be best. And it'll be slower than usual, even by Earth's standards."

"What about your bandages? Do you need any help changing them?"

Samael shrugged. "If you want," he said, somehow making it sound like he did her some huge favour.

"We should get some weapons," Grace said. "It's not fair to have every battle rest on you."

Daniel frowned. "Are weapons really necessary? Perhaps we could get some tranquillisers?"

Samael snorted. "You can't be serious," he said. "What will you do if they don't work? Sing them a lullaby and hope they fall asleep? This is war. We need weapons more lethal than a tranquillizer. We need guns."

"And where are we going to get guns from?" Daniel demanded to know.

"It would've been easier if we'd still been in the States," Samael admitted. "Not that it'll be hard. Not in this kind of neighbourhood."

"This kind of neighbourhood," Grace repeated. "We're literally surrounded by a picket fence. Isn't this the last place we'll find a gun?"

Samael snorted. "Hardly. These suburban areas can get surprisingly paranoid. I'll bet there's at least one guy on this block with a weapons permit. The trick is how to get a hold of whatever he has. And to figure out which house it's in."

"We can ask Grace about that part," Daniel said. "But if these neighbourhoods are as paranoid as you make them out, they probably have all sorts of fancy alarm systems. I can get an old car open. I can't break into a house."

Samael smirked, looking terribly smug. "That's the beautiful part," he told them. "We're not going to break in. They're going to invite us."

"Why?" Grace asked. "Dick has probably already told the entire neighbourhood how rude you were."

Samael shrugged, indifferent. "It seems you forget how charming I can be." With these words, he speared the last piece of pancake with his fork and looked at them with glittering eyes. "And I do have all day to get that invitation."

* * *

"Oh, you're thinking of buying?" Jennifer asked, smiling at them from across the dining room table. Her husband Eric was sitting next to her, busy pouring a generous amount of sauce over his potatoes.

According to the apple, their house had a gun somewhere inside of it, and Samael had gotten an invitation to dinner within fifteen minutes of conversation.

"We are," he said, taking Grace's hand. "It's such a lovely neighbourhood. Don't you agree, darling?" He smiled at her.

There was something undeniably wrong about that smile. It was too gentle, too *un-Samael*.

"It is," she agreed.

"And it's a wonderful place to raise children," Jennifer told them with a smile. She touched her stomach gently.

"There's a great school nearby," Eric added. "English-speaking. Competent teachers. If you're planning for children, that is."

"We've just started trying," Samael lied smoothly.

Grace felt her mouth pop open and quickly closed it again.

Jennifer practically glowed. "Oh, that's wonderful! I hope you'll get pregnant soon. If you move here, our children could be friends. I'm three months along. Wouldn't that just be darling?"

Samael smiled, appearing completely at ease. "Just darling," he agreed. "Grace here wants four, but I've always been partial to two myself."

"There's certainly room enough for four," Eric said. "Except for the Peterson house. They only have four bedrooms." He shook his head.

"How dreadful," Samael said.

Grace thought she could detect a hint of sarcasm in his voice, but neither Eric nor Jennifer appeared to notice. Samael truly seemed to have them wrapped around his finger, and Grace decided that it was time for her part of their plan.

"Excuse me, would it be alright if I used your bathroom for just a minute?" she asked.

"Of course," Jennifer said. "Up the staircase, third door on the right. We're having the one downstairs remodelled," she added quickly.

Grace thanked her and headed upstairs. Behind, she could hear Samael tell their hosts how they met — a story that took place in Africa, where she was vacationing, and he was working for a charity that protected the local wildlife. Apparently, he had been accidentally led to believe that she was a poacher. Grace felt comfortable that he would make their hosts completely forget about keeping track of time as she went on her search.

Upstairs, she asked the apple for the location of the nearest gun and followed her new-found knowledge to the master bedroom. Once there, she removed several books from a positively enormous bookcase and was met with the sight of a steel safe.

"Well, fudge," she muttered. Of course, they'd lock it in. She wondered what to do. Perhaps it was all about asking the right question. She couldn't ask what the code was. But maybe they'd written it down somewhere. Then she'd be able to find it.

Closing her eyes, she asked herself for the location of the code.

She received no knowledge of any kind.

Grace sighed. She would have to figure out her next move downstairs. She put the books back in place and made her way back to the dining room.

Samael gave her an inquiring look, and she shook her head slightly. He frowned, standing up.

"Darling, did you bring my insulin pen?"

"Your insu... Yes?"

He smiled at Jennifer and Eric. "Would you excuse us for just a moment?"

"She's going with you?" Eric asked.

"Yes. It's silly, I'll admit, but I've never been able to do it myself. But she doesn't mind, do you, darling?"

"Not at all," she said and gave a last smile to Jennifer and Eric before she followed Samael into the hallway.

"What happened?" he asked as soon as they were alone, all traces of embarrassed humour gone.

"They have a safe. We need the code."

He nodded thoughtfully. "Follow my lead," he said. "I have an idea. But let's wait a minute. I don't know how long it actually takes to inject someone with an insulin pen."

"Just a couple of seconds."

"Oh. Never mind then. Let's go back."

They went back to the dining room, Samael smiling at Jennifer as they sat down.

"I have to ask you, Jen," he said. "Grace here was considering a spring wedding, but I'm more partial to the winter time myself. What do you think?"

Jennifer looked delighted at the change of topic. Eric did not.

"I didn't know you guys were engaged," he said, scrutinising Grace's bare hand. "She's not wearing a ring."

Perhaps Samael was right about the whole paranoia-suburbia thing.

"We're having it resized," Grace said.

"Well, I'm partial to a summer wedding myself," Jennifer said, ignoring her husband's interrogation. "We were married in June."

"Ah! A June wedding. We considered it, but we thought it might be too hot."

"Oh, no, not at all," she assured him.

"Early or late June?" he asked.

"Late. The twentieth." Jennifer smiled fondly at the memory.

"The twentieth," Samael repeated. "Last year?"

She laughed. "No, it's been three years."

"Really? You guys seem like newly-weds."

Jennifer giggled, and Samael smiled at Grace.

"You heard that, darling?" he said. "The twentieth of June. Lovely date, isn't it?"

And a possible code as well.

"Lovely date," she assured him, wondering how long she should wait before she could pretend to go to the bathroom again. Maybe if she drank a lot, it would seem less conspicuous.

"So, tell me," she said. "When are you due? Like, the exact date?"

* * *

Groaning in frustration, Grace bumped her face against the bookshelf. They had spent the last two hours grilling Jennifer and Eric about every important date in their life (which was something Samael did much more subtly than she), but not a single of the dates had opened the safe. She was grateful, at least, that it allowed more than three tries.

Something hit the window.

Grace looked over in surprise but there was nothing to see. Must've been a bug or something.

Something hit the window again. Too big to be a bug, but not big enough to be a bird. Curious, she made her way over and looked down.

It had gotten dark by now, and she could only see her own reflection. Not wanting to miss whatever it was, she hurried over to turn the light off before she made her way back to the window and looked down once again.

Daniel and Gregorian were down on the street, throwing pebbles at the window. Daniel was dressed in black and was hardly visible, while Gregorian was back in the costume, he'd worn during their first meeting.

Opening the window, she strained her ears for any indication that Samael hadn't been able to keep Jennifer and Eric at the dinner table. Not hearing anything, she took a chance.

"What are you doing here?" she whispered-yelled.

"We got worried," Daniel called back. "What's taking you so long?"

"They have a safe. We've been trying to open it, but it's not working. Would you be able to?"

"No. How would I know how to break open a safe?"

"Well, it never hurts to ask," Grace said before she turned her attention towards Gregorian. "What about you?" she asked.

He hesitated.

"You *can* open it," Grace guessed.

"No."

Even in the darkness, she could practically see the lie shining out of him from underneath his green facial mask.

"Yes, you can. Get up here."

"Fine, I can open it. *Obviously*. I'm a Gatekeeper. But even if I can open the safe, how do you expect me to get up there? I can't crawl up walls."

"I'll unlock the front door. If you're quiet, I don't think they'll hear you. This house is ridunculously big. Just head upstairs, fourth door on the left."

"And if I refuse?"

"I'll tell Lucifer that you've turned traitor."

It was hard to see his skin colour, but Grace would bet the

Voice that he was a pale pink.

"Fine," he hissed. "I'll come up!"

She smiled at him. "Lovely," she said before she shut the window and made her way downstairs. Unlocking the front door was a matter of seconds, and when she made her way to the dining room, Samael met her eyes with a questioning look. She smiled at him.

"So what are we talking about?" she asked, and Jennifer immediately got her up to speed on their trip to Cuba.

Grace did her best to keep the conversation going, and Samael followed her lead.

Jennifer and Eric had already cleared the table after dinner, and now Jennifer made a move to begin clearing up after the coffee as well.

"Stop that," Grace ordered. "We can do that."

"Oh, I couldn't ask that of you. You're our guests."

"I insist," she said, imagining Jennifer stumbling upon Gregorian on his way out.

"If you're sure?"

"Positive. Sammy, a little help, please?"

He willingly helped her clear the table, assuring Eric that the cake had been delicious.

Once in the kitchen, he dumped the plates on the counter.

"My name is Samael," he told her with an annoyed expression. "First Follower of Lucifer, warrior of Hell, and destroyer of Paradise. Don't call me *Sammy*."

"You'd be welcome to call me Gracie."

"I think not. But never mind the ridiculous nickname. Did it work?"

"No."

"Damn it." He looked at the dirty plates on the kitchen counter. "Suppose we could always tie them up and force them to tell us."

"We can't just tie them up," Grace said. "We're their guests."

"So?"

"So, it's *wrong*. Besides, we won't need to."

"And why is that?"

"We've already begun plan C."

"What's plan C?"

A scream sounded, unmistakably coming from upstairs.

"Please," Samael said, "tell me that's not plan C?"

"It might be?"

Hurrying upstairs, they just had time to see Eric running into the master bedroom, desperately calling his wife's name. They got there seconds after him, stopped and stared at the scene in front of them.

There was Gregorian, still in his pink robe and green facial mask. His bathing cap was gone, however, and there was nothing hiding the curling horns sprouting from his head. At the bottom of his robe, a tail poked out. He was holding a gun in each hand.

On the floor in front of him lay Jessica, deadly pale, pointing at him with a shaky finger.

"Monster!" she screamed.

Gregorian looked up at Grace and Samael. "Sorry, guys," he said. "I didn't hear her come up."

Eric spun around to stare at them. "He's with you?"

Grace opened her mouth without having any clue what she was going to say. "Yeah?" she tried.

Eric stared at her for half a second before he turned back towards Gregorian.

"Get away from her," he demanded.

"I'd love to, but she's kind of in between me and the door."

Grace thought this to be a remarkably sensible argument, but evidently Eric didn't agree. With a shout, he jumped over his wife and threw himself at Gregorian, seemingly with the intent of physically fighting the demon off.

Gregorian gave a startled shout, dropped the guns — and burst into flames.

Chapter Thirteen:

Left Behind

With a half-choked yell, Eric just barely had time to avoid collision with the now flaming demon. For several seconds, everything was chaos. Jennifer was screaming, the fire alarm was blaring away, Samael threw himself over Eric, and Grace had only one thought in her head: She had to put out the fire.

In three strides she was over by the bed where she grabbed the bedspread and threw it over Gregorian, only to see it burst into flames.

"Stop, drop and roll!" she yelled at him and looked over to where Samael and Eric were fighting. Samael was on top of Eric, who seemed to be attempting to get his arm around the shapeshifter's head, while Samael himself had claws and fur growing from his hands.

Grace hurried over to Jennifer instead.

"Jen, do you have a fire extinguisher?"

Jennifer merely stared at Gregorian in silence, her eyes huge in her pale face.

"Monster," she whispered.

She had to be in shock. Taking a deep breath, Grace rearranged her features into something relaxed and kind. Then she took hold of the other woman's face and forced her to look at her. "Jen," she said. "I need a fire extinguisher. There's a fire."

Jennifer's eyes slowly focused on Grace. "Under the bed," she said. She looked back at Gregorian. "There's a monster," she said. "It's on fire."

Grace didn't bother with a response as she hurried back to the bed, dropped to her knees and felt around under it until her hand met cold metal.

She pulled the fire extinguisher out with one strong yank,

got to her feet and tried to pull out the pin. It was stuck. Suddenly, Jennifer was there, holding the fire extinguisher still for her. No longer having to lift the entirety of its weight, Grace successfully pulled the pin out. She aimed the nozzle towards Gregorian and pushed the lever down.

White foam shot out and surrounded him, and Grace swept the fire extinguisher from side to side until she was convinced the fire had been put out.

Finally, she put the fire extinguisher down, trying to determine whether or not Gregorian was still moving underneath the large body of foam.

"Greg," she asked. "Are you dead?"

"No," the answer came. "But why did you cover me in… what is this, bottled clouds?"

"You were on fire," Grace informed him.

"It's called self-defence," Gregorian said. He clumsily began to brush off the white foam.

"You attacked my wife!"

Grace looked over at Eric, who had lost his wrestling match with the shapeshifter, and who was currently pinned to the floor by a pair of bear paws. Besides these, however, Samael had for the most part remained in human form, although he looked quite a bit… bulkier than usual.

"I did not!" Gregorian said. "She just saw me, and she started screaming. It was pretty offensive, actually."

Grace turned towards Jennifer, who was looking at Gregorian with wide eyes. Gregorian's clothes had been burned off, but he appeared otherwise unharmed. Jennifer, however, was shaking.

"Maybe you should sit down," Grace suggested. "This kind of shock can't be good for the baby."

Jennifer practically collapsed on the bed.

"I'm terribly sorry about this whole thing," Grace told her. "But we need your guns, and we didn't think asking politely would work."

"Are you going to kill us?" Jennifer asked, her voice small. Still, Grace thought that she could sense a certain sense of calculation behind her eyes.

"Of course not," she assured her quickly. "We just need to make sure you won't call the police. At least right away."

"Let's just knock them out," Samael said. "Use the fire extinguisher. That should be heavy enough."

"Don't you dare touch her!" Eric hissed. He jerked his head to the side and sunk his teeth into Samael's paw.

Samael swore but didn't let go. Instead, he looked at Daniel. "Are you going to help or not? I can't hold him down forever. Grace, the fire extinguisher. Now."

"Um... excuse me," a voice said. Jennifer. "I have some sleeping pills in the medicine cabinet in the bathroom. If we take one of those, will you please just leave us alone?"

Grace considered it. That did seem like a good idea. No muss, no fuss.

"We can't trust them," Eric said. "Jen, they'll kill us in our sleep."

"We could kill you while awake," Samael told him. "But I don't think Grace or Daniel would approve — and I'd have to listen to them moan about it for the rest of the trip. So how about you thank them politely and eat your bloody pill? Grace, go get it."

Grace willingly went to locate the glass of sleeping pills as well as a glass of water before she returned to the bedroom.

"Have you asked your doctor if it's okay to take them while pregnant?" she asked Jennifer as she handed her the glass and one of the pills.

Jennifer nodded shakily. "I... yes. She said it was fine, just not too often." She was terribly pale but swallowed the pill willingly enough.

Satisfied, Grace walked over to Eric.

"Open up," she said, kneeling down next to him.

He merely glared at her.

Daniel cleared his throat, looking distinctly uncomfortable. "We could... tie him up," he suggested. "His wife's here to untie him when she wakes up."

"That would probably be a good idea," Grace noted. After all, the sleeping pills *had* been prescribed to Jennifer.

She looked around for something to tie Eric up with, and her eyes landed on two robes thrown carelessly over a comfortable-looking armchair. The sashes from them should work well enough, and together she and Samael succeeded in tying up Eric quite thoroughly.

"What now?" Grace asked.

"Well, we only need one person to stand guard," Daniel said. "And I think it should be me. Samael is far too malicious, and you are..."

"Overly naïve?" Samael suggested.

"Very trusting," Daniel said.

Grace wondered what the difference was.

Samael snorted. "I don't trust you to stand guard either," he said. "Eric here will complain of sore wrists, and you'll loosen his bonds. And probably make him a cup of tea while you're at it."

"Why don't Gregorian and I stand guard together then?" Daniel suggested. "You and Grace can wait downstairs."

Samael sighed. "I suppose it would be nice with a bit of quiet before the next step."

Grace quite agreed, and she was only too pleased to leave the somewhat sooty bedroom behind her as she dragged Samael with her downstairs.

"What do you want to do until we leave?" she asked as they reached the bottom of the stairs.

"You mean until Gregorian, Daniel and I leave?" he asked. "I thought we'd agreed that you weren't coming with us."

"No, you agreed on that," she said. "There's no way I'm

staying behind while you guys charge off into danger. You're my friends. Would you have been willing to stay behind?"

"That's different."

"Why?"

Samael took a deep breath. "Grace, I know that you're... impetuous, but you must admit that it just makes sense to keep the Voice safe. And it certainly won't be safe if we take it with us."

"But why should I be the one who stays behind? I understand why you need Gregorian there, but Daniel can stay behind and protect the Voice just as well as I."

"Grace, you've eaten an apple from the Tree of Knowledge. You can find a safe place. Daniel can't."

"I'll just tell him where there is one. Besides, we've already seen how fickle this apple can be. I only need to ask the wrong question once, and all is lost. Daniel knows his brother. He'll have an advantage that I don't."

Samael gave an exasperated sigh. "There must be something I can say to convince you to stay?"

"There really isn't. Sammy, I'm not going to sit back and wonder if my friends are okay. I'm just not."

He looked at her with determination written across his face.

"Yes, you are," he said. "Because I'm going to force you if you won't stay behind willingly." He didn't even comment on her use of Sammy, proving just how serious he was.

"You can't do that."

"But I can. I'm infinitely stronger than you. If necessary, I'll force-feed *you* a sleeping pill. Grace, you're staying behind."

His eyes met hers with steely-eyed resolve, and Grace realised that he wasn't going to give in. And that there was nothing she could say that would make him change his mind.

"Fine," she said.

Samael's shoulders visibly relaxed. "Wonderful," he said. "Grace, you'll see that it's for the best. Eventually."

Grace didn't answer. She was busy making plans.

* * *

Forty minutes later, Samael, Daniel, and Gregorian left in Eric's car.

Three minutes after that, Grace followed them in Jennifer's.

Humming softly to herself, she considered how difficult this would have been without the apple. Not that the trip went entirely without difficulties. The suburban labyrinth of entirely identical streets was Hell to get away from, apple or not.

In the end, the trip took almost an hour, partly due to a small, but necessary detour.

She ended up downtown, surrounded by people in varying degrees of intoxication. The street itself consisted of town houses that had been converted into restaurants, bars, and clothing shops, and both sides of the road were packed with parked cars. Despite the late hour, the street was positively buzzing with life.

A large, graffitied Leonard Cohen looked down upon her from a skyscraper not too far away, but none of the townhouses were more than a couple of stories high. The architecture reminded her more of Boston than anticipated, and everyone seemed to be in good cheer. If the situation had been different, she would've loved to stick around and get a cappuccino on one of the outdoor terraces, watching people pass by. As it were, however, there were only three people she was interested in finding.

Looking around, she realised she would need a miracle to find a free parking spot, and so she parked illegally instead, accidentally hitting someone's Mercedes as she did so.

She stepped out into the cold night air, thankful that she'd had the foresight to "borrow" one of Jennifer's jackets.

Having asked the apple for directions, she walked past several bars and multiple groups of chattering friends. Around her, people were speaking in English, French, German, and a myriad of other languages, and Grace wondered absent-mindedly if the Gateway to Hell had been placed in the midst of a tourist destination. She walked past a large restaurant with red awnings and turned down an alley next to it, leaving the crowd behind as she did so.

She found the others at the end of it, barely out-of-sight from the busy street behind them. If they looked up, they'd see her, but they seemed entirely engrossed in an argument of some sort. Remaining silent, Grace considered her options. If Samael saw her, he might send her back, and she couldn't risk that.

Instead, she took a step to the side and crouched down behind some wooden crates. The others couldn't be more than twenty feet away, but the noise from the street behind her entirely drowned out their argument.

As she peered around the wooden crates, however, she could see them relatively clearly. Apparently, she'd just made it to the end of the argument, and she watched in fascination as Gregorian lifted the lid of a manhole cover. Samael and Daniel disappeared down into it, and Grace realised that this was the Gateway. Which meant that this was her only chance if she didn't want to be left behind.

She hurried forward, and Gregorian looked up in fright, only for his eyes to widen in surprise at the sight of her. She ignored him as she made a jump for it, aiming for the hole that was evidently a portal to Hell.

She screamed as she suddenly fell, only to land on something that was simultaneously hard and soft, and which gave off a grunt of pain at impact.

Looking down, she saw Samael partly sitting and partly lying beneath her, face half-transformed into its familiar feline form. It slowly returned to its human shape. Next to them, Daniel was pointing a gun at her, which he slowly lowered. Another gun was tucked into his belt.

Grace looked around. It didn't look anything like Hell as

she knew it. Instead, circular stone walls surrounded them, and they were sitting in at least five inches of water. A rotten stench hung in the air, and Grace wrinkled her nose in distaste. Maybe it wasn't just water.

She looked back down at Samael, who was scowling up at her.

"Hi?"

"*Grace*, what the never-ending staircase are you doing here?!" Samael hissed.

"I couldn't just leave you guys behind."

Samael snorted. "You mean you couldn't stand being left behind yourself?"

"Maybe a bit of both," she admitted, looking around. "Where are we?" she asked.

"Where does it *look* like we are?!"

"Well, it kind of looks like a sewer," Grace said.

"That's probably because *it is one.* Now get off me."

Grace stood up and offered Samael a helping hand, which he ignored. They were both covered in slimy more-than-water, and Grace's stomach gave an unpleasant lurch.

"You shouldn't have come," Daniel said. "We needed you to keep the Voice of God out of harm's way."

"I didn't bring it," Grace said.

"*What?!*" Samael said. "Where the burning pit did you put it?!"

"Somewhere safe," she answered before she wisely decided to change the topic. "Why are we in a sewer?" she asked. "I thought this was one of the Gateways."

"It *is*," Samael said. "But the coward up there refused to come down and open it unless we checked it through for traps. I thought we'd actually found one when over a hundred pounds suddenly landed on top of me."

"Oh. Sorry about that."

"Never mind that! Just tell me where the bloody Voice is! Are you sure it's safe?"

"Positive," she said.

Samael slowly closed his eyes. "Always," he muttered.

"What?"

"Never mind. Is it locked in?"

"Well, no."

Samael stared at her. "*No?!*" he repeated.

"Try to trust me, would you? They're not going to find it. It's *safe.*"

Samael looked at her in dismay before he sighed. "I suppose it might be safer the fewer people know of it. In case we're captured and tortured, we only need to make sure Grace gets away."

"Tortured," Daniel repeated with a croak.

"That is something people occasionally do during war times," Samael said. "And don't start on the whole 'my brother would never do that'. Let's just *pretend* that he would."

Daniel hesitated. "Perhaps his followers," he said.

"Sure," Samael said. "His followers." He turned around to glare at Grace. "Just stay behind me," he ordered. "And if something happens, *run.*"

"Sure," she said, relieved that he wasn't sending her back. Staying behind him, she tried to keep quiet as they made their way through the tunnel, realising that Samael would probably calm down the fastest if she left him alone. Her resolution held all of forty seconds.

"Why are we walking through the sewer?" she asked. "If there's a trap, shouldn't it be at the Gate itself?"

"The Gate is down here," Daniel explained. "We're just not there yet."

"We are now," Samael said, and Grace peered out from behind him. The Gateway to Hell was... kind of gross, actually.

Apparently, this Gateway was one of those iron gates that sewers use to keep rats out of toilets and inmates inside of prisons. At least that was how Grace had understood their function.

They were all standing in a pipe that had to be close to seven feet tall. Around four or five feet off the ground a hole led into another, smaller pipe, covered by an iron gate. They would have to crawl. Not exactly ideal when you were checking for an ambush.

Samael looked at it with obvious dissatisfaction, closed his eyes and said something in the same unfamiliar language as last time. When he tried to open the gate, however, it didn't budge.

"Is it locked?" Grace asked.

Samael frowned. "I don't think so," he said. "Just kind of... stuck."

He proved to be right, and in the end it took the strength of both Samael and Daniel to force the gate open, inch by inch.

"You crawl first," the shapeshifter told Daniel.

"Why him?" Grace asked.

"He's disposable."

Daniel grimaced. "You do say the nicest things." Despite his words, however, he still lifted himself up into the smaller pipe.

The sight was bizarre. Staring with large eyes, Grace barely kept herself from gasping outright as Daniel disappeared piece by piece as he struggled his way into the smaller pipe. The second a part of him crossed the threshold it disappeared, until Daniel was ultimately gone altogether.

"Wait here," Samael said before he lifted himself up and stuck his head and upper body through the smaller pipe. Grace watched in fascination as his legs hovered in the air, seemingly entirely detached from any upper body.

Then the fingerless hands let go of the edge, and Samael reappeared before her.

"It seems to be safe," he said and interlaced his fingers in order to create a makeshift stepping stool. "But scream if anything seems out of the ordinary."

Grace nodded and stepped on his interlocked hands. He then gave her a push upwards, and she crawled into the smaller pipe.

She wasn't quite sure what out-of-the-ordinary meant in this world of Hell, Heaven, and drugging your dinner hosts, but she felt relatively sure that this didn't count.

She'd expected this Gateway to look like the other. Instead, she found herself in a shallow, clear stream. It was around three or four feet wide and entirely closed off by what appeared to be green walls.

Daniel was there, already offering her a hand up. He was standing on one of the many stepping stones leading down the entirety of the stream. They were quite slippery, Grace discovered, once she was standing on one of them.

The green walls weren't really walls at all, she saw now, but rather a thick layer of lianas and vines, on which blossomed enormous rust-coloured flowers. Above their heads, a thick fog made it impossible to see any ceiling or sky, but Grace was confident that she could hear birds chirping. A pale light was shining through, comparable to how sunlight looked through thick glass.

"This is a Gateway to Hell?" she asked.

"To the In-Between," Samael corrected her, having manifested behind her. "The place where Heaven and Hell meet. And technically the Gateway is over there at the end."

Grace looked, squinting her eyes. The stream ended suddenly, appearing to hit nothing and follow it upwards, like it was flowing up a wall.

"What happens if we go through the water without Gregorian?" she asked, curious as to why the Gatekeeper was even needed.

"We get wet," Samael said. He made his way down the stepping stones, fingers dancing across the vines on his right side as he went. Checking for traps, Grace realised.

Samael went all the way to the end of the stream, and all the way back, checking the other side of the foliage. He meticulously searched through the water and even went as far as to walk into the water wall at the end of the stream.

He came out wet, but clean, and Grace suspected that he'd mostly done that last part to get the slime off of him.

"It appears to be safe," Samael said.

"Lovely," Grace said and made her way over to him.

"What are you doing?" Samael asked, once she was there.

"I just want to be clean again," she said and stepped into the vertical water.

It was like stepping into the most powerful shower she'd ever been in. Water immediately got in her nose and ears, and when she tried to stumble out of it, she found that she wasn't sure which way *was* out.

A hand grabbed her upper arm and pulled her out of the up-going waterfall, and Grace looked up at Samael with a sheepish expression. "Thanks?"

"Grace, you're exhausting, you know that?"

"I just wanted to be clean," Grace said again. She put her head to the side and shook it to get the water out of her ear.

"Does this mean we should go retrieve the Voice of God?" Daniel asked, carefully making his way over to them.

Samael grimaced. "Grace clearly isn't going to stay with it," he said. "And it's too dangerous to take it with us." He looked at the wall of flowing water. "We'll get Gregorian to let Daniel and I through first. Grace, you can wait here until we get back." His voice brooked no argument.

Grace considered it. There wasn't really anything stopping her from jumping in after them, and so she kept her mouth shut.

Samael appeared pleased that she didn't argue, and he languidly stretched himself, reminding Grace of his familiar feline form.

"If you feel certain that the Voice will remain safe for now, we should return without it," he said. "Since we can't be sure where choir boy's lunatic brother is. Lucifer will retrieve it, once we've told him of its location. All we really need is to get Gregorian down here."

"And then what?" Grace asked. "We're going home?"

Samael grinned, looking happier than she'd seen him in a long time. "Yes," he said. "Home to Hell. Finally."

CHAPTER FOURTEEN:

Setback

Samael's good mood held all the way up to the surface.

It disappeared, however, when they got there and found Gregorian gone.

"That lily-livered coward!" Samael spat.

"He must have left as soon as he thought it was safe," Daniel said.

Grace frowned. "I can't believe he just left," she said.

"Why not?" Samael bit out. "It's not exactly the first time."

"But he promised us. I can't believe he'd just let us down like that."

"I can," Samael said darkly. "And if I'd spent a little less time with you, I never would've given him such an atrociously perfect opportunity to escape!"

"What's that supposed to mean?"

"It means that you are without a doubt the most infuriatingly *naive* person I have ever met, and I should have known better than to let that influence me to act so foolishly myself!"

"Oh, poppycock!" Grace said. "This isn't my fault. We trusted Gregorian when we shouldn't have, and now we have to deal with it. There's no reason to cast blame. We'll just have to find him and start over."

"*Fine.*"

"And I'd like an apology."

Samael stared at her. "What?" he said.

"I'd like an apology."

"I don't apologise."

"You rarely apologise," Grace corrected him. "You're bad at it. And when you're bad at something, you should practice."

"And why should I? Because it's the *right* thing to do?"

"Because it's hurtful," Grace said. "I'm not the one to blame, and you're my friend. You shouldn't try to make me feel bad."

"You never feel bad."

"Yes, I do. I felt bad when you got stabbed."

Samael went quiet, something flickering in his eyes. He sighed.

"Fine," he said. "I'm sorry."

"Thank you."

Samael shot a warning look at Daniel. "Don't you dare tell anyone about this," he said.

"About what? How you were acting like a decent human... eh, demon?"

"Exactly. I'd never live it down."

"Your secret is safe with me. We should probably go find Gregorian though. Grace, where is he?"

Grace didn't answer.

"Grace?"

"What? Oh, I'm sorry. It's just that, well, the answer doesn't really make sense, you know?"

"How so?" Samael asked.

"Well, he's over there." She pointed towards a couple of dumpsters, no more than fifteen feet away.

"He's *hiding?* But he knows what you can do. His only chance of getting away is to keep running."

"Unless he's planning an ambush," Daniel noted.

"That would be ludicrously dumb," Samael said, frowning. "Even for him. If nothing else, he must be aware that he doesn't stand a chance against me."

"Maybe your reputation isn't as scary as you think," Daniel said.

Samael glared at him. "Yes," he said. "It is."

"You don't seem that scary to me," Grace said.

Samael scowled at her. "Well, you're not exactly an enemy of mine, now are you? You're my… ally."

"You mean friend?"

"I mean *ally*. Now come. We should get Gregorian before he does something stupid. Again. And stay behind me."

"Sure."

"I mean it, Grace."

"And I'll stay behind you. Would you like a pinkie promise?"

Samael didn't dignify that with an answer as he walked away. Grace followed, taking care to stay one step behind the cranky shapeshifter.

Samael's sour mood certainly didn't improve when he had to transform halfway into a bear in order to pull the first dumpster out of the way, only to be rewarded for his effort by the sight of concrete and insects. Nor when the second dumpster generated the same result.

"He must be inside one of them," Grace said with a frown as she reached out to open the one closest to her. It was heavier than anticipated and Samael helped, his bear-like strength causing the lid to practically fly open.

Grace screamed.

There, in the trash, lay Gregorian. Dead.

Grace stared. This wasn't like the corpse of the old woman, or the Gatekeeper they'd found in New York. They knew Gregorian. He'd really just been a frightened demon in over his head.

Who'd met a most horrifying end by the looks of it.

His stomach had been cut open, and his guts had been spread out on the trash surrounding him like some sort of macabre art piece. Out of the corner of her eye, Grace could see Daniel leaning heavily against the wall, and as she glanced up at Samael, he was deadly pale.

"He's dead," she said. The words fell heavily between them, utterly pointless.

"So he is," Samael said, voice carefully devoid of emotion. He was slowly turning back to human form. "I seem to owe him an apology as well."

"How can you joke at a time like this?" Daniel demanded to know. "He was our friend, and he didn't deserve this. He must have been terrified."

"I wasn't joking. And he wasn't our friend."

Grace looked down. Samael's hands were clenched so tightly that his knuckles had turned almost entirely white.

"He chose to stay up here," she told him. "It's not your fault."

"Of course it isn't. He was a foolish coward. He should've stayed with us. We would have kept him safe."

Grace reached over and took hold of his hand. She squeezed it gently. "He's..." she trailed off. "It's not your fault."

"We should give him a proper burial," Daniel said. He still hadn't taken his eyes off the corpse. "It's... it's the right thing to do. Isn't it? Even if he was a demon."

"Why?" Samael asked, freeing his hand from Grace's. "Piling dirt on him won't make him any less dead. And we don't have the time to spare. We need to figure out what to do now. We were so bloody close."

"We'll... we'll fix this," Daniel said. "We'll make things right."

"Getting the Voice to Hell won't make the coward any less dead," Samael sneered.

Daniel flinched, and Grace put her hand on Samael's arm.

"Don't lash out," she said. "It won't change anything. We need to focus on finding another Gatekeeper. And we'll be more careful next time."

"We need to get the Voice back first," Samael said, running a hand through his hair.

"Why?" Grace asked. "It's safe. Wouldn't it be better to leave it there for now?"

"I'd feel better if we didn't leave it unsupervised longer than necessary," Samael said. "The apple isn't infallible. As we've already seen. What exactly did you ask yourself when hiding it?"

"Um... well, technically I didn't really ask it anything."

Silence.

"*What?!*"

"Well, I couldn't figure out what to ask it."

"A safe place! You ask it for a safe place, Grace!"

"But what constitutes safe?" Grace asked. "Daniel's brother clearly isn't planning on destroying the Voice, so it would technically be safe with him. Every question I considered seemed kind of risky. So, in the end, I just decided to go with common sense."

"Common... sense..." Samael repeated.

"It's in the safest place I could think of on such short notice. Why is that so bad? You weren't planning to take it with you either."

"No, but I didn't leave it unsupervised," Samael said. "And my trip to Hell would hopefully have been both short and temporary. If we need to find yet another way in, I don't even want to think about how long this might take. I really thought it was finding the Voice that would prove the difficult part. Not getting back."

"What about Gregorian?" Daniel asked.

Samael sent him an annoyed look. "We don't have time for another burial, just because you feel that it's the *right* thing to do."

"We still need to stay practical," Daniel said. "Gregorian doesn't exactly look human. What happens when somebody finds his corpse?"

"They won't. We'll burn it."

"We can't just burn it," Grace interjected. "Corpses are really hard to burn."

"Someone is bound to notice us," Daniel said. "And we'll need things that we don't have. Fuel for one thing. Fire, even."

"We don't need fuel," Samael said. "It isn't a human corpse. Gregorian was a fire demon. And unlike humans, they are highly flammable. All we need is a bit of fire."

"I saw at least a dozen people smoking on the way here," Grace said. "Fire isn't going to be hard to come by."

Walking out of the alley's darkness, she made her way back to the illuminated street. Looking back, she could just about see the dark outline of the others. If they were going to start a fire, they were going to have to make a quick exit.

Walking away from the alley, she wished that the restaurant next to it had been a little less popular. She hoped demons burned fast because she had a feeling the fire wouldn't burn for long.

She made her way over to a group of smokers not too far away.

"Excuse me?" she said to the man nearest her. He was skinny, heavily tattooed, and currently lighting a cigarette. "But could I borrow your lighter?"

He smiled at her. "Sure thing, doll," he said. "Care for a cigarette as well?"

"She does not," Samael said, coming up behind her. "Just the lighter."

The young man frowned. "I wasn't talking to you."

"I think you were," Samael said, putting a hand on the young man's lower arm. The young man gave a shout of pain.

"Okay!" he said. "Just take it. Jesus. It's like a dollar at the gas station."

"Lovely," Samael said. He took the lighter from his hand and began to walk back the way they'd come.

"Thank you," Grace added a bit more politely before she followed him.

She came back to the alley just in time to see Samael open the lighter with a flick of his wrist and throw it at the corpse, which immediately burst into flames.

"Why is he burning now?" Grace asked. "He wasn't hurt in the fire earlier."

"He was alive back then."

In the dumpster, Gregorian's face was melting into an unrecognisable lump of flesh. Samael watched it with a passive expression. "He'll be unidentifiable in three minutes, ashes in fifteen."

"We should leave," Daniel said. He looked pale even in the light of the flames. "Before we're discovered. Even if the corpse is gone, we're hardly going to get away with starting a fire."

"It's surrounded by concrete. I doubt it'll spread."

"But maybe it'd be better if we didn't have to explain that to the police department?"

"A valid point," Samael admitted before he turned towards Grace. "Well, lead the way," he said. "To the Voice of God. Again."

* * *

"Grace, why are we at the park?"

"The Voice of God kind of looks like a stick."

"So you decided to hide it between other sticks?"

"Well, I would've never found it in the graveyard if I hadn't been able to ask the apple where it was."

Samael sighed. "Just... let's go get it. Before my brain comes up with every way this could've gone wrong."

Grace led them to where she'd hid the Voice in between the roots of an old maple tree. It was too dark to rely much on her sight, and so she merely felt for the intertwined wood of the Voice.

"Here it is!" she said, holding it up victoriously, only to realise that she was merely holding a somewhat unusual stick. "Oops, never mind. Just hold on a second." She went back to looking. "Here it is!"

"Sure it's the right one?" Samael asked sarcastically. "Wouldn't want to walk up to Lucifer and hand over a *stick*."

"I'm sure," Grace assured him.

Samael frowned at her. "This was ridiculously stupid of you," he declared. "Just leaving the Voice of God in a park."

Grace tilted her head slightly, looking up at him. She found his reaction a bit excessive, considering that nothing had happened. "All's well that ends well?"

"No!" Samael said. "It most certainly is not! It was *stupid*. And irresponsible."

"Irresponsible," Grace repeated, trying to remember when he'd used that word before.

"Yes! Irresponsible. Grace, you need to bloody think things through."

"Okay," she said.

"Don't contradict me!"

"I wasn't."

"But..." Samael trailed off. "You're too irresponsible," he repeated. He sighed, running a hand through his hair.

"We shouldn't fight," Daniel said. "If nothing else, we have more important things to worry about. Like how to get back to Hell. Unless, of course, Gregorian wasn't the only Gatekeeper still alive." He looked expectantly at Grace.

"You'll have to phrase it as a question," she reminded him. "And it has to be about a location."

Daniel hesitated. "Grace, where's the nearest Gatekeeper?" he asked.

"In the alley we left behind."

Samael sighed. "Grace, where's the nearest Gatekeeper who's alive?"

"In Hell."

"In Hell?" Daniel repeated. "Someone got there alive?"

Grace frowned. "I wouldn't know," she reminded him.

Samael sighed. "Grace, where's the nearest Gatekeeper who's alive and here on Earth?"

"I don't know," she said.

"And without a Gatekeeper, the Gates aren't an option," Samael said.

"We could try praying again," Grace suggested.

Samael sent her a look. "Because it worked so well the last time."

"Well, I don't hear you coming up with better ideas."

"Maybe we just need a more powerful prayer," Daniel suggested.

Grace broke into a smile. "Yeah! Like a super-prayer."

Samael stared at them before he closed his eyes in dismay.

"We could get a priest to pray for us," Grace said. "Or the pope."

"Yes, I can just see how that will go," Samael said, opening his eyes. "Dear Pope, would you please send a word upwards so that we can bring the Voice of God to *the Devil?* But don't worry, he's really not that bad a guy, once you get to know him. Love, Grace."

"There's no reason to snipe at us," Grace said. "Do you have a better idea? Besides killing Daniel, which really ought to be our last option."

Samael frowned at her. "No," he said. "But let's at least start with someone a bit more attainable, and work our way up to the pope."

"Sure," Grace said. "He's probably kind of busy anyway. Now, where can we find a church with an open-minded priest?"

* * *

In the end, they found a synagogue not ten minutes' walk from the park. Despite the late hour, the apple insisted that the rabbi was inside.

They were making their way through the small room before the sanctuary of the synagogue when Grace stopped.

Samael, who already had a hand on the door handle, looked back at her with an annoyed expression. "Are you coming?" he asked.

"Should I wear a hat?"

He stared at her. "What?"

"A hat," she repeated, gesturing towards the small basket that was filled with little, round hats. "Or are those just for the men?"

"Who cares?!"

"Well, we want to make a good first impression."

Daniel reached out and took a small hat from the pile. "Grace is right," he said, putting it on. "And I suppose it wouldn't hurt."

Grace reached out and took one as well before they both looked expectantly at Samael.

"*Not. Happening.*"

"Fine," Grace said. "Suit yourself. Now, are we going in or not?"

Samael gave her an exasperated look but threw open the doors, nonetheless.

Stepping inside, Grace looked around curiously. She'd been in a church often enough, but she'd never stepped foot inside a synagogue. She was actually somewhat disappointed by how similar the two places seemed.

Just like in a church, they found themselves in an elongated room with an aisle between two rows of pews. A raised platform was located near the end of the room, and the most significant difference — as far as Grace could tell — was a set of closed curtains at the end of the room and an utter lack of any depictions of Jesus. She tried to remember what Judaism believed of him but came up short.

Instead, she focused on the couple standing at the end of the aisle. The rabbi was a Black man in his best age. A man who lifted an eyebrow at their entrance, but who otherwise didn't react to their presence.

He was currently talking with a young girl (who, Grace was pleased to notice, did wear one of the little, round hats), and Grace and Daniel politely remained where they were, waiting for them to finish their conversation. Samael did not.

"We need you to do something for us," he declared, striding up to the rabbi.

"You know, it's moments like these," Grace whispered to Daniel, "where I just can't believe that he actually convinced Eve to take a bite of the apple."

The rabbi didn't look impressed as he turned towards Samael.

"Francine, dear," he said. "Would you mind terribly if we have this discussion tomorrow? If you're adamant about not returning home, go to my place and call your parents. They must be worried sick. There's a key underneath the green pot."

The curly-haired girl didn't answer. Instead, she was staring at Samael. Grace wondered if she could sense that he came from Hell. And then the girl sent the shapeshifter a flirtatious smile, and Grace realised that she was staring for an entirely different reason.

"Francine, dear," the rabbi repeated.

"Of course, rabbi," the girl said. "I'll come back tomorrow." She sent Samael another flirtatious smile before she left without so much as a glance towards Grace or Daniel.

The rabbi looked at Samael with a calm expression. "I won't help you, son of Lilith," he said. "Hurt me if you will, but I won't change my mind."

"He's not going to hurt you," Grace said and hurried up next to Samael. "And he's not Lilith's son. He's just a regular demonic shapeshifter."

Samael smiled at the rabbi. "Far more capable of hurting you than a common demon," he said.

"He's joking," Grace said. "He's actually a really nice guy, once you get to know him."

Daniel snorted, and Grace glanced back at him.

"Well, decent enough," she said. "And we're just here to ask you a favour."

The rabbi lifted an eyebrow. "A favour?" he said. "For a son—shapeshifter?"

"Or for me," Grace said before she changed her mind.

"Actually, for this guy." She gestured towards Daniel who was making his way over to them. "A real good guy," she said. "Wouldn't hurt a fly, trained mechanic, allowed entrance into Heaven, the whole nine yards. And he would *really* appreciate a teeny tiny favour."

"Would he now?" the rabbi wondered, keeping his eyes on Samael. "And why should I help you?"

"My brother has done something bad," Daniel said. "And he's going to do something even worse. A lot of innocent people are going to get hurt. Well, maybe not entirely innocent, but they certainly don't deserve the fate that my brother has intended for them. And to avoid this, we need you to say a prayer for us."

"A prayer," the rabbi repeated.

"Yes, please," Grace said.

"You wish to be saved?"

"Saved?" Grace repeated, uncomprehending. Then she realised what he meant. "Oh! Oh, no, thank you. We're quite good. But if you could send a message upwards saying that we could really use some help keeping the Voice of God safe, that'd be great."

"The Voice of God," the rabbi repeated.

"Yeah," Grace said, waving the Voice in the air. "If you could tell them that we got it but kind of need a ride home?"

The rabbi stared at her. Then he looked over at Daniel and Samael, the latter of which looked highly annoyed. Seconds ticked by.

"Very well," he said. "I shall pray for you."

"Just like that?" Samael demanded to know.

"Sammy, maybe we shouldn't look a gift horse in the mouth," Grace said.

"Of course we should. I've *been* a gift horse. I should know. It could be a trap." He sent her an annoyed look. "And don't call me Sammy."

"He's just going to pray," Daniel said. "And unless my brother has reached angelic stature, he's not going to hear him."

Samael ran a hand through his hair. "That's true," he admitted before he sent the rabbi a warning look. "But I'm watching you."

"I'll keep that in mind," he answered, not sounding all that impressed. He hesitated. "Should I pray to God?" he asked.

"One of the angels would probably be better," Daniel said.

"I imagine God has rather much to do," Grace added.

"God always has time," the rabbi said.

"Well, we kind of need an angel so perhaps you could cut out the middle man?"

The rabbi sighed. "Very well," he said. "An angel it is."

He closed his eyes and began speaking in an unfamiliar tongue. Hebrew, Grace realised.

"Could you pray in English?" she asked.

The rabbi opened his eyes to look at her. "A prayer should be said in the language of God."

"But if you speak English, we can correct you if there's something you've misunderstood."

The rabbi sighed and closed his eyes again, but Grace could have sworn that he'd given her an exasperated look.

"Angels in the sky," he said. "Hear my prayer."

"That's a bit formal," Grace noted.

"I'll keep that in mind," the rabbi said.

"Whatever works for you."

"Angels in the sky. Hear my prayer. These people need your aid. They have gotten into their possession the Voice of God, and they need your help to guide it to safety."

"Not that we wouldn't have found a way to do it ourselves eventually," Samael interjected.

The rabbi continued as if he hadn't heard him. "Angels; hear our prayer. Please come to our aid. Amen."

Silence befell the synagogue once again.

"That's it?" Grace asked. "That was rather short."

The rabbi *definitely* looked exasperated.

"But nice," she quickly added. "Very succinct."

"Did they answer?" Samael asked.

"In a way."

Samael stared at the rabbi. "In a way," he repeated. "Meaning what exactly? Did you *feel* that they heard you because that really doesn't mean squat in the real world! We need verbal affirmation here!"

"They're coming," the rabbi simply said, absolute certainty in his voice. "You may not trust my feelings, but I do."

"I believe him," Grace said.

Samael snorted. "You would."

Grace shrugged. "Let's just wait around for a bit," she said. "You can plan Daniel's murder as our back-up plan if that'll make you feel better."

Samael considered if. "I suppose it would." Then he grimaced. "Guess we might as well make ourselves comfortable." He sat down and leaned against one of the benches of the synagogue.

Grace sat down next to him with a sigh. She hated waiting. She leaned against one of the benches as well and looked up at the rabbi.

"Do you... I'm sorry, what was your name again?"

"Stefan. Stefan Abramovich. But my friends call me Steve."

"Steve," Grace repeated. "You don't look like a Steve."

"I know. My friends think they're being witty."

Grace laughed. "Samael would've done the same thing," she said.

Samael sent her an annoyed look. "Well, I wouldn't have made friends with a priest to begin with," he said.

"He's a rabbi," Daniel corrected him, a smile in his eyes.

Grace noted that he only ever seemed amused whenever someone was quarrelling with Samael. She decided not to comment on it. "I think his friends sound amusing," she said instead. "But that wasn't my point."

"Then, by all means, make it," Samael said.

"Stefan," Grace said.

"Yes?"

"Do you have a deck of cards?"

Stefan blinked. "Excuse me?"

"Do you have a deck of cards lying around?" Grace repeated. "Who knows how long we'll have to wait for? It'd be nice with something to pass the time with."

"I... I suppose I could go find a deck of cards, yes."

"No," Samael said. "You're not going anywhere. You're staying here so that I can keep an eye on you. For all we know, you might come back with a horde of torch-bearing villagers."

"It's been quite a while since we've used torches as a common light source," Grace noted. "Not to mention that he'll have to travel pretty far to find villagers of any kind."

Samael rolled his eyes. "Then a horde of flashlight-bearing, knife-wielding city-people," he said. "The worry still stands. The rabbi's staying until we know if the angels are coming or not."

Grace looked up at Stefan. "I'm sorry, rabbi," she said. "But when he gets that look in his eyes, there's really no changing his mind. The last time, I actually had to stalk them, do you believe that? I hope we're not too much of an inconvenience." She smiled hopefully at him. "But maybe you could tell me where the cards are, and I'll go get them myself?"

"They're coming," Stefan told her.

"The cards?"

"The angels. They're coming. I could feel it."

"Feel it?" Samael repeated with a snort. "Feel it like you feel the love of God?"

"They're *coming*," the rabbi repeated. "Now silence, shapeshifter. If we're to wait together, that might be the only way to remain civil."

Samael opened his mouth, no doubt to say something scathing, and Grace reached out to place a hand on his arm.

"Samael," she said, softly. "He's been an enormous help."

Samael sighed but remained silent. Well, sort of.

"Well, then get to it, *Stevie*," he said. "Tell her where those cards are. Who knows how long those goody two-shoes are going to take?" There was something sinister in his smile. "And you're sure as Hell not going anywhere," he said, hand transforming into a clawed paw. "Not if you know what's good for you."

"And for humanity," Daniel quickly added.

Stefan looked at Daniel. "Is that what you keep telling yourself in order to remain patient in his company?"

"Samael grows on you," Grace assured him.

"So does fungus," Daniel said.

Grace grinned, and though Samael glared at them, his right hand was back to normal, and his shoulders relaxed in a way Grace hadn't seen since they'd found Gregorian's body.

"So what do you guys wanna play?" Grace asked. "I vote for a tournament of Spit."

CHAPTER FIFTEEN:

Where There's Smoke

In the end, neither Daniel nor Samael was much in the mood for Spit. Instead, they walked restlessly around the synagogue under the curious eyes of Grace. It was just after four in the morning, and both of them appeared tense and on edge.

"Does it hurt being in a synagogue?" she asked.

Daniel turned around to look at her with bewildered eyes. "What?"

"Not you," she said. "Samael. Being a demon and all. Because I'm a resident of Hell, and I feel fine. I felt perfectly alright in the church as well, come to think of it. I thought it was meant to be a safe place for believers and whatnot. Weren't we supposed to, I don't know, burst into flames or something?"

"Hardly," Samael said. "I do feel the blessing put upon the building, but it's more like an itch you can't reach. Annoying, but ignorable."

"I can't feel anything," Grace said.

"Well, of course you can't," Samael said. "You're human. No amount of sinning will make a place of worship give you any kind of physical distress. Otherwise, you'd never see a thief or an adulterer enter one."

"I see," Grace said. She leaned back and looked at the ceiling. "Will they let Stefan into Heaven?" she wondered out loud.

"How would I know? I'm not his guardian angel."

"I know that. I was just thinking that… well, he's not… which religion gets into Heaven anyway?"

"You get a chance to convert," Daniel said.

They all looked at him.

"When you die," he clarified. "As long as you believe in God, you will be given a chance to convert to Christianity and be allowed entrance into Heaven."

Samael smirked and leaned back against the benches. "How ridiculous," he said.

"Excuse me?"

"Do you really think that one religion got it all right?" He smirked at him. "A bit arrogant, are we?"

"I believe in the bible. That's not *arrogance*."

"That book written centuries after Jesus' death? Yes, nothing flawed about that."

"Does Jesus really exist?" Grace asked, only partly to change the subject. She hadn't seen anything of him when they'd been in Heaven. Though, of course, she supposed Heaven was large.

"Of course." Samael snorted. "A real stick in the mud, if you ask me."

"We didn't," Daniel muttered.

"And he's really God's son?" she asked.

"Of course he's God's son!" Daniel exclaimed. "Sent from Heaven to save us from ourselves."

Samael rolled his eyes. "Relax, choir boy," he said. "Before you give yourself an aneurysm. Learn a little from the rabbi here. He *listens* when his betters talk."

"I listen when everyone talks," Stefan said. "As you can see."

Grace laughed but quickly turned it into a cough when Samael glared at her. "God's actual son, huh?" she said. "That's pretty wicked."

"That *was* how his followers described him," Samael said drily. "Yah, for we do say unto you: Our Lord Saviour is pretty wicked." He glanced at Daniel, smirking ever so slightly. "And Jesus' parentage is really up for discussion," he added.

"How so?" Grace asked.

"When Maria was pregnant with Jesus, a *mortal* child, he had died in her womb. God came to Earth to bless the dead child and send a little of His spirit into him. A little of His essence, if you will. This part of God brought Jesus back to life, a little of

God's spirit trapped inside his mortal body. Every angel can do this as well, though of course when it's God himself, the result is a little more... intense. Whether or not you believe that counts as making him God's son..." Samael shrugged. "That's really up for interpretation."

"It is not!" Daniel snapped.

Samael smirked. "Sure it is," he said. "Ever heard of something called genetics, choir boy?"

"I don't see how it really matters," Grace noted absent-mindedly. She was examining the decorations of the synagogue, fascinated by the golden lettering of some plaques decorating one wall.

They turned to look at her.

"Matters?" Daniel croaked. "Of course it matters!"

"Why? He existed, right? He was a good man. I don't see why his parentage matters."

Daniel didn't look like he agreed. "Jesus is the Son of God," he said firmly.

The rabbi frowned.

Grace shrugged, still not seeing the big deal. Hoping to change the topic, she decided to ask Stefan some casual question about the design of the synagogue.

Instead, she frowned.

"Doesn't it smell kind of weird?" she asked.

"You're changing the subject," Daniel accused her.

"But doesn't it?"

The others sniffed the air.

"I can't smell anything," Daniel said.

"I can," Samael said. "At least I think I can. Just give me a moment."

Slowly, his face half-transformed into the snout of a wolf, eliciting a strained gasp from the rabbi. Samael transformed back, a frown marring his features.

"Smoke," he said. "Something's on fire."

"What's on fire?" Grace asked and sniffed the air once again. This time there was no mistaken the smell of something burning.

Samael was already walking towards the entrance. "The building, if I'm not mistaken," he answered her with a grim expression. "Someone set fire to the synagogue."

"Fire?" Grace repeated and looked over at the main entrance. The door was closed but smoke was coming in from underneath it, slowly filling the room.

"You can't think my brother's here?" Daniel said, following Samael.

"I can think of few others who'd have a reason to set us on fire," Samael bit out and grabbed the handle of the door. He swore. "Blocked," he said. "Something's in the way."

"But he wouldn't burn us alive! Even if it is on fire, and he did do it, he's probably just trying to smoke us out."

"Yes, that's why they sent that nice message to warn us! We need to get out of here. *Now*." Samael glanced up at the synagogue's windows, which were all placed much too high to be of any use. Swearing, he turned towards the rabbi. "Is there a back door?"

Stefan nodded and ran over to a large curtain in the corner of the room, which he pulled aside to reveal a door. He pulled at the handle but it didn't budge.

"Hell!" Samael swore. "I guess we'll need to use the main entrance then."

"How?" Grace asked. "It's blocked." She looked over at it. Smoke was still coming from underneath it, and she blinked rapidly as her eyes began to burn.

"It won't be for long," Samael answered. "Do you still have the guns?"

"Of course," Daniel said, holding one up.

"Get ready to use them. I'm going to get us out of here, but they're probably waiting for us. Keep Grace safe. She's holding the Voice." He began to transform.

"It's going to be okay," Grace assured the rabbi. "Samael will get us out of here."

Looking back at Samael, she saw that he'd chosen to transform into a rhinoceros and that he was currently backing down the aisle. Grace hurried out of his way and over to Daniel.

Her throat was beginning to feel parched.

"Could I get a gun as well?" she asked him.

"Do you know how to use one?"

"Point and shoot?"

"There's a little more to it than that."

"Well, we don't really have time for a class right now," Grace said and reached for a gun.

Samael was now standing half-way down the aisle. He stomped one of his feet a couple of times before he hurled himself towards the door and crashed into it. The door shook at the impact but stood firm. Snorting, Samael succeeded in sounding frustrated even as a rhinoceros, and he backed up further than before.

Grace looked upwards, where the smoke was gathering above them. She was thankful they were in a relatively high room. Reminding herself to breathe through her nose, she looked back at Daniel with an impatient look.

"Fine," he said and handed her a gun. "Just try not to shoot me."

"Wouldn't dream of it," Grace assured him.

"Could I get one as well?" Stefan asked.

"You're a rabbi!" Daniel exclaimed. "You shouldn't be handling firearms!"

"I'm also a sharpshooter," Stefan told him. "And I'd prefer not to die."

Daniel looked a bit lost. "We only have two guns," he said.

"You can have mine," Grace told him and handed it over. "You're probably less likely to be the cause of friendly—" She was cut off by a coughing fit.

She looked back at Samael. He had reached the end of the aisle, where he stood motionless for a couple of seconds. Suddenly, he raced towards the door and crashed into it with the weight of a couple of tons. This time the door gave in, and smoke billowed into the synagogue. Grace gave a shout of triumph.

"Let's get out of here!" she yelled at the others before she ran directly into the smoke.

That had been a mistake. She immediately started to cough violently, and the air itself seemed to burn in her lungs.

Grace knew that it would only get worse the longer she stayed in the poisonous smoke, but there was no way to know which way would lead to sunlight. Instead, she ran blindly, hoping for the best.

And then she was out of the smoke and breathing relatively freely once again. A dozen or so people were waiting for them, each of them wearing a white cloak that looked entirely bizarre against the background of parked cars and concrete.

"There's one over there!" one of them yelled, just as Grace stumbled over a small rock. Falling to the ground, she heard a swishing sound above her. She hit the concrete hard, barely having time to reach out to break her fall.

Pain shot through her arms, but she didn't give herself time to feel it. Instead, she rolled around and scrambled to her feet, actions fuelled more by instincts than by thought.

In front of her stood a man, holding a broadsword of all things. Behind him, a rhinoceros was barging through a group of people as if they were bowling pins, their screams piercing through the air.

The man in front of her lifted the broadsword once again, and Grace threw herself to the side as it came down at her. She turned her back to the man and ran towards Samael.

She only made it a couple of steps before a shot sounded somewhere behind her, and she instinctively spun around. The man with the broadsword was falling to his knees, holding a hand to his stomach, where blood was gushing out. His face was contorted in pain, and Grace took an involuntary step backwards. The man looked at her with desperate eyes and released his hold on the sword, which fell clattering to the ground.

Grace saw something move out of the corner of her left eye. She spun around again and came face to face with another of the white-cloaked men, the second before he slammed into her.

For a fraction of a second, she was flying through the air before the back of her head hit the concrete. Black spots danced before her, and when Grace could finally see again, she was looking directly into the face of the white-cloaked man. His hands were ransacking through her pockets, and she could see the victory in his eyes as one of them closed around the Voice of God.

Grace kneed him in the groin.

Gasping in pain, the man's grip on the Voice disappeared as he fell on top of her. Grace pushed him away and scrambled to her feet once again. Knowing that she didn't have time to think, she seized the Voice and ran towards Samael. The rhinoceros was bleeding from several shallow cuts, and three white-cloaked men were lying on the ground around him. It was impossible to see if they were unconscious or dead.

In the background, fire engulfed the synagogue, sending dark smoke up against the golden background of the sky.

Behind her, she could hear footsteps closing in. They were getting closer, and she knew that she couldn't get to Samael before the man caught up with her. She wondered wildly if she should simply hurl the Voice of God away. Surely the rhinoceros would get to it before the white-cloaked men.

And then she heard a voice from above; so beautiful and bright that it was as if lightness itself became sound.

"Grace," it said, and she looked up, shielding her eyes.

An angel was hovering above her, offering her a saving hand.

"Angel!" she exclaimed in relief, not knowing its name. Smiling, she grabbed its hand. The angel pulled her upwards, away from the white-cloaked man. Protective arms wrapped themselves around her waist.

But rather than flying towards the others, they flew upwards and hovered about fifty feet or so above the battle. The angel's powerful wingbeats caused her hair to fly wildly around her face, blowing away the dark smoke from the fire.

"Do you have the Voice of God?" the angel asked her.

"Yes!" she yelled back, holding it up victoriously.

One of the angel's arms let go of her, but the angel seemed to have no trouble supporting her weight with only one. It reached out and took the Voice from her grasp.

"The Voice of God, two of the pieces," it said.

"Yes. We found it like that. We just need to bring it to Hell, and all will go back to how it should be."

"No," the angel said. "As it was. Not as it should be. But that will all change now."

It let her go.

Screaming, Grace fell. The ground seemed to advance towards her at an almost impossible speed. People were yelling, but she could barely hear them over the loud rush of the wind. Then she hit the ground, the back of her skull smacked against the pavement, and all sound disappeared from the world.

She could still see. Her eyes were open, and they took in the scene in front of her, but there was no sound of any kind. Nor was there any pain.

Stefan was lying on the ground, unconscious, while a giant of a man held Daniel in a tight grip. A rhinoceros stood frozen not far from her, two armed men between him and Daniel, who was suddenly and inexplicably wearing a white cloak.

No, that wasn't right. It wasn't Daniel. The man's nose was a bit shorter, his face a bit softer. His brother. Jacob.

The angel landed beside him. It was holding up the Voice of God and looked at it with fascination before it handed it over to Jacob.

Jacob's hand closed around the Voice, and his lips moved. Slowly, the rhinoceros turned back into Samael. He was staring at Grace with a horrified expression, and yet he didn't move a muscle. That was wrong. Samael wouldn't just stand there.

She wanted to ask him what he was doing, but she couldn't move her lips. Instead, she watched as Jacob reached out to put a hand on the angel's shoulder, smiling. A second and a third angel landed on the ground beside them. One with impossibly blue eyes and the other with hair so red that it almost appeared to be made out of fire.

And sound returned.

She could hear the roaring from the flames of the burning synagogue as well as sirens blaring in the distance. Daniel was yelling, struggling against the gigantic man's hold on him. It was much like seeing a young child being held back by an adult.

Samael, however, remained still. No, not still: His entire frame was shaking, but he didn't move an inch even though nothing was holding him back.

Grace wanted to ask him why, but as she finally forced her lips open, all that came out was a small bubble of blood.

Jacob stepped forward, his entire focus on Daniel.

"Is this the side you picked, Dan?" he asked. "Over mine?"

"Let me go, Jake!" Daniel demanded. "She's dying! She needs help."

Dying? Who was dying?

Jacob shrugged. "She's just a girl," he said. "A girl and a demon. And you chose them over me."

"Jake... *please.*"

"You could've been my Peter," Jacob said. "You should have understood how wrong it all was. I told you what had happened to me. Where they sent me. And you *still* took their side!"

"Jake... what you're trying to do..."

"I'm making things right! And I told you! I told you how it was! Sinners walking around in Hell, without so much as a rap on their knuckles, while good people are sent to *that place!*"

"God acts in—"

"Oh, shut up! There's nothing mysterious about this! It's just *wrong.*"

"It's not our place to—"

"Somebody has to! And I *can*. Shouldn't I then?" He took a step towards Daniel. "I thought it would be like when we were children," he said, his tone almost pleading. "You and me; fighting demons."

"We were *children!* Playing a game!"

"We were preparing for war! We just didn't know it yet!"

"It's not too late, Jake. Just... just put it back the way it was."

"Back?" Jacob almost sounded confused. "I can't put it *back*. It was horrible. If you can't see that, you aren't my Peter." His face contorted in disgust. "You're Judas."

"Jake, please!" Daniel said. "She's *dying.*"

"*I* died! And now you're begging for *her* life, when you never cared about *me!*"

"Of course I cared!"

"Don't lie to me! I was there! I saw you turn away!"

"Jake! *Please!*"

"Is it because she's female?" Jacob asked. "Is that why you care? Or is it because she was welcome in Hell?" He laughed without joy. "Do you think she'll go back there if she dies a second time?"

"Don't!" Daniel exclaimed "Don't kill her, Jake!"

Jacob took a step back. "I won't," he said. He sounded hurt. "How could you think that of me?"

"Thank you, Jake," Daniel said, relief clear in his voice. "Now let me go. If she doesn't get help, she's going to die."

"She'll die anyway," Jacob said. "Have you forgotten whose company you've kept?" He gestured towards Samael. "A *demon*. A sadistic creature who's only waiting for his chance to murder. Who *revels* in it!" Jacob laughed again. "And I'll prove it. Maybe then you'll come to your senses." He turned towards Samael. "You! Demon! Kill the girl," he ordered before he said something in an unfamiliar language.

Grace would have chuckled if her mouth hadn't been full of blood. *That* wasn't going to work. How could he possibly think Samael would be willing to kill her?

And yet, Samael took a halting step towards her. A white-cloaked man walked over to him. It was the same man who'd wrestled with Grace during their first meeting outside the church. He handed a sword to Samael.

The shapeshifter accepted the sword stiffly before he made his way towards Grace. There couldn't have been more than fifteen steps or so between them, but the distance seemed to stretch on forever as Samael slowly made it to her side. His face was pinched, and Grace wanted to ask him what he was *doing*.

"Sammy..." she finally got out, not even discernible to her own ears.

"I'm sorry," he said.

"Sammy... what..."

"I'm sorry," he said again. "I have to. I can't stop. I'm sorry."

I thought you didn't apologise, she wanted to tell him. *Not unless I force you.*

Samael raised the sword with both hands. The tip of it was pointing straight at her. His arms were shaking, and he looked down at her with an anguished expression.

For a long moment, he remained frozen.

"What are you waiting for?!" Jacob demanded. "This is what your kind does! Kill her! Prove what you are!" He said something more in that unfamiliar language.

Grace met Samael's eyes.

"Sammy… What are you doing?"

"I'm sorry," he whispered.

He brought the sword down and speared her heart.

CHAPTER SIXTEEN:

Limbo

Grace's eyes flew open.

Samael, the angels, Jacob; they were all gone.

Instead, she was looking up into a shimmering fog. While pretty, it was a somewhat unexpected sight.

She brought her hand up to her chest and let her fingers slide over the tear in her shirt that was located directly above her heart. Following the tear, she felt smooth skin become rough and sore. A scar. She frowned. If she'd been healed, why hadn't she been *healed?* Why wasn't she dead? Well, deader than she'd already been?

She let her arm fall to her side and looked up into the fog, thinking. Jacob had killed her, using Samael as a proxy to do so, and now she was someplace unlike anything she'd ever seen.

Limbo.

Sitting upright, she examined her surroundings. The ground she was sitting on was grey, smooth, and seemed to give in slightly beneath her as if it could just barely hold her weight. As if it wasn't quite *there* enough to be able to fully withstand her presence.

Looking around, she saw nothing but glittering fog surrounding her, quickly establishing that her recently improved sight was of little help. If she'd been standing ten feet away from a Gate to Hell, she would have no way of knowing. Looking up, she tried to discern whether it was night or day, but all she saw was fog. She squinted at it. It appeared to give off a slight light.

A fluorescent fog, Grace mused to herself.

"Hello?" she called out.

Hello. Hello. Hello.

The echo was loud enough that for a second, she thought

that someone had answered.

"Is anyone there?"

Anyone there. One there. There.

Getting to her feet, she scanned the fog. What now? If a person was lost, it was generally a good idea to stay put, but she felt relatively sure that no one was coming to get her. If this was Limbo, she needed to find her own way out.

Suddenly, she smiled victoriously, realising that the apple could show her how to get away from here, where to find a Gate to Hell, and from there…

Well, from there she would simply have to figure out her next step.

And so she closed her eyes and asked where there was a way out.

Nothing.

Frowning, she asked for the location of a Gate to Hell, and then of the Staircase to Heaven. None of her attempts produced any sort of result. Frustrated, she asked herself about the location of her own hand. Still nothing.

The apple was worthless.

There was no sudden knowledge, no inner sense of direction. There was nothing but fog and silence.

Well, that wasn't entirely true. It actually seemed like the world around her was getting louder.

Listening intently, she tried to pinpoint the sounds. It almost sounded like a rushing river, mixed with an insisting beating, which got louder by every beat.

It seemed to come from everywhere and nowhere at the same time. A heavy pulse from inside her own body.

Her heart. She was hearing her own heart and the blood flowing through her veins. The sound of her own breathing was rapidly gaining the strength of a howling storm. An insisting screech joined in as her brain started to produce sound itself, if only to fill out the silence.

A person could grow mad in this world.

Quickly pushing that thought aside, Grace started walking, if only to do something.

She needed to find a way out, apple or not. If she walked for long enough, eventually she'd have to see something besides fog.

* * *

She could have been walking a year.

Or maybe just half an hour. It was impossible to tell.

Nothing changed around her, and Grace chose not to focus on it. Not to focus on the time that was surely passing by, even if nothing changed to prove it.

It hadn't taken long before she'd started singing in an attempt to fill out the silence. Every word out of her mouth had been flung back to her, and she'd amused herself for a while, attempting a duet with herself. The more noise she made, the less loud everything became.

Then she had tried storytelling. There was no one to listen but herself, but it filled out the silence almost as well as singing had, and her audience was very impressed by her work. She even gave herself a standing ovation after a particularly clever plot twist.

At one point, she had started counting steps. Her voice had already grown hoarse by then, and when she'd reached 8,548, it gave out entirely. After that, she'd counted inside her head until the numbers were flowing together.

She had tried not to think. Instead, she had merely walked, every step sending a nearly everlasting echo out until it was finally swallowed by the fog.

She hadn't thought that she would ever get tired in this land of pseudo-existence, but her legs had grown increasingly heavier until they had finally given out, refusing to bear her weight any longer. She had laid down, closed her eyes, and waited for sleep to overtake her. It'd never happened. Instead, she'd laid still until her legs had stopped aching. Then she'd resumed walking.

She'd lost count of how many times she'd done this. She still hadn't slept, hadn't peed, hadn't felt hungry. She had simply walked and rested.

Feeling her legs ache once again, she lay down on the ground and gazed at the fog above her. She'd tried finding shapes in it but had eventually declared defeat. She'd stopped noticing its prettiness a long time ago.

Trying to ignore the heartbeat pounding inside of her, she let her eyes drift closed. Even though she couldn't sleep, she could still let her thoughts wander.

She thought back on her meeting with Jacob. In hindsight, she probably shouldn't have given the Voice of God to the angel. Though how could she have known that the angels were the bad guys?

Of course, she didn't know if *all* the angels were bad. It wasn't like three unsatisfied angels equalled them all. Otherwise, the story of Lucifer's rebellion would have looked a whole lot different.

And surely, Daniel was proof that you couldn't judge one person for someone else's actions?

It was odd, really. How Jacob could look so much like his brother and yet be so different. They'd had the same upbringing, the same parents. And Daniel had turned out quite well, for the most part. She hoped he wasn't feeling guilty over her death.

Knowing Daniel, however, he probably did.

Grace wished she could tell him how ridiculous that was.

And it wasn't like Daniel wasn't blaming himself enough already, even if he was too dense to realise it. He was rather like a puppy in that regard.

Wait. Did a puppy blame itself when it shouldn't? Grace frowned, distracted by the thought. It probably didn't. Never mind. He was like... something that blamed itself a lot when it shouldn't.

Humming to drown out the ever-lasting beating of her

heart, she thought back on Jacob's words. He'd called Daniel his Judas. She'd give Daniel a big hug, next time she saw him. Poor dear could probably use one. He was hurt enough as it was, blaming himself like he did. And it wasn't like it was Daniel who went around, ripping the fabric of reality apart.

He'd just gotten his own life; no longer putting his older brother in the centre of it. Grace could certainly remember worse things she'd done than occasionally putting herself first.

Considering she'd gone to Hell, though, maybe that wasn't the argument to use with Daniel.

She'd probably know what to say the next time she saw him. It couldn't be too hard to convince him that he hadn't sold his brother for 20 pieces of silver. Or was it 30? Never mind that. He definitely wasn't Judas, and she'd make sure to tell him just that.

Besides, if he were Judas, what did that make Jacob? Jesus? Drumming her fingers against the soft ground, she considered it. Eleven followers. Wishing Daniel were his twelfth. Calling him Peter and Judas. Jacob really did consider himself some warped version of Jesus, didn't he?

And she thought Christians were supposed to be humble and whatnot.

Snorting, she stopped her fingers' drumming.

And then she heard a sound.

Her eyes snapped open.

That sound hadn't come from her. It hadn't been her footsteps, her heartbeat, her own mind. Though she was only relatively sure on that last count.

Listening intently, she waited with bated breath.

There! The same sound. A step echoing through the air. The tiniest quiver going through the ground. It could've come from miles away, but it didn't matter. A step meant a person and a person meant company.

Holding her breath, lest the storm of it would drown out the next step, Grace waited. And waited. And waited.

There! Again. This time there was no doubt where it came from, and Grace scrambled to her feet and hurried in its direction.

Several times she stumbled, unsure if she was going the right way. Every time this happened, she forced herself to be patient and listen for the next step. And every time the sound was a little louder until it was as if someone was hitting the world's biggest gong right next to her.

And then she was there.

It was a woman. A woman who might have looked dignified once upon a time before her face had become pinched and desperate. A woman whose brown hair had been torn out in several spots, who was wearing rags that had at one point been a dress at least three decades out of style.

A woman who screamed at the sight of her.

"Hello," Grace responded, and the word echoed around them.

The woman threw herself at Grace and clawed desperately at her face.

"Shut up!" she screamed. "Shut up, shut up, shut up, *shut up.*"

The words were thrown back at them a thousand times over.

Grace struggled to keep the woman's hands away, feeling blood trickle down her face. It hurt, and she finally caught the woman's wrists in her hands.

"Calm down," she told her, in the soothing tone she'd used with panicked soldiers.

The woman was crying. "Quiet," she whispered. "I just want it to be quiet."

"Well, screaming at me certainly won't help," Grace said. "Well, it probably would, considering how dreadful silence is here, but never mind that. If I let go of you, would you please try not to scratch me to pieces?"

The woman stared at her. She nodded, a tiny little jerk of her head.

Grace let go of her and watched as the woman scrambled away from her, looking at Grace as if she might hurt her.

"I'm Grace," Grace said. "What's your name?"

"I'll hurt you," the woman said. "If you hurt me, I'll hurt you."

"Hurt you? Why would I want to hurt you?"

Then she realised why: This was Limbo, meaning that this woman was an Undesirable. Quite a few people here probably enjoyed hurting others.

"Why are you here?" Grace asked. "What did you do?"

"*DO?!*" the woman screamed. "I did nothing! *Nothing!*" Her eyes were flickering wildly as she spoke, and she desperately combed through her hair with sudden, jerky movements.

"I believe you," Grace hastened to assure her and took a step back. The woman didn't seem to notice.

"He was mine, and nobody else's, and he didn't do as I said. If he'd done as I said, I wouldn't have gotten angry. I didn't do anything wrong; I didn't, I didn't, *I didn't!*"

"I'm sure that you didn't," Grace said.

The woman screamed, lunging herself at her. Grace took a quick step to the side, avoiding the woman's frantic attack.

"If you hurt me, I'll hurt you," she said, turning the woman's words against her.

The woman bared her teeth at her, but she didn't attack again.

"You're no better!" she hissed instead. "You're here too, aren't you? Probably deserve it as well. But I don't. He was mine. He belonged to *me*. I had to!"

"Had to what?" Grace asked.

"Shut up!" the woman screamed. "I had to, you hear me?! I was *supposed* to punish him! I was his mother! And he was too weak, and it was an accident, and they shouldn't punish me for an *accident*. They shouldn't! They're the evil ones. You are. I'm not. I'm *not*."

"You hurt your son?" Grace asked, surprised.

The woman stared at her with wild eyes.

"No! It was an accident. I'm a good woman, you hear me? I don't deserve this place!"

"It kind of sounds like you do," Grace said.

The woman sneered at her. "You didn't get in either, did you?" she mocked her. "So don't you dare pretend you're any better than me. We're the same, me and you. Except that I shouldn't be here. I only got here because of an accident. I should be in Heaven."

"Hell really isn't so bad either," Grace noted. She regretted the words the second they left her mouth.

"*Hell?!*" The woman screamed. "You got into Hell?! *You got in?!*"

Grace stumbled backwards, deciding that a tactical retreat was her best choice of action. She turned around and fled, the echoes of the woman's screams following her as she did so.

"You got in! You got *in!* You've gotta get me in! Help me, get me in! I'm going crazy here, *crazy!*"

Grace just kept on running until her legs gave out underneath her, and she collapsed on the ground.

Looking at the fog above her, she yearned for the sun and the sound of birds chirping. By Samael's fluffy tale, how she missed sunshine. And stuff. Tangible *stuff*.

At least she had time on her side. An eternity to find a way out.

She wondered if Jacob had killed Samael and Daniel. Perhaps they were here in Limbo with her. She should continue tracking down sounds. She would most likely run into other Undesirables, but if there were just the slightest chance it was one of them...

She should get up and search. It was just so very hard to do so. But she needed to get out and help them.

And she needed to get out and tell Samael that she didn't blame him. That it hadn't been his fault she'd died, for all that he'd led the sword. That had been Jacob's doing, but judging from the expression on Samael's face, Grace didn't think he'd forgive himself until she did. And told him about it, that was.

Samael really was the type who needed to hear things said out loud. Just look at how he was with Lucifer.

Maybe she should have a talk with the Devil. Samael shouldn't have given the apple to Eve, but hadn't anyone ever told Lucifer that you punished a misbehaving child by taking away toys and privileges, not love and attention?

Grace imagined the Devil's expression if she told him this. Maybe she could rephrase it. It was true though. Samael was clearly desperate for his idol's approval, and sure; he'd played a small (or perhaps not so small) role in the Fall of Man. But you didn't see Adam and Eve still being punished.

Just all their descendants.

Okay, so *maybe* the Devil wasn't so harsh (in comparison and all), but Grace still thought he could tell Samael that he was proud of him. Samael did, after all, find the Voice of God when no one else could. Sure, they'd accidentally handed it over to the anti-Christ, but that one was really on Grace's head. And she'd tell the Devil just that.

She thought back on how he'd simply disintegrated the Undesirable who'd sneaked into Hell.

Maybe she could tell him in writing.

She thought back on Samael and the look in his eyes when he'd been forced to kill her. Looking at the shimmering fog above her, Grace made a vow. She'd find a way out somehow and tell him that she didn't blame him. Someone else had gotten out once.

Why not her?

* * *

Time passed. Possibly. Her heart was still beating, and if she counted the beats, she could count seconds, and if she could count time, surely it had to be there? She stopped wondering when she got a headache.

She found eight people after that first one. It got easier after she'd learned how to lay down, put her ear on the ground, and listen. Sure, it would cause the blood flowing through her head to sound like a tsunami ready to tear her away, but she could also hear the faint echoes of footsteps.

Eight times she followed them, and eight times she encountered Undesirables.

On the bright side, she only faced attempted murdered twice.

Which meant six times of merely being threatened and cursed. At least it had sounded like threats and curses. As four of them hadn't spoken neither English nor French, she really had no way of knowing for sure.

Her headache was growing more insistent, and she ignored it as best as she could.

Lying with her face pressed against the ground once again, Grace listened.

There. Footsteps. Heavy ones. She wished she'd paid more attention to the footsteps of Samael and Daniel. This would have been a lot easier if she'd been able to discern whether it was them or not, without having to go check for herself.

But she did, and so she got to her feet and went searching for the person making the footsteps, only to be disappointed for the ninth time.

The man was enormous, and an eternity without food and plenty of exercise had apparently had zero effect on that. She estimated that he'd been here a century or two, judging by his clothing, and he positively lit up at the sight of her.

Grace stopped, not used to the sight of joy on someone's face. Not in Limbo.

"Hello," she said hesitantly. "I'm Grace. What's your name?"

"Such a pretty one!" the man said, seemingly close to crying with joy. "Such a pretty one. It's been a while since I've been allowed one like you."

Grace took a step back. "Allowed to what?"

"You look just like my second one," he told her, grinning manically. "She was really special."

He threw himself at her, horrifyingly quick for his size, and Grace just barely had time to throw herself to her side, falling over her own feet in the progress.

"Come here, pretty bird," the man crooned. "Let me wring your pretty, little neck."

"I'd rather you didn't," Grace said, struggling to her feet.

"Come now; it'll feel wonderful."

"I doubt it."

"No, it will. I know. I've seen it in their eyes. The peace, fleeing with the last of the life. It feels wonderful to die with someone else's hands around your neck. So fly this way, pretty bird."

"Did it feel wonderful when you died?" Grace asked, inching away.

The man looked displeased. "I didn't get to try it," he said. "I was hanged using that new method. The one that breaks your neck. I begged them to strangle me, but they refused. I died by the pull of a lever when the only way to go is with the help of warm flesh." He smiled at her, and Grace saw that two of his teeth were missing. The others had almost entirely rotten away.

"I didn't do it right with the first one," he confided. "It took too long, and I got impatient and used a knife. How I regret that." He reached for her with a pleading expression. "I didn't get to see the peace in her eyes, the gratitude when I freed her using my warm flesh. The second one was wonderful. You'll go like that, I promise."

He made a move for her, and Grace stumbled backwards, successfully staying out of his reach.

"The third one," the man continued as if their little dance

hadn't happened. "The third one was awful. I thought I was done, but I wasn't. She only lost consciousness. But I learned from my mistake. And here I just listen for the heart."

He jumped at her, and Grace felt his fingertips grace her upper arm before she once again got out of his reach. This man wouldn't allow her to simply inch away from him, and so she turned around and ran.

Footsteps sounded behind her, and then the man slammed into her back, sending both of them tumbling to the ground. Grace could feel his warm breath against her neck, could hear him gasping in ecstasy. He grabbed her shoulders and turned her around so that she was looking directly into his joyful face, and he smiled at her with rotten teeth and shining eyes.

Then he put his fat hands around her neck and squeezed.

Grace tried to tear them away, but she might as well have tried pushing away a wall. The strength of this man was unfathomable.

And then, suddenly, the man loosened his hold on her.

He was still sitting on top of her, holding her down, but his focus was no longer on her. Instead, he was looking around, a frightened expression on his face. Grace wondered what could make this man looked *scared*.

And then she heard it.

A sound.

Not footsteps. Not anything she could relate to this world of fog. Something unknown.

The man jumped to his feet. He seemed to have forgotten her entirely. He stood perfectly still for two long seconds before he suddenly set off in a run. Grace wondered if he could hear what direction the sound came from. She couldn't even determine what it *was*.

It almost sounded like someone hitting a spoon against a glass. Except the glass was full, and she could hear the water flowing around the glass in its own little maelstrom.

She took a step back and spun around to see if she could see any sign of whatever was producing the sound, but the fog was as thick as ever.

Then the ground disappeared beneath her left foot.

Barely keeping her balance, Grace stumbled backwards, watching with big eyes as more and more of the ground collapsed, a domino effect seemingly created by one little misstep.

Where the ground had fallen away, there was now a large pool of liquid, thicker than water but thinner than molasses, spinning around on its own accord.

It was a vortex. The maelstrom she'd heard.

It was dark and foreboding, and Grace stared at it with her mouth slightly open, entirely disregarding her mother's rule for 'not wanting flies.'

Finally, the ground became stable once again, leaving her with a vortex that was covered partly by the shimmering fog. It was almost like a black hole.

A hole. Perhaps it was. A crack in the wall.

She had no way of knowing. It might obliterate her the moment she touched it. But she had neither time nor patience to test it out safely, lest it suddenly closed again.

It was the one chance she had.

Grace looked up at the shimmering fog, which had decidedly lost its charm long ago, and took one last deep breath.

And then she plunged in.

CHAPTER SEVENTEEN:

The New Hell

She never landed.

She fell, all right; the feeling reminding her unpleasantly of when the angel had dropped her. But she didn't crash into the ground. Instead, she was falling one second and standing upright the next, her stomach churning uncomfortably at the feeling.

She was surrounded by a mass of people. A man next to her was vomiting, bile splashing on the ground. Looking around in confusion, she tried to determine where she was, but it was impossible. Everywhere around her there were people, pushing and shoving at each other.

People whom she could now recognise by the ticks of their faces, and their constantly shifting eyes. Undesirables. They must have come from Limbo, just like her. Grace wondered if they'd gotten out the same way she had. Had the border between the worlds truly grown so thin?

She gnawed on her bottom lip as she contemplated the ramifications of this. Lucifer had enough trouble as it were, and Lilith had already looked like she was at Death's door. Could she even *survive* a further crumbling of the walls? Hopefully, the damage wasn't bigger than a couple of additional holes, allowing a few more people to sneak in.

Except, they weren't few, and very little sneaking was taking place. People were crying, yelling, throwing up.

Feeling sweat drip into her eyes, Grace took off her jacket and fanned herself with her shirt. It was indescribably hot; a dry, tormenting heat. It was as if someone had opened an oven and was forcing her to sit directly in front of it.

She could hear screams far away, and the air was thick with the stench of sulphur. Looking up into the sky, she tried to find the vortex she'd fallen from, but it wasn't there. Instead, black snow was falling from a white sky, landing softly on her cheeks. It didn't feel cold against her bare skin, and she realised that it wasn't snow. It was ash.

Wiping it away as best as she could, Grace stood on her toes and tried to get a look at what was ahead of the mass of people. It was impossible. There must have been thousands, if not hundreds of thousands of them. This was nothing like the worlds Grace knew.

This wasn't Hell. Where was the smell of barbecue? The chatter, the laughter, the arguing of its many inhabitants?

Neither was it Heaven. There was no nature, no sunshine, no garish pastels.

It reminded her most of the whiteness of the In-Between, even though she couldn't see a stairway or a conveyor belt anywhere. She was also relatively sure she would have remembered the falling ashes, the unbearable heat, and the stench of sulphur.

Figuring that it was best to remain unnoticed, she tried to blend into the crowd around her. A man not far from her was yelling up into the darkened sky; screaming that he'd finally made it through the test and into the Kingdom of Heaven. Grace decided to stay away from him.

A voice suddenly rang out, and they all became quiet. Not that anything could have drowned out that voice. It was loud and booming, and if Grace hadn't been so curious as to what it would say, she might have held her hands up to shield her ears.

"Listen!" the voice called out. "For we are to enter a new time, where the righteous and the sinners are divided as they ought. Salvation or condemnation. Praise the Second Saviour!"

"Look!" a woman gasped not too far from Grace, pointing upwards.

An angel was hovering above them, his eyes resting on the crowd, and Grace quickly looked down. The image of him was burned into the inside of her retina. An angel surrounded by falling ashes, face twisted in fury. He looked... rather intense, actually.

"Do not attempt to hide!" the angel warned them. "For we know every face and every name. Though you have not entered through one of the Gates, your soul has been judged. We know you all; every soul damned into the Wasteland of Limbo."

He looked down at the people beneath him with contempt. Some were crying. Some were desperately trying to claw their way away from him. Others were reaching for him, light shining in their eyes as if they were seeing their salvation. Their gaunt faces lit up with timid smiles, and a woman next to Grace was murmuring the Apostles' Creed over and over, her lips moving rapidly even as her eyes never wavered from the angel above them.

Grace glanced up from underneath her eyelashes. The angel was holding a roll of parchment, which now seemed to be unfolding itself. It tumbled down and spread across the ground, becoming an ever-growing pile of parchment in the midst of the crowd; soon taller than the people in it.

Grace frowned slightly, looking down. She hadn't been damned to Limbo, had she? She had gained entrance into Hell. Her name had been written down in Hell's Chronicle. It shouldn't appear on the angel's list.

She risked a third glance upwards and saw that the angel didn't seem to be searching through the crowd as she'd expected. Weren't they aware that she was here?

"Go," the angel ordered them, gesturing with his arm in the direction behind him. "Go to your salvation. Your damnation. Your judgement."

People started moving, and Grace was amazed to see that most of them were willingly moving in the direction the angel had indicated; hope shining in their eyes.

Grace turned around and tried to push against the flow of

the crowd. She wasn't the only one; others were fighting to get away from the angel, not caring who they hurt in the process.

But they were outnumbered by the people with the hope of a better future. They were pushing forward, and Grace was swept along with them. She might as well have tried to break a tidal wave. It was difficult enough to even keep standing as the excitement grew, and Grace found herself forced to tread on fallen men and women, lest she should be among them.

"Look!" a woman said, her voice trembling with excitement, and only a hint of apprehension.

Grace craned her neck to see as well. There, in the distance, she could now see an enormous door; seemingly placed in the middle of nowhere. There were no walls surrounding it. Nothing but a white background filled with black ashes. The horde of people were travelling towards it.

The door looked nothing like the Gateway she'd travelled through the first time she'd gone to Hell. This was larger, far more intimidating, and on fire.

It was also wide open, inviting in the crowd surrounding her. Around her, more people started to fight their way back. The flaming doors certainly looked nothing like salvation, and someone elbowed Grace in the face as more and more people started to panic.

"It's Hell!" someone screamed.

"It's Purgatory!" someone else yelled. "The last test. I'm finally getting into Heaven!"

Around her, people were screaming at each other, as one part of the horde struggled to get to the gate, and the other part was fighting to get away from it. Unfortunately, there were still far more people going towards the burning gate, and everyone else was forced to follow along with them or be trampled down on their way.

Looking up into the sky, Grace saw angels fly above them. Each angel was carrying a person, seemingly not even noticing their desperate pleas not to take them.

Grace realised that these were the people who'd tried to get away. The angel had meant what he'd said: There was no escape.

The heat only became stronger as they neared the gate, and with a last glance backwards, Grace was forced through it. The heat was now close to unbearable. Grace's throat was parched, and her eyes were burning from lack of moisture. Blinking rapidly did little to help, and so she could only hope that she would eventually grow accustomed to the heat. Or that they'd turn on the air conditioning. People were screaming, crying, begging.

They were standing on an enormous Hill, looking out into the darkness. If she squinted, she could make out the silhouette of Lucifer's palace, dark and ominous in the distance. They were definitely in Hell. But the little lights in the valley had been put out and replaced with other lights that were bigger, orange, and which seemed to dance in the distance. Fire, she realised with dismay, and turned her eyes away from the sight. An explosion went off, and Grace's entire body tensed; her eyes instinctively scanning her surroundings for cover.

Bombs and grenades exploded in the distance, and men around her were screaming in pain. She could feel a familiar liquid drip from her fingertips. She stared down at her hands, expecting them to be covered in blood.

They weren't, and Grace took a deep breath, closing her eyes. She was in Hell, not France, and she clenched her fists tightly as she reminded herself of this. Her nails dug into her palms, and the pain helped. Slowly, she opened her eyes.

Though the blood hadn't been real, the explosions and screams still were, but they were the screams of fear and anger rather than excruciating pain.

There were demons, but they weren't the chattering group she remembered. Instead, they all wore identical, hard expressions, and Grace realised that they were shepherding the humans through Hell; dividing up the men and women as they did so.

A push from the back sent Grace falling to the ground, and she hissed in pain as her right hand bend at an unnatural angle underneath her body. Someone stepped on her other hand, and Grace gasped in pain. Then someone grasped the neck of her shirt and pulled her up with a hard yank.

Trying to regain her balance, Grace felt a cloak being folded around her. A hood was pulled over her head, her peripheral vision now blocked by white fabric.

"Do not turn around," a voice told her, the unmistakable musical tone of an angel.

Angrily, Grace spun around, about to give it a piece of her mind if it were the last thing she ever did.

A hand was placed over her mouth, just as she looked into a set of impossibly blue eyes.

"I told you not to turn around," the angel whispered, and Grace hadn't even known that angels *could* whisper. He looked young. If he'd been human, she would have put him around the age of twenty. He was also one of the angels that had stood at Jacob's side. She felt anger well up in her.

"You should consider yourself fortunate that the Second Saviour has forgotten you," the angel said, removing the hand that was covering her mouth. "Now follow me. We need to hide you before you are recognised."

Grace looked at the angel in disbelief. The last time she'd seen him, she'd ended up getting stabbed by her friend.

But... she glanced over at the demons. She couldn't trust that they would help her. Not after she'd seen what the Voice could make Samael do. The angel *seemed* to have changed sides, and she really did need someone to explain this inexplicable chaos to her.

"Fine," she whispered, turning away from the angel as if they weren't talking. "But if this is another trick, I'll make you regret that you were ever born."

"I was not," the angel answered. "Now look down and follow me." He started to walk through the crowd, and Grace struggled to keep up.

"Do not let anyone know that you are here," the angel said. "If someone talks to you, answer them with as few words as possible. Do not react to anything you may see, and if the Second Saviour appears, step out of his way, but do not leave unless he tells you to. Refer to him only as the Second Saviour. And *never* show your face. Even if it is not recognisable for all of them, you are still a woman."

"So? There are no female followers?"

"No. The Second Saviour does not believe that women should have a mission. Now come. We need to hurry."

Grace wasted a few seconds gaping at the angel's back before she pulled herself together and hurried after him.

They walked through the crowd far easier than Grace would have been able to, had she been alone. Demons and humans alike moved aside as they saw the angel approaching, and Grace made sure to stay close behind him. They walked continuously downhill, and Grace struggled to keep up with the angel who seemed to have no trouble moving in the darkness.

Suddenly, something landed on her shoulder.

Frowning, Grace took hold of whatever it was and looked at it, squinting her eyes to see it properly in the darkness. It was a wiggling worm, and Grace let go of it with a gasp. Another worm landed on her cheek. Hurriedly, she brushed it away, only for a third to land on her arm. They were falling from above. Looking towards the angel for an explanation, she realised that he hadn't waited for her.

Running to catch up to him, she remembered his advice not to look up, but she still couldn't keep herself from glancing out from underneath the hood. The crowd was thinning out as they moved through it, and she saw that there was more order to the chaos than she'd initially thought.

There were no more women. Everywhere around them, there were only men and male demons, and Grace wondered what was going to happen to the women. She couldn't see any children either, and Grace tried to remember if she had ever seen any in Hell. Did all children go to Heaven? And if they did, would they still do so now?

Grace could only speculate what was happening to the women and children, but she could have no doubt what was happening to the men. They had all been put to work. The kind of work which people didn't tend to survive long term. At least they wouldn't have, if they'd still been alive. Jacob had taken an entire world and turned it into a labour camp.

She and the angel walked past buildings that were being torn down and flowers that were being ripped from the ground. Once, Grace had to jump aside to avoid being completely smashed by an overturned statue of Lucifer, and the destruction of Hell only worsened as they neared the Palace.

They were now walking amongst the fires she'd seen from the hill, and Grace came to realise that they weren't only there to give Hell a more classic fire-and-brimstone kind of look. Everywhere around her, men were swearing as they tore down buildings, carelessly cutting through electrical wires and waterpipes. Accidental fires were a constant source of alarm, and the equally accidental bursts of water could only do so much when they weren't directed towards the flames.

A screaming man suddenly ran out from the midst of a fire, flames engulfing his entire form. He threw himself in the path of a burst waterpipe before he fell to the ground. The smell of burnt flesh mixed with the sulphur in the air and without thinking, Grace took a step forward to help.

The angel grabbed her arm and pulled her back. "We cannot help him," he said. "We need to hurry before someone realises who you are."

"But he's in pain! And I could help!"

"So is almost everyone else. And I assume that you want to save them all." He dragged her along with him, and Grace stumbled on beside him, struggling not to look back at the man. She wasn't sure she'd be able to leave if she did.

"Save them all?" she said. "How?"

"Not now," the angel said. "Not here. We shall go to a safe place."

"Where?"

"One of the Second Saviour's conference rooms."

"You want us to walk directly towards him?"

"They will not be searching for escapees there," he told her.

Grace considered it.

"That's true," she allowed. "But there'll also be a lot more of his followers to worry about."

The angel looked back at her.

"They're all his followers," he said.

"But you're not."

"I am. If he orders me to hand you over, I shall have no choice but to do so."

"*Everyone* follows him?" Grace repeated, thinking back on Daniel and Samael. Daniel was human, but she'd already seen what Jacob could force Samael to do.

Even if she found the shapeshifter, he might just turn her in.

She took a deep breath. "Okay," she said. "How far to the conference room?"

* * *

They got to the palace without any incidents. Here was even busier than outside of it, as thousands of paintings were torn from the walls, and innumerable artefacts were smashed against the stone floors. Grace stumbled over a torn-off cover of a book titled How to Integrate Yourself in Hell, and she wondered if they'd raided the library of any books that might have shown what Hell had once been like.

There were fires here as well, though these were definitely not started accidentally. Instead, she'd seen countless paintings and books being fed to the flames. It didn't seem to matter much what they were about. Grace saw a collection of Doctor Seuss as well as beautiful, leather-bound books that could have belonged to Lucifer himself. A lot of them had without a doubt been priceless, but all of them were turned into ashes.

Winding their way through increasingly deserted back passages, they slowly left the ruination behind. They were now the only two people travelling through the halls, and Grace almost walked directly into the back of the angel as he suddenly stopped. They were standing in front of a white door, and the angel signalled Grace inside before he closed the door behind them and carefully locked it.

"There," he said. "We are as safe as we will be."

They were standing in a somewhat normal conference room. Wooden flooring, white walls, and a large, marble table in the middle. It was inlaid with gold and surrounded by twelve chairs. The walls had several squares on them that had a slightly different colouring than the rest, and Grace realised that paintings had been removed from Jacob's inner sanctuaries as well. She supposed it made sense, though the sight still made her frown.

Impatient, she took her cloak off and threw it over the back of one of the chairs before she perched herself on the table and started drumming her fingers against its marble top.

"What *happened?*" she asked.

"Four days ago," the angel said. "The Second Saviour united the three pieces of the Voice of God and took it with him to Hell. He has since then enslaved demons and angels alike, recreated Heaven and Hell, and is currently reallocating the souls."

"Four days ago?" Grace repeated. "But... why wait so long? Not that I'm not thankful he did!" It was quite a relief to know that Hell hadn't been like this for more than a few days.

"He was unable to change anything before he got the Voice of God into his possession."

"But… it's been *months* since he did! Or at least weeks."

"It has not. You were in Limbo. Time moves differently there. You were killed four days ago."

"Four… days," Grace repeated incredulously. "Four days." She felt dizzy. She shook her head, forcing herself to move on and not think about it too deeply. "Why do you call him that?" she asked instead. "The Second Saviour. There's no one around to hear us, and you don't seem to like him very much."

"He has ordered us to."

"Oh." Grace considered it. "Why did you save me?" she asked. "Even if you aren't with him, then why risk yourself over me when you wouldn't for the man on fire?"

"Because you are the only one who is unaccounted for," the angel said.

"Yeah, I figured as much. I'm written down as a resident of Hell, not Limbo. But what difference does that make?"

"The demons have been ordered not to hurt the Second Saviour," the angel said, flicking his wings ever so slightly. "As have the angels. Neither are they allowed the steal the Voice of God. The people written in Heaven's Chronicle are re-evaluated, as are the people of Limbo. The location of every last one of them is known. Every resident of Hell has been captured. He keeps his brother in his personal chambers. He has even contained Lucifer. You are the only creature that is not under his control. He forgot about you."

"Even then, I'm hardly able to do much," Grace said. "He has the Voice of God."

"So did you," the angel said.

"But I didn't know how to use it."

"The brother of the Second Saviour did. He still lost it. The Second Saviour can lose it as well. You are not forbidden to take it from him."

Grace shook her head. The angel had to be desperate if he was putting all his eggs into her human, magic-less basket. Though she supposed there weren't many other options left.

Resolutely, she nodded.

"Okay," she said. "What do you want me to do?"

The angel hesitated, and Grace grimaced. "You don't have a plan, do you?"

"I need you to take the Voice of God from the Second Saviour."

"I got that. But you have no idea how?"

"No," the angel admitted, and Grace groaned.

Gnawing on her bottom lip, she considered her options. She wondered if the apple worked here when it hadn't in Limbo.

"Where is the Voice of God?" she asked.

"With the Second Saviour in the throne room," the angel told her.

"Well, don't answer me."

"What?"

"I wasn't asking *you*. I was asking the apple."

The angel's blue eyes widened in surprise. "It is true then? You have eaten an apple from the Tree of Knowledge?"

"Yeah. It was pretty good." She thought about what else she could ask herself. She wondered what had happened to the rabbi who'd helped them, back in the synagogue.

"Where is Stefan?" she asked. She frowned over the answer that came to her.

"What is Stefan doing in Hell?" she asked the angel.

The angel didn't answer.

"What is Stefan doing in Hell?" Grace repeated, thinking that he hadn't heard her.

"You are not speaking to the apple this time?" the angel asked.

"Well, no. It can only tell me where stuff is."

The angel nodded thoughtfully but remained silent. With a

sigh, Grace repeated her question for the third time.

"Why is Stefan in Hell?"

"He was killed off for his attempt to help you."

"He was *killed?!* Because of us?!"

"Yes."

"But wouldn't he have gone to Heaven?"

"The Second Saviour does not allow entrance for anyone helping his enemies."

Grace considered it. Stefan had *died* because he'd helped them. She hoped that it had at least been a merciful death. She realised that it wouldn't matter. Even if he'd been killed in the most painless way possible, he still would have been condemned to an eternity of punishment.

"Okay," she said. "Jacob has the Voice of God. Can't I just... you know, yank it out of his hands?"

"Even if you got close enough to do so, every angel and demon have been ordered to immediately return the Voice of God to his possession. I myself would be forced to do so until a new order is given."

"Meaning that I'll need to immediately give it to someone who can give that order. Daniel would be the best choice."

The angel looked at her with contemplative eyes. "Then we shall need to get you in a room with both him and Daniel, and we need a distraction if you are to take it from his hands. He will not let it go willingly."

"Well, shouldn't we be able to find some fireworks in this place? Setting that off in his vicinity is sure to create a distraction."

"There are no longer any fireworks in Hell."

"What about a normal fire? You know, bigger than the ones they've already got going."

The angel considered it. "I do not think that it will be enough," he said. "I shall ask the others what they would advise."

"The others?"

"The other angels who refuse to accept this new world."

"There are others?"

The angel bowed his head. "There are," he said. "Not all angels are pleased with the changes the Second Saviour has brought. Less and less each day. He makes himself a lot of enemies."

Grace tried to imagine the underground resistance of the angels. The majestic, powerful creatures; enslaved by a mere human.

"We'll make it right," she tried to comfort him. "How many allies do we have?"

"There is a handful of other angels that I have chosen to trust. Dissatisfaction is growing amongst us, but it is unclear how deep it is seeded. I do not know how many have turned against him. He promised us a world that was more than just a battlefield for God and the Devil. He promised us equality. Instead, he turned us into slaves."

"We'll stop him," Grace promised. "All we need is a distraction." She considered the dissatisfaction that was apparently brewing against Jacob. "What about a riot?" she asked.

"We cannot go against him. It is against our orders."

"Not you guys. The humans. I can't imagine that they're pleased with him. They should be willing to fight if only they feel they have a chance."

"They do not."

"I'm not asking them to defeat the angels and demons. Just to serve as a distraction."

The angel seemed to consider it.

"What about Lucifer?" Grace asked. "Didn't he lead a rebellion once?"

"Lucifer has been ordered to stay in the room of the highest tower in the palace," the angel told her. "There he has been condemned to forever look out the window and see what his Hell has become. He cannot leave. He cannot fight."

"Oh." Grace considered it. That was rather sad. "What about a bomb then?" she asked.

The angel contemplated it. "There are many weapons found in Hell," he allowed.

Grace nodded resolutely, jumped down from the table, and threw the cloak over herself once again. Off to find a bomb then.

"Wait," the angel told her.

"What?"

"You need a better disguise than that. We need a mask."

"A mask? You don't think that seems a tad suspicious?"

"No."

Grace sighed. Leave it to angels to keep their answers simple. "Well, it will," she said. "People don't just randomly wear masks."

"The Second Saviour's most trusted followers do. He insists. There are eleven of them, and they all wear masks. You will pretend to be Benjamin."

"Benjamin?"

"He has a slight build and a light voice. If you do not speak too much, they will assume that you are him."

"Okay," Grace said. "Benjamin it is. How will we get ourselves a mask?"

"I shall bring it here."

"You want me to *wait*?" Grace asked. She could hardly fathom anything she wanted to do less. Not when there were so many reasons to *act*. Though acting too fast might ruin everything. She sighed.

"I'll wait," she said. "Wearing my super-hero cape, and not looking at anyone, and not talking to anyone."

"I would advise you to pray."

"What? To God? You think he might help?"

"He does not involve himself in matters regarding free will."

"Of course, he doesn't."

"But every angel can hear a prayer sent to us," the angel said.

"The Second Saviour uses this to gain information of everything that happens in Heaven and Hell alike. He keeps one of the archangels at his side at all times."

Grace considered it. "Wouldn't it have been simpler to just get a phone?" she asked. The angel didn't deign to answer. "So, you want me to pray to... look like I'm talking with this archangel?"

"Barachiel," he said. "Yes. If it appears as if you are passing on information, no one should disturb you."

"I can do that," Grace said. "A good girl, down on my knees to pray."

"I shall hurry back," the angel said. He gave her a grave nod and walked towards the door. Grace frowned slightly. It seemed like he did all the work, and she looked forward to doing something productive herself. *Anything*, really.

"I shall bring a weapon as well so that you can kill Benjamin," the angel said before he opened the door.

"Wait, *what?!*" Grace hurried over and closed the door, staring at the angel in disbelief.

"I shall bring a weapon as well so that you can kill Benjamin," the angel repeated flatly. "I am not certain that you are physically strong enough to defeat him without one, and it would be foolish to take unnecessary risks."

"Absolutely not," Grace said promptly. "I'm a nurse. I don't kill people."

"We cannot allow him to remain in this Hell alongside you. It is too dangerous."

"But... I can't kill someone," Grace said.

"I am aware that he may be physically stronger than you. That is why I shall bring you a weapon."

"No. I mean, I probably *could* kill him. I just mean I won't. I can't take someone's life."

"But he is not alive," the angel said.

Grace shook her head. This was confusing, though she

supposed it was true. If Benjamin had come from Limbo, he must already be dead.

"Then what does it help to kill a dead man?" she asked.

"His re-death will send him back to be judged once again, which should give us at least two days."

Little of that sentence made sense to Grace. "What?"

"The Second Saviour has broken down the walls of Limbo. People are flocking in. It will take at least two days until he is judged."

Grace considered it. She wondered if it still counted as killing someone if they were already dead. "Can't we just... give him a sleeping pill and be done with it? I've had great success with them in the past."

The angel seemed to consider it. "We will risk someone finding him."

"Won't we run the same risk if he's sent back in line? One of the angels might see him and report back to that Barachu guy."

"Barachiel," the angel said. "The Leader of the Guardians."

"Sure, that guy. Isn't it safer to just... put him to sleep and lock him in somewhere?"

The angel hesitated. "It might be," he said. "A powerful sleeping draught should buy us three days."

"Perfect," Grace said. "So, you'll go get that, along with the other things. Do you need a list?"

"No," the angel said.

"Lovely," Grace said. "Now, just one last thing before you leave."

The angel looked at her inquisitively.

"I don't know your name," Grace said. "And if it weren't for you, I would probably have been found by now. So thank you. And it feels wrong that I don't know your name."

"I would rather that you did not."

"Why not? Is it hard to pronounce?"

"If you knew my name and were captured, you might be

forced to reveal it under torture."

"Oh. Right." Grace tried not to think too much about that. "No names then. I can do that. My name's Tobias Harker."

The angel looked at her with bewilderment. "It is not," he said.

"No, but if you're asked who you were with, you can honestly say that the person in question introduced themselves as Tobias."

The angel still seemed confused. "Who is Tobias Harker?"

"A boy I had a crush on back when I was twelve. As good a name as any."

The angel sighed. "Very well. I shall henceforth refer to you as Tobias Harker."

"And I'll call you Blue-Eyes. Until it's safe to know your real name. Now shoo. I'll be here, praying like a fourteenth century monk."

With these words, she pushed the angel towards the door, and he left with a last worried glance back at her.

Grace looked at the closed door and pulled the cloak closer around her. Then she knelt and prepared herself for hours of waiting.

* * *

The angel returned after what seemed like an eternity, and Grace hurried over and took the mask he was holding out to her.

"Lovely," she said. Then she actually looked at the mask. It was entirely white, with a rather generic face on it, but there was still something about its features which seemed... familiar.

"Eh, Blue-Eyes," she said. "Is it just me, or does this mask kind of look like Daniel?"

"It does," the angel said. "It is not something that should be commented upon."

"That's..." Grace said. "Well... okay." She forced herself to put the mask on. "Did you get the other stuff?" she asked, once she was adequately disguised.

The angel handed her three grenades and a glass vial of purple liquid, which Grace carefully placed in her pocket. Hadn't these people heard about plastic? He also handed her a piece of cloth, and she looked at it in confusion.

"For the sleeping drought," he clarified. "Soak the cloth in it and press it against his mouth."

"Blue-Eyes, that's genius!"

"I... yes. Thank you." The angel shook his wings a bit, and Grace suddenly got the feeling that he was fidgeting.

"I am not aware of the location of Benjamin," he told her, his wings folded motionless behind him once again. "I thought that questions regarding him might raise unwanted suspicion."

"That's okay," Grace assured him. "Apple. Remember? Just ask me a question."

The angel frowned. "Where is Benjamin, follower of the Second Saviour?"

"In Purgatory," Grace promptly answered. Then she frowned. "Wait, isn't Purgatory just another word for Hell? That isn't very helpful."

"No," the angel told her. "Purgatory never existed. It was a story made up by people who wanted to believe that they could sin and still be allowed entrance into the Kingdom of God."

"Kind of like a hangover?" Grace suggested.

The angel raised his eyebrows ever so slightly. "A hangover?" he repeated.

"Well, yeah. They want to be able to party as hard as they want, and then just deal with the hangover later. And, you know, only temporarily."

"I... yes," the angel said. "I suppose that it is a viable metaphor. They were wrong, of course, but the Second Saviour believes that Purgatory is a necessary part of Heaven and Hell. He forced us to create one, where he can burn the Original Sin out of women."

"Wait, what?" Grace said. "Just women?"

249

"Yes."

"But... *why?!*"

"When Eve took a bite of the apple, she committed the very first sin, and the Second Saviour believes that this sin is part of the female nature, poisoning you from within. He wishes to burn this sin out and leave your gender pure."

"But that's *ridiculous*. He can't send all women through Purgatory."

The angel was silent.

"He's sending *all* women through Purgatory?"

"It is still being tested. But he ultimately plans to do so, yes."

For several seconds, Grace was speechless. Her mother. Her grandmothers. Her sisters, once they passed. Her nieces.

"But that's... that's ludicrous," she said, thinking of the bite she'd had herself. It hadn't *felt* particularly sinful. "You can't send all women to burn just because Eve took a bite out of a stupid apple!"

"He can," the angel answered her.

Grace considered this, stunned.

"We'll stop him," she finally said. "We'll make this right. I want my Hell back."

CHAPTER EIGHTEEN:

Purgatory

It took about an hour for things to start going wrong.

Not that things hadn't been going wrong for a while now; but it took about an hour for things to *continue* going wrong. They'd gone through Hell easily enough, Grace mumbling an almost inaudible greeting to every enemy they passed.

Stone walls gave way to a deserted village, which took them through a landscape consisting entirely of black rocks and mountains. The angel led her towards one of these mountains, and Grace saw that a two-story tall door had been built directly into it. A window was placed on either side of the large door, giving it the impression of being ready to swallow up anyone who dared enter. There was no glass covering the windows, but a red glow shone from within.

The angel, however, wasn't leading her to the door.

"Isn't that Purgatory?" Grace asked, realising that the angel hadn't actually told her they'd arrived. She'd just assumed, due to the red glow and face-looking entrance. It certainly looked purgatorial.

"It is," he said. "But it would be foolish of us to use the front entrance."

"Eh..." Grace had fully intended to do just that. He was probably right, though, now that she thought about it. Discretion was everything. It would, after all, be preferable if no one saw them.

"Alanadiel!" a voice sounded above them, and Grace froze. The voice was too intense to belong to anyone but an angel, and she slowly turned around to look up at the new arrival.

The newcomer landed elegantly beside them and gave Grace a quick bow before he turned his attention towards Blue-Eyes.

Alanadiel, she realised. So much for not knowing his name.

"Heraphesius," Alanadiel said, greeting the newcomer.

"The Second Saviour demands your presence," the other angel said, sending Grace an unreadable look as he did so.

Grace forced herself not to check if the mask was still properly in place. They couldn't afford to be found out.

Then she wondered if perhaps they'd already been. It could hardly be a good sign when a rebellious angel was called to present himself in front of his dictator.

Looking at Alanadiel, Grace tried to figure out what he wanted her to do, but she might as well have tried to read the emotional state of a brick wall. His face was completely impassive.

"I would never let the Second Saviour wait," he said and followed the other angel away without so much as a spare glance at Grace, who was left behind alone.

She fidgeted for a second, unsure of what to do. Should she go to Purgatory herself and get rid of Benjamin? It'd been her job anyway, and the lack of her angel side-kick shouldn't change that. She had to get this done, cheerleader or no cheerleader.

Taking a deep breath, she closed her eyes and asked the apple for the location of the side entrance to Purgatory. Using her new-found knowledge, she followed the mountain wall away from the front entrance for a good five minutes or so before she came to a small door of dark wood. Unlike the main entrance, this one was hardly noticeable against the mountainside. To her great relief, it was unlocked, and she hurried to let herself in before anyone saw her loitering around outside it.

She found herself in a narrow hallway consisting of crude stone, lit by the occasional burning torch. Grace wondered if they had accidentally cut the wire to the electricity, or if IKEA lamps just weren't Hellish enough.

Walking down the hallway, she felt the air grow even hotter, and she noted to herself that — if nothing else — she needn't worry about catching a cold in this new Hell.

Finally, she came to a second door, which had about half an inch of empty space between it and the wall.

Looking out through the crack, Grace saw a pillar of stone a few feet further into the room. The floor was dark and littered with rocks, reminding her of a construction site. She remembered what Alanadiel had said about Purgatory still being under creation, and she realised that in many ways this *was* a construction site. A red glow came from the right side of the room, but she couldn't see what was causing it. Knowing the interior design of this new Hell, however, she could only guess that it came from a very large fire. If there were people in the room, they weren't in front of the small door.

Grace slowly opened the door, slipped out and hurried behind the pillar. It was only then that she realised she'd left the door slightly ajar behind her. With a shrug, she told herself that going back and closing it completely was riskier than merely letting it be. Instead, she leaned forward and glanced out from around the pillar; getting her first view of Purgatory.

Grace wasn't sure how the stories had described Purgatory, but the real thing was a dreadful sight. A large room met her eyes, four pillars on each side holding up the ceiling above them. Rocks lay scattered on the floor, and while the floor itself was smooth and polished, the walls and ceiling still consisted of rough stone. To her left side was the large door Alanadiel had steered her away from, but none of these details were what caused Grace to gape at the sight in front of her.

She'd assumed that the red glow came from a big fire, and she had technically been correct. The wall on her right side didn't consist of dark rock like the other three. Instead, the entirety of it consisted of nothing but flames. Even from where she was standing, she could feel the scorching heat of it against her cheeks, hotter here than in any other place in Hell. The flames were too red to be natural, and they seemed to dance playfully around, almost as if they were alive.

Two white-cloaked men stood not far the dancing flames along with a demon, and Grace gave a start as she recognised Reigh. A crying woman was standing next to him. Her hands were tied in front of her with a thick rope, and a miserable-looking Reigh was holding the other end of it.

Neither of the men wore a mask. One of them was the brown-haired young man she'd fought after their first attempt to contact the angels — the one she'd knocked out with a knife. Due to his (lack of) size, she deemed him to be Benjamin.

The other man wasn't familiar at all: He was of medium height and handsome, with dark hair and olive skin. He was currently writing in a small notebook, a concentrated look upon his features.

"Test subject number four," he said out loud. "Height, 171 centimetres. Weight, 63 kilograms. Of Caucasian descent. Born, 1876. Name, Cornelia Parker." He closed his little book, pulled out a pocket watch and looked at the woman.

"Insert the test subject," he ordered Reigh.

Grace's eyes widened. She shouldn't be surprised that they were planning to put the woman into the fire, but somehow, she still was.

Realising she couldn't just stand around and do nothing, she looked around for something to distract them with. Maybe she could hurry out the way she came, and hammer on the main door before running away. She's seen enough kids do the trick to believe she might just pull it off. She'd figure out her next move then. All she needed was a bit of time.

Reigh pushed the woman towards the fire, and Grace admitted that she didn't have that kind of time. And that it hadn't been that good of a plan. She needed a plan B, and she scrambled through her brain for ideas.

And then Reigh gave the woman a last push, and the fire *reached* out and curled itself around her arms and legs. The woman screamed and stumbled backwards. She fell and landed on the stone floor with a painful thump before she turned around and desperately began to crawl away from the flames, hands still tied in front of her. It was a futile struggle. The woman screamed with fear as the flames pulled her into their depth.

The woman's screams turned into something animalistic and inhuman. She was screaming in the exact same manner that Grace had once heard, back when she'd been twenty-three, and she'd had a young soldier on her stretcher with his right leg blown off. Grace could still vividly remember the exact pitch of his screams.

The woman's screams died out as her form was swallowed by the flames.

The flames were still dancing playfully, almost looking happy to be fed. Reigh still held the end of the rope, which was stretched out and disappeared into the flames. The fire didn't seem to affect the rope at all. It was almost as if it wasn't interested in the physical act of burning.

Grace forced her eyes away from the sight. Instead, she looked at the two men and Reigh. While the unknown man was looking at the flames with a sort of detached interest, Benjamin seemed joyful. His eyes were shining as he looked into the dancing flames. Reigh, however, looked anything but joyful. Tears and snot were streaming down his face, and his loud sobs were echoing through the hall.

"Forty," the unknown man said, nodding at Reigh, who gave the rope a hard tug and pulled the woman out of the flames. She came tumbling out, and immediately Grace saw that something was definitely off with her.

She wasn't screaming any longer. Nor was she sobbing or crying or any of the other things you could expect of someone in her situation. Instead, she almost seemed bored.

She was staring out into the air with an indifferent expression. The unknown man had been scribbling in his little book, and he now looked at the woman with interest.

"What is your name?" he asked her.

The woman didn't react.

The unknown man reached out and snapped his fingers in front of her face. Slowly, the woman looked at him.

"What is your name?" he asked her again.

"My name," the woman murmured, a confused tone in her voice.

"Yes. What is your name?"

The woman was once again staring into the air. The unknown man snapped his fingers until he once again had her attention.

"What is your name?"

"My name." The woman frowned slightly, for the first time showing a hint of emotion. "I don't know," she said.

The man scribbled something in his little book.

"Your name is Beatrice," he told her.

"Beatrice," the woman murmured. "Beatrice." She shook her head slightly. "Beatrice."

"Yes," the man said, his attention focused on his book. "Your name is Beatrice."

"No," the woman murmured.

The man looked up sharply. "What did you say?"

"No," the woman repeated, a bit more strength in her voice.

"Yes, it is."

"No." The woman was shaking her head. "No."

The unknown man sighed and wrote something in his book. "Perhaps we need to recalibrate it," he muttered. "Either that or add to the allotted time frame. However, with the square footage available, and seventy-five thousand new subjects per day, notwithstanding the already substantial waitlist, we cannot allow an unlimited time frame." He frowned, speculatively tapping his pen against the pages of his book. "I suppose we could ask him for a larger area and add to the time. It would certainly be the simplest solution, though perhaps not the most effective in the long run."

Effective in the long run. Grace felt the anger in her grow. They were planning to send every woman and girl through that fire, and they worried about each of them taking *too much time.*

The unknown man looked up at Reigh. "Get the next test subject," he said. "Subject number five. And take this one with you."

Reigh flinched but picked up the woman, nonetheless. She made no move to stop him. She didn't even appear to notice she'd been moved. Reigh left the room with her in his arms, his feet dragging on the floor as he did so.

"Let's just use this one again," Benjamin said.

The other man frowned. "She's been compromised," he said. "The results won't be viable."

"But she needs to be cleansed entirely anyway," Benjamin argued. "Might as well get her done properly. Save ourselves the time."

The other man shook his head. "She'll be sent in again, once we have perfected the procedure. The rigidity of the experiment takes precedence." He looked down in his notebook. "We shall try fifty seconds," he added.

"Why not just use a minute?" Benjamin argued.

The other man frowned. He looked over at the woman. "Perhaps you're right," he said. "There's still a lot of work left. While less emotional than the earlier subjects, she does showcase a lack of amiability. The cleansing of her memory also leaves much to be desired." He shook his head. "No," he said. "I'm a scientist. We shall add the allocated number of seconds to each test subject until we find the ideal time frame. With any luck, we shall be done with the initial experiments by tomorrow. The larger cleansing will have to wait."

The larger cleansing. Grace gnawed on her bottom lip, contemplating his words. That must mean all women. She thought of the woman they'd already pushed in. What had been her name? Cornelia? Cordelia? Grace wondered if she'd had a family. A husband or wife or children. She'd probably had interests. Hobbies. Something she'd been passionate about. Now all gone.

The other man looked at the door. "Where's that demon?" he asked.

"Attention!"

Grace flinched. The shout hadn't come from either Benjamin or the other guy, and for a confusing second, she'd thought someone had snuck up on her. Then she realised that it was Jacob's voice she could hear, seemingly coming from nowhere and everywhere at the same time. Did Hell have an intercom she hadn't heard of?

"The inner circle is called together for an immediate meeting," Jacob said. "Excepting Yuanzhen, who shall remain in his current location."

Silence followed this message, and Grace realised that Jacob had finished speaking. Well, that'd been brief. And inconvenient, since it pretty much made it impossible for her to get rid of Benjamin until after the meeting was over.

The other man shut his book with a sigh. "I suppose we shall resume our experiment later," he said.

Benjamin frowned. "He's always late anyway," he said. "Going through one more test subject won't take more than a couple of minutes, and we would still be at the meeting before him. Whatever this meeting is for, he'll probably be ranting about it to his brother for half an hour before going himself."

The other man laughed softly. "True," he allowed. "Nonetheless, the test subject will still be here when we return. And we cannot let our impatience disrupt the experiment."

Benjamin turned around to look at the dancing flames. "I'm not your assistant," he said. "We're equals in this experiment."

The other man said nothing.

Benjamin turned towards him once again. "I'm staying," he said. "I don't wanna wait around for an hour before he finally deigns to show up. I'll be there in plenty of time anyway."

The other man seemed to consider it. "I do have some notes at the lab, it would be nice to retrieve before going," he mused. "And I would still be there in plenty of time. Looking through them while we wait would certainly be a more productive use of time than staring into the air." He looked over at the main door with a frown. "What is taking that demon so long?" he asked.

"I picked out test number five myself," Benjamin said. "I thought we would be close to finished by now. He might not be so pleased with my choice."

"I hope you haven't asked him to get Lilith," the other man said. "Jacob's orders were very clear. He wants the method perfected before he fixes her." Then he frowned thoughtfully. "Do you think his reluctance might cause him to act slower on an order?" he asked. "That would be a fascinating thought. We shall have to carry out some experiments to see if there's any basis to it."

"It's not Lilith," Benjamin said. "Though I definitely want to be here for that."

Grace breathed a sigh of relief. Lilith was still alive then.

The other man pocketed his notebook. "Do try to come to the meeting before him," he said, ignoring Benjamin's words. "I'd rather not have another fit on my hands."

Benjamin gestured dismissively. "The demon will be back any second now. And the experiment won't take more than a few minutes."

The other man nodded thoughtfully. "Remember to take notes," he said, moving towards the main door. "An experiment is pointless without notes." With these words, he left.

Grace felt her heart pounding in her chest. This was it. This was the moment she'd waited for. They were alone. It was *perfect*. She took a step forward, stepping away from the column.

And then Reigh entered once again.

Grace hurried back behind the column. Looking out at the demon, she felt the air get knocked out of her lungs. There, held in Reigh's arms, was Mei Lien.

She wasn't screaming or fighting against Reigh's hold. Instead, she was speaking to the crying demon; her voice too soft for Grace to hear.

"There you are," Benjamin said. "It's about time you came back. Now hurry up."

Reigh walked the tiniest bit faster, and Grace realised that Jacob must have ordered him to follow his apostles' instructions. That couldn't be good.

Grace stared at the couple, a lump growing in her throat. She couldn't let Reigh push Mei Lien into the flaming wall; she just couldn't.

Resolutely, she looked over at Benjamin once again. She had to subdue him, and then order him to let Mei Lien go. Hopefully, her cloak would pass her off as one of Jacob's apostles.

No. That wouldn't work. She couldn't possibly have time to do all that before the flames had taken hold of Mei Lien. She didn't have the time. She needed a new plan. A better one.

Except, Reigh and Mei Lien were only fifteen feet away from the fiery wall.

She could call out to Mei Lien, ask her for assistance. No, even with the two of them, it was too risky. Benjamin might send a prayer and alert Jacob. She needed something else.

Reigh and Mei Lien were eight feet from the wall.

She needed to subdue Benjamin *before* he called for back-up. She needed to take him by surprise. She needed stealth. Sneakiness. She needed to remain undetected.

Reigh and Mei Lien were now at the wall, and the flames seemed to flicker with anticipation. Reigh was sobbing so hard that his entire body was shaking. He was about to push Mei Lien towards the fire, and Grace was out of time.

She looked around in desperation and grabbed the only thing there was there. A rock by her feet. Two quick steps got her out from behind the pillar, and she threw the rock with all her might.

Too late did she realise that her aim had been off. It was never going to hit Benjamin, and Grace frantically searched her brain for a plan B.

And then the rock hit Reigh squarely in the head, and he stumbled, causing Mei Lien to tumble from his arms and down to the floor. She didn't hesitate but scrambled backwards to get away from the reach of the flames.

Slowly, with a more stunned expression than anything, Reigh reached up and touched his temple where the rock had hit him. His fingers came back bloody as he held them in front of his face. He then turned his eyes inside out and passed out.

Oh. Well, that turned out better than expected. Reigh really did look tougher than he was.

Benjamin looked at the unconscious demon with disbelief before he looked up in the direction the rock had come from. Spotting Grace in her white cloak, his confusion only grew.

He walked towards her, and Grace scrambled in her pocket for the sleeping draught, wishing she'd had the foresight to have already put it on the piece of cloth.

Keeping her head held high, she hoped that Benjamin's confusion would buy her enough time. Uncorking the bottle with one hand while never taking it out of the pocket was challenging but doable. It did, however, take far too long. Benjamin was only a few steps away from her when she succeeded. She turned the bottle in her pocket and felt the liquid slosh out, thoroughly drenching the piece of cloth. Benjamin was in front of her now, and with a pounding heart, Grace's hand closed around the piece of fabric. She was ready to slap it across Benjamin's face before he'd had time to realise what had happened.

"What do you think you're doing?" Benjamin demanded to know, and Grace knew that this was her one chance.

With one smooth movement, she pulled the piece of cloth from her pocket and thrust it towards Benjamin's face. He gave a startled yell and grabbed Grace's wrist.

Time seemed to stand still. For one long second, Grace could only stare at her arm, held tightly in Benjamin's grip. Then she came to her senses and pulled with all her might. Benjamin, however, held on.

He still had a confused look upon his face, and with his other hand, he reached out and tore her mask off, eyes widening in surprise as he saw the woman hiding underneath it.

Slowly, his confusion gave way to anger; a burning fury that twisted his features until they were almost unrecognisable.

"*You!*"

Grace took a deep breath, readying herself to kick him as hard as she could. She still hadn't let go of the soaked piece of cloth in her hand, and Benjamin wasn't a big man. As long as he didn't call for help, she stood an honest chance. Glancing around, she noted which weapons could be found around her (rocks). She was going to win this fight.

Then Grace felt cold steel press against her abdomen. Her eyes darted back to the man in front of her. She realised it was a knife she felt pressed against the bare skin of her stomach — a knife that had sliced through the fabric of her cloak and shirt as if they weren't even there.

"I remember you," Benjamin said, fury burning in his eyes. He was armed with a dagger, and she was armed with a sleeping draught. All he had to do was to move a few inches, and that'd be it.

"Well, fudge," she whispered, mind frantically searching for a way to save her life and coming up short.

"Drop it!" Benjamin hissed at her. "Now."

Grace let go of the piece of cloth, and it fell uselessly to the floor.

"Good," Benjamin said. He spun her around and pressed the knife against her throat. His other hand grabbed both of Grace's arms and forced them behind her back before he started to push her towards Purgatory.

It was a slow process. Grace couldn't get herself free with a knife pressed against her throat, but Benjamin wasn't a strong man. She could still slow them down considerably.

Not that it helped much. They were now only a couple of feet away from the fire. The heat was almost unbearable, and sweat was trickling down her face and back. Each breath seemed heavier than the last. In front of her, the dancing flames were reaching towards her, brushing ever so slightly against whatever skin they could reach. Surprisingly enough, it didn't hurt, but her skin tingled wherever they touched her. It was almost like a gentle caress, luring her in. She wondered when exactly they would start to hurt.

She looked away from the flames and twisted around to look at Benjamin's face. He looked joyful as he was staring at her with the dancing flames at her back.

Taking a deep breath, Grace got ready to kick him with every ounce of strength in her body. She wasn't going in there. She would rather take her chances with the knife.

And then a figure showed up behind Benjamin. Mei Lien. Grace had completely forgotten about her. For half a second their eyes met, and then Mei Lien lifted a rock and hit Benjamin in the back of the head.

With a groan, he dropped to his knees. Unlike Reigh, however, Benjamin didn't fall unconscious. Already, he was struggling to his feet.

Grace launched herself at him and tore the knife out of his hand before she sent it flying across the floor with a flick of her wrist. Frantically, she turned the pocket in her cloak inside out. It was soaked in the sleeping draught and would serve as an excellent replacement for the cloth. She felt triumph well up in her. And then Benjamin's hand closed around a rock, and he turned around and swung it at her.

Grace threw herself backwards. A flame took hold of a lock of her hair, and Grace tore it out of its grip. Another inch or two further back, and the flames would pull her in. She looked at Benjamin with a wary expression, realising that she'd just thrown away a perfectly good weapon. Mei Lien was on the other side of Benjamin. Her ally was still holding the rock, but Grace would have preferred it if the delicately built woman had held a weapon with a little more oomph.

They needed Benjamin unconscious before he remembered that he could just call for angelic help. Unless he already had?

"Benjamin," she said, meaning to distract him. She could feel the heat of the flames as they were reaching out for her.

"How did you get here?" he demanded to know. His hand tightened around the rock until his knuckles turned white. "We killed you."

Grace shrugged nonchalantly, doing her best to emulate Samael. He seemed to have a gift for pissing people off, and Grace wanted Benjamin angry. Angry people didn't think straight, and she couldn't risk him starting to think about his options. He had far too many of them.

"I walked," she said.

Benjamin inhaled sharply. "You—!" His eyes glittered with rage. "It will be a pleasure to improve you," he said. "The perfect girl."

Grace shrugged again. "Well, I think it takes far more than a bit of fire to make you the perfect man," she said calmly. "Or even a man at all. I can recognise a lost cause when I see one."

For a long moment, Benjamin only stared at her in incredulity. Then he shrieked in fury and charged at her.

Grace yelped and threw herself to the side, watching in disbelief as Benjamin found himself unable to stop his momentum. He stumbled past her, and Grace felt her mouth pop open as the flames got hold of him and pulled him towards them.

Benjamin screamed, reaching out towards Grace. She took a step backwards. Was he asking her to save him or hoping to take her with him? She hesitated, and the moment was over. The flames had pulled Benjamin completely into the fire, and she could see the shape of him writhing in pain as his screams echoed throughout the hall.

Forcing her eyes away, Grace stumbled backwards; away from the flames.

"Are you okay?" Mei Lien asked her.

Grace looked over at the other woman.

"Yeah," she said. "I think so." She looked over at the flames. She could no longer see the shape of Benjamin, and her stomach did an unpleasant flip. Grace had been the one who had riled him up. She felt nauseous.

She hadn't known that he would run directly into them, she reminded herself. She'd just meant for him to make mistakes, which would make it possible for her to somehow knock him out. Besides, they'd needed to get rid of him. The life (or death, technically) of countless people depended on it. And he was just one man. One malicious, spiteful man. And yet Grace's eyes continuously strayed towards the flames. She felt as if there was a little ball of lead in the bottom of her stomach.

She wondered what would happen to him without a demon to pull him out. Would he be in there forever? He wasn't screaming any longer. Was he still in pain?

She realised that Mei Lien was talking to her and forced herself to focus on the other woman.

"I'm sorry, what?"

"What are you doing here?" Mei Lien asked. "How come you aren't with the rest?"

"What? Oh, Jacob killed me. Or, Jacob had Samael kill me, and I spent a bit of time in Limbo. Then Limbo got full of holes, and now I'm here."

"But… they always find the people who escape. Always."

"Oh, they're not actually looking. Jacob kind of… forgot about me," Grace said. "Since I'd been supposed to be in Hell, but wasn't… it was quite confusing." She gave a shaky laugh. "Who'd have known I'd end up grateful for bureaucracy?" She looked towards the flames, straining her eyes for a glimpse of Benjamin. "I'll take back the Voice of God," she said. "Do you want to join me?"

Mei Lien shook her head. "No," she said. "They're going to look for me, and they're going to find me. It's better if you're not dragged down with me."

Grace was about to argue. Then she saw the wisdom in what Mei Lien was saying. If they could really find people that easily, it'd be better if they weren't looking for her.

"How long do you think you can evade them?" she asked, looking at the flaming wall. There could be no doubt that they were going to throw Mei Lien in there, once they found her. Perhaps she *should* insist they go together.

"I don't know," Mei Lien admitted. "In the confusion about what happened, it might be a while before they remember me and start looking."

"We should go together," Grace said. "If they find you… they're going to put you in there."

Mei Lien shook her head. "Absolutely not," she said. "You're going to fix this, and you won't be able to do that if I lead them straight to you. The best thing you can do for me is to fix this mess. So go. Stay safe."

Grace hesitated. Then she nodded resolutely. "I will," she promised. Her eyes fell on Reigh. "I'll just give him a quick check first," she said, kneeling down next to his unconscious form.

Mei Lien shook her head. To Grace's surprise, she was

smiling ever so slightly. "Don't bother," she said. "You'd be surprised by the amount of times Reigh has bumped his head into something and passed out. He's not good with blood."

Grace smiled, but couldn't resist the temptation to give his pulse a quick check before she stood once again. "I'll leave then," she said and sent one last look at Purgatory before she left it behind.

Or she would have, if Benjamin hadn't stumbled out of it.

Mei Lien gasped, and Grace readied herself for battle. Then she realised that there was no reason to do so. Benjamin's body might have come out of the fire, but his mind had been left behind.

His eyes were entirely glassed over, and he was staring emptily into the air. A bit of drool trickled down his chin.

Grace took a step forward.

"Benjamin?" she said. "Are you still... can you hear me?"

Benjamin slowly opened his mouth. A small bubble of spit formed before it burst against his lips, followed by another and then another.

Grace looked at him in silence. She'd contributed to that. She wondered if his mind (his soul?) was still burning inside the fire or if it had been obliterated for good. Whichever it was, the same fate awaited countless women if Grace didn't pull herself together.

She looked over at Mei Lien. "We need to hide him," she said.

"I'll do that," she said. "You just leave. It's only a matter of time before they finish that... *thing*, and you need to get our Hell back before then."

Grace nodded. Then she took one last look at Benjamin before she forced herself to turn away and go pick up her mask. Mei Lien was right. She needed to fix this, and she needed to do it fast.

CHAPTER NINETEEN:

The Meeting

Having decided that she needed to make sure that "Benjamin" came to the meeting, Grace made her way back to the palace. The meeting should give her information if nothing else. And with any luck, Daniel might be brought there as well. And she might end up alone with him and Jacob. Smiling slightly, Grace admitted that she probably wouldn't get that lucky.

Having made her way down the blackened road leading to the palace, she stopped. On each side of her were burnt-down houses, and they looked oddly familiar. She and Alanadiel had walked this same road on their way to Purgatory, but she'd been too busy pestering him with questions to notice much of the details. Frowning, Grace resumed walking, looking around for something recognisable.

Suddenly, an image flashed before her. Dandelions growing in the cracks of the street, and demons and humans intermingling. This was the street she'd walked down with Samael on her first day in Hell. It was now utterly deserted, and the charred remains of the houses stuck up from the ground like twisted, black teeth.

A similar French village flashed before Grace's eyes, and nausea overcame her. The metallic scent of blood filled her nostrils, and an uncomfortable pressure settled on her chest. She saw stretcher after stretcher of dead boys, but it was a shattered image, several pieces to multiple puzzles. And yet she saw them again and again, a horrific carrousel spinning around in her head.

There didn't seem to be enough oxygen in the air around her, and so she forced herself to take a deep breath and hold it for several seconds. With shivering hands, she smoothed down the fabric of her shirt, focusing on how different the texture was from her nurse's uniform. She slowly released her breath and took another one as she looked at the village around her. This wasn't France, and she forced herself to list all the ways in which it wasn't, whether it was the broken street sign written in Demoniac or the obvious lack of sky above her.

Slowly, the images disappeared, but Grace carefully kept at her list as she once again made her way toward the palace.

Once there, Grace entered through the grand entrance door, ignoring the two angels standing on each side of it. They paid her no attention beyond a quick glance at her white cloak, and Grace felt her spirits rise. She walked down dark, bejewelled hallways, occasionally asking the apple for directions.

The palace was mostly deserted but every once in a while she'd walk past someone wearing a grey cloak. They usually ignored her, except a short bow in her direction, which she answered with a polite nod. Thankfully, no one stopped to chat.

Finally having made her way to the meeting room, Grace took a deep breath and opened the door. Three bare faces and one masked one turned in her direction, and Grace blinked in surprise. She'd expected ten people in here, if not eleven, depending on whether Jacob had shown up yet. She wondered if everyone had decided to take their time the same way Benjamin had. The other man from Purgatory had said that he'd stop by to get some papers before going. He had, however, still made it there before Grace.

"Benjamin!" he said eagerly. "Any success with the experiment?"

Grace shook her head, hoping that he didn't find "Benjamin's" lack of verbal response odd. She made her way into the room and promptly sat down in an empty seat, keeping her head down as she did so. This idea had seemed better when she hadn't been in the middle of it. Surely, someone would recognise that she wasn't Benjamin?

They didn't. Instead, they talked over and around her, not a single one appearing to notice that Benjamin was entirely mute. Slowly, Grace's heart returned to a more normal rate, and, with a deep breath, she looked up and studied the men around her.

Directly across from her sat an elderly man with an impressive mane of white hair. He was impatiently drumming his fingers against the table, a frown marring his features.

Next to him sat someone wearing one of the Dan-masks, but with the hood of the cloak pulled back. The man was black-haired, and his cloak was splattered with specks of blood.

On her left side sat the man she'd seen in Purgatory. He was even more handsome up close. Beautiful really, with soulful, brown eyes. He looked like someone you expected to write poetry; not push women into a torturous fire.

On her right side sat a blonde man. His mask lay on the table in front of him, and he sat perfectly still. He might as well have been a statue. Suddenly, he turned his face and looked at Grace.

"Did you meet any of the others on the way?" he asked.

Grace shook her head.

The white-haired man leaned back in his chair. "I'm sure they'll be here in time," he said. "It'll probably be a while before Jacob arrives. And Reginald, of course, will arrive with him."

The man from Purgatory laughed. "He certainly will," he said. "His loyal dog. It wouldn't surprise me if he slept outside his door at night."

"Don't laugh, Alessandro," the blonde man said.

"Why ever not, Nicolas?" The man from Purgatory — Alessandro — asked with a provocative smile. "We all know where the dog is."

"Don't let the Second Saviour hear you speak thus."

Alessandro shrugged. "What he doesn't know, won't hurt me," he said. "It's not like he has punished you."

The blonde man — Nicolas — frowned. "And why should he punish me?" he asked.

Alessandro's grin only widened. "Well, he wouldn't be pleased with your comments about the masks." He looked down at his own, which was currently left abandoned on the table. "Though I'll admit that I'm not fond of wearing *his* face either."

The man with the bloodstained cloak turned his head and looked at him. Slowly, he took off his mask. The face underneath it looked tired and worn, like he needed a good hug and a cup of hot tea.

"It's not like we have much of a choice," he said.

Alessandro snorted. "I'd say. Did you know, he actually called me Dan the other day?"

"Perhaps we shouldn't talk of this," the white-haired man said. "We don't want to be overheard. He certainly wasn't pleased when I asked when we were going to Heaven."

"When *are* we going to Heaven?" Alessandro complained. "Why leave Limbo for Hell when we could leave it for Heaven?"

"He's scared," the man in the bloodstained cloak said.

"Of what?" Alessandro asked. "God?" He scoffed.

The man in the bloodstained cloak merely shook his head before he put on his Dan-mask once again.

"Of not being welcomed," the white-haired man said. "He wants them to welcome him, and he knows that they won't."

Alessandro frowned. "It's no reason to keep the rest of us down here! Do you know the kind of research I could get done in *Heaven?!*" He gestured wildly with his hands. "I could be the first man who understands the soul. But no! Because he's *scared*. And how long are we supposed to wait for him? I would like to return to my experiments, even if I can only do them here in Hell."

"We all know why Cecil isn't here yet," the white-haired man said. "James and Tegbessou are with the angels. I met James on the way. He said they were forming a search team."

"Searching for what?" Alessandro asked, leaning forward.

The white-haired man shrugged. "He didn't say. Did you hear anything, Patrick?"

The man in the bloodstained cloak — Patrick — shook his head.

"And Yuanzhen?" Alessandro asked. "Why isn't he coming?"

"I've ordered him to remain where he is," a familiar voice answered from the door.

Grace took a deep breath. It would have been impossible to forget the voice who'd ordered her best friend to kill her, and so Grace was prepared when she turned her face and looked directly up at Jacob.

He was entering the room with an angel and an unknown masked man. Around Grace, everyone else got to their feet, and Grace hurried to do the same. They all remained standing as the trio made their way to the middle of the room, and Jacob sat down. Grace was about to sit as well but caught herself at the last moment when no one else did so. Then Jacob made a gesture with his hand, and everyone sat down, Grace half a second after the others.

If things continued in this rate, she'd need a miracle to remain undiscovered.

The man, who'd followed Jacob in, leaned forward and whispered something in his ear.

Jacob nodded, and the masked man hurried out of the room. Grace noted that the others seemed surprised, though no one said anything. The angel remained standing, and Grace took the opportunity to look him over, once her eyes had gotten used to his light. He was handsome with silver hair and skin the exact colour of a starless night sky. There was a burning rage in his eyes, and Grace wondered whom he was angry at. Jacob, hopefully.

For several long seconds, no one said anything.

"Where are the others?" Jacob demanded to know.

The blonde man — wasn't he called Nicolas? — cleared his throat. "They've been delayed," he said.

Jacob's jaw tightened. "Delayed," he repeated. "I thought I'd said this meeting was important."

Nicolas fell silent.

"You did," the white-haired man agreed. "I'm sure that they've strived to be here as quickly as they can, but Hell is a large kingdom. It might take a while to come to the palace, even if they do everything in their power to fulfil your order."

Grace smiled underneath her mask. Alessandro and Benjamin sure hadn't seemed to strive all that hard.

Jacob relaxed. "I suppose that's true," he said. "But they need to be here."

"What has happened?" Alessandro asked.

Jacob leaned back in his seat and rubbed his temples.

"Alanadiel has betrayed us," he said.

Grace started. They'd learned about Alanadiel. If he'd been forced to tell Jacob about her, there'd be Hell to pay for both of them. Literally.

"One of the *angels?*" the white-haired man asked.

"No," Jacob said. "He wasn't an angel."

A surprised murmur went through the room, and Grace lifted a doubtful eyebrow. Not an angel? Alanadiel with the intense voice, the frightening aura, and the utter lack of humour? He was the very epitome of an angel.

"He wasn't?" the white-haired man asked, having apparently thought the same.

"Angels are *good,*" Jacob said. "He was a demon." He made a disgusted face. "He must have laughed at us behind our backs."

Jacob's hand was trembling as he slowly lowered the Voice of God on the table. "He thinks I'm... *we're* stupid," he said, voice brimming with anger. He looked stiffly into the air, not meeting the eyes of any of his followers. "But just because he can't hear my orders, doesn't mean that he'll get away! I've sent the angels after him, and I'll make sure they get him!"

Grace struggled to remain silent as she realised what this meant. Not only had Alanadiel escaped, but, apparently, the

Voice of God only worked if the demon or angel in question could *hear* the speaker. With enough noise, the Voice would be virtually worthless. A stick, only useful as a weapon if you stabbed someone in the eye.

"Is it wise?" the white-haired man asked. "To send out the angels to search for ano— a demon disguised as one? Shouldn't we... think this through?"

"Are you saying I haven't, Immanuel?" Jacob asked.

The white-haired man — Immanuel — frowned. "Of course not, my Saviour," he said. "However, we can't act insensibly. There might be other angels, who are... disguised demons."

"There are not," Jacob said. "I have ordered any of them to step forward if they were truly a demon. No one did."

"Perhaps someone did," Alessandro said, a grin stretched across his face. "It was just a minuscule step that was hardly noticeable."

Jacob turned his eyes towards him. "Are you trying to be funny?"

"Of course not, my Saviour."

"But Alessandro may have a point," Immanuel said. "We must think things through. Expect the worst. Be sensible."

"What could be more sensible than what I'm doing?!" Jacob demanded to know, jumping to his feet.

"We just need to think it through."

"So you're saying I'm not thinking?!"

"Of course not," the blonde man — Nicolas — said. "You were the one who saw how senseless the worlds were."

Slowly, Jacob sat down again. "Yes," he said. "I was." He leaned forward and put his face in his hands. "I'm being sensible," he murmured.

"What about the walls?" Immanuel asked.

"I have rebuilt them," Jacob said. "People are now being sent to where they belong. Heaven, Hell, or Purgatory."

"And what of... that place?" Nicolas asked.

Around the table, people stiffened.

"It's gone," Jacob said.

"You have destroyed it?" Alessandro asked, cautious excitement in his voice.

"I have closed it off," Jacob said.

"Closed it off?" Nicolas asked. "But you were going to destroy it! You said—"

"Shut up!" Jacob said. "I have closed it off. That's how it'll be. It can't be destroyed."

"Maybe it could!" Nicolas argued. "If you just—"

"*I said it can't!*"

Nicolas fell silent.

"Perhaps," Immanuel said carefully. "Perhaps if you would spend a little less time on your brother, you would have more time to discover how it could be done."

Jacob slowly turned towards him. "What did you say?"

Immanuel avoided his eyes, but spoke, nonetheless. "You are ruling a world, my Saviour," he said. "But you spend most of your time with your brother, trying to convince him that—"

"I'm trying to *save him!* We need him!"

"No one else is offered that salvation," Patrick said, anger clear in his voice. "Why is your brother?!"

"Because I said so! I saved you, and now you listen to me!" He lifted the Voice of God. "*Does anyone have a problem with that?*"

Immanuel looked down. "No, my Saviour," he murmured.

"Does anyone else?"

No one met his eyes. "No, my Saviour," they murmured. Grace hurried to do the same. She noticed, however, that none of them looked particularly pleased.

Beside her, Alessandro was drumming his fingers against the table, Nicolas and Immanuel were both sitting with slightly displeased looks, and though she couldn't see the expression of Patrick, Grace still remembered the anger in his voice.

It seemed that Jacob's apostles weren't as loyal as she'd assumed.

She considered it. Was there any way to use that to her advantage? Would they support her or Jacob, if she revealed herself to them?

They would support Jacob, she admitted to herself. He might not be the leader they'd hoped for, but he was still their only option. After everything they'd done, they would have to realise that they'd be severely punished for their part in this travesty if Jacob failed. Even if Lucifer somehow agreed not to punish them, they would still be sent back to Limbo. And she understood better than most why no one would ever want to go back there.

She snapped back to the conversation when she suddenly heard Lucifer's name mentioned. It seemed the room had relaxed slightly, though Jacob continuously fidgeted with the Voice.

"Foolish," Immanuel said.

"No one said the Devil was anything but," Nicolas reminded him.

Grace strongly disagreed. She was actually quite certain that she had once heard the exact opposite. How did that saying go? The Devil is no fool?

"We must have overlooked something," Immanuel said. "He couldn't possibly have thought that he could have won. Weak humans against angels and demons? It doesn't make sense."

"He did try to rebel against God," Nicolas noted. "It's not the first time he's fought a war that he couldn't possibly win."

"He's a fool," Jacob said, his voice cutting through the room. "There's nothing special about the Devil. And I refuse to treat him as if there were!"

Grace rather thought that locking him in a tower was treating him like he was special. If anyone else thought the same, they said nothing about it.

"He's dangerous," Immanuel said instead. "Is it safe to keep him here?"

"He's harmless," Jacob said and held the Voice of God up in order to examine it. "I have absolute control over him. One order, and he was blabbering away. Disloyal."

Grace found that to be a somewhat unfair assessment. It couldn't possibly count as a lack of loyalty when you were magically forced to do it.

"Are we sure that it's over, though?" Immanuel asked. "He's the Devil. Cowardly or not, he's sly."

"I'm sure," Jacob said. "The riot he'd planned for was *pathetic*." He smiled; a fragile, forced smile. "I forced him to give me the name of every general he had ordered around, every scout he had used. None of them will be able to help him again. Ever."

"Do you know if he had some other plan?" Immanuel asked. "You can't expect the Devil to only have the one."

"I ordered him to tell me if anyone contacted him again," Jacob said. "And I told him not to lie. That's what we're making here! A world without lies!" Jacob tightened his hand on the Voice until his knuckles turned white. "This is *my* Hell now!"

"Yes, of course," Nicolas said.

Jacob inhaled deeply before he exhaled once again, and Grace recognised a standard breathing exercise. Jacob was trying to calm himself down.

"And in my Hell, things will make sense," he said.

Around the table, people were muttering their agreements, all avoiding Jacob's gaze. Jacob took another few, deep breaths.

"Yes," he said, voice overly moderate. "The true Hell."

It had nothing to do with what Grace considered the true Hell, and she sure liked *her* version a whole lot better.

But she had other things to focus on. Lucifer wasn't giving up his Hell without a fight, but whatever he'd planned had clearly failed. Still, it was nice to know that she wasn't the only one fighting. Especially now that Alanadiel had been forced to flee.

And Jacob was definitely obsessed with his brother. Which meant that if she found Daniel, Jacob would be sure to show up sooner or later, giving her the very opportunity she was waiting for. Both brothers in the same room.

"It's still early," Immanuel said, and Grace focused back on the conversation. Jacob seemed displeased once again, and Grace was starting to see a pattern.

"It isn't," he answered. "We promised we would fix the inconsistencies and this... lack of information is one of the biggest ones."

"I understand," Immanuel said. "However, it would be wise to allow Hell and Heaven to settle before we focus on Earth."

"It's a travesty," Jacob bit out. "People don't know the rules and can only guess what they are. Some of them don't even know there are rules! What use are they if they don't know what they are? I'm sending the angels to inform them once they've captured the traitor, and *that's final!*"

"Have the new rules been finished, my Saviour?" Nicolas asked.

"They're finished," Jacob said. "We merely need to distribute them. *The Saviour's words are a guiding light through the darkness.* This is the future we're creating. A clear path through the darkness of uncertainty and loneliness."

A sound came from next to Grace, and she glanced over at Alessandro. Had he just snickered? When she looked at him, his expression was neutral enough, though his eyes were shining with amusement.

"How many rules have we added?" he asked. "To create this... path of light?"

"815," Jacob said proudly.

"Do we really need that many?" Nicolas asked.

"*Yes!*" Jacob said. "We're building worlds that make *sense!* We need rules for this. We all know this. I've told you so! Unless someone here doesn't think that I'm right?" He looked around the table.

Silence.

"Good," Jacob said. "Now let's go over the current rules."

Grace was eighty percent certain she hadn't imagined the light groan from Alessandro. She certainly felt that way herself. She was on a tight schedule, and it looked like she was about to waste hours of it.

Gosh dangit.

CHAPTER TWENTY:

Jacob's Obsession

When the meeting (finally) ended and everyone hurried out, Grace thought it wise to do the same. She felt like she was back in middle school, and all the students were rushing out of the classroom, scared the teacher would call them back.

The other apostles had eventually arrived, all offering apologies for their tardiness. Some of their excuses sounded rather implausible, and Grace couldn't help but think that they all wished they'd arrived even later.

It turned out that it took quite a while to go through 815 rules. The meeting had ended with Jacob's right-side angel leaning forward and telling him that they hadn't been able to locate Alanadiel. It was believed that someone might be harbouring him, and Jacob had slammed his fist into the table, only to immediately (and obviously) regret it. It did tend to hurt when you decided to hit something made of marble.

Finally, they'd been allowed to leave, and Grace had hurried out along with the others, taking care to keep her head down.

A few questions to the apple gave her the location of Daniel, and Grace hurried through the hallways. With any luck, she would get to him before Jacob arrived and she would be able to tell him about her plan.

Daniel was kept in the centre of the palace, and a little, odd part of Grace was somewhat disappointed that he wasn't kept in the tallest room in the tallest tower. It would have been reassuring somehow. After all, the knight in shining armour always won in the end.

Instead, Daniel was kept in a room at ground level. There was nothing extraordinary about the hallway nor the door leading into the room, and Grace hesitated in front of it. What if

Daniel weren't alone?

A few silent questions to the apple led her to the unfortunate conclusion that there were no secret entrances into the room, nor any windows to climb through. Jacob, however, was not in there either, which lowered the risk dramatically.

"C'est la Mort," Grace murmured to herself. Then she took a deep breath, checked her mask one last time, and opened the door.

For half a second, she was sure she'd gotten the room wrong, apple or not. Daniel should have been kept in a dungeon: Chains hanging from the ceiling and a rat scattering across the bare stone floor. Sure, it would be a ground floor dungeon, but a dungeon, nonetheless. She shouldn't find him in a medium-sized living room that was decorated in a calming (if somewhat outdated) dusty green. Not that she could see him anywhere.

The room was utterly deserted, and she walked around among the couches and sitting tables in a sort of haze. Bowls of pomegranates and peaches were placed around the room, and a large painting on the wall portrayed a group of young ladies out for a stroll in Victorian London. It was a lovely room, and it had absolutely nothing to do with a dungeon. Especially considering that the expected prisoner was nowhere to be seen.

And then she heard a voice. Grace looked around the empty room in confusion. Finally, she noted a pair of drawn curtains on the wall furthest from the door. As she already knew the room had no windows, the curtains had to cover something else, and a quick question to the apple assured her that Daniel could be found on the other side.

She walked over and pulled one of the curtains an inch or so to the side. She'd expected to see Daniel (and possibly a rat scattering across a bare stone floor). Instead, she saw a small sitting room and Samael. He wasn't tied up or restrained in any way, but he probably didn't have to be. Grace had seen first-hand how little free will demons had against the power of the Voice.

The shapeshifter was currently pacing the small room, looking so angry and impatient and *Samael* that she could almost pretend that the last few days hadn't happened.

But they had, and she couldn't let the shapeshifter see her.

It would have been a lot easier if she'd known what Jacob's orders to him had been. *Stay here and make sure my brother doesn't leave?* With that kind of order, Grace could start a fire to smoke them out, and all she'd get was two dead friends. She needed to think this through.

And then she heard the door behind her open.

Not giving herself time to think, she stumbled through the curtains and into the room, falling over her own feet as she did so and landing on all four. She looked up, hoping against all common sense that Samael had somehow not seen her.

He was staring at her fallen form, mouth slightly ajar.

He didn't know it was her, she reminded herself. She still looked like someone from the inner circle. He might just leave her alone.

"Grace?" Samael asked.

Well, that couldn't be good. But considering that she could hear steps coming from the other side of the curtains, she might have more pressing concerns.

Scrambling to her feet, Grace looked frantically around the small room. Two comfortable-looking armchairs and a small side table were placed in front of a large fireplace. There was a bookcase, a chest (which she definitely did not have time to empty and hide in) and three green pillars lining each side of the room. The curtains she'd fallen through covered the entirety of the entrance wall, and Grace wasted a second trying to decide whether to hide behind the curtains or the pillars. The curtains were thick and heavy, and she would simply have to keep her feet from poking out at the bottom.

Looking back at Samael, she wondered wildly what orders he'd received. She just had to take a chance and hope for the best.

She put a finger up to the mask's mouth and saw Samael's eyes grow comically large. She then hurried towards the curtains, only to have Samael grab her arm and yank her back, slapping his other hand across her mouth.

She didn't even have time to despair before he dragged her to the pillars on the left side of the room. Evidently, he was going to hide her behind one of them, and Grace felt relief well up in her.

And then he pushed her *into* the pillar, which absorbed her with no more difficulty than a sponge would absorb water. Grace felt her mouth pop open. She could still see the living room clearly, and as she reached out, she felt cold stone against her fingertips, despite the fact that nothing seemed to be there. An invisible pillar? Why would anyone have an invisible pillar? To hide treasures in? No, she realised. To put people in. A prison. What was it Reigh had said, once upon a time? Something about Lucifer not even pillaring people any more.

It was certainly practical if all you wanted was a bit of peace and quiet. Samael had effectively locked her up, and she wondered if she could bluff her way out once Jacob entered. Keep her voice low and say the demon had trapped her?

Samael wasn't even looking at her. Instead, he looked at the pillar next to hers.

Jacob entered the sitting room followed by his walkie-talkie angel, and Grace waited for him to realise that she was there. He never did. Instead, he threw himself in the chair closest to Grace and sprawled out in it. He looked exhausted. The angel stood behind Jacob's chair, looking into the air with an expressionless face and eyes burning with rage.

They couldn't possibly have avoided seeing Grace. Unless... unless they couldn't see through the pillar. If that was true, Samael hadn't captured her. He'd hidden her. And quite effectively at that.

Jacob lifted his head from the back of the chair and looked

around the room, proving her theory as his eyes ran past her without a moment's pause. Instead, they lingered on the pillar next to hers, and Grace had a growing suspicion as to what or whom it was hiding. The apple had said that Daniel was in here.

Silence stretched out into the room, and Grace did her best to breathe without sound. Did she even need to breathe? She was dead, wasn't she? Maybe it was just an old habit. Experimentally, she held her breath.

"Anything to report?" Jacob asked Samael.

Samael didn't as much as glance at Grace's hiding spot. "There has been a white-cloak here," he said, his face carefully blank.

"One of my apostles?" Jacob sounded surprised but not overly worried. "Cecil, I presume?"

"No. I don't know all their names though. A dark-haired one."

Jacob opened his eyes and glared at him. "Didn't you think to ask?!"

Samael shrugged.

Jacob sighed. "Well, how long ago was it?"

"Sometime after Cecil left but before you came back."

"That's not very specific," Jacob said, clearly annoyed.

Samael shrugged again. "I'm not counting the seconds," he said. "And it's not like you've left a clock behind. You just told me to stay in here and make sure Daniel didn't go anywhere. After you told me I wasn't allowed to hurt any of your followers. And when I pointed out I might not know who your followers were, you told me not to hurt anyone wearing one of the white or grey cloaks. And to hand over any human not wearing either. Except you, apparently. And then you told me not to lie. You sure do give a lot of orders."

He wasn't telling Jacob, Grace realised. He was telling her. If she lost her white cloak, he'd have to hand her over.

Jacob sent the shapeshifter a sour look. "Never mind," he

said. "I'll ask them during the next meeting." He gestured towards the pillars. "Pull him out of there."

Samael went to the pillar next to Grace's, and she watched in fascination as his arm went through it and pulled out an unconscious Daniel.

Jacob pointed at the chair next to his, and Samael placed the unconscious form in it.

"Wake him," Jacob ordered the angel behind him.

The angel looked at Daniel, who groaned and opened his eyes. Slowly, they focused on his brother.

"Move behind him," Jacob ordered Samael.

Samael moved to stand behind Daniel's chair.

Seconds stretched by as Daniel looked at his brother.

Jacob's expression was unreadable. "Still with the silent treatment?" he asked.

"I'm not giving you the *silent treatment!*" Daniel said. "Jake, you've gone too far this time! Just... put it back the way it was."

"The way it was," Jacob repeated. "The way it was?! It was broken! Horrible, twisted, sick, and I'm the one who's *fixing it!*" He took a deep breath, appearing to calm himself down. "You must be able to see it, Dan," he said. "The hypocrisy of it all. Limbo. The guidelines for getting into Heaven. Nothing was clearly stated. Getting into God's so-called Paradise was a question of luck rather than morality. But I've changed things. They make *sense* now!"

For several seconds, Daniel only stared at his brother. When he spoke again, his voice was calm and quiet. "I know that you think that, Jake. I do. And we can fix what is wrong with the worlds. Come on, Jake. But this isn't fixing it. You're just... making it worse."

"Worse?" Jacob repeated with a half-strangled sound. "Changes require sacrifice, Dan."

"People are suffering, Jake. *Innocent* people."

Jacob snorted. "They're hardly innocent. And what else

could I have done? Nothing? What if Lincoln had shied away from a bit of conflict? Slavery would still be thriving. You must see reason here, Dan. In the real world, change doesn't just happen."

"But you *brought back* slavery, Jake."

Jacob rolled his eyes. "They're demons, Dan. They hardly count."

"They do. And even if they didn't, you've hurt people. Innocent people. Friends of mine."

Jacob sighed. "You're still thinking about the girl?"

Daniel's hands tightened into fists. "You killed her, Jake!"

"I got rid of her," Jacob said impatiently. "She was clouding your judgment. Just like that other one did."

"April?! She wasn't *clouding my judgment*, Jake."

"She did! She tricked you into giving up your ministry and then she just left! And this one is even worse! Hanging out with demons! She was *sent to Hell*, Dan! And when I got rid of her, you just kept going on about how I shouldn't have. Your infatuation kept you from seeing sense, and it would only have grown worse if I'd kept her around. I did it for you, Dan."

"I wasn't infatuated! We were friends. And you just... killed her off like she didn't matter. Do you even know what happened to her, Jake?"

Jacob stood up and turned around to face Grace's pillar.

Gulping, she wondered if he'd figured it out. Then she realised that he'd merely turned his back on his brother.

"It doesn't matter," he said.

"You don't," Daniel concluded. "And you don't care either. Don't care that you killed someone. Jake, this isn't... I can't do this any more."

Jacob turned around to face his brother once again. "You can't... What are you talking about? You can't what?"

"I can't do *this*. Making up excuses. Fixing things. I can't fix it this time, Jake. You just... you went too far. I'm *done*."

"I... I don't..." For several seconds Jacob didn't seem to know what to say. Then his hands tightened into fists and he straightened up. "There's nothing to fix, Dan. I only need to make you see reason."

"I am seeing reason! Perhaps for the very first time! You've hurt people, Jake! You've destroyed Heaven and Hell! I can't help you this time. This time you need to face what you've done. I'm not going to help you any more. I just... I just *can't.* I'm done."

For several seconds, silence filled the room.

Then Jacob reached out and grabbed the lamp from the small side table, hurled it to the floor and shattered it into a thousand pieces.

Grace gasped, and even Samael gave a little start. The only ones who didn't react were the angel and Daniel, the latter of which seemed more resigned than anything.

"You're done?!" Jacob screamed. *"I'm done!* I've given you a thousand chances, Dan! Trying to make you see reason! I've *begged* you to come to your senses! Well, I'm done! This time, I'll *make* you see reason, even if I have to force it upon you!"

Wait, what?

Jacob looked up at Samael. "Break his leg!" he ordered.

"What?!" Samael and Daniel said in unison.

"Break his leg!" Jacob repeated wildly. "Make him see reason!"

"Jake!" Daniel said, sounding so hurt that it just about broke Grace's heart. "You can't mean that!"

"I do!" He still wasn't looking at Daniel. "Break his leg," he said once again to Samael.

Samael merely looked at him in shock. "No," he said.

"Do it!" Jacob ordered. "שבור לו את הרגל!"

No. Grace looked on in desperation. He couldn't do that to his own brother. Couldn't do that to Samael. He'd already been forced to kill one friend. He couldn't now be forced to torture another.

Except that he could.

Slowly, Samael walked around the chair until he was in front of Daniel. Daniel who wasn't tied down but who seemed to be too shocked to move.

"Jake," Daniel said, sounding more confused than anything.

Samael knelt before him. Slowly, he reached out and grabbed Daniel's right leg with both hands. Grace could only look on in muted terror as his hands and lower arms transformed into something clawed and furry.

Daniel wasn't looking at Samael. Instead, he was looking at his brother. "Jake," he said.

"Do it!" Jacob ordered.

There was a crunch, and Daniel's scream echoed through the room.

"*No!*" Grace yelled, throwing herself towards them only to crash directly into the invisible pillar.

No one even glanced in her direction. They didn't seem to be able to hear her either.

Grace clawed at the wall. She couldn't let this happen.

"Again!" Jacob ordered, his voice breaking. "The other leg!" He said something in Hebrew, and Grace could only watch helplessly on as Samael took Daniel's other leg in his hands.

Another crunch. Another scream. And then only Daniel's laboured breathing.

"הכה בו!" Jacob ordered.

Slowly, Samael stood up. He looked down at Daniel. Then he slapped him across the face.

It didn't look like he hit him all that hard to Grace, and it seemed like Jacob agreed.

"Not like that!" he screamed. "Hit him properly!"

Was he crying? It sounded like he was crying. He said something in Hebrew.

Samael pulled his deformed hand back, and Grace noted that he'd retracted his claws. Then he hit Daniel.

Grace gasped as red splattered across the armchair. Blood was dripping from Daniel's face. His eyes were closed, and his head lay limply against the back of the chair. Had he fallen unconscious? Or... or had Samael accidentally killed him?

Silence stretched across the room, every eye on Daniel. Then a groan came from him, and his eyes opened. Slowly, they focused on the shapeshifter in front of him.

"I'm sorry," Samael said in hardly more than a whisper, his words clearly heard throughout the quiet room.

"'s okay," Daniel rasped. "Not your fault." His words were slurred together, and the clinical part of Grace noted that it sounded like he'd had a couple of teeth knocked loose. "Still friends," Daniel muttered.

"*Friends?!*" Jacob repeated. "Jesus Christ, Dan, you can't be friends with a *demon!*"

Samael looked at Jacob with hate in his eyes. "He certainly has better friends than he does a brother," he noted coolly.

"It's not my fault!" Jacob screamed, stomping on the floor. "He did this! It's his fault!"

Grace looked at him in surprise. She'd seen him angry before, but this was the first time she realised exactly how... childish Jacob could be. She couldn't imagine growing up with someone like that.

Jacob turned towards Grace, away from his brother, and Grace saw tear tracks on his face. It didn't make sense. If hurting Daniel hurt him then why do it?

"It's your fault," Jacob told his brother. "All you had to do was pick my side. Why was that so hard? We're brothers! We're supposed to pick each other's sides! But you *weren't there*, and I was all alone!" He spun around to face his brother once again. "Break his arm!" he ordered.

"Master, there is a message."

They all looked over at the angel. Grace had almost forgotten he was there.

"What?" Jacob said.

"There is a message," the angel repeated. "You ordered me to tell you whenever someone sent a prayer."

"I'm busy!" Jacob hissed.

The angel looked at him expressionlessly. "You ordered me to tell you whenever someone sent a prayer," he repeated.

"Well, what is it then?!" Jacob demanded. "What do they want?!"

"I do not know," the angel said calmly.

"*What?!*"

"I do not know. Whoever sent the prayer was disturbed. All I got was that they found something."

"Found what?!"

"I do not know."

Jacob stared at him. He looked absolutely deranged, and for a second Grace worried he might order the angel to commit suicide.

"Connect me to the intercom!" he said instead.

Grace frowned. The intercom. He was calling for a meeting again?

The angel made a waving motion with his hand, and suddenly Grace could see Jacob's vocal cords glow through the skin of his throat.

"Attention!" he called out, his voice coming from the top of the room as well as from the man in front of them. "Someone has been interrupted while passing on information to me! This will not happen again. It is absolutely forbidden to disturb someone who's praying." He said something in Hebrew, and Grace assumed that he was repeating the order in the only way he knew that would be obeyed.

Jacob gestured towards the angel, who waved his hand again, causing Jacob's vocal cords to stop glowing.

Jacob took a deep breath followed by another and then another. He then turned towards his brother and looked at him.

Grace wondered what he saw. The broken legs? The bloodied face? Or did he only see someone he thought had betrayed him?

Jacob stepped forward and knelt next to his brother, silent for a few seconds. "It doesn't have to end like this," he said softly. "It's your choice, Dan. Just admit you were wrong. I won't hold it against you. But I can't afford to give you any more chances."

Daniel looked at his brother in disbelief. "You're sick," he said.

Jacob flinched back. "Why are you still on their side?!" he demanded to know, jumping to his feet. "They *lost!* Look at my side. We make sense! We have *angels!*"

Daniel coughed; a hoarse, raspy sound. "They're not all on your side, Jake," he said.

"They are! They'll stop anyone attacking me. I told them to, right from the beginning!"

Daniel coughed again. "That's not the same thing, Jake," he said.

Jacob took another step back. "I can see you're still against me," he said. "It seems the work done by your so-called friend has not convinced you." He shot a quick look at Samael before he turned his attention back to Daniel. "I suppose it would be pointless to keep trying," he said. "I've already tried so many times. It's too late. I don't even *recognise* you any longer."

Grace nervously gnawed on her bottom lip. Jacob had stopped torturing his brother, but Grace had the unpleasant feeling that he wasn't just going to send Daniel back to Earth and be done with it. She looked over at Samael, expecting him to look as worried as she felt.

Instead, he almost looked cautious. The shapeshifter was slowly inching away from Jacob and Daniel and towards the pillar where Grace was trapped inside.

Jacob was only looking at Daniel. "You turned your back on me," he said. "You betrayed me. *You weren't there!*" The Voice of God was shaking in his hand. "You weren't there," Jacob repeated, "and I realise, you never will be. You don't care that we're brothers. And soon, we won't be. I won't have to think about you at all."

Wait, what? He meant to kill Daniel? That would hardly make much of a difference, considering that Daniel would just be thrown right back into Hell. Certainly wouldn't make them any less brothers.

"You won't matter any longer," Jacob told his brother, his voice rising in volume. "Because after tonight you won't even *exist*."

Grace stared at Jacob in disbelief. Wouldn't exist? He couldn't do that. Could he?

Samael was now by Grace's pillar, his back towards her. He almost appeared as if he was leaning up against it. Not that he had any reason to pretend. Jacob's attention was solely focused on his brother.

Slowly, inch by inch, Samael reached backwards and into the pillar. His clawed hand closed around Grace's arm and pulled her out, only to immediately push her behind the pillar instead. Less well hidden, but no longer trapped. She peeked out from around it.

Jacob was saying something in Hebrew, looking at the angel.

"Don't!" Samael said, stepping away from the pillar and towards the angel, clawed hand raised as if ready to strike.

"עְצוֹר!" Jacob ordered, and Samael stopped.

The angel disappeared.

"Jake," Daniel said, looking vaguely ill. "You can't possibly…"

"Don't talk to me!" Jacob spat.

Grace waited with bated breath for his next words. They never came, and silence filled the room. The seconds ticked by. Grace wondered what had been supposed to happen.

Suddenly, Daniel's body started to convulse so violently that he fell from the chair. His screams tore through the room, and Grace could only stare at him in shock. Nothing was happening, and yet Daniel was clearly in excruciating pain. The screams stopped just as suddenly as they'd started. Next thing she knew, Daniel looked completely healed.

She blinked, but nothing changed. It didn't make any sense. Healing Daniel was just about the last thing she'd expected Jacob to do.

The angel reappeared from thin air as suddenly as it had gone, and Grace tried to read his expression. A futile task when looking at an angel. Wherever he had gone, it had to have something to do with Daniel's inexplicable pain.

"So you had someone kill my body," Daniel said as he staggered to his feet.

Oh.

Daniel's body was still somewhere on Earth. Through his angel, Jacob had just killed his own brother.

Jacob looked at Daniel with an unreadable expression.

"If I hadn't changed the worlds," he said slowly, "you would be making your way up a staircase. I wonder if they would have let you in. If you'd been in *luck*. I wish you would see it from my point of view, Dan. See how… random it all was. How they were playing dice with your fate. How *sick* it all was."

Daniel merely stared at the floor, ignoring his brother's rant.

"I'm not surprised that you can't look me in the eye," Jacob continued. "You who turned your back on your own brother! You refused to do the dirty work. It didn't matter how necessary it was. You were a *coward*! But I had the guts to do what needed to be done!"

Daniel finally looked up at his brother. "You've broken it all," he said dully.

Jacob gasped. "*I* broke it?! I gave you every chance I could!" he yelled. "I *loved* you. And you weren't there!" He lifted the Voice of God. "I can't stand the thought of you being my brother," he said. "Soon, you won't be. I'll rip your soul apart!"

Grace gaped at him. Ripping a soul apart. Was that *a thing*?

Jacob started speaking in Hebrew.

And Daniel screamed.

Jacob stopped talking. Instead, he looked down at his brother in silence. Daniel had fallen on his knees and was holding a hand up against the right side of his face. Slowly, he lowered it, and Grace gasped in horror at the sight that met her.

A good part of Daniel's face was simply... gone. The skin and muscle on the right side of his face was entirely missing, leaving behind nothing but bone. There was no gushing blood, no open wound. The flesh was just... not there.

Jacob stared at his brother with wild eyes. For half a second, Grace was convinced he'd changed his mind. Then a new resolve entered Jacob's eyes. If he'd had any sanity left, Grace was pretty sure that had been the moment he lost it.

Jacob spoke again in Hebrew, and Daniel screamed, curling up in a fetal position. A few moments later, the brothers fell silent once again.

This time it was Daniel's torso that took the brunt of it. Grace stared. Almost the entire left side of his chest was missing. It was like one of those anatomy dolls they'd used in nursing school to show the organs. She could see his heart, half of one of his lungs, what little was left of his ribs. But unlike the dolls, Daniel was an actual *person*. Grace could see his lung expand and contract, his heart beat in a chest that was no longer there.

Grace felt herself grow sick. She'd seen some twisted things, but nothing like this. She couldn't watch on any longer, doing nothing as her friend disappeared piece by piece in front of her.

Instead, she fumbled in her pocket for the grenade Alanadiel had given her. Once found, she pulled the pin out, knelt down, and sent it sliding across the floor, under the curtains, and into the adjoining living room. The following blast would undoubtedly attract attention, but it would also cause the confusion Grace needed. She waited with bated breath for the explosion.

The seconds seemed to stretch on forever. Had she gotten a dud? Or hadn't she done it properly? She fumbled in her pocket for the second grenade, and the living room exploded.

Everything went black.

Grace blinked, finding herself lying on the floor. When had she fallen over? Something was ringing, and Grace struggled to her feet. She had definitely miscalculated the size of the explosion. The formerly pristine room was filled with rubble and dust. The others were slowly getting to their feet as well. Even the otherwise expressionless angel seemed confused and dazed.

Grace, however, only had eyes for Jacob. Somehow, he had held on to the Voice of God. Grace reached up to touch her mask and was relieved to determine that she was still wearing it. She stumbled closer to Jacob, and he looked at her with confusion. She was now standing right next to him, wearing the cloak of the inner circle. The angel didn't even glance in her direction. With a pounding heart, Grace reached out and let her fingers close around the Voice of God. This was it. This was victory.

She had severely underestimated the speed of the angel. Suddenly, he was just there, grabbing Grace's arms and forcing her backwards. Away from Jacob. Away from the Voice. She screamed something, but she didn't know what. Her mask was pulled from her face.

Jacob stared at her with a baffled expression.

"The girl," he said, sounding more confused than anything else.

Grace struggled against the hold on her, but the angel didn't even appear to notice, let alone loosen his grip.

Reality hit her, as horrible as only reality could be.

They'd lost.

* * *

For a full eight seconds, Grace felt utterly hopeless.

Then her eyes flickered between Jacob, Daniel, and Samael. There had to be another way.

She couldn't do anything herself.

And Lucifer definitely wasn't an option. Imprisoned, forced to submit, and unaware of the current situation.

Samael was no good either. He couldn't go against the Voice of God. He'd proven that when he'd killed her.

Daniel. Daniel was an option, wasn't he? He was human, so the Voice had no power over him. But if Daniel tried to hurt Jacob or take the Voice, the angel would stop him as well. Shoot, even Samael would be forced to.

Still. Daniel was unrestrained, human and present. He could also speak Hebrew, meaning that he only needed a few seconds with the Voice of God in his hands.

There had to be a solution to their problem, some obvious answer that they just couldn't see.

"You!" Jacob said, snapping her out of her train of thought. He wasn't speaking to her, however. Instead, he was looking at Samael. "Did you know about this?" Jacob demanded to know.

"That an explosion was about to occur? I did not."

"So just a foolish girl then," Jacob muttered. He ran his hand over his face. "I'll have to punish her," he said with a regretful expression. He looked at Grace, though he still didn't meet her eyes. "I know you won't understand," he said. "I can't expect a female to realise the necessity of sacrifice. But I've created a world of justice, and terrorists must be punished. Even those who can't understand the consequences of their actions." He looked back at Samael. "Break her arm!" he ordered before he repeated his order in Hebrew.

Samael looked at Grace with a horrified expression. He stepped towards her ever so slowly.

"Your gender is no excuse here," Jacob said.

Grace stared at him in disbelief. She wondered what *his* excuse was.

Samael was right next to her now. The angel held out her left arm for him to take. Samael's anguished eyes met hers. He grabbed her arm, and the angel let go of it.

You told me not to hurt anyone wearing one of the white or grey cloaks.

Those had been Samael's words. But she was wearing a white cloak, and Samael was clearly about to hurt her. He went against an old order in order to follow a new one. What was that thing Jacob had said about the angels?

They'll stop anyone attacking me. I told them to, right from the beginning!

Right from the beginning. Meaning that almost every order he'd given must have come after that one. Meaning that...

There was a crunch and a snap.

Grace screamed, pain shooting through her arm. It was impossible to think beyond the pain. It felt as if her arm had been covered in ice, and someone was pouring burning embers inside of it. She'd *had* it. She'd had the solution, but she couldn't for the life of her remember what it was.

Slowly, a numbness mixed with the pain, and Grace found herself able to think around it.

Every order Jacob had given had most likely come after that one. Grace's mind frantically ran through all the orders she knew about.

"Crush her elbow!" Jacob ordered before he repeated his words in Hebrew.

Crush? What?

Grace screamed again. The pain of before had been nothing in comparison. Samael had taken her elbow between his transformed hands and simply... crushed it.

By now it was a good thing that the angel held her up, or Grace would have collapsed. She needed to think around the pain, but it wasn't going away, wasn't to be ignored. She ground her teeth together.

An order Jacob had given that could be used.

Pain.

Something that could be twisted.

Pain.

He'd given so many stupid orders.

Pain.

Women in Purgatory.

Pain.

Undisturbed praying.

Pain.

Torturing one's friends.

Pain.

Undisturbed praying.

"Daniel," Grace croaked. Jacob frowned at her, but made no move to stop her. Daniel was only a few feet away from him. "Do you trust me?"

Daniel blinked at her. He was a ghastly sight as he stood there with half a peeled-off face and an open chest.

"I... yes," he said.

"Enough!" Jacob ordered. "Crush her jaw." He began translating the order but only got a few words out before Grace interrupted him.

"Pray!" she screamed at Daniel. "And attack! They won't be able to stop you while you're praying!"

Daniel wasted almost a second staring at her. Then he threw himself at his brother, the Lord's Prayer falling from his lips.

"Stop, Dan!" Jacob yelled. "Stop him!"

Neither Samael nor the angel moved. It hadn't been said in Hebrew, and they couldn't disturb someone praying.

Of course, all it took was one new order and that would change. Daniel needed the Voice in his control as soon as possible.

"Samael!" Grace shouted. "Can you barricade the door? Before the explosion brings anyone here?"

"The door?" Samael stared at her in incomprehension before he seemed to pull himself together. "Yes," he said. "I can't hurt them once they're in, but I can keep them out." He disappeared into the living room.

Grace looked back at the two fighting brothers, only able to watch as Daniel drove a knee into his brother's chest. He had one hand desperately clasped over Jacob's mouth, while the other was struggling to free the Voice of God from his brother's grip.

Suddenly, Daniel seemed to give up on pulling the Voice from his brother's hand. Instead, he pulled his fist back and slammed it into his brother's liver. Jacob's muffled scream was clearly heard even through Daniel's hand, and the Voice of God fell limply from his grip. Daniel let go of his brother and scrambled for it, and Grace gave a shout of triumph as she watched him lift it victoriously into the air.

Another scream from Jacob. He reached upwards, and Grace instinctively yelled out a warning to Daniel. He needed to keep the Voice out of his brother's reach.

Rather than grasping for the Voice, however, Jacob's hand closed around his brother's exposed heart and squeezed.

Daniel's scream was like nothing Grace had ever heard. The Voice of God fell from his limp fingers and onto the floor, inches away from Jacob's face. Jacob let go of Daniel's heart to grab for it.

Grace looked on in horror. She needed to get free and help Daniel. She jammed her elbow backwards, hitting the angel in his lower abdomen. He didn't react. At all. Grace wasn't even sure he'd noticed.

Maybe physical violence wasn't the answer here.

And then Grace got an idea, and she looked up at the angel with a hopeful expression. "He didn't order you to hold me," she informed him.

He looked down at her. "He ordered us to stop anyone trying to take the Voice of God. You did so."

Grace looked in desperation at the two fighting brothers. Then she gasped as she saw Jacob's fingers close around the Voice.

Daniel punched his brother in the throat, and Jacob let go of the Voice. Pulling his fist back while disjointed bits of prayer fell from his lips, Daniel punched Jacob again. He hit him square in the nose, and Grace could hear the crack even from where she was standing. Jacob screamed and reached up for Daniel's heart.

Again, Daniel hit him. And again, and again. Jacob's hand fell down on the floor. He was lying completely still.

Above him, Daniel was still saying the Lord's Prayer; the words hardly more than a sobbing. He let his arm fall down and took hold of the Voice.

Daniel's English prayer turned into Hebrew words, and the angel released his hold on Grace. She hurried over to Daniel, who was still sitting astride his brother. Daniel was sobbing uncontrollably, and she hesitated, unsure of what to do. Jacob's face was a bloody mess, but she could see the rise and fall of his chest. He was unconscious but alive.

Reaching up around Daniel's neck, Grace hugged him. Daniel's arms wound themselves around her waist, and he was clinging to her, bawling. Grace let him, even as pain was shooting through her crushed arm.

Finally, it became quiet. Daniel was no longer crying, though he was still clinging to Grace.

"Daniel," she said. "He's still alive."

Slowly, Daniel unwound his arms from her. "I know," he whispered.

Sluggishly, Grace rose to her feet, suddenly aware of a banging noise coming from the living room. She made her way in there and gaped at the sight that met her.

The formerly cosy living room was completely destroyed, but for now, Grace didn't focus on the havoc. Instead, her eyes were drawn to the (thankfully still intact) main door, where a ten-feet anaconda was twisted around the handle. Samael, she presumed.

The banging came from the other side of the door as someone was desperately trying to break in, but the anaconda didn't budge. He was hissing furiously, and Grace was pretty sure that Samael's rage wouldn't allow him to lose this fight. She briefly contemplated rushing to his side, but the shapeshifter honestly didn't seem like he needed it.

"Um, Daniel," Grace called out. "You may want to use that glowing throat-thing and get some angelic help. Someone's trying to break in."

She waited just long enough to hear Daniel's affirmative answer before her legs gave out under her, and she fell to the floor. Exhausted, she leaned against a fallen bookshelf. Adrenaline was still pumping through her body, but it seemed the pain in her arm was only growing worse now that the biggest threat had been overcome. Black spots were dancing in front of her eyes.

Daniel's voice, magically broadcast across all of Hell, was the last thing she heard before she passed out.

CHAPTER TWENTY-ONE:

A Visit from God

Jacob's apostles did put up a fight, but it was rather like watching a group of toddlers try to keep out an invading army. Their power had come from the Voice and without it they were just a group of desperate men with life skills a few centuries out of date.

Grace had little to do with the capture of them. Instead, she was hurried over to Hell's infirmary where she was happy to discover that a crushed elbow was deemed an easily fixable thing. She was still told to keep her arm in a sling for a couple of weeks, an order which she promptly ignored. It was a matter of minutes to convince the young nurse to simply bandage it up instead. Immediately thereafter, Grace got to work. Dying hadn't made her any less capable at her chosen profession, and there were countless of wounded people to tend to.

Thankfully, not every hurt person was their responsibility. Plenty of people who'd been dragged from Heaven were returning there as fast as they could, only too happy to leave Hell behind.

Grace's mother had been one of these people — though she had stopped by to see her youngest daughter. It had taken quite a bit of time for Grace to convince her mother that, yes, she truly was fine. And, no, Hell really wasn't so bad. And, yes, she'd see if she could get one of the angels to pass messages back and forth.

Her mother had ultimately gone back to Heaven with a last hug and plenty of tears. She hadn't seemed convinced that her daughter would be happy in Hell. In fact, Grace rather got the impression that her mother would hound the angels to let Grace gain entrance into Heaven, despite her lack of faith. If her mother succeeded, however, it could possibly turn into quite an awkward conversation when Grace turned them down.

The days seemed to fly by after that, though Grace was much too busy to count them. Samael got into the habit of stopping by once a day to say hi (though he always did have some excuse as to why he was forced to be there). It was he who let her know how the restoration was going, which angels had been Jacob's accomplices, and how Daniel spent his days carefully undoing Jacob's many, many orders. He also kept her up to date on Lilith's recovery now that the walls had been rebuilt.

Grace herself had caught the occasional glimpse of the queen, who seemed to be working constantly despite her prevailing exhaustion, and she knew from Samael that Lilith was blithely ignoring the advice of both her doctors and her husband.

Due to these visits, Grace was far from surprised when she looked up from where she was gluing a 10 feet tall demon's horn back on, doubtful if this was *really* the correct procedure, and saw the shapeshifter standing in the doorway to the infirmary. Even after several visits, he still looked slightly uncomfortable, though Grace wasn't sure why. For a hospital, Hell's infirmary was certainly one of the cosier ones.

Every long-time patient got their own room, which admittedly was only possible because every part of the infirmary shared the same space — and the same main door. It had taken Grace quite a while to figure out how to open it to *her* part of the infirmary.

Well, not entirely hers. She shared it with two other nurses, and it consisted of a rectangular room with six beds on each side, each made up with fluffy pillows and a duvet in a pale blue. Several cheerful paintings hung on the walls, and each of the nightstands had its own potted plant, only some of which were recognisable to Grace.

She was pretty sure that the magenta one, which gave off light puffs of pink smoke, wasn't native to Earth, and the blue one, which kept trying to fly away, definitely wasn't. She'd been told, however, that each of them was there for medicinal purposes, and she couldn't wait to learn all about them.

The infirmary itself had two adjoining rooms (an office and a storeroom), which made it possible to keep the main room looking much like a shared dormitory.

Grace was quite proud of her new workplace.

"Hi," she said, when Samael made no move to talk.

Samael merely frowned as an answer; a response Grace was more than used to and therefore felt free to ignore. She sent her current patient out with a smile and an admonishment to refrain from scratching his newly glued horn, even if it did itch.

"I heard Lucifer finally got rid of Purgatory," she told Samael, expecting him to take on a smug expression and say that *he* didn't have to listen to idle gossip, but was told these sorts of things by Lucifer himself.

Samael remained silent, however, and Grace looked at him a bit more closely. It was hard to say with a shapeshifter, but she thought that he looked a tad pale.

"You okay?" she asked.

Slowly, the shapeshifter walked to her side.

"God's here," he said, too softly for the other two nurses and remaining three patients to hear.

"God," Grace repeated, surprised. "As in God-God?"

"No, as in the God of capybaras," Samael snapped, sounding far more like his usual self. "Now come on."

Grace frowned. "I can't just get up and leave," she told him. "I have a job to do."

Samael rolled his eyes. "Grace, this is important."

"So is this."

"Oh, for the love of—" Samael looked around the room and caught the eye of its head nurse. "The Devil has requested Grace's presence," he told her.

The head nurse was a no-nonsense demon, who'd made it clear that Grace and Russell (the other assistant nurse) shouldn't expect much free time until Hell resembled something a little less apocalyptic.

"Of course," she said, apparently deciding that a summons from the Devil was worth an exception. She looked over at Grace. "I expect you back here afterwards," she said. "We still have a lot of work to do."

"Sure," Grace said. "Thank you."

That was all she had time to say before Samael grabbed her by the arm and pulled her out of the room.

"Where are we going?" Grace asked as he hurried her through the palace hallways.

"The throne room," Samael said. "Daniel is waiting for us outside of it."

"Did Lucifer really ask for me?"

"Of course not. The Devil isn't going to waste his time on a mere human."

"I did kind of save Hell," Grace noted.

Samael spun around and stared at her, almost causing Grace to walk directly into him. "After putting it in danger in the first place," he said. "Grace, you gave the Voice of God to an angel."

"Well, yeah," Grace said. "How was I supposed to know any different? We thought they were on our side."

"*I* never trusted them," Samael said.

"No," Grace agreed, willingly enough. "But you did plan to ask for their help anyway. Meaning that they still would've gotten the Voice."

"I only considered it because of you!" Samael said. "I did fine before I started hanging out with you. You were always too bloody impulsive, and it was bound to rub off on me."

Grace smiled. There was something undeniably amusing about having a demon accuse you of being a bad influence.

"Well, don't smile!" Samael spat. "You didn't think your actions through and gave the Voice to the enemy!"

"I wasn't smiling because of that," Grace said. "And it worked out in the end, didn't it?"

"That isn't the point," Samael said, his voice rising in volume. "And it wasn't just then! You never think things through! If you continue like this, you'll never be like him!"

Grace frowned, confused. "Like who?"

"Like Lucifer!" Samael was breathing heavily, and for several seconds they merely looked at each other in silence.

"I don't want to be like Lucifer," Grace finally said.

"I... Why not?"

"Well, I wouldn't be happy," Grace said.

"Sometimes it isn't about being happy!"

Grace tilted her head to the side, considering it. "What is it about then?" she asked.

"It's about... it's about *dignity!* And pride!"

"It is?"

"Yes!"

"I don't think it is," Grace declared. "I think it's about being happy. And making other people happy."

"Don't be ridiculous. One's existence can't just be about having fun."

"Well, I think it should be."

"Yeah, well, I'm not you."

"That's true," Grace said. Then she grinned. "Though we do remind a bit of each other, don't we?"

"We most certainly do not! I'm nothing like you. I'm Samael! *I* am part of the nobility of Hell, and you—"

"Are a puny, little human," Grace finished his thought. "You've mentioned."

"You're impulsive," Samael told her.

"That's true," Grace agreed. "Is that bad?"

"Is that... of course, it is!"

"Why?"

"Because that's not how real demons should behave!"

"I'm not a demon, though," Grace noted. She looked at the

shapeshifter in contemplation, choosing her next words carefully. "Samael, you won't ever be like Lucifer," she said.

Samael took a step back almost as if she'd hit him. A painful expression flickered across his face. "I..."

"And that's not a bad thing," Grace said. "You're not him. You're you. And you're... great. I wouldn't have wanted to go through this adventure with Lucifer. And I think we did pretty good. I know that I'm impulsive, and that it's going to get me in trouble. But other times, it'll get me out of it, so I think that's a pretty fair trade."

Samael looked at her with an almost lost expression. "I..." He fell silent. Seconds ticked by. Then he turned around and walked away.

Grace hesitated, unsure if she should follow.

"Are you coming?" Samael called over his shoulder. "Daniel's waiting, you know!"

Smiling, Grace hurried after him.

Samael was silent for the rest of the walk (probably due to him being deep in thought), and Grace followed his example (which required quite a bit of willpower on her part).

Finally, Samael broke the silence.

"I am pretty great," he mumbled to himself.

Grace grinned and forced herself not to comment.

Finally, they arrived outside the door to the throne room. Daniel was there waiting for them with his half-a-face and a blue T-shirt covering his exposed chest cavity. Grace was surprised to notice that he was impatiently tapping his foot. "There you are!" he exclaimed, relief evident in his voice. "Finally!"

"We had a little chat," Grace said.

"About what?"

"Never mind that," Samael said. "Are they still in there?"

"Yeah."

For a while, both men looked at the closed door in silence. Grace wondered if any of them were planning to open it.

"Shouldn't we go inside?" she asked.

Samael fidgeted nervously. "We haven't really been... officially... invited," he said. "They've been in there for almost an hour."

Grace frowned. "If we can't go in, what are we doing here?"

Samael grimaced. "Daniel and I have been talking," he said. "And we think there might be some small areas — minuscule, really — where Jacob might have... you know."

"Where my brother might've had a point," Daniel said.

Grace stared at them, unsure if she'd heard them correctly.

"You think Jacob was right?" she asked.

"Don't be daft," Samael said. "Of course not."

Grace frowned. "What?"

"I'm going to Heaven," Daniel said.

Grace blinked, thrown off by the change of topic. "Why?" she asked, disappointed. "I know Hell didn't make the best first impression, but it's actually quite lovely."

Daniel smiled at her. "I'm sure a lot of people will be a lot happier in Hell than they would have been in Heaven," he said. "I, however, am not one of them."

Grace considered it. If Daniel went to Heaven, they were never supposed to see each other again. But surely, they'd find a way. If she could get out of Limbo, getting visitation rights into Heaven couldn't be *that* difficult.

"Besides," Daniel said, "I've been thinking. What you and my brother have told me about Limbo... it isn't right. I know that only bad people go there, but there must be another way. Some way to *teach* them to be good."

"So you want to what?" Grace asked. "Create a rehabilitation centre for the Undesirables?" That was exactly the kind of idea she would have assumed Samael would have deemed idiotic. She looked at him, hard pressed to believe that he agreed with Daniel.

Samael shrugged. "I don't really care about that aspect," he said. "But it's about more than that. I know that you haven't been in Hell long, Grace, but most people don't usually go touristing in Heaven. Typically, when people die, there are plenty of friends and family members they'll never see again."

"Like my mom," Grace mused. Then she smiled at Samael. "I'm so proud of you!" she said. "Thinking about other people!"

Samael spluttered. "I am not!" he said. "I just..." He glanced at Daniel. "It's a matter of *principle*," he said.

Grace smiled. "You're just sad you won't see Daniel again," she said. "I knew you guys would make friends! Eventually."

"We. Are. Not. Friends!"

"Sure, you are," Grace said. "And if you want things to change, shouldn't you go to Lucifer with that? Especially now that God's in there as well? Two birds and all that."

"It's God and the Devil!" Samael hissed at her.

"I know that," Grace said.

"We don't want to disturb them," Daniel said. "In case it isn't... a good time."

"And we need to prepare our arguments," Samael added. "We can't just — Grace, what are you *doing?!*"

Grace looked at him, fist still raised from where she'd been knocking on the door. "What?" she asked. "It's not polite to just barge in."

"That's not what I meant!"

"We'll just ask them if they have a minute," Grace said.

"Grace, you don't just—"

The door swung open, and the frightened eyes of a young boy met them. "Yes?" he asked. Behind him, they could hear thunderous yelling. Quite literally. Whenever one of the two shouted, thunder could be heard in the background. Grace started to wonder if this had really been her best idea. Still though. In for a penny, in for a pound.

"May we come in?" she asked.

"*Grace!*" Samael hissed.

"What?" she looked back at them. Samael was as white as a

sheet, while Daniel was whimpering ever so slightly. He didn't look much like a war hero right now.

She looked back at the boy, who was as pale as Samael. A furious shout came from behind him, and the boy made a sound not unlike a dog who had gotten his tail stepped on, bolted past Grace, and ran down the hallway, door falling shut behind him.

"Well..." Grace said. "I guess this means we let ourselves in?"

"But... they're clearly having a fight," Daniel said. "God and the Devil. Do you think God might kill him?"

Grace considered it. "I think if God could kill the Devil, he'd be dead a long time ago," she decided. "And you wanted to talk with them, right?" She had to admit that it seemed like a worse and worse idea by the second. Perhaps they really should come back later. Any situation with an angry God rarely turned out all that great. Grace remembered something about a flood and falling frogs. "Would you like to wait until later?" she asked.

Daniel took a deep breath. "No," he said. "This is important." He stepped forward, opened the door and walked inside. With a quick glance between them, Grace and Samael followed.

The throne room was enormous. At least the size of a football field, if not larger. The ceiling towered above them, painted with intricate murals, and the white, marble flooring was put in strong contrast to the almost black walls. Two long rows of behemoth columns stretched themselves to the ceiling, each of them decorated with a complex pattern of gold. There were murals decorating the walls as well, but these had been smashed to pieces.

And not far from the entrance, stood the two most powerful creatures in the universe.

The Devil and God were facing each other, and for a second Grace thought she was having a stroke as God appeared to be constantly changing before her. As she looked at him, his skin went from alabaster white to jet black before it lightened to a russet brown. His features changed both shape and size, and his body itself seemed to grow and fill out, while his hair grew several inches before it shrunk once again. He looked nothing like she'd expected (the Santa-beard was entirely missing), and yet she didn't have an ounce of doubt in her that this was God.

"It has been millennia!" Lucifer yelled at God, fury clear in his voice.

"I made it for a reason!" God replied thunderously. His voice was as multi-facetted as his appearance, with an underlying hint of wind, thunder, and crashing waves. It was an entire chorus of voices working together in perfect harmony. And each of them furious beyond belief.

"It's a liability! Even your haloed pets agree!"

"Everyone has a place in this universe, and I created it to make sure this balance was upheld!"

"My place is *not* on my knees in front of a human!"

"Your place is where I say it is!"

"My siblings may believe such foolishness, but I certainly—" The Devil cut himself off as he saw the trio standing by the door, staring at him and God. "Samael," he said, frowning. "What are you doing here?"

Samael winced. "I... I..." He looked helplessly at Grace and Daniel. Grace sent him an encouraging smile, but it was Daniel who went to stand by his side.

"We... eh, we were thinking," the shapeshifter said.

The Devil frowned. "Can't this wait?" he asked, already turning back towards God.

"No!" Samael exclaimed and winced as soon as the word was out of his mouth. Then he squared his shoulders. "It can't!"

The Devil turned back towards him. "Excuse me?" he said, voice foreboding.

God, however, appeared almost amused.

"It can't wait!" Samael said, his voice gaining confidence as he spoke. "This is important. Or it might be." He looked over at Daniel.

"We were thinking," Daniel picked up. "About some of the things my brother said."

The Devil lifted an eyebrow. "Am I to have the same problem with you as I did your brother?"

"Of course not!" Samael hurried to say. "Daniel isn't trying to take control. There were just certain aspects that we thought we might be able to do... a tad differently."

Grace looked back and forth between the four of them. For someone who'd worried about taking up the entities' time, Samael and Daniel sure seemed to have trouble getting to the point.

"We want visitation rights between Heaven and Hell," she said. "Oh, yeah, and Daniel would like a rehabilitation centre set up in Limbo."

"Grace!" Daniel hissed at her.

"What?" If anyone were going to hiss at her, she would have assumed it'd be Samael. "Did I misunderstand?"

"A rehabilitation centre?" Lucifer repeated. "In Limbo?"

"It doesn't have to be in Limbo," Daniel hurried to explain. "But both Jacob and Grace told me about the place, and it shouldn't exist. Even if some people aren't welcome in Heaven or Hell, it isn't fair to just forget about them. If they don't know how to do the right thing, we should teach them."

For a long time, the Devil said nothing.

"Not everyone can be taught," he finally said.

Daniel looked down. "Still," he said, "we should try. If not for them, then for us."

"Ah," the Devil said as if he suddenly understood something. "You could not save your brother, so now you wish to save everyone else."

Daniel recoiled. "I... maybe," he said. "But that doesn't make it any less true! People like my brother's so-called apostles shouldn't be the way they are. No one should enjoy hurting other people. Or just be indifferent to their pain. But Limbo shouldn't exist either. It's not there to help or protect anyone. It's just some place to throw away people we prefer to forget about."

"An impressive consideration to have," God said, for the first time speaking directly to any of them. His voice no longer carried thunder and crashing waves but was instead quiet and unassuming. If she hadn't already known, Grace wouldn't have been able to hear that it was God speaking.

Daniel gaped at him. "Thank you, your... eh... thank you."

Lucifer, however, appeared far less impressed. "I have a world to clean up," he said. "I have sixty billion inhabitants who have been tortured and frightened. I do not have time for Undesirables."

Daniel took a deep breath. "But will you ever have time for them?" he asked. "Or will there always be something more important?"

The Devil looked at him in silence before he turned his attention towards Samael. "And you?" he asked. "Do you agree with this?"

Samael avoided his gaze. "Of course not, my Lord," he said. "It's only reasonable that you prioritise your own inhabitants first."

The Devil nodded thoughtfully and looked over at Grace. "And do you—"

"I think Daniel has a point, though!" Samael interrupted him. "My Lord," he added quickly.

The Devil looked back at him, surprise in his eyes. "Do you now?"

"About the border between the worlds," Samael said. "The... visitation rights. So many people are separated from their friends and family because they got into different worlds. Like Mei Lien. She's—"

"I know who she is," the Devil said. "You want people to be able to visit Heaven? If you think I can make that happen, you severely overestimate my power."

"I was just thinking," Samael said, "that you could open Hell up for visitors from Heaven. I mean, if people don't want to go to Heaven, they can still go to Hell, right?"

Lucifer tilted his head to the side. "Yes," he said. "Though no one has ever actually done so."

"And if they can choose Hell, why shouldn't they be able to also just kind of choose it... temporarily? For long enough to make a visit."

"I would like the chance to see my mom again," Grace said.

"It might help the people overcome what they've been through," Daniel added. "If they get a chance to reconnect with their lost ones."

"And it's better this way," Samael said. "Better than how you... how it's been done before."

Lucifer looked at him with a pensive gaze. "It seems several things have already changed," he mused. "But it is not merely my permission you need."

Slowly, the three of them looked over at God.

Grace took a deep breath and forced herself to meet his eyes, only to find that she couldn't look away. She had the weirdest feeling that he saw everything: Every mistake she'd ever made, every uncharitable thought she'd ever had. She gulped. It was like those nightmares where you were giving a presentation and discovered that you were naked, except that this was far, far worse.

God looked away from her to look at Daniel and Samael, and Grace found herself shivering. She took a few deep breaths. All he'd done was look at her. No biggie. Except, somehow, it definitely, definitely was.

Beside her, she could *feel* Samael's and Daniel's discomfort. Another few deep breaths and she opened her mouth to talk to God, only to discover that it wasn't cooperating with her. Her tongue suddenly seemed to be too big for her mouth, and her throat was oddly parched.

"You want me to send my children to Hell so they can associate with the sinners here?" God asked them.

"Eh..." Grace looked helplessly at Samael and Daniel, who seemed to be just as tongue-tied as she.

"That was hardly what they said," Lucifer said, apparently not experiencing the same difficulties. "They want the people of Heaven to be *allowed* entrance into Hell. No one is forcing them. But perhaps you're worried you might lose them if they're allowed to see that there is... another way?"

"A worse way," God said.

The Devil remained impassive. "Another way," he said. "You always were so worried. Remember a certain bet we made, once upon a time?"

"A bet which I won!" God said, the storm back in his voice.

"But it seems you're afraid of losing this one."

"There is no 'this one'," God said. "We are not betting."

"But you're still worried about your precious children seeing Hell. What are you afraid of? That they'll realise the lies they have been told?"

"I have not told lies!" God said, lightning flashing from the ceiling.

"But you sure did little to stop them," the Devil rebutted. "You were especially pleased about that little rumour of my supposed attempt of tempting the kid. And with stale bread, no less. You always loved it when lies were spread about me."

"Do not try to provoke me!"

Around them, the entire throne room shook, and Samael sent Daniel a desperate look. What good was it that the Devil would help them if God refused?

"Um, excuse me... eh, God," Daniel said, stepping forward.

Grace looked at him with surprise.

God's expression, however, was unreadable: Possibly because his face kept changing. "You're one of mine," he said, pride warming his voice. "I look forward to welcoming you home."

"Thank you," Daniel said. "And..." he trailed off.

"And?" God asked, yet somehow Grace got the feeling he already knew.

"And... Um... And..."

With an impatient grunt, Samael shoved Daniel forward, almost sending him sprawling across the floor. It did, however, cause Daniel to stop mimicking a broken record.

"And I would like you to reconsider," he blurted out. "Please."

"Are you trying to change your God's mind?" God asked him, a warning in his voice.

Daniel took a deep breath. "Yes," he said. "I am. My friendship with Samael and Grace hasn't damaged me. They haven't caused me to lose my way. They've just... they've made me think more about things. And maybe that'll be a good thing for... for everyone."

"Have they not caused you to sin," God repeated. "So, you have not stolen and taken what was not yours?"

"I... Well, I mean, I have, but—"

"And you have not caused someone physical harm?"

"I have, but—"

"And have you not lied?"

"That's not fair!" Daniel exclaimed.

God looked at him, his face and body now that of an old man of Asian descent. "Not fair?" he repeated.

Daniel, however, didn't back down. "No," he said. "It's not fair. I know I have sinned, but sometimes you have to commit the small sin to keep someone else from committing the big one. It was a choice I made. And if... and Lucifer is right!"

"You're agreeing with the Devil?"

"On this, I am. People... people are faced with sin all their lives, and I always thought it was to test them. Why can't they be tested after Death as well? To refuse them to visit Hell because you worry about their association with its inhabitants, it's... it's..." Daniel trailed off. Then he took another deep breath. "It's cowardly!"

Grace gaped at him, not sure if he was being very, very brave, or very, very stupid. Probably both.

"Cowardly?" God repeated.

"Yes! You need to trust us!"

"And if the Devil won't allow you to leave again?"

Daniel gaped at him. "Why wouldn't he let us leave?"

"He is the Devil."

Grace *almost* thought she saw Lucifer roll his eyes.

"Well, yeah, but..." Daniel considered it. "I'm sure he will," he said. "And even if he won't, you can get us out." The last part was said with such certainty that Grace knew that a part of Daniel still felt that God could fix everything. Which led her to think of something else.

"Why didn't you help us?" she asked.

God looked at her, and Grace took a step back. But if Daniel could stand up to God, then so could she.

"Why did you refuse us when we asked you for help?" she asked, forcing herself to meet his gaze.

"Humankind made its choice. You wanted the knowledge of Good and Evil. With this knowledge comes evil, which you alone must face."

Grace frowned. Someone took a bite out of an apple once upon a time, so now God wouldn't stop a maniac madman. That seemed... less than ideal. Which was a thought she didn't have the courage to voice, but as God looked in her eyes, she realised that it didn't matter. He already knew.

"I created the Voice of God to give humankind a chance to defeat the Devil," God said.

"You created the Voice of God to punish me," Lucifer bit out. "And even you realised it was a mistake. Why else would you split it up?"

Next to Grace, Samael gasped. "God split it up?" he asked. "I thought it broke during the war?"

"It did," Lucifer said. "By God's hand. And now it's time he destroys it entirely. It's too dangerous to keep around."

With a scornful expression on his face, God grew until he was thirty feet tall, and lightning cracked between his fingers.

"Do not tell me what to do!" God thundered. "I created you!"

"And so you have reminded me for millennia now! It's not the argument you think it is!"

Feeling like they were about to enter into another shouting match, Grace cleared her throat, gaining the attention of both God and the Devil.

"It seems that the two of you are rather... occupied," she said. "And I think we have said what we came to say?" She looked over at Daniel and Samael who both quickly nodded. "So maybe... we should just go and let the two of you... eh, talk it out?"

"Yes," Lucifer said, looking just as angry as God. "Maybe you should."

None of them felt the need to be told twice. Seconds later, they were outside the room, the door falling shut behind them. They could hear thunder from the other side.

"So... what now?" Grace asked.

"I suppose we wait," Daniel said. "They must come to an agreement sooner or later."

Samael snorted. "They've been fighting for millennia without ever coming to an agreement," he said.

"Well, then I suppose it's about time," Grace said optimistically.

Samael just groaned.

* * *

It turned out, however, that Grace was the one who got it right.

Well, sort of.

It seemed that God and the Devil had been arguing about the destruction of the Voice since the War in Heaven, and they were probably going to fight about it for the next several millennia to come.

But they did come to some agreements.

Instead of destroying the Voice, they decided to break it into its three pieces and this time keep each piece in a different world.

And while God still refused to let his people visit Hell, he did agree that they could leave Heaven and then meet whoever they wanted in the In-Between. Grace decided to count it as a success.

Regarding Limbo, however, God proved to be the amiable one. Not that the Undesirables would ever be allowed entrance into Heaven, but maybe throwing them into a fog and forgetting about them hadn't been the *best* way to handle them. Instead, it was Lucifer who seemed to think that the idea of a Limbo rehabilitation centre was 'overly idealistic' as he'd later called it.

Samael later admitted to Grace that he'd overheard Lilith tease the Devil to submission by telling him that people had called *him* idealistic when he'd started the War in Heaven. But perhaps he'd grown old and world-weary? Which was hardly the man she'd fallen in love with. Lucifer had given in.

It was God's and the Devil's last agreement, however, that Grace had never seen coming. God had decided to take Jacob with him and keep him in lock-down in Heaven, and Grace wondered if Jacob himself considered this a blessing or a curse.

He would finally be let into Heaven, but he didn't go there as a beloved servant of God. Instead, he travelled there as a prisoner, guarded by the very angels he'd enslaved.

At the moment, however, Grace was far more occupied with Jacob's brother.

She was standing in front of the Gates to Hell, saying her goodbyes to Daniel, who was finally done with his part of the restoration. He'd chosen Heaven over Hell, and Grace couldn't help but be disappointed by his choice. Not that her disappointment kept her from hugging him tightly as they said their goodbyes.

"Remember our next visit," she said. "Two weeks from now."

Daniel smiled at her. "I will," he promised her.

"And ask my mother if she can meet me the week after. Around noon."

"I will," he said again.

Grace let go of him and stepped back.

Daniel looked at Samael, who was standing behind Grace.

"I'm grateful that you allowed me to be part of your mission," he said.

"I guess you were slightly more useful than I imagined you'd be," Samael said.

Daniel smiled at him, holding out his hand. "Goodbye," he said. "I wish you all the best."

Samael shook it. "Do remember the visit," he said. "She'll be so disappointed if you don't, and *I'll* have to hear all about it."

"Hey!" Grace said, elbowing him in the side. "You'd be disappointed too."

Samael scoffed.

Grace looked back at Daniel. "Goodbye," she said.

He smiled at her. "Goodbye," he said. Then he turned around and walked out.

Grace looked at the Gates, closing behind him. She sighed. "It's kind of odd, isn't it?" she said.

"What is?"

"That it's over. Our whole adventure."

"And thank Lucifer for that."

Grace shrugged. "I don't know," she said. "Except that last part, it was awfully exciting. And, well, I was thinking…"

"About what?" Samael asked warily.

"Well, Lucifer did mention that he'd do us a favour…"

"And you've thought of something you wanted? Since you declined the title he offered you."

Grace shrugged. "Well, could you honestly have seen me as part of the nobility?" she said. "Besides, there's something I want more."

"Which would be what?"

"An adventure."

"A what?"

"I want another adventure," Grace said. "Something with excitement. And danger."

"How about forgetting about that second part?" Samael suggested. "We could... we could go surfing."

"Surfing," Grace repeated. "Just, like... on water?"

"Or cliff diving, or sailing, or bloody baking. We saved Hell *four weeks ago*. Can't you wait a bit before your next adventure?"

Grace considered it. Samael did look like he could use a bit of rest. "Maybe I could wait a bit," she allowed. "We can use the time to work on Lucifer."

"Yes, let's— Did you just say *work on Lucifer?!*"

"Well, yeah. We still have a long way to go before we're where you and Daniel wanted us to be."

"That's not... Grace, we got them to change the worlds. It was a *success*."

Grace smiled at him. "That's the spirit! And yes, it was a success. The first of many."

"The first of... are you planning to single-handedly pester the Devil until he gives in to all of our requests?!"

Grace frowned. "Well, I thought you would help," she said. "You do know Lucifer better than I do. And I was planning to recruit Daniel to take care of the Heavenly side of things."

Samael stared at her. "Grace, they just changed the worlds. Maybe give them, and the people, a chance to get used to the changes before you push for new ones?"

Grace considered it. He did have a point. She sighed.

"Fine," she said. "I suppose we could wait till next week."

Samael gaped at her. "How about a few decades?"

"How about a month?" she offered.

"A year," Samael said. "At least."

"Two months?"

"A. Year."

Grace sighed. "Fine," she said. "But just because our political work has to be postponed doesn't mean we have to wait a whole year for another adventure."

"I suppose it was… interesting," Samael said. "Though I'd like a pause before I leave Hell again. And I'm not talking about a couple of days, Grace!"

"Fine," she said. "How about three months? And then we'll ask Lucifer for a new mission."

Samael sighed. "I'll grow old before my time because of you."

"It'll be good for you. And you're already old."

"I am not."

"No, I guess you're not," Grace agreed. "*I'm* old. You're ancient. And I believe you said something about cliff diving?"

"I thought you wanted to wait three months?"

"For a mission. I can't wait three months for *fun*. Besides, you only live… eh, thrice, I guess? And the start of my third life wasn't the best, so I'm thinking that I kind of have to make up for it."

Samael groaned. "It's times like these, I regret I ever met you."

"Oh, hush," Grace said. "You're happy we're friends."

"We're not friends," Samael said. "Now, come on. You can help me put the Book of Souls back in something resembling order, and *then* we'll go cliff diving. And maybe afterwards we can go to a concert like you've been badgering me about."

Grace merely grinned at him.

She was going to enjoy her third life.

ABOUT THE AUTHOR

Maria Sjöstrand is a Danish author whose first writing endeavours started at the age of 12. A true bibliophile, she taught herself to read at the age of 5, and she has dreamed of adding to the wonderful world of literature ever since.

Maria has a BA in Popular Fiction from the South Gate School of Creative Writing, and an MA in Creative Writing from the University of Dundee in Scotland.

Born with two holes in her heart, Maria found herself on the operating table at the age of 4. It is perhaps not surprising then that she likes to play around with the thought of what comes after death — for believers and non-believers alike.

More from Guardbridge Books

Sherlock Mars
by Jackie Kingon

When a diner is murdered at Molly's restaurant on Mars, she helps the police solve the crime. Could it be the dreaded Cereal Serial Killer? Fine dining, virtual reality, and murder. Delightfully Weird.

Now with a sequel, **P Is For Pluto**. Molly is opening a new branch on Pluto — send in the clones!

Soul Searching
by Stephen Embleton

South African police use a device that can track souls in a harrowing search for a serial killer. But when one's soul can incriminate them before birth, can there be justice?
NOMMO Awards Best Novel 2020 Finalist.

Drakemaster
by EC Ambrose

A desperate race across medieval China during the Mongol conquest to locate a clockwork doomsday device that could destroy the world with the power of the stars.

"Expertly researched with unforgettable characters and superb writing, this is one not to be missed." — Brendan DuBois

All are available at our website and online retailers.
http://guardbridgebooks.co.uk